MW01047278

THE IMPENDING STORM

Rebecca + Elana,

May your adventures be magical!

[illegible]

The Imperium Saga

THE IMPENDING STORM

Fall of the Imperium Trilogy
Book 1

Clifford B. Bowyer

Silver Leaf Books
HOLLISTON, MASSACHUSETTS

THE IMPENDING STORM

Cover Art by Logan Lubera, Norman Lee and Lisa Lubera

First printing November 2003

ISBN 0-9744354-4-9
LCCN 2003096031

Silver Leaf Books, LLC
P.O. Box 6460
Holliston, MA 01746
+1-888-823-6450

Visit our web site at **www.SilverLeafBooks.com**

To all of the family members and friends who have supported and helped me along on this amazing journey: You have been my inspiration, my motivation, and my faith.

Thank you.

ACKNOWLEDGMENTS

Without the support, hard work, and dedication of many people, this book and the new Fantasy world created would not have been possible. Thanks to you all for your patience, feedback, assistance, and excitement in this endeavor. I truly appreciate it. I wish to acknowledge the efforts of the following people:

My mother and my father, my two biggest supporters and champions of my efforts. I would also like to mention my sisters, their husbands, my nieces, and my nephews for their insight, suggestions, and help in bringing some of the characters to life.

Shannon Horton and David LaPointe, my Fantasy experts and initial readers. Through discussions with you, I have been able to take an idea or plot, and develop it into a highly polished masterpiece.

Norman Lee, and Logan and Lisa Lubera, my art team, who took my preliminary profiles and script and brought the characters of the Imperium to life.

Stacey Rizoli, who has tinkered time and again to make the logo turn out perfectly.

Sue Collier for her superb editing, along with Deb Ellis, Kate Deubert, Cathy Bowman, and Marilyn Ross for their efforts in the publication process from the beginning to the end.

I would also like to thank my entire Test Market group. These individuals have provided opinions, commentary, and feedback on a variety of things throughout the life of this project. In those indecisive times, their perspectives have truly been appreciated. There are far too many of you to name here, but I want you to know that I value each and every comment you have made to me.

And finally, to all of my readers, with whom the fate of the Seven Kindgoms hangs in the balance.

Thank you, all.

CAST OF CHARACTERS

Warlord Braksis	human male from Falestia
Solara	mystral female from Suspinti
Empress Karleena	human female from Dartais
Admiral Morex	human male from Dartais
King Sarlec	human male from Danchul
Captain Centain	human male from Dartie
Kai	elven female from Madrew
Kyria	human female from Frocomon
Winton	human male from Danchul
Arifos	elven male from Madrew
Thamar	dwarven male from Vorstad
Ferceng	troll male from Falestia
Rawthorne	human male from Falestia
Durgin	human male from Suspinti
Prime Minister Torsceen	human male from Dartais
Angel	human female from Falestia

PROLOGUE

The Forbidden Regions filled a vast portion of the sea with a misty atmosphere so thick one felt weighed down when trying to walk within its boundaries. These Regions were famed and feared. Sailors the world over turned away rather than risking the dense fogs and uncharted dangers that could reside within. Tales were told of ships that had sailed in and were never heard from again. Certain catastrophe was widely accepted.

For the Madrew elves, this venerable death trap had become their sanctuary, if not their home. Several years before, an evil plague swept the land, and those fortunate survivors fled to the seas seeking salvation in the unknown. Of a once proud race of elves, only a few hundred remained in hiding and seclusion. This island, which they hoped that they would not be at long enough to name, was fortunately large enough to sustain life after their fleeing vessels crashed into the rocky shores.

Existence here was harsh and at times unbearable. The elves unanimously decided they needed to find a way to go in search of a new home similar to the one they were forced to leave behind. At the same time, they needed to find some way to oppose the evil plague if they were to come upon it once again. To complete both tasks, the Elders, the most magically attuned elves, went into isolation and fasted while focusing on visions of the future. After several weeks of contemplation and self-imposed suffering, Eldiir, leader of the remaining Madrew elves gathered all around to speak of the Elders' revelations.

The Madrew elves strained to see their leader through the thick fog, but what they saw troubled them immensely. Eldiir, once so strong and vibrant with life, looked frail and weak. His muscles were depleted, leaving nothing more than skin and bones. Where once he had a rich shade of pink skin, now he seemed pale and white. His gray hair flowed over his face and down his back in disarray. The only remaining aspect the people could cling to was the sheer determination and fire that remained in Eldiir's eyes.

He stood before them and spoke softly. All around grew silent and strained to hear his words: "My fellow Madrew, we have come upon unfortunate times that have led us here. This avenue. This path, where once we saw happiness and prosperity, now we see only despair and hardship. Our livelihood and way of being are but a memory." Eldiir paused as he erupted into a fit of coughing. Slowly, he took several deep breaths and began again. "Yet our memories will motivate us to reunite our people, to find a new homeland, and to defend against our adversaries. What we were may seem to have been taken from us, but nothing can tarnish our will and spirit."

Several of the elves cheered and clapped in response to their leader's words.

"The Elders have spent many long days and nights in isolation trying to clearly ascertain our future. At long last, we have done so." He paused again as he looked around. Although he had difficulty seeing all of the elves, he knew they were listening closely. "Our future lies in a faraway land, a land that we have never known of before, a land which is beyond the Forbidden Regions."

"Beyond the Forbidden Regions?" one elf yelled out.

"That's ludicrous! We crashed here when we even tried to get into the Forbidden Regions!" another chimed in.

"How would we get to this new land? We no longer have a boat!" screamed a third.

"Listen, my people, listen," Eldiir pleaded. "There is a new land. We have seen it clearly. Yet we are unable to get there ourselves. That is not within our abilities."

"Then how can that be our future?" inquired a member of the crowd.

"It can be our future, because the future is clearly written. A trio of Madrew elves will be sent via a portal the Elders will open for them. This trio will be in search of a young child, a human female we have foreseen as being the savior of all. The Chosen One."

"A human female?" a tone of disbelief was clearly evident in the words.

"Yes, a human female. She has no knowledge of her future. Her power is locked within her. Without the success of the trio, she will never meet her destiny."

"How will the success of the trio get this girl to change?" one elf yelled.

"Yeah, and who will be trusted as the trio?" inquired another.

"If you allow me to continue, all shall be answered. The Elders will have the trio go through a transformation. Each will then have the ability to unlock the potential within the Chosen One. She will then be a pure mystic, unlike anything this world has ever seen before. When trained, she will have the ability to save us all. Even to take all of us to her world."

Eldiir looked around waiting to be interrupted again. He could tell his people were on edge and scared of what had happened and what might happen. He had seen much over his nine hundred and twenty-four years, and he patiently allowed them to interrupt. Still, seeing them listen when he asked them to, a tear formed in his left eye. "This girl also holds the key to defeating the horde which displaced us."

This last comment garnished a gasp from many and shrugs of doubt from others.

"We have not selected the trio. We have some people in mind, but would like volunteers who truly believe and wish to see our people living in harmony once more. The transformation, so that one can unlock the girl's potential, is not an easy one. The three will go through many changes. Only the truest of soul and heart will be able to complete this task."

"If you need a volunteer, then I am at your service." Arifos approached Eldiir with cheers from the crowd chanting his name. "There is none braver or stronger than Arifos." He had been a famed Madrew for three centuries as both a hunter and warrior. An elf who was noble, honorable, and compassionate. He had dark pink skin and braided silver hair with light blue strands. He carried a bow and two lightweight handcrafted swords wherever he traveled. Arifos was considered an expert in physical weapons, but also possessed a strong affinity toward combative magic, both offensive and defensive. For Arifos, sitting on this island was like being in a prison. This quest was exactly what he needed to feel he was an asset, that he was helping his people. Against the horde, he was the only Madrew who managed to battle valiantly and claim minor victories. He also was primarily responsible for the survival of this segment of elves.

Eldiir smiled at his people's champion. "Excellent, Arifos. You were naturally one of the people we anticipated going on this journey. We need two more now."

In reply to the request for a second champion, Rulysta, a powerful female mystic, rose above the crowd and floated toward Eldiir. Rulysta spent much of her six centuries learning the ways of magic and developing her powers so acutely that the mystical arts accompanied her as easily and normally as clothing. With age taking its toll, Rulysta's pink hide had also begun to fade, though not as much as Eldiir's. Her hair had not yet lost any of the vibrancy of her youth and was still a reddish brown. Without ever touching the ground, she turned and remained afloat next to Arifos. When she spoke, the words were not loud, but every elf present heard her as if she were directly in front of them. "I, too, shall join this expedition."

Eldiir nodded his assent at his longtime friend. The Elders should have known she would volunteer, but had not really considered her as an option. Still, as a powerful Mage, he could hardly think of anyone more suited to go on this most imperative mission. "Do we have a third volunteer to join with these two legends of our people?"

The third volunteer stepped forward full of confidence and poise. The light pink pigmentation of the skin portrayed the youth of the volunteer. Kai had in fact not yet reached her one-hundredth birthday. Like all Madrew elves, her skin pigmentation would continue to darken with age, before lightening again in the elder years. Her hair was a slightly darker shade of crimson and flowed down to her shoulders. As she spoke, none would suspect she was youthful and full of innocence. The experiences of the past few years had a way of aging everyone quickly. "It would be my honor to help restore our people to our former glory."

The Elders had suspected Kai would volunteer despite her youth. Although she had no mystical abilities of her own, she was well versed and skilled in the theory of magical abilities. She also worked hard to make up for her lack of powers by increasing her flexibility, dexterity, motion, and speed. She was acrobatic and possessed intricate knowledge of various strategies of physical hand-to-hand combat.

Eldiir paused as Kai approached the other two volunteers. "Our trio has been assembled. From now on, they shall be referred to as the Triad. May fables and legends be written in their honor for years to come." He then gestured for the Triad to go to the isolation area where the Elders convened. After they nodded and turned to leave, he addressed the crowd once more. "We shall now transform them so that they can unleash the powers within the child. These three will be the keys to our salvation."

With the conclusion of his words, the crowd erupted in cheers again, chanting, "To the Triad!"

A young elf walked over to Eldiir and assisted him as he made his way back to rejoin the Elders and the Triad. "Are you ready for your journey to begin?"

In one voice, the three responded with a confident "Yes."

"Very well. This process of transformation will be like a light flowing over you. It will happen very quickly, and when done, you will not feel any differently. However, you will have the ability to find the Chosen One and unlock her potential."

At the close of Eldiir's words, the Elders all joined hands and closed their eyes. The Triad looked around, then felt a burning sensation deep within themselves. Although Eldiir mentioned it would be painless, the trio felt as if their insides were on fire. Light erupted from the pores of their skin, mouths, and eyes. Then as quickly as it began, it was over. The trio collapsed to the ground and struggled to rise and regain their footing.

"Is everyone all right?" Eldiir questioned.

Arifos looked at his two companions and answered for the group. "But a little price to pay for the salvation of our people. We are fine."

"Excellent. Now, we will open up a portal for each of you to go to the land that we spoke of. This land will present new challenges and obstacles that will get in your way. You must overcome them and remain focused on your true mission. Each of you will start off alone, hopefully to expand the search area, yet you all will be in the same land mass. Do you all understand?" All three nodded yes to Eldiir's query. "Excellent. The future of our people, and quite possibly the world is in your hands. Be brave, be strong, and be successful."

As the three adventurers watched the Elders, a slice in the fabric of reality opened beneath each of them and slowly moved up their bodies. Below the slice, the Elders could no longer see the trio's legs. As the slice slowly moved up, more and more of the three disappeared until finally all were gone and the slice dissipated as well.

Eldiir closed his eyes as the exertion from the Elders' combined effort sapped him of most of his strength, and spoke softly to his colleagues. "Our future now lies solely with them. There is nothing more we can do but wait and hope."

CHAPTER 1

As an inn, Springs's was better than most in the kingdom of Dartie. With the land full of hunters, innkeepers began to capitalize and create lodgings that a hunter would find useful. A place where they could get drunk, tell tales of the hunt, and sleep on mattresses that often had not been cleaned. The hunters would break their fair share of tables and chairs, so most inns lost their desire to maintain a clean atmosphere, and grew darker and grimmer. Springs refused to give in to this trend. He ran a clean operation and prided himself on it. His nine children created a full-time staff to wait on people from the moment they first walked in. His lounge area served alcohol to its patrons and had tables for comfort and privacy, as well as a well-lighted atmosphere so all could see. His youngest son played the piano throughout the evening with calm and soothing tunes for people to enjoy. His family also spent extra time cleaning the entire area whenever a patron had moved on so that the next guest would receive a clean, warm, and friendly experience.

His rooms were also far more luxurious than his competitors'. No bed would ever be remade without cleaning the garments. Springs's wife and daughter-in-law saw to the upkeep of the rooms, and they took great pride in it. In terms of size, his rooms offered more space than others in Dartie as well.

Springs liked to consider himself an entrepreneur of a fine establishment. One that royalty would be willing to occupy when traveling in his area, and quite frequently, royal families did check in when they wished to go hunting in the Dartian Woods. These occupants he gave special care to and catered to their every need so that more royal families would return in the future.

Springs's Inn had been in the family for seven generations. Each firstborn son took on the name Springs to follow in his father's footsteps. Springs himself was the eleventh, with the name lasting even longer than their time as innkeepers. He was relatively short for a human, and gray hairs covered what remained of a balding head. He dressed in comfortable blue pants with leather shoes rather than boots, and a lighter blue shirt with a red ribbon around his neck. A small set of spectacles rested on his nose to help eyes that at one time could spot a customer long before they stepped foot into his establishment. Springs's elder son was the twelfth to take on the name, and eagerly was learning all aspects of the business.

As Springs proudly looked over the patrons on this warm afternoon, he thanked the gods as he did so often for the way things turned out. Unlike other inns, he couldn't recall the last time a brawl broke out. He remembered something from when he was a child and learning from his father, but he was young then and that was during the Great Wars. Wars have a way of upsetting even the most peaceful of places.

With all of those thoughts flowing through his head, he would later think that he must have jinxed himself, because his entire world turned upside down the minute that five hunters walked through the doorway.

As the bell on the door rang, Springs the twelfth went to great the new patrons with a warm welcome. He was repaid by being shoved aside by the first hunter inside the door, with a yell to get out of his way.

The elder Springs quickly moved over to the five new patrons to try to prevent hostilities in advance. "Welcome, hunters, to my establishment. If you would please leave your weapons by the door and wipe the mud off your boots, it would be greatly appreciated."

The man that pushed his son took two steps closer to Springs. His breath smelled of liquor and his teeth were rotted. The dirt and grime smeared on his face and tattered clothing looked as if he had not bathed in months. He looked down at the shorter Springs and grinned. "Greatly appreciated? Well we would greatly appreciate it if you would get the hell out of our way so that we can get a decent drink!" With that, he took his foot and smeared it along the floor, leaving a trail of mud as he walked over to the bar area. "Barkeep! Drinks for my men and I!"

The barkeeper was Springs's second son, Barrow. He preferred hunting to staying and working, but enjoyed talking to the customers about their latest games. At the age of thirty-three, Barrow often gave in to his emotions and did things that would embarrass his father. Yet never has he acted inappropriately here at the inn. He looked up at his father with a plea in his eyes to let him do something, anything, to try to remove the new group, but his father just shook his head no and gestured for him to serve them.

Disappointed that his father wouldn't do anything, he realized that the hope must be for these people to have a quick drink and leave. "Anything in particular, gentlemen?"

"Har, har!" Another hunter bellowed. "Ya hear that, Jenks, he calls us gentoilmen."

The man he addressed as Jenks turned out to be the same man who had pushed the younger Springs and smeared the mud on the floor. He looked at his grubby companion and hit him in the chest. "Other than you, Riff, we are gentlemen. Hell, you can't even say the word!"

Springs closed his eyes and prayed this would end quickly. He could see the disruption and watched as several patrons packed up and got ready to leave. Something like this, if it got out, could ruin him.

As the customers slowly left, he thanked them all and apologized for the disruption. Most seemed to regard him warmly and stated that they understood. He truly hoped they did. Looking back inside, there remained only a few patrons sitting at tables, and the five hunters at the bar. He noticed one man in the back corner lean back into the shadows and watch the newcomers intently. He was wearing a red cloak that covered most of his features, but Springs could tell that his eyes had not swayed from the direction of the hunters since they first walked in.

As the five men drank more, they began to speak more freely. Conversations moved from the hunt, then twisted into derogatory remarks of the Imperium.

"I'm tellin' ya, Syke, ever since that old geezer Conrad kicked the bucket, the Imperium has fallen to pieces."

The man addressed as Syke swatted at a few insects swarming around his head before providing a drunken retort. "Emperor Conrad knew how to keep things going. His whelp of a daughter is a joke."

One of the other hunters was leaning against the bar looking for more liquor. "Who wants a chick to be in command anyways?"

Syke laughed with the deep tone of a man under the influence. "Yeah, Wolmn, you tell 'em!"

The original speaker looked to add some more insightful commentary. "Hell, even Lord Braksis himself can't keep the Imperium together for little Karleena!"

The leader of the group, Jenks, knocked the speaker off his stool. "Quiet, Vrent. We all know that the time of Zoldex is coming, and that the Imperium will fall. Stop advertising. That goes for all of you!"

Standing back up, Vrent lashed back at his leader. "Come on, Jenks, the army Zoldex assembled here in Dartie alone will march all over the warlord and his troops. We can celebrate a little."

The man sitting in the corner continued to watch the exchange intently. He was becoming intrigued by the conversation and wanted to hear much more.

"I told you to shut up, Vrent!" Jenks screamed to his fellow hunter. With the steadily rising voices and potential for increased hostilities, all the remaining patrons jumped up and ran outside—except for the man in the shadows.

The innkeeper lowered his head and sobbed. How could things have gone so poorly? He had such a reputable inn. Now, five vagrant ruffians had run off his entire clientele.

With the conversation of the hunters dying down, they started to vandalize some of the surroundings. Wolmn jumped behind the bar and started tossing bottles to his comrades. Both elder and younger Springs, as well as Barrow, tried to reason with them. The youngest son and six daughters fled the inn to the safe haven of their mother who was cleaning the rooms.

The cloaked man in the corner had heard and seen enough. He stood up slowly and took a few steps to place himself between the five hunters and the door.

Jenks looked at the man quizzically. "What the hell do you want?"

The man lowered the cloak from his head and allowed it to open to reveal the armor underneath for the first time. As his greenish-blue eyes bored into the hunters, they could feel a sense of intimidation and self-doubt. He stood a little taller than six feet and with the confidence of success. He had light brown hair that feathered back in layers down to his neckline. His face had a perfectly trimmed goatee of the same color. Certainly an attractive man, but a man not to be trifled with.

His suit of armor beneath the red cloak, which flowed to the floor, was predominantly black. The breastplate was intricately designed and portrayed a flaming bird rising from a sea of darkness that burst through with the flood of a raging inferno. The emblem of the phoenix quickly identified the man who opposed the hunters. The armor itself had its own unique origins: It was forged from illistrium, a material located in the molten magma of the planet terra itself. It fit on his body and was as malleable as regular cloth, yet at the same time the fabric was harder than any known metal. An enigma to even the best blacksmith throughout the Seven Kingdoms.

The eyes of the hunter known as Riff widened. "That's, that's, that's..."

"Shut up, Riff. We know who it is," Jenks ordered. "Warlord Braksis." He sneered.

Braksis focused on Riff specifically and yelled out a loud and piercing "Boo!"

Riff screamed and ran toward the closest window and crashed through it as he fled the inn.

Springs watched with horror as he realized what was about to happen. Myriad reactions flowed through him. The most honored and revered warrior of their time was here to rid him of the infestation of the hunters, but at the same time, his poor inn was about to become a battle zone. Without saying a word, he gestured for his two remaining sons to follow him, and they walked out the door praying that when they walked back in, they'd still have a bar for the inn.

Warlord Braksis looked at the remaining four hunters and smiled, watching as they pulled their swords and prepared to fight. They were shaking in either fear or intoxication, it mattered little. "I'll give you this one chance. Surrender and leave now, or face my wrath." His voice was stern and full of authority. From the tone, one could ascertain that very few would ever disobey an order once given by Braksis.

"Wrath, huh?" Jenks screamed out. "There are four of us, armed, and only one of you. Not a weapon in sight."

Continuing to smile, Braksis nodded as he began to taunt the hunters. "If you are so confident, then shall we begin? I know from your comments how little you think of me and the Imperium. Of course, four hunters of your ilk can take one defenseless man."

Jenks started to spout orders. "Ready, men! We're going to enjoy this!"

Leading the charge, Jenks ran toward Braksis, who remained where he was. The smile never left his face. "I'm going to enjoy this, too," he commented under his breath as Jenks arrived and lunged toward him with his sword. Braksis motioned quickly, parrying to the side and allowing Jenks's sword to find nothing but air. Finishing his movement, he brought his open hand down in a chop on the back of Jenks's neck. As the man crumbled to the floor, Braksis uttered another challenge. "Next?"

The remaining three looked at each other in awe. None of them could believe that Jenks had fallen, much less how quickly it had happened. The three charged together. Braksis began to loop around them, weaving in and out, creating confusion as the three kept trying to connect with him.

In the doorway left open by Springs, a woman walked up and leaned against the arch. She was of good height but not as tall as Braksis. She had long, silvery-white hair flowing freely down her back. The left side of her face had the mark of the mystral, a dragon-shaped birthmark of intricate detail. She was garbed in a skintight red outfit that appeared strong as armor, but also flexible, which would allow her to be agile. The outfit itself displayed all of her features, revealing bare arms and legs that clearly showed signs of muscle tone and strength. She wore boots that came up to her knees in the same shade of red as her one-piece armor. On her right leg, she had a ring around her bare skin that held small throwing blades. Latched to her waist was an elongated sword. Crossed upon her back she also had two holsters holding swords in each.

The woman watched the scene inside and spoke to Braksis. "Need any help?"

Braksis swirled around dodging the thrashing sword of Syke. "Nope. I'm having too much fun with these imbeciles."

"How about a sword?" the woman inquired.

"Come on, Solara, that would take the fun out of it," Braksis retorted while still smiling.

Wolmn ran toward Braksis with his sword held high above his head. Braksis dropped and rolled onto his back, lifting his legs to catch Wolmn's torso and using his own momentum to launch him through the air and into a wall. Wolmn started to scream but was silenced as he broke through the wall and lost himself to unconsciousness.

Solara watched the move. "Not bad, but destructive. You'll be paying for that wall."

"I know," Braksis replied as Vrent started swirling his sword trying to hit him.

Syke approached Braksis from behind trying to end it quickly, if cowardly, now that the numbers were slowly losing their favor. He stabbed forward as Braksis dodged and found his sword clanging with Vrent's. Braksis then turned and jumped, launching a kick at Syke's head while in midair.

Vrent momentarily lost his balance when Syke's sword impacted his. He watched as Syke fell and he was alone against Braksis. As the Warlord came back down to the ground, he picked up a barstool and tossed it toward Vrent. Vrent dodged, but the stool hit his sword hand and he dropped his blade.

Unwilling to surrender, the hunter Vrent, who had always believed he could best any beast with his bare hands, threw a punch at his foe. Braksis caught the punch in midair, and simply smiled at Vrent. He then twisted Vrent's arm back and punched him in the face with his other arm.

As Vrent fell, he heard a few last words before he slipped into unconsciousness: "Did you enjoy it?"

Standing straight up, Solara took a step into the inn. "Not bad. Not bad at all."

"Thanks. Did you get the fifth man who fled when this all started?"

"Tiot has him. He's not going anywhere."

Braksis stepped outside and saw his faithful timber wolf atop Riff, growling at the cowering hunter. From his nose to the tip of his tail, Tiot was six feet in length and weighed close to one hundred and fifty pounds. He was predominantly gray, with white legs and paws, a white outline around his nose and mouth, as well as a much darker shade of gray flowing to the tip of his tail.

Seeing that Tiot did indeed have things under control, Braksis walked back inside the bar, opened the cabinet by the door, and reclaimed the sword that was famed throughout the Seven Kingdoms. His trusty blade, the Phoenix, handcrafted just like the armor he wore.

The innkeeper Springs slowly walked back inside and surveyed the damage. Tears were streaking down his face. "I'm ruined."

Braksis reached into a pouch hung behind his back and pulled out a small bag. He looked inside, tossed it up in his hands a couple of times, then tossed it over to Springs. "I apologize for the mess. On behalf of the Empress, this should cover the damages."

Springs opened the small bag and his eyes widened as he saw the contents: pure grains of gold, untampered and worth more than his entire inn combined. "Why, thank you. This is most generous, kind sir."

"Think nothing of it. I apologize again for the destruction. However, I could not sit back any longer. I am Lord Braksis, after all."

Springs thanked him again and quickly called his sons over. "Go bring this to your mother," he told them. Next he addressed Barrow. "You go contact the ISIA and have them pick these five up."

With his work done, Braksis walked over to where Tiot had Riff cowering. "We're leaving now, but if I hear that you ran off, I'll have Tiot here track you down, and this time, I'll let him do what he wants with you. Understand?"

Stuttering, Riff complied. "Y-y-y-yes, y-yes, sir! Not going nowhere is I."

"Good." Braksis stood and walked to his horse, Solara, in stride. As they mounted their horses and started to head off, Braksis let out two short whistles. Tiot jumped off Riff and ran alongside the two riders.

Springs stood there watching as they slowly vanished over the horizon. Dreams of an even bigger and more luxurious inn danced through his head.

CHAPTER 2

The kingdom of Dartie was predominantly plain lands and forests. Wild creatures and animals had always found the land of Dartie to be their home. Hunters from all around were drawn to the kingdom primarily seeking sport and game. The people of Dartie prided themselves on having a deep sense of the hunt and tales of their feats grew with each passing year. This however was not always so.

Generations ago, twin brothers Sarkod and Bosik were heirs to the throne of the Kingdom of Dartais, a land prominently known for fishing and exploring. One brother, Sarkod, looked to the sea and found the peace he craved doing what his father and his father's father did before him. His twin brother Bosik was not as allured by the tranquility of the sea. Rather, he questioned the ideals of his people and felt that his true calling was not on the water, but on the land. He began to lead a small following of people who felt they should test their own might against the beasts and other creatures that often terrorized the kingdom. These feelings grew and finally Bosik led an expedition to the west where he entered the Dartian Woods. When they walked out again, this small group had conquered their fear of the unknown, and had claimed victory over nature and the beasts.

As tales of Bosik and his hunting party grew, many of the younger Dartais residents flocked to his influence and also wished to test their might against the beasts. Following the trends of his people, Sarkod felt a tension growing, and dread in this dangerous development. The two brothers quarreled over the path of their kingdom and a rift grew between them. The people of Dartais also began to split between the two. Many to remain true to their upbringing and many to venture into the woods and plains and feel the exhilaration of pitting their strength against a creature of nature.

Ultimately, the two brothers were unable to mend the gap that developed between them, and Bosik led his followers out into the plains to create a new kingdom of their own. Thus, this group slowly established the kingdom now known as Dartie, a land of hunters and warriors. A land where the people felt they were stronger and better than any other. A land that suddenly was erupting with violence and uprisings.

During the last Great War, Conrad led his forces and united the Seven Kingdoms into a period of prosperity that never had been felt before. During his reign, he proclaimed himself Emperor, and began to oversee the royal families of each kingdom. After the war, he gave much of Dartie's land to their neighboring cousins and supporters of Conrad, Dartais. King Rentios of Dartais however wished to reunite his people who had been separated for so long. Not into one kingdom again, but at least have the two begin to grow closer. With this foresight in mind, he turned down the offer to expand his land, and allowed Dartie to retain that which it originally possessed.

Grateful of the generosity of King Rentios, the young King Palenial, who ascended to the throne when his father was slain in the Great Wars, began to mend the wounds that time had created for both kingdoms. The two kingdoms, although separate, enjoyed close to fifty years of open trade, alliance, and increased interaction between their people.

A dark shadow was cast the day that Emperor Conrad had been assassinated at the palace, and the tranquility of the Seven Kingdoms soon was broken. Conrad's young daughter Karleena assumed the title of Empress, but found herself faced with frequent uprisings and revolts. The land slowly returned to chaos.

Although Palenial became an avid supporter of the new Empress, and had no desire to return to war, the people of his nation seemed to have a different perspective. Many of the hunters banded together and attacked those loyal to Karleena, as well as King Palenial and the royal families. Dartie was thrown into turmoil as Palenial's efforts to restore order to the land were thwarted. Finally, in desperation, Palenial called upon the young Empress and requested her support.

Unlike her father, Karleena had never been hardened by the turmoil of war. She sent diplomats and envoys to attempt to bring the people back into the Imperium peacefully. With her efforts failing, she ultimately sought the solace of her military leader, Warlord Braksis. Under his leadership, legions of Imperial troops marched into Dartie to eliminate the uprisings. This, however, spurned others and more incidents occurred.

As Braksis returned to the encampment upon Blaze, his faithful steed, he thought back to the recent encounter at Springs's. The people of Dartie were becoming more hostile and violent. But he had heard the name Zoldex mentioned before. A new name, only mentioned since the death of Conrad, but one that must be explored. If he truly were the one responsible for these uprisings, he would need to be dealt with quickly.

Any soldiers Braksis and Solara passed quickly stood at attention in respect for their leader. Watching closely, the Warlord knew these men would bring honor to the Imperium in the upcoming days.

Arriving at the command tent, Braksis and Solara dismounted. A lower ranked soldier came over and took both horses to be bathed and fed. Looking down at Tiot, Braksis commanded his faithful wolf to stay. Obediently the animal shook its head as if in reply, then sat by the entrance to the tent.

The tent itself was the largest of all those around. The purpose was not for the officers to sleep. They, too, slept in the smaller tents that were scattered throughout the encampment. This tent however was where the officers assembled to review the reports and strategize. As Braksis and Solara walked in, they saw the four generals under his command reviewing maps and charts. Several other soldiers were also present, one of whom was presenting a report. All stopped what they were doing to acknowledge Braksis's presence.

"As you were," he stated as he walked to the table in the middle of the tent and viewed the maps his command staff had been analyzing. "What is there to report?"

The first man to speak was the eldest General, Kronos. He had originally fought in the armies of Danchul during the last Great War, fifty years before. Over time, he rose in rank and assumed control of the entire Army of Danchul, which was famed for its vast size and strength. After serving there for several years, Conrad requested that the kingdom of Danchul allow Kronos to command not just his own kingdom's army, but also the combined forces of the entire Imperium. A respected leader and warrior, he maintained this position until age started to set in, and Warlord Braksis was given command of the Imperial forces. Kronos remained in the military as a top advisor, and still retained his rank.

The man himself seemed to defy his age, and at seventy-eight he still remained vibrant and full of life. His short gray hair and beard were perfectly trimmed and represented the order he valued so highly. His eyes showed strength and the wisdom of the ages. When he spoke, there was no sign of frailty, but rather a thunderous pitch that demanded attention. Even his uniform was in perfect order and fitted flawlessly to his form. The underlying skintight black leather flowed from his throat down to his feet, revealing no skin below the neckline. A finely designed white breastplate covered all of his chest and torso. He also wore separate armored attachments on each arm and leg that allowed the joints to be free and have full range of motion. His hands were covered by gauntlets, and his feet were protected by armored boots. Hanging from the back of his spaulders, armored shoulder pads, was a long emerald green cape, which was worn only by the officers. Along the black leather on his neck, he also had five small white diamonds, which showed his rank as a senior general in the army.

"Our scouts have returned with information on the enemy's forces."

Braksis glanced at the man who had been giving the report then back at Kronos. "Continue."

"Our forces are encamped here." As he said this, he used an elongated rod to point at the map. "According to the scouts, the antagonists have joined forces here." Once again pointing at the map. "Several scouts did not make it back. However, we have learned that the forces amassed are quite formidable."

"How big?" Braksis inquired.

"No real number was presented. Nothing organized, just a large contingent of these hunters. Varied weapons and supplies."

"Recommendations?"

Kronos looked at the other three generals and nodded at each in succession to provide a recommendation.

The first General to speak was Hinbar. Like Kronos, he was similarly garbed, but with four small white diamonds, showing that he was a general but not as highly ranked. When not on duty, Hinbar resided in the mountains of the kingdom of Falestia, a home he cherished and believed was the most beautiful in all of the Seven Kingdoms.

More than twenty years younger than Kronos, Hinbar sported long brown hair that now flowed freely down his back. He also had a mustache of the same color that hung down the sides and below his chin. He traditionally commanded the infantry and oversaw the majority of the land forces. Hinbar was hand-selected by Braksis when he first was put in command of the Imperium's forces. Hinbar was always unyielding and relentless. He understood and studied his opposition's forces, and used his studies to help him strategically overtake his enemies. He placed a strong value on the lives of the men under his command, but when the advance was sounded, he would neither ask nor give any quarter.

"Based on the information provided from our scouts, I am hesitant to suggest a direct confrontation without having a better representation of the forces amassed against us. I therefore feel that more scouting missions would be imperative prior to advancing." Pausing to allow the suggestion to sink in, Hinbar continued. "With that said, the people of Dartie are strong, proud, and naturally inclined toward hunting and hand-to-hand activities. Without further information on numbers, I would advise that the archers play a key role in this engagement, striking from afar and dwindling the opponent's numbers long before we advance. The last thing we want here is a close confrontation with them. The infantry and cavalry can advance next to try to add confusion to the ranks, splitting their forces and making them easier to overcome."

Kronos nodded at Hinbar for his recommendation, then looked up at Lowred.

General Lowred was part of the military long before Braksis was given command. He fought alongside Emperor Conrad when the Imperium was challenged by outside nations. His tactics and abilities helped the Imperium stand strong and remain unscathed, although he lost his left leg in the skirmish. Unable to command the regular army any longer, Lowred utilized his abilities by teaching others. He still journeyed with his troops, but remained atop his horse where he could direct the archer units he commanded and not allow his disability to endanger those around him. Similarly garbed as the other generals, his neck displayed his rank with four small white diamonds. Instead of a left leg, he had a prosthetic wooden peg to keep him erect. He also carried a cane that unsheathed a sword when he needed a weapon.

Like Kronos, Lowred came from the kingdom of Danchul. Rather than giving in to the despair of his disability, he often found himself treating activities outside of the military as trivial and humorous. He truly enjoyed his life, and fathered five sons and two daughters, all of whom inherited his vibrant red hair. Four of his sons joined the Imperial army like their father. The rest of his family remained at home enjoying the utopia that Danchul had become.

"I will agree with General Hinbar. My archery units will definitely play a key role in the upcoming skirmish. However, I feel that we can also use the cavalry to a distinct advantage. With the archers attacking and the infantry advancing, the cavalry could circle around and attack from behind here." As he said this, he pointed with his cane to an area where the woods thinned out but still could allow the cavalry to move behind the forces without discovery. "This way, we would attack from multiple fronts and squeeze the enemy forces between us."

Acknowledging Lowred's perspective, Kronos then addressed the final general, Sevlow.

Unlike the other generals, Sevlow was much younger at the age of thirty-two, and had only recently been advanced to the rank of general by Conrad shortly before his death. He had dark brown hair slicked back using a resin from a tanctun tree. He otherwise appeared plain and unobtrusive. However, his eyes were constantly in motion and watching everything that transpired around him. His brown eyes took in every detail, missing nothing. Also unlike the other generals, he only had two white diamonds, which represented him as the lowest ranking general present.

Originating from the swamplands of Tenalong, Sevlow was raised to be aware and cautious of his surroundings. Many criminal elements thrived in those swamps, and he managed to maintain his distance, but also to observe as much as he could. Those who knew him best called him an information broker. He seemed to know everything about everyone.

His background and special talents were uncovered by Emperor Conrad and put to use in his employ. Neighboring nations had begun to take an interest in the Imperium, and Conrad wished to learn as much about these potential threats as he could. Sevlow then spent most of his years of service to the empire in other nations with scouting parties and espionage groups. His reputation became well known in the Seven Kingdoms, and his activities and abilities brought him acclaim. Upon his return, Emperor Conrad was grateful for the information provided, and promoted him all the way to the rank of general. In this capacity, he led the scouts directly, but usually with guidance from other generals until his tactical abilities and leadership skills increase along with his naturally inclined stealth and information gathering attributes.

"Information is key here. My first unit of scouts got us some information, but not as much as they could. I recommend sending three separate units out in different directions to gain as much information as possible. One of these units would assuredly return unscathed. We could do this during the next nightfall. Then, we could have a better estimate of how to proceed."

As Sevlow finished his recommendation, Kronos addressed Braksis. "Which option would you like to pursue, sir?"

"You all bring up excellent points. As Hinbar said, we do not wish to spend excess time engaging this enemy up close. Lowred's archers will play a key role here. Lowred also has a good suggestion to have the cavalry circle around and attack from multiple fronts. However, I must agree with Sevlow on this matter, we need more information prior to advancing. Send out the three scouting parties, then we shall proceed from there."

The three generals bowed first to Braksis, then to Kronos. They walked out of the officers' tent to prepare their men. The nonofficers present left with them, leaving Braksis and Solara alone with Kronos.

"Lord Braksis, with the option set to delay, there is another matter that needs to be brought to your attention."

"I'm listening."

Kronos handed Braksis a scroll that had been delivered earlier. "This arrived today by rider from Suspinti. Queen Zerilla requests Imperial assistance. Apparently, her kingdom has fallen under siege by a man-eating dragon."

"A dragon? They left the land over a thousand years ago."

Solara grew very interested in this news. Her people, the mystral, had once shared a common alliance with the dragons. They had worked together to help maintain peace and order in the land. When the early Race Wars erupted, the mystral and their dragon counterparts were unable to hinder the assaults, and often found themselves as targets of others aggressions. Dragons were hunted, forcing them to travel north and seek safety in a land where they were alone. The remaining mystral, strong in the belief of honor and justice, faltered without the support of the dragons, and likewise went into hiding. "If dragons have returned, this would be of great interest to my people."

Kronos looked intently at the mystral warrior. In all of his years, he had seen what the prejudice of humans could do. There would be no peaceful resolution if dragons were to return to the land. "Great interest perhaps, but it does not alter the fact that it is feeding on humans at Suspinti. This dragon will need to be stopped, not cherished."

"I was not implying that my people would condone the actions of this dragon. Only that the return of the dragons would be of interest."

"Enough," Braksis whispered as he put his hand on her shoulder. "What is Queen Zerilla requesting?"

"She wants the army to deal with her problem," Kronos curtly replied.

"That is not possible. We are preparing for war. If we don't stop these uprisings, the forces amassed could march against Trespias. The Imperial City would be defenseless. We cannot allow that, regardless of what is happening in Suspinti."

"I know that, my lord, but we also cannot neglect our duties to the kingdoms under our reign."

"Agreed. Solara and I will go to investigate personally. However, I wish to be here for the assault. I am leaving you in command, Kronos. If you feel we should not delay our assault, proceed. If not, await our return."

"I understand, my lord." Kronos bowed before turning to exit the tent.

Braksis took one last look at the map of the battlefield. "Let's go. I want to get back in time for the battle."

Solara followed him out silently. The return of a dragon sparked a reaction deep within her—a part of her history and heritage that longed to be restored. She needed to face the past of her people, and perhaps in doing so, plot a new course for their future.

CHAPTER 3

The journey from the Imperial encampment in Dartie to Comonor, home of Queen Zerilla, took five long days atop Braksis's and Solara's thoroughbred horses. The bulk of the time was spent riding in silence, as Braksis's thoughts were plagued on the length of this trip and his desire to be in two places at once. The travel itself was preventing him from helping either the Imperial army or Suspinti's dragon encounter.

Suspinti bordered Dartie, but was more than twice the size of its neighbor. As a kingdom, the bulk of the land within its borders was dense forestland. After the final Race Wars several hundred years prior, many of the remaining races fled into the forests they now called home. Elves, mystral, lupan, simian, centaurs, gnomes, fairies, feline, gorn, and numerous other races called the various forests of Suspinti their home and flourished there once more.

Fearing these civilizations within the forest, especially the largest forest in the Seven Kingdoms, the Suspintian Forest, Suspinti was a kingdom that lived in fear. The cities and towns on the outskirts had great walls of stone built to enclose and keep them safe from the trees beyond. Guard towers were constantly manned with the Suspintian Guards, keeping a constant vigil on the foliage beyond the walls.

Although the races within the forests primarily remained in their new homes, the people of Suspinti were raised to look at the forest and pray for another day without incident. Overall, the people of Suspinti seemed overly paranoid and cautious.

This new incident with an alleged man-eating dragon certainly would not help the spirit of the people. In fact, Braksis questioned the validity of the reports. Perhaps the people's overactive imagination ran away with them, and there was no dragon. He wouldn't be surprised if he got there and determined that the big threat was nothing more than the branch of a tree blowing against the city walls in the wind. If that were so, being separated from his forces would enrage him even more. Still, if they were being assaulted by a dragon, it was better for him to address their concerns sooner rather than later.

Comonor was built at the southern tip of the Suspintian Forest and about half the distance from its borders east and west. It was currently ruled by Queen Zerilla, whom the people perceived as just a peasant and really not a member of the ruling class. Her former husband King Noroat had defied his family and wed a servant girl. The two were very much in love and produced three sons and two daughters. Two years ago, shortly before Noroat's thirtieth birthday, he was infected with a deadly plague that swept through the kingdom of Suspinti and stole many lives.

Left behind, Zerilla faced the scorn and deceit of her mother-in-law, Dascony, as she began to rule the kingdom. With her background, she ruled her people compassionately and won their hearts. Dascony continued to look down upon her daughter-in-law and tried to tutor the children in the ways of royalty.

As they approached the walls of Comonor, Braksis dismounted his steed. Blaze showed no sign of fatigue, even though he had been pushed more than usual over the past five days. His hide was a light brown, with a darker brown mane and tail. His head had a white blaze down the middle like his namesake, with similar color stockings around his lower legs.

Solara rode a thoroughbred like Braksis, but her mount, Myst, was all white with the exception of a black star on his head, and a matching black mane and tail.

Braksis walked up to the gates of the city and pounded three times on a gong hanging by the entrance. Looking up, the walls towered a good thirty feet into the sky to prevent anything that couldn't fly or climb from getting in. Atop the wall, a sentry dressed in a combined yellow cloth and chain link mesh looked down. The guard leaned back and yelled something to someone below.

A small window in the gate opened up and another guard peered out. This guard was similarly garbed as the sentry atop the wall, but his face was almost completely covered by a yellow tinged helmet of armor. "What's your purpose?"

"We received a message from Queen Zerilla requesting Imperial aid against the attack of a dragon."

"Only two of you?" the guard responded incredulously.

"Only the two of us," Braksis replied with impatience in his voice.

"Very well, I'll let you pass." The hatch in the gate closed, followed by the sound of gears turning and grinding. Slowly the massive gates opened inward allowing the riders to pass.

Several Suspintian Guards were stationed inside the gates to defend against subterfuge. As Braksis and Solara led their mounts in, with Tiot by their side, one guard stepped forward to address them. "If you will follow me, I shall take you to her majesty the Queen."

They followed the guard as he walked them into the small city. Small residences were grouped together in parallel lines throughout the inner portion of the city. Nothing directly touched any of the walls, nor the direct middle of the city with the exception of what was obviously the royal home. It was much larger than all of the other building, and seemed far more eloquently designed. Small shops, inns, and stables were also passed along the center portions of the street.

Two stable boys approached and offered to feed and bathe the horses. Both Braksis and Solara thanked them and continued to follow the guard.

As they approached the royal home, several other soldiers guarded the entrance. The door opened and a man walked out to greet them. He also wore the yellow fabric of the guards, which covered his shoulders, trailed down his chest, and was tied together by a black belt at his torso. Beneath the belt, the material flowed freely down another twelve inches. Underneath the tunic, he wore a gray body suit that fit snugly and covered both arms and legs. Yellow gloves covered his hands, and his legs were in knee-high yellow boots. Unlike the guards seen outside, he did not wear any chain-link mesh around his head or underneath the uniform.

The man himself looked to be in his mid-forties, with short brown hair and a full mustache. His eyes displayed weariness, as if he had seen much frustration, and little sleep of late. "My name is Captain Vector. I am in command of the Suspintian Guard. We welcome you and thank you for any assistance you could provide."

Braksis nodded briefly. "Lord Braksis of the Imperial Army."

"Yes, Warlord, your reputation precedes you. Although we have never met, I would never have been able to mistake you." Gazing beyond the

Warlord to Solara, Vector seemed to have energy flow through him and reinvigorate him. "And you must be the beautiful Solara who stands by his side."

He stepped forward, raised her hand and kissed it gently.

Flattered, Solara smiled back. "Why thank you, sir. So very kind."

"Yes. If I may be of any assistance, you only need to ask."

Beginning to grow annoyed because of his desire to be with his troops, Braksis coughed a couple of times to attempt to get Vector to return to business.

"Ah yes, my apologies. Come this way and we shall see the queen." Looking down at the timber wolf by Braksis's feet, he glanced up at its master one more time. "If you would please, the wolf must remain here."

"Understood. Tiot, guard the door."

Releasing a quick bark then a soft growl, Tiot turned and let his senses search for any hint of danger. With the command given, Tiot would not allow anyone to approach the door without at least a challenge and warning for his master.

The trio entered the queen's home and moved toward the back of the building. As they walked, Braksis and Solara noted the inconsistencies of the decor. In certain areas, furniture and possessions were finely kept and quite fashionable. In other areas, items appeared more homely and lived in.

Vector led the two visitors into the dining hall where the entire royal family was seated to dinner. The hall fit more with the decor of the fancy rooms and clearly had a lot of effort put into maintaining the elegance of the room. "My apologies for the disruption, my lady, but the people you sent for are here."

One woman stood with a clear smile on her face. She appeared to be in her early thirties, with a kindness about her. Her features, Braksis thought, were nearly perfect, and any man would have to look twice in admiration. Her pale skin was lightly colored on her cheeks. Her long blonde hair was in numerous braids and locks, flowing down her perfectly curved body almost to the floor. She wore a simple white dress with a pink ribbon tied at her waist.

"No apologies necessary, Captain. I am grateful for the disruption." The words were practically sung with compassion and honesty.

"Allow me to introduce Lord Braksis, commanding officer of the entire Imperium's army, and his personal colleague, Solara."

"Welcome and thank you for coming. I am Queen Zerilla, and this is my family. Please, join us and we shall discuss matters that have transpired."

Braksis took a step forward. "We appreciate your offer of hospitality, but we do not wish to intrude. We shall wait until your dining is complete."

One of the younger girls leaned over to her sister and whispered something. Both girls began giggling. Zerilla looked down at them and shook her head. "Girls, what are our guests to think?" Addressing Braksis, she continued. "I insist. It's no intrusion."

With those words, two servants set two more places at the table next to the queen.

"Well then, we thank you. It has been several hours since we ate last."

As they sat down, Zerilla continued to smile at her visitors. "Before we begin discussing business, please allow me to introduce my family. I would like us all to feel comfortable before going into the tragic details."

On the opposite end of the long dining table, an older woman who could be none other than Dascony stopped eating, disgusted that two visitors who were of lesser stature had joined them at the royal table.

Once again, the two girls let out a little giggle.

"Allow me to begin by introducing my two daughters first. They clearly seem to have something to say, so we might as well begin with them."

The two girls quickly jumped up knowing that the attention was on them. Both had long blonde hair, although not as long as their mother's. "The oldest one is Trella, she is thirteen, and the younger is Partha, at eight."

Trella laughed out loud and started to goad her younger sister by singing four short words. "Partha has a crush."

"Hey, do not!" the younger daughter screamed.

"Do too!" Trella shot back.

Not knowing what to do, Partha began to tremble and pout.

The older woman, Dascony, leaned forward staring at her two granddaughters. "That will be enough of that. Ladies do not carry on so in public."

Seeing the enthusiasm and joy quickly being deflated, Braksis leaned forward himself and addressed Trella. "Well, I'll tell you this much, there is not a lovelier girl in the entire Seven Kingdoms that I would prefer to have a crush on me."

Partha immediately smiled again, then looked at her sister and stuck her tongue out.

"Okay, let's move on." Zerilla giggled. "Partha is a twin to little Savic here."

Savic did not stop eating his food when introduced, which garnered another sneer from his grandmother. The youngest son had disheveled light brown hair and the formation of a tummy that would certainly keep on growing if he continued to eat the way he was doing now.

"Next to Trella is my eldest son Trong, who is fifteen."

Trong also had light blonde hair like his mother. Unlike Savic, it was perfectly clipped and styled. His demeanor was the most regal of all the children present. He had none of the spirit and fire one usually finds in the eyes of a teenager. He acted as if he were better than others. His attire also displayed that of one accustomed to fine living and royal descent. "Charmed," was the only word he said in greeting.

Braksis looked back at Zerilla. "No offense meant, but you look no older than me, yet you have a son who is fifteen? This I find hard to believe."

Pleasantly surprised, Zerilla smiled back. "No offense taken, Braksis. Noroat and I fell in love when we were Trong's age, and wed soon after that. Trong was born when I was seventeen."

"Ah, that would explain a lot," Braksis commented.

"Finally, this brings us to Mivo. Mivo is twelve years old."

Mivo seemed out of place with shadow-black hair. He quickly jumped up and addressed the visitors with enthusiasm. "Wow, a real-life warlord! Pleased to meet you, sir! Can I see your sword?"

"Mivo, sit down," Dascony scolded.

"Yes, ma'am. I'm sorry, Grandma."

Braksis winked at the boy. "I'll show it to you after dinner."

Jumping back up in defiance of his grandmother, Mivo cried out in elation. "Really, that's just swell!"

This time Trong addressed his brother. "Mivo, you heard our grandmother."

"Sorry," Mivo uttered back, but the anticipation of seeing a real-life warrior's sword, especially the famed Phoenix that Lord Braksis wielded wouldn't allow his mood to be sullied.

Still smiling at her children, Zerilla went to introduce her mother-in-law. "Finally, that brings me to my mother-in-law, Dascony."

Dascony was elegantly dressed in regal fashion. Jewels hung from around her throat and wrists. Her brown hair was graying as age took its toll. Wrinkles also had begun to form around her eyes. Scornfully, she looked at Braksis. "Unlike my daughter-in-law, I do not approve of this intrusion. Royalty should never be interrupted by common folk."

Quickly ready to get up and leave the table to allow the family to continue its meal, Braksis stood, but found Zerilla reach out and take his hand, dragging him back down to his seat.

"Mother, you are dishonoring our noble guests, and in fact, dishonoring me." This last statement was the first time since they arrived that Zerilla had taken a harsh tone. The smile she had been brandishing since they first entered had been replaced by cold determination.

"Well, I never," Dascony panted in disbelief. "If this scoundrel doesn't leave, then I shall not stay and sully myself with their presence." She waved to a servant who came and pulled the chair back for her to stand. She glared at Zerilla, then turned and walked out, her elongated dress swishing as she walked.

"I'm sorry, Queen Zerilla, I did not intend..."

Zerilla raised a hand and quieted him. "She is old-fashioned and set in her ways. It is not you she disproves of, but rather me." After a brief pause to collect herself, her smile and euphoric demeanor quickly returned.

Solara chuckled softly before speaking. "Imagine her surprise if she were to learn that Braksis here is the true heir to the Falestia throne."

Partha sighed and rested her chin on her hands as she glanced at Braksis. "Handsome—and a king, too."

Trella elbowed her sister lightly forcing her to move back.

"What did you do that for?" Partha shot back.

"To keep you from daydreaming," Trella rebutted.

"Children, please, shall we finish dinner?" Zerilla inquired. Looking over at Braksis. "Are you truly the heir to the throne of Falestia?"

"Yes. I am. Though it is a long story—and one that shall have to wait until your plight has been remedied."

"A story that I think will be well worth listening to. I look forward to it."

"Mama?" Savic spoke for the first time.

"Yes, dear?"

"I want more."

"I think you've had enough, dear. Why don't you run along now and play."

The young twin did not need to be told twice. He jumped up and ran out the door heading for his room and the toys within.

Zerilla looked at the rest of her children. "If you are all finished eating, would you please allow us to have some privacy?"

Trong stood up, bowed formally to his mother and to Braksis, then walked out of the room.

Mivo quickly ran over between his mother and Braksis. "I'm still going to see your sword later, right?"

"You have my word," Braksis replied.

"Yippee!" He cheered before leaving to join his brother.

"Mom, Partha doesn't want to leave," Trella stated as she was pulling her younger sister by the hair.

Zerilla leaned over and kissed her youngest daughter. "You'll see your love again. Say so long for now."

With a frown, Partha stood up and waived goodbye to Braksis. Then the two sisters were also off.

As the last of the children left, Braksis smiled after them. "Handsome family."

"Why thank you." Seeing him turn his gaze intently to her, she knew it was finally time to tell him of the woes her kingdom has been suffering. "Shall we get down to business?"

"Yes, please."

"About a month ago, one of our sentries sounded an alarm in the dead of the night. When the guards went to investigate, all that they found on the walls and guard towers was blood. At first, we thought that it was one of the races attacking, but during the day, Captain Vector and his men returned with no evidence of this.

"Vector doubled the guards, and torches were lit throughout the night to illuminate the walls. That night we were attacked again. This time there was no doubt, it was a large reptilian creature that plucked the soldiers right off the walls."

"Reptilian creature?" Braksis questioned. "The message said a dragon."

"We have no other means to describe it. It is similar to a dragon, but also different."

Solara searched her memory with great unrest. She had both hoped and feared that the beast attacking would indeed be a dragon. Now, she was uncertain.

"Hunting parties were sent into the forests after the beast, but very few returned. Any that actually encountered the beast have yet to escape with their lives intact. Captain Vector began to run out of options and looked for other means to stop the beast. He first contacted a pair of brothers. Famed hunters who claimed to have gone to Darnak, the Dragon Territory and actually hunted and killed numerous dragons."

"What happened to them?" Solara inquired, hoping that dragon hunters met their fate with much pain and agony.

"They claimed to have sighted the beast and chased it into the forest. We have not heard from them since."

Although she did not crave the loss of life with those helping to fight the beast, Solara quickly warmed to the fact that these dragon hunters most likely perished. They deserved to die for tracking down and hunting such noble beasts.

"Finally, Vector indicated we should contact the Imperium and request official assistance. Which has brought you to us. How many troops did you bring?"

Looking down, Braksis slowly replied. "Unfortunately, none. The bulk of the army is currently in Dartie preparing for battle against those who have been pillaging villages and wreaking havoc. The rest of the troops are fortifying the defenses of Trespias."

"You mean you two are alone?" Zerilla gasped incredulously with a sudden sense of foreboding.

"Yes, we are alone. We will help you. I promise you that."

"I'm sorry to sound so grim, Lord Braksis, but what is it you can do that others have not?"

"I shall personally assess the situation, direct your troops, and face the creature this evening. I should speak with Captain Vector and see what has already been attempted. Traps, strategies, and things of that nature."

The conversation was interrupted as Braksis heard Tiot outside barking and howling. Something was coming, and the timber wolf wanted its master to be aware. Immediately in defense mode, Braksis spouted orders as he rushed toward the front door. "You there–take the queen and get her family down below to safety. Solara, with me."

As the two approached the door, they could hear Tiot growling, and giant bangs thundering against the door. Inside, Braksis could hear the screams of the younger children. He would not allow anything more to befall and harm this family.

Unsheathing his mystical blade, the Phoenix, in preparation, the doors suddenly burst open before them. Braksis and Solara both braced for the attack as a bluish-scaled creature plummeted through the entrance.

CHAPTER 4

The creature flew threw the door and landed lifelessly upon the ground. Behind were two men trying to get Tiot to stop growling and barking.

Poking the carcass upon the floor with the Phoenix, Braksis was satisfied that the beast was dead. He sheathed his sword and let out a low whistle to Tiot, who immediately stopped growling and lay down.

The two men in the doorway were identically garbed in red armor with silver outlines. It encompassed their entire bodies except for their heads. The armor fit loosely but was bulkier and heavier than anything the Imperial Army would wear. The joints of the armor around the shoulders, torso, and knees revealed a smooth silver lining. From their backs hung red capes that stretched from shoulder down to the ground. Both men appeared heavily armed with a variety of weapons, but most noticeable was the elongated bastard sword that each had sheathed across their backs. The blades were almost as long as the warriors that wielded them, and slanted from the hilt above their heads down to the tip, which was slightly raised off the ground.

The two warriors themselves were of different features and dimensions. The taller one was clean-shaven with short blonde hair. A smile was stretched across his face as he looked at the slain beast by his feet. The second of the two was about a head shorter, but much more muscularly built. He had brown hair pulled back into a ponytail and a long mustache with ends that turned down toward the chin. He had a wild look in his eyes; Braksis felt he could not be trusted.

The taller of the two took a step forward, still grinning with pride. "Not bad, if I do say so myself. This here beastie we tracked for close to two weeks, but we got him."

Braksis could hear footsteps behind him. In his peripheral vision he could see it was Queen Zerilla and Captain Vector.

The shorter of the two men looked at the queen. "Hey, Queenie, we told you we would get this here beastie. I think it's time for a reward." Stepping forward and past Braksis and Solara, the shorter man grabbed the queen and attempted to kiss her.

Queen Zerilla struggled against his advances and attempted to pull her head away, pleading for him to stop.

As he struggled with Zerilla, he pulled a small blade from his back and held it steady at Vector's throat so the captain could not come to the queen's aid. "No distractions."

The second man by the door laughed uproariously.

In an instant, Braksis was in motion. He grabbed the newcomer by the arm holding the blade and twisted it back so the dagger would drop. He then applied force, pulling the man toward him. As he did so, he used his leverage to send the armored man hurtling through the air.

The taller man was no longer smiling. He quickly attempted to retaliate, but Solara had dodged behind him, and grabbed him by the throat with a knife of her own, rubbing it against his neck in warning. "I think he can handle himself on his own, what do you think?"

Not wanting to move, the taller man let out a low whisper. "Sounds reasonable to me."

"I thought you'd see things my way," Solara replied.

The shorter man stood up and saw both Vector and Braksis looking down at him. Glancing at his companion, he felt that this was a hopeless scenario. "Okay, okay, man, no kiss. I get where you're coming from. We still got the beastie."

Zerilla stepped forward and looked at the creature on the floor. She instinctively felt something was wrong but wished to put a close on the hostilities within the room. "Everyone, if you please, I hired these two men several weeks ago. Although I think Drew went a little far, we are all friends here."

The taller man smiled again. He reached up and moved the blade away from his throat with his index finger. "That's right. Friends. I don't think friends need knives at their throats, do you?"

Solara released him and resheathed her knife.

The taller man stared hard at his brother. "Idiot. You know who you just got in a fight with?"

"No," the man Zerilla called Drew responded with scorn.

"You just had the privilege of being manhandled by none other than Lord Braksis."

"Braksis?" Drew repeated.

"Yessiree, Braksis. Dolt." Taking a step toward the warlord, the taller man continued. "Allow me to introduce ourselves. My name is Boudie, and that there is my idiot of a brother Drew."

Braksis nodded, then addressed Zerilla. "You hired these two?"

Without allowing Zerilla to respond, Boudie spoke up. "Oh yes, my brother and I are the two best hunters in all of the Seven Kingdoms. Darnak, too, for that matter."

Solara brushed past Boudie. "If I knew you were a dragon hunter, I would have slit your throat instead of just restraining you."

"A good sense of humor you have there, lass."

"Who says I'm joking?" Solara rebutted with no sign of humor.

Wanting to resolve this situation and possibly get back to his troops, Braksis walked over to the dead creature. "So this is the man-eating dragon?"

"It's not actually a dragon," Boudie answered. "We've killed many a dragon and never seen one like this. I've been calling it a tragon since I've never seen one before. Tragon, get it? Three-headed dragon?"

"How inventive," Solara mumbled.

Looking at the creature, which had bluish-white scales, four legs, three heads, and a tail, Braksis felt uneasy. "Awfully small to cause such a disturbance."

Zerilla soon realized that was bothering her as well. "How could this thing have gotten over our walls? It doesn't have wings. Are you sure this is the right creature?"

"Hey, you've got the Boudie and Drew seal of approval. Like I said, we tracked this thing for close to two whole weeks!" Boudie beamed.

Zerilla seemed to pale with the news. "Two weeks? We were attacked just last night."

"Impossible, we were deep within the Suspintian Forest last night."

"This must not be the creature," Vector surmised.

"What? Not the creature?" Drew asked. "I still want to get paid for this."

Zerilla looked at the beast, then at her guests. "Please remove this from my house. I would like you all to stay for the evening and see whether the attacks have halted or not. If so, then you will be paid as agreed and not by a kiss or anything physical. The gold we agreed upon."

"Of course, your majesty. I apologize for my brother's inappropriate behavior. Of course we shall wait and confirm that we killed the right beast. I'd hate for our reputations to suffer. We are the best, after all." Quickly grabbing his brother's cape, Boudie yanked Drew over to him, and the two begin to lift the tragon back up.

As they slowly made their way back out of the house, the tension in the room subsided.

"Are you okay?" Braksis asked, genuinely concerned.

"Yes, I just don't know why he attempted to kiss and grope me like that," Zerilla responded shakily .

"A night in the dungeon would do him well," Vector offered.

"That won't be necessary, Captain."

"How about house arrest?" Vector tried one last time.

"No, but thank you for trying. You can go now and check on the defenses for tonight."

"Yes, ma'am." Vector turned and walked out of the royal household to administer to his duties.

"Are things always this entertaining?" Braksis jokingly asked.

"Humph. No, it seems like the past month or so has been exceedingly difficult." With a deep sigh, she composed herself, then seemed to be glowing once more. "Thank you both for your assistance. I appreciate it."

"Anytime," replied Braksis.

As Solara watched the two, she was amazed this was the same person she traveled with. Braksis had been so determined to return to his armed forces and the battle at Dartie, but now he seemed to be growing soft, gentle. Could he be falling for this troubled queen?

Suddenly feeling out of place as the two began talking to each other, she slowly edged her way back toward the doors. She could always check on the horses. Yes, the horses would be good. She looked back and realized Braksis and Zerilla both seemed oblivious to the fact that she was leaving. Her last thought for Braksis as she walked out was contradictory. She felt he deserved some happiness in his life, but she also felt a deep sense of resentment toward the queen.

❖ ❖ ❖ ❖ ❖

The minutes turned into hours, and Braksis and Zerilla seemed to lose themselves in each other's eyes. Zerilla was amazed she could begin to have feelings so quickly for another man so soon after the death of her husband.

Braksis seemed to lose all sight of the warrior he was and turned into a little kid himself. He told her all about his royal lineage. How his parents were the rulers of Falestia, and one night, when he was a child, his cousin Rawthorne came to the castle seeking power. His parents were slain, but a servant fled with Braksis in his arms. How Rawthorne's men ultimately caught up to them, killed the servant, and almost killed Braksis, if not for the intervention of a troll by the name of Ferceng. A troll who would hide Braksis and raise him as his own son.

Although Braksis was the true king, he seemed inclined not to reclaim the throne. Rawthorne was removed from power, and Emperor Conrad granted Braksis the right to reclaim that which was rightfully his. Instead, Braksis went to his uncle, Lorrents, and requested that he claim the throne. Lorrents had always been highly respected and very close to his brother, and he accepted. The people quickly clung to their new leader, and Lorrents had ruled a peaceful land ever since.

As he finished his story, he looked deep into Zerilla's light blue eyes. He knew that life would never be the same again after meeting her. He couldn't explain it, but just by looking at each other, a sense of elation grew within them both. He wished he never had to leave.

Slowly as they gazed at each other, the two grew closer, then magically, their lips touched. Her kiss was soft and gentle. Tender and warm. A sense of warmth and passion fluttered through them both. The two clung to each other savoring the moment. A moment that seemed poetic, surreal, and heavenly. If one could live forever in a moment, this would be it. Unfortunately, life often has ways of interrupting the most pleasant and enjoyable of circumstances.

From the forests beyond the city's wall, a loud and deep roar pierced the tranquil air. Braksis jumped up and held Zerilla as if to defend her right here and now.

She stared at the door to the house. "It's the beast. It has returned."

A thunderous banging and crash could be heard. Screams ensued.

Braksis looked at the queen who meant so much to him and yet was also a stranger in so many ways. "Get the children and go underground. I don't want anything to happen to any of you."

She nodded agreement, distress clearly etched on her face.

"Don't worry, I won't let anything happen to you or the children." He leaned over and kissed her one last time. The passion of the moment quickly flooded both of them, as both had thoughts that this may be their last embrace.

He pulled himself away and ran to the door, and to the unknown threat waiting for him. As he opened the door and saw what was happening outside, he quickly wished that his whole army had come with him after all.

The tragon killed by Boudie and Drew was clearly nothing more than an infant. The beast in front of him towered over the crumbled stone wall it had just walked through as easily as a fish swimming through water. Soldiers and people were running rampant, as the giant three-headed tragon leaned over and snapped at anyone within its range and swallowed them whole.

Braksis could see Boudie and Drew rushing into action. Captain Vector was doing his best to reorganize his troops. Solara was riding her horse toward the house, bringing Blaze to him as well.

The tragon raised its three heads and released a giant roar that could awaken the dead. As he looked on, Braksis suddenly wondered whether his promise to Zerilla could be kept or not. He honestly could not see any way they could fend off a beast this size. A deep sense of foreboding overcame him like none ever before. He must be triumphant. Somehow. He refused to accept that he found Zerilla, only to lose her so quickly. Life could not be that cruel.

Seeing the tragon lower its heads and start snapping at the fleeing people of Comonor, he was not so sure.

CHAPTER 5

The torrents of fleeing people vastly slowed down Solara's attempt to reach Braksis with the horses. All seemed to be screaming and reaching desperately for the unmanned steed that they hoped could help whisk them away to safety.

Not wanting to hurt the scared people, Solara tried to keep a steady pace and get past the citizens, but as often in crowds, she was slowed to a near halt. Screaming for them to get out of her way and allow her to go to confront the beast, her pleas were lost in the hysteria.

She felt someone grasping her leg, then many hands joined it. Before she knew what was happening, she was being pulled from her horse. Still unwilling to confront these terrified townsmen, she opted to relinquish the horses without much fight. From the ground, she looked up and saw small fights erupting over who would ride the captured steeds. All reason was lost on these people, and Solara had no time to remain to try to soothe things.

Unable to see Braksis through the scrambles of the crowd, she slowly edged her way to one of the buildings. Most of the people were fleeing by the main roads, so her only hope was to bypass them until the crowds dwindled down. Hearing another roar from the beast, she doubled her efforts and slowly forced her way through the dense bodies.

Reaching the porch of what was Comonor's Inn, she quickly ran inside the open doors. The inn was empty. All citizens had fled when they first heard the commotion. She spotted large drums of alcohol and quickly filed that to memory as she raced toward the stairs.

Ascending to the top floor, she saw a door to a room on the same side as the main street. She tried the knob; it was locked. Unwilling to waste the time by trying the next room over, she kicked the wooden door in with one swift jolt. The door swung open with wood chips spraying as the frame splintered.

She raced to the window and peered out. She could see the beast much more clearly from here. The body of the tragon was large and bulky. Standing on all four legs with a long tail swishing behind it, buildings seemed to crumble with every movement. On the front of the body were three elongated necks attached to heads that would bring nightmares to those who survived for years to come. The heads were relatively narrow, with large teeth jutting out of mouths that looked like a birds beak. A sharp horn extended through the top of each head's nose, with two small slit-like eyes that were scanning the area for prey.

Solara could see a mesh of the yellow-garbed guards attempting to organize. The two red-armored hunters were rushing in to face the giant creature. Braksis, too, was hustling into action after losing sight of her and the horses.

Reaching up and grasping the edge of the roof, she hoisted herself up and began swinging back and forth. After building up a decent amount of momentum, she angled herself upward and spun up onto the roof. From this perch, she wished that she had a bow to fire arrows at the beast. Looking at the building next to her, she was grateful that the architects here built the town condensed in the middle and away from the walls. She leapt from rooftop to rooftop, getting closer to the beast with each jump.

Her only remaining desire was to get to Braksis and fight by his side. He had once sacrificed himself to save her, and in return, she bonded her life to his as his protector and friend. To watch him entering battle with a creature of this magnitude, and not be by his side, she feared that her vow would be broken. Guilt and regret filled her and fueled her to move across the rooftops more quickly. If only she had not left Braksis and Zerilla alone, then they would be together now.

❖ ❖ ❖ ❖ ❖

Watching his men running rampant, floundering and undisciplined, Vector tried to rally his troops and organize them with little avail. The only people who seemed to be attacking the beast were the two Dartian hunters who had sprung into action as soon as the tragon was heard.

Vector spied Braksis walking out of the royal residence and wondered again how any one man could truly help win this day. It seemed to him that Braksis was more interested in swooning the queen than defending Comonor—a task Vector did not willingly grant to anyone but himself. After all, how could an outsider understand what he cherished so deeply?

Curious at what could have caught Braksis's attention over the beast they were facing, he followed his gaze, and saw the mystral warrior attempting to reach him with the horses. Looking to flee was all that Vector could think. As the fleeing people dragged Solara off of her horse, an unusual sense of satisfaction seemed to overcome Vector. It was a feeling she had received what she deserved, and it served her right for trying to abandon the people in their time of need.

Refusing to give any more thought to these outsiders, Vector returned to unsuccessfully trying to corral his men. It seemed as if they all lost their discipline and could not handle the pressure of the situation unfolding. If they survived this, he would need to train the troops better. Suspintians seemed to give in to fear far too quickly. Even if he had to recruit elsewhere, things needed to change.

Another roar from the creature, and those few troops who had stayed with him also began to flee.

❖ ❖ ❖ ❖ ❖

"Well, brother, it looks like we caught the wrong beast after all," Boudie pointed out as they advanced toward the tragon, using the buildings and fleeing people as cover.

"Yeah man, oops."

"Very big oops," Boudie laughed in return.

Peering around the corner, Boudie watched the head closest to them lunge for an old woman desperately trying to seek cover.

"Now!" Boudie ordered. While the head was not looking their way, the two hunters sprinted out below the beast and stopped for cover directly behind its forward right leg.

Boudie looked at the leg and gently touched it. "The scales are going to be tough to get through."

"Hey, we can do it," Drew declared in a cocky tone. "We've hunted just about everything alive; this is no different."

"Yeah, you're right, brother." Drawing his elongated bastard sword, Boudie signaled his brother to do the same.

The tragon took another step, and Boudie and Drew had to jog farther up the street to stay with the giant step.

The creature remained oblivious to their presence, which was exactly how the two hunters wanted it.

"On the count of three," Boudie suggested. Both men stood on one side of the large circular foot, grasping their swords with both hands, ready to strike. "One, two, three!"

As they hit the number three, both hunters swung their elongated blades with all of their might and cut deeply into two sides of the tragon's foot. The beast raised all three heads and let out a piercing scream as they did so.

"Um, brother, weren't we supposed to sever the limb?" Drew asked looking befuddled that the foot had only been cut and not removed.

Before Boudie could answer, one of the heads lowered to look at the brothers and opened its fang-filled mouth in a giant roar at the two. The scent of human death and decay permeated the air being blown at them.

The two brothers stood staring at the mouth and wondering what to do now. The decision was soon taken away from them. The injured leg lifted up and swung both men aside into the ruins of what was once a residence.

One head swung over and picked up the unconscious Boudie in its mouth and started to chew. The hunters' armor, which was much thicker and stronger than those of the fleeing guards, only gave way slightly to the chewing of the tragon. Unable to taste the flesh underneath, the hunter was spit back out, hurtling through the air and impacting one of the remaining walls.

With another roar, the creature continued its advance and left the battered hunters behind, seeking other townsmen that would be easier to feast upon.

❖ ❖ ❖ ❖ ❖

After losing sight of Solara, Braksis turned his attention on the matter at hand. He refused to allow this beast to bring harm to Zerilla or the children. He would gladly die before he would allow anything to happen to them.

He watched the two Dartian hunters charge valiantly against the creature. Both men arrived at one of the beast's feet and swiped at it, resulting in another roar from the three heads.

As the tragon released its scream, many of the remaining guards fled in terror. If they had any hope of surviving this day, all forces needed to pull together and attack in an organized and strategic fashion.

Braksis jogged toward the fleeing troops to gain their attention himself. He saw that Vector's efforts thus far were in vain.

Another roar from the creature quickly drew his attention. He watched as the beast lifted its leg and sent both Dartian hunters hurtling through the air into wreckage. One head reached over and grabbed a hunter in its mouth and started chewing.

Braksis turned his head and refocused. Even though they were arrogant, cocky, and not very likable, they had fought and fell valiantly. Fell, as all those confronting this beast may yet do this day.

Drawing the Phoenix, he waved it in the air trying to gain the attention of the fleeing troops. The sword itself was famed throughout the Seven Kingdoms, as was the man who wielded it. The Phoenix, crafted from the molten magma of terra itself, had been a gift from his surrogate father, Ferceng. The hilt was handcrafted and detailed in gold to resemble the great bird. It was detailed with the shape of wings arching skyward toward the blade, and tail feathers flowing at the bottom of the grip. The center was shaped as a bird's head, leading into the blade. The blade itself had finely detailed designs of flames swirling about it.

"Soldiers of Suspinti, hear me! We must stand and fight. Organize and protect the people of Comonor." Looking around, he saw that only a few stopped to stand with him, and not for the first time, wished that his own men were here this day.

Captain Vector approached Braksis with several troops of his own with him. "I see that you decided to stay and fight after all."

Not knowing where this sudden verbal attack was coming from, Braksis ignored the statement. "As we saw with the Dartian hunters, we can hurt the beast, but attacking in close proximity is not wise. Do you have long bows?"

Captain Vector turned to look at the advancing creature, then at the few men who remained with them to fight. "Yes, each guard tower is stocked with weapons in case of invasion."

"Excellent. I want you and your men to circle around then. Get to those towers and start sending volleys of arrows at the beast from behind. If it turns to attack you, keep moving along the walls so that the barrage can continue."

"What will you do?" Vector sneered.

"I will provide you with time if nothing else. Now go."

His final words left no room for doubt. Vector turned and ran toward the western walls, which still stood and were not barred by the advancing beast. His remaining men followed suit, and they were only too glad to be able to attack from afar and not from the ground. They all had seen what happened to the famed hunters, and none of them wished to meet a similar fate.

Braksis turned and faced the beast straight on as it approached. The streets were growing barren, and he was all that was left to face the growing rampage. Experience taught him that even the mightiest force could fall, but he still could not yet see how he would overcome the creature before him.

Unwilling to let its master face the creature alone, Tiot stood next to Braksis and growled in defiance.

"Tiot, my faithful timber wolf. I'm afraid our luck may have finally run out." From above him, he could hear a shout. He looked toward the voice and saw Solara standing atop a building. She was trying to tell him something.

"Meet me at the inn!" she yelled. "There are barrels of alcohol. We could set the beast ablaze!"

Finally, a plan that seemed to have merit. Braksis nodded his acknowledgment, and he and Tiot ran toward the inn.

Unlike when Solara struggled there moments ago, the streets were clearing and the crowds were gone. He ran in the open doors and saw what Solara was referencing. The lower portion of the inn served food and spirits to its patrons. There were three large drums of alcohol. Not much, but something.

Solara quickly appeared as she ran down the stairs. "We can use these to at least turn the beast back."

The two quickly flipped the kegs over and rolled the first one out. The size of it required both of their strengths to get it in motion. The process of moving the drums was slow. They could hear the beast roaring in the distance. A distance that was growing ever closer.

As they brought the first keg outside, they saw that the tragon had arrows jutting out all over its body. Captain Vector and his men had clearly made it to the armory and had begun their volley. Braksis hoped that the captain would buy them enough time to get all three drums in place.

Satisfied with the placement of the first keg, the two ran back to retrieve the second one. Solara looked at Braksis briefly and saw his demeanor was grim. "You know, if we don't start seeing some excitement in our travels, I may have to leave you. Your life is too dull. There is nothing I need to protect you from."

Braksis toppled the second keg over and considered his companion for a moment. "What?"

"Just trying to lighten up the atmosphere. You're too grim."

"Are you seeing what I'm seeing?" Braksis questioned astonishingly.

"Yes, but by the look on your face, you seem like deep down you have already admitted defeat. Today is not your day to die."

"How can you be so certain?"

"Because I am here with you. It is when you are alone and I cannot reach you. That is the day you should fear for your life. Not today."

The seriousness and confidence in her statement was inspiring. Although he still did not see how they would triumph this day, he refused to give in to the despair of the moment. That would only slow him down. If he thought that he would lose, then it would be a self-fulfilling prophecy and he would. "Thank you."

"Anytime."

"Well, let's get these drums moving so we can incinerate that bitch."

"That's what I like to hear."

The moment of talking was gone, and both pushed the keg as it slowly rolled out of the inn and onto the street. They saw the beast was closer to their first drum, but it was clearly distracted and trying to retaliate against Vector along the walls.

The second keg seemed easier to move than the first, and they quickly were back for the third. As they rolled it down the central street, they saw that this would be cutting it close. The tragon was almost upon the royal house, and Braksis did not want to allow anything to disrupt the patrons inside.

Taking the Phoenix, he jabbed the final keg near the bottom sending alcohol streaming into the street. He and Solara then went in opposite directions toward the other two kegs and cut an opening in the bottom of each. They had placed one on each side of the road, with the final one in the middle.

As the liquor flowed onto the road and toward the tragon, Braksis felt a sense of success overcome him. As the alcohol started flowing below the tragon's feet, Braksis signaled Solara to light it.

She impacted two small knives several times until a spark finally hit the flowing alcohol. The rest ignited quickly as the fire encompassed the entire stream of liquid on the ground. The tragon let out a roar as the fire engulfed its feet and lower body. Flames shot up and the creature began to burn.

Braksis smiled at Solara as she walked back toward him. "Nicely done. Good plan."

"Why thank you."

Their conversation was interrupted by a scream close to the tragon. As Braksis looked over to see where it came from, he saw the young Mivo trapped by the flames.

"Damn," was all Braksis said as he started off toward the boy. He would have to go through the flames himself if he were to reach Mivo. Looking for water or something to douse himself in before jumping into the fire to save the child, time seemed to run out.

One of the heads of the tragon also heard the petrified child and reached out to find him. As it approached, its head caught on fire, but still it snaked toward the sound of fear. As it grew closer, Mivo saw it and screamed even louder.

Braksis swore under his breath as he jumped into the flames and raced toward the boy. He only prayed he could get there in time. A roar of triumph from the tragon, and his heart sunk as he saw he would arrive moments too late.

CHAPTER 6

As Braksis ran through the dancing flames, his cloak burst into flames and his armor began to overheat, but the Warlord did not allow any of this to deter him from his goal. He could still hear the boy crying, and he would not stop until he reached the child and was able to protect him.

❖ ❖ ❖ ❖ ❖

The tragon's head was slowly closing in. Mivo was terrified as he saw the flame-engulfed mouth moving toward him. He looked to his left and right but saw no way to flee. The flames had indeed trapped him.

All he had wanted was to see the soldiers in action. He thoroughly enjoyed seeing warriors fight, and he particularly wanted to see the famed Braksis. He hid and then snuck out of the house as his mother was rounding his siblings up, never realizing he may put his own life in jeopardy by doing so.

The tears flowed freely down his face but almost immediately dried up from the heat of the fire. Out of the flames he saw the open jaws of the tragon as it reached out to him, widening. He screamed one more time in terror, realizing for the first time, that perhaps life was not all fun and games for warriors. He knew all about death. His father had passed from plague recently, but he felt that a warrior would fight valiantly and could never truly die if his course was true. As the tragon's mouth closed around him, he wished dearly to be inside with his mother. In her gentle arms and caress. Never again did he think he would see her.

Then, the mouth did not close; it just fell right there around him, wide open and ready to bite. Mivo was terrified, yet also curious. What had happened?

❖ ❖ ❖ ❖ ❖

Braksis had seen the tragon stretching for the child, and realized that he was too late. He hoped and prayed that he could stop the beast before it brought any permanent damage to the boy. He leaped high in the air with the Phoenix held above his head. As he came down, he thrust with all of his might at the neck of the beast.

Expecting merely to slice into the neck and startle the beast as had happened with the Dartian hunters, Braksis was amazed when his blade sliced through it, severing its head from the rest of its body. He knelt on one knee in amazement. The neck of the beast jerked away quickly back toward its body. Its severed head lay there on the ground, twitching slightly, but with its mouth remaining open.

Moving around the head quickly, he saw Mivo shuddering as he looked at the teeth of the creature lying lifeless in front of him. The flames burned at the flesh, and the head soon was engulfed in flames.

Braksis removed what was left of his red cloak and put it around the terrified boy. "Here, I will use this to carry you."

Mivo looked away from the decapitated head for the first time. "I'm sorry; I'll never leave my mother again." The tears flowed once more.

Both Braksis and Mivo coughed slightly from the smoke emanating from the tragon's charred head. "We need to go—now."

Knowing his armor would scald the boy, Braksis used the remains of his cloak to support the child and cradle him in his arms. He ran quickly back through the flames where Solara was waiting, concern painted on her face.

Finally escaping the flames, Braksis put Mivo down and instructed him to roll around to put out any fire that caught his clothes.

Breathing a deep sigh of relief, he looked at Solara. "Take the child to his mother. Make sure they are safe. I will stay here and face the beast. The neck is tender and weak. I need to relay that to the men."

Solara reluctantly picked up the child and looked at Braksis one last time. She did not wish to leave him. How could she protect him if they were apart? But this innocent child must also be protected. "I will be back as soon as I can."

"Not before you make sure the family is safe. Tiot, go with them. Guard the family."

Tiot barked in acknowledgment and fell in step next to Solara. With one last thought of the man she vowed to protect, she was off to bring the child to his mother.

Braksis turned and looked at the flame-engulfed road in front of him. He needed to spread the word of the weakness quickly. As he looked toward the western wall, another head reached through the flames too quick for him to react.

❖ ❖ ❖ ❖ ❖

Vector and his men were having trouble seeing the tragon through all of the smoke. As they continued their volley, merely aiming at the sounds of the beast's roars, he lost himself in bitterness toward Braksis.

Before Braksis had come, Suspinti had been losing people but never had the damages been this vast. Suddenly, on the day he arrived, the northern wall had been crumbled leaving them vulnerable to all forms of attack from the forest. Residences and businesses lay in ruins. Now, Braksis had set the streets on fire. Who knew what the damage would cost?

Even worse, the cretin had spent time alone with the queen, undoubtedly romancing her and turning her heart away from the people. This disgusted Vector even more. He realized that was truly the origin of his scorn. Could it be jealousy? After all, he was the one who failed to slay the creature when he had the chance. Then in comes the mighty warlord, and his queen seemed smitten by him. He was not truly angry with Braksis, but jealous.

Regretting such primitive reactions, Vector vowed that from this moment on, he would follow Braksis's commands, and not include the emotional baggage that he brought out after the tragon attacked.

After all, if this warlord made the queen happy, then who was he to stand in their way?

"Men! Keep firing until your very last arrow!" he found himself ordering.

"Sir, I can't see anything."

"It doesn't matter, you can still hear it. Aim for the sound. It's large enough that we are bound to hit it!"

Loading arrows and launching them in unison, the remaining guards continued their volley with the remaining shafts at their disposal.

❖ ❖ ❖ ❖ ❖

Slowly Drew opened his eyes. The glimmer of the fire hurt his eyes as they adjusted. He lay there for several moments trying to recall where he was and what he was doing. He could see that he was lying in a pile of rubble. The remains of what used to be a house. Debris from the northern wall was also scattered about.

The memory of the tragon quickly flooded back into his mind. He looked at all the death and destruction left in its wake. Attempting to stand, he felt pain compressing his chest. The armor he wore was damaged from when the tragon barreled its foot into the two brothers. Drew slowly strained to reach behind him and unfasten the straps holding the armor in place.

With the straps removed, taking the armor plating off was much easier. It still took effort and time, but Drew managed to get it off and dropped it next to him. With the armor off, he could breathe much easier, and his wits returned almost fully.

Below the armor, he wore nothing more than a spotted vest designed from the pelt of one of his many kills over the years. Not much protection against a tragon. Drew scanned the debris for some of his weapons. He found an axe and two smaller swords. He tied them across his back as he wondered how he could use these small weapons to bring the tragon down.

He stared out at the flames and could see the shape of the tragon smoking in the midst of the tempest. There was time. First, he needed to find his brother.

Looking around, he saw small pieces of red armor scattered along the ground. Not much, but certainly chunks that had been removed from Boudie's outfit. Following the trail, he quickly came across his brother, collapsed against the wall.

Running to his brother's side, Drew turned Boudie over. The armor he wore was dented, impacted and overall a mess. Drew struggled to take the breastplate off, and saw that Boudie was still breathing.

"Brother?" Drew called out trying to awaken Boudie. His only response was moaning. "Stay here then. I will kill that beastie for you and we will dance around its dead carcass."

Drew sat his brother up against the wall, and placed one of Boudie's weapons by his hand on the ground in case he were to awaken. Vowing he would see the creature slain, Drew ran off toward the tragon, leaving his battered brother behind.

CHAPTER 7

As the tragon reached out for Braksis, his eyes widened in shock, not realizing how close the beast had come to him. Behind him, a bright light glowed, momentarily startling the creature.

Braksis dropped and rolled out of the way, and looked toward the light from behind one of the remaining buildings. The light appeared to be slicing through space, and a figure leapt right out of it.

Straining to see, the figure appeared to be elven, but she had pink skin, like nothing he had ever seen before. Not knowing who this girl was, but accepting the fact that her appearance just saved his life, he yelled out to return the favor. "Over here, girl!"

The elf joined him behind the wall, and looked him over briefly. "I am looking for the savior. What is this place?"

Not certain to whom the elf was referring, Braksis decided to reply with a joke. "I don't know who your savior is, but you just became mine. Thank you. I am Lord Braksis; this is Comonor."

"I do not recognize the names. The Elders must have completed their mission then, and I am in the land of the savior. My name is Kai."

"Well, Kai, pleased to meet you." A roar from the tragon interrupted pleasantries. "How about we continue this little conversation later? Are you any good with that bow?"

Kai let out a cocky grin. "I am one of the best."

"Good. We are facing a giant reptilian creature we have dubbed a tragon. So far, its neck seems to be vulnerable. I caught it by surprise last time. I do not have much faith in that working again. However, if you could blind it, we may have a chance."

"Blind it?" Kai inquired.

"Yes, shoot out its eyes. Do you think you can do it?"

Kai smiled a second time in response. "Just watch me." With that, she vaulted away from their protective perch, spinning and leaping throughout the street, dancing through the flames without once touching them.

She had trouble seeing the tragon through the smoke, but by concentrating, she could make out the remaining two heads of the beast. "You're a big one, aren't you?" Kneeling down, she removed arrows from her quiver and fired them at the tragon in a rapid-fire motion. Her hands moved in a blur as four arrows were quickly launched in succession, leaving the tragon roaring in pain as the arrows pierced its eyes.

One head blindly dashed out looking for the instigator. Kai continued launching arrows as it approached. Arrows kept impacting the roof of its mouth, and when it jerked away, she used her marksmanship to pierce its throat. The head could not retreat from her barrage quickly enough, as it began to swirl back and forth slowly, and finally plummet to the ground lifelessly.

Braksis raced out to join Kai. "Impressive. Most impressive."

"Thank you. I told you I was one of the best."

"Look, it's starting to back away. It's retreating!" Braksis shouted.

The tragon was indeed turning to leave. The one remaining head roaring in defiance, but it was unable to handle the pain any further. Yellow ooze dripped from its pierced eyes, and the beast was listening to every sound, attempting to avoid a further attack.

What it heard was motion near the side of its head. Reaching out and snapping, the tragon bit air.

❖ ❖ ❖ ❖ ❖

On the roof close to the tragon's head, Solara stood waiting to attack. She had brought the child to his frantic mother, and left Tiot to guard them. Now, she desperately desired to be back and to make sure that nothing happened to Braksis.

She could see the head as it came toward her, and noticed the arrows that had pierced the eyes. Realizing the tragon was blind, she hovered and waited. As it bit out, she jumped out and caught the horn on the tragon's nose.

The tragon jerked its head back and forth trying to dislodge her. Solara held on to the horn tightly. At the base, the horn was not sharp, so as long as she did not touch the tip, she was in no danger of harming herself.

The tragon stopped jerking and walked forward again. Solara eased her grip and gently unsheathed her sword. Without moving her legs, she raised the sword up high, and brought it down, plunging it into the tragon's snout.

The beast roared again and shook its head violently. Solara held on to her sword and continued to apply pressure.

The pain to the tragon was overwhelming. It wanted the pain to stop. The neck from the first severed head came up suddenly and plowed into the final remaining head. Unprepared for the tragon to attack with its severed limb, Solara lost her grip and fell from her perch.

As she fell through the air, she was shocked that this was how she would die. She always envisioned being bested in combat with a humanoid. Yet this was not her time to perish.

From out of nowhere, Kai swung out and snatched Solara from the sky. The cable she was swinging on was not strong enough to support both their weight, but it did allow them to decrease the speed of the fall.

"Hold on and trust me."

Solara listened in shock as they once again plummeted through the air. Who was this? Why was she trying to save her?

The pink-skinned elf seemed to have complete control of her body and motion, and twirled several times in the air, each time bringing herself closer to one of the buildings remaining erect. A hand shot out and clasped tightly to Solara. The other hand found a ledge and held on.

The strain was immense for Kai, but she managed to hold on to both Solara and the ledge. "This is something I can live without trying again."

After holding on for several moments, Kai released the ledge and both mystral and elf fell to the ground, which was only one level from where she had grabbed on.

Amazed and slightly mystified by the aerial rescue, Solara stared intently at Kai. "Thank you."

Kai smiled back. "The one called Lord Braksis seemed concerned for you. I apologize that my original cable arrow was insufficient to maintain both of our weights."

"No need to apologize. You just defied the odds as far as I am concerned. I am in your debt."

"I seem to be hearing that frequently this day," Kai responded as she caught her breath.

"Who else did you save?"

"Me," Braksis proclaimed as he finally caught up to the two women.

Solara looked up at him, then back to Kai. "It appears I am in your debt twofold then."

❖ ❖ ❖ ❖ ❖

The tragon continued its blind rampage back toward the entrance and to a Dartian hunter who demanded revenge.

Drew pulled out his two short swords and rushed over to the bleeding leg he had attacked earlier. He jabbed both swords into the beast's legs, then used his tremendous strength to lift himself up and climb.

The tragon roared out again, as pain was quickly overcoming all of its senses.

Drew removed one blade at a time and kept jabbing it higher and higher, dragging himself up the tragon's leg. His muscles were shaking from the strain of supporting his weight in the air, but his determination kept him going.

As he approached the neck, he continued his way up the back side until he reached the tragon's remaining head. Pulling out his axe, he grinned sinisterly as his eyes glared with the glory of a kill, then plunged the axe down into the tragon's head, slicing into the creature's brain.

The tragon shook and quivered, then the final head fell as the entire body stumbled and dropped lifelessly to the ground. Drew held on by his axe, which was hoisted beneath the creature's skull.

As the head impacted the ground, Drew jumped off and rolled away from the writhing creature. Standing up, he looked at the smoldering carcass with disgust, and spit on it. "That was for my brother."

A second longer, and Drew was off to get help for Boudie.

CHAPTER 8

Soot and debris covered the faces and bodies of most of the people in the streets of Comonor. For hours after the final head of the tragon had fallen, those who remained within the city walls had pulled together to fight the growing blaze and save the remainder of their home.

Looking back at the idea to set the creature ablaze and the damage that it inflicted on the surrounding buildings, Braksis regretted his decision. It had been a wise strategy that could have worked, but he lamented the aftermath.

After the erupting inferno had finally been quenched, Braksis, Solara, Tiot, and the newcomer, Kai, searched for survivors. Tiot's enhanced senses helped them to find many buried citizens that morning, and the three champions quickly strove to uncover them.

Their efforts continued throughout the day and night with no pause for rest or concern for themselves. With every tense exclamation from Tiot, they were in action looking for another survivor, speaking soothing words of comfort and optimism as they worked.

Many other efforts were underway that night as well. Captain Vector organized a sentry party and had them secure the fallen northern wall. With their guard down, he did not wish to lose the rest of the capital to the creatures within the forest. Tensions already high, guards leapt into action at any movement in the trees.

Zerilla opened her home as a makeshift hospital for the injured, much to Dascony's dismay. Along with the servants of the house and her older children, she tended to the injuries of all being brought inside her walls. The twins, Savic and Partha, remained upstairs where they would not bear witness to the tragedy that had struck their home. Zerilla feared this would haunt and scar the youngest children for years to come.

Drew also remained within the royal household, refusing to leave his brother's side. He still clutched and twisted the axe in his hands, fidgeting while he waited for Boudie to regain consciousness.

❖ ❖ ❖ ❖ ❖

As the night turned back into day, the relief efforts were beginning to slow down. It had been hours since Tiot had uncovered anyone alive and weariness was beginning to set in.

Taking a step back to truly look and see what was transpiring around him, Braksis could see that the people were pulling together to overcome the disaster that had befallen their home.

Many of the lesser injured survivors were already released into the care of their families, friends, and neighbors. Tables were set up along the road with soup, drink, and bread for those who had lost their homes. Everyone seemed to pull together in light of this tragedy. Everyone, except perhaps for the Suspintian Guards.

Braksis noted that Vector now had the trampled walls completely guarded with troops, and that architects were already on hand discussing the rebuilding of the city walls.

"Our work here is done. We are needed elsewhere," Braksis announced. "Let's say our farewells and be gone."

Solara slowly rose from where she had paused to rest and fell in line beside him. Tiot, too, jumped up and walked at his side.

Kai looked at her new companions and opted to march in line with them as well. "If you have no objections, I shall travel with you at least until we have hit the road."

Braksis considered the small elf he had not even known a day, but to whom he owed so much. "You saved Solara's life, and in fact, may have saved many lives here over this past day. Although the Seven Kingdoms will look down at you for not being a human, know that this day you have earned the respect and admiration of its champion."

Walking to Zerilla's home, Braksis entered and sought out the queen. Instead, Mivo found him first.

"Can you believe all that happened? I mean, wow! I was so terrified, but I should have known that you would rescued me."

"Well, Mivo, remember this: I was there this time to help you but will not always be. You should not have left your family to venture outside. Be more careful in the future."

"Yes, sir," Mivo said, but the fire quickly returned to his eyes as he ran over to see Kai. "Wow, a real elven bow! Can I see it?"

Zerilla slowly approached Braksis and gently touched his hand. "I'm afraid he has a flare for adventure. I am just grateful you were there to protect him when the time came."

"Um, yes. Well," Braksis stammered as he gazed into the eyes of Zerilla. "What I mean to say is, we shall be taking our leave. I am needed in Dartie, and we have uncovered all of the survivors. Captain Vector is also making arrangements to refortify the defenses, so my presence here has come to an end."

Closing her eyes and taking a deep breath, Zerilla tightened her hand around his. "I pray we shall meet again, under calmer circumstances."

"I look forward to such a reunion."

"Until then, safe journey brave knight."

Seeing a tear forming in her eye, Braksis gently wiped it away, then raised her hand and kissed it gently. "Until we meet again."

Standing atop a staircase, Dascony stared down at her daughter-in-law in horror. To defy the memory of her own son by entertaining this heathen? With her fury of the unfolding events growing, she could contain herself no longer when she saw Mivo was speaking to a nonhuman. "Mivo!"

The scream pierced the cries and commotion that filled the lower levels with those being cared for. All seemed to grow quiet and look at the exquisitely dressed Dascony. "Step away from that foul creature!"

Kai looked up at the former queen with rage in her eyes. She had always been loved, then hunted, but never discriminated against simply for being.

Braksis walked over to Mivo. "Why don't you head on up and check on your little brother and sister?"

"Yes, sir," Mivo drawled out in clear disappointment.

Zerilla waited for Mivo to leave. "This elf is a champion of our people. She risked her own life to save that of many of ours, and you would speak poorly of her."

"I would not speak of it at all, a nonhuman is beneath me. It is beneath all of us," Dascony raised her voice as if attempting to persuade those within.

Kai looked at Zerilla. "Your hospitality and kindness has been quite generous in these trying times. I apologize for any burden I have played to add upon that. I, too, shall take my leave now."

"And good riddance," Dascony muttered.

Looking back with annoyance, all frustration seemed to leave as Zerilla addressed Kai. "You have added no burden and will always be welcome within these walls, regardless of what some of the elders may think. There will always be a setting for you at my table."

As the group of champions turned to leave, they faced Drew and a now-conscious Boudie. "Well, maybe I hit my head a bit harder than I thought. I'll be damned, but that there looks like a pink elf!" Boudie declared.

Drew started laughing.

Braksis walked over and extended his hand. "Gentlemen. We faced a beast far greater than any of us, and managed to pull together in victory. We shall part as friends until the day we meet again."

"Friends, huh?" Drew snorted, still remembering the circumstances of their meeting.

Boudie leaned on his brother's shoulder, and held out his hand. "Friends it is." Looking to Kai, he added, "As for you, I only wish I was not unconscious so I could have seen you in action. We shall cross paths again, you and I. I foresee we will share many adventures together."

She looked at the grin deeply etched on his face and was curious at his words. Customs here were strange and new to her. Yet with the task appointed her, she needed all the friends and allies she could find. "Until those adventures then."

As Braksis led his group back out the door and down the street, all whom they passed turned, clapping and cheering. The champions that saved Comonor. Their names and deeds of these past few days would grow into legend.

Mounting their reclaimed horses, Braksis and Solara waited for Kai, who had never ridden a horse before. The stable owner provided her with a tame steed as a gift. She thanked him graciously for the new mount. Under instruction of Zerilla, the stable boy also prepared a pony that had supplies and provisions for a full week's journey packed on its back. Collecting their things and finally ready, the trio of riders left the walls of Comonor and the cheering crowds behind them. Though they did not know it yet, the destruction and disaster they had just survived would pale next to the adventures they all were about to embark upon.

CHAPTER 9

After a pair of days' traveling, Braksis wished he were back with his troops already. Not because of any feelings of foreboding or longing for war, but because he wanted to get away from the near-constant barrage of queries and jokes Solara had been spinning on his behalf.

This was the type of relationship the two had shared for years since she indebted herself to him, but typically there was a back-and-forth flow of remarks and needling. So far this journey, he has remained quiet and contemplative.

Solara looked over at Kai and winked before she continued harassing her companion. "That's right, one of these days he's going to be giving up his sword, armor, and army for the gentle caress of a queen. A queen!"

Braksis remained focused on the road and stared straight ahead as if he did not hear her words at all.

"This one is a tough egg to crack lately. Could it be? Is he happy?"

"That's enough, Solara," Braksis spoke evenly.

"Enough of what? Enough travel for the day? The day is still young. Isn't the day still young, Kai?"

"The day is indeed young, Solara."

If the girls concentrated enough, they thought they could actually hear his teeth grinding in frustration.

"Fine then. Have it your way. I'm happy. I'm also confused. Your needling isn't helping."

"My needling? Well, clearly someone is confused!" Solara declared. "Needling aside, perhaps we should speak?"

He paused for a great while in thought. Looking around him, he absorbed the world as it was, seeing things he had never truly seen before. To his left was the Suspintian Forest, for they had not yet traveled beyond its borders. Yet he saw more than just the trees. He seemed to see life. From the swaying leaves, down to a small lizard crawling on a branch. Birds singing in the trees. Other small animals going about their daily tasks around the ground.

To his right, there was open land. Still many miles to the borders of Danchul, this was all land that in the future could be built upon by the Suspintians if need be.

Random thoughts flowed through his mind, where military strategy once dominated. If this was the lingering effect of Zerilla's lips, then Braksis wanted none of it, yet desperately craved for more. Conflicted, he had a hard time trying to focus. He wished to return swiftly to his troops, then lead a battle where many of the enemy would die. To be seeing and absorbing the surroundings of nature, he could not contemplate how he could have missed so much through a life focused on combat.

"Braksis? You in there?" Solara tried again.

"Sorry, my mind has been wandering," he replied.

"Like I said, all jest aside, let's talk. She's a very lovely woman. Beautiful children, too. The mother-in-law is a witch, but you can't have everything."

Kai watched her two new companions closely. Everything in this new world seemed so strange to her. The same sensations and perceptions Braksis seemed to be noticing for the first time, Kai, too, was absorbing. This land was contradictory. So much seemed to be at peace, but yet from her newfound friends, it also seemed that things were falling apart around her. She was beginning to love it here, but also feared what might happen if this tranquility were to suddenly be interrupted.

Looking at Braksis biting his lip, Kai opted to add her own comments. "I may be new to this part of the world, and perhaps things are indeed different here than they are from where I come from, but if you can find happiness with another, is that not to be cherished?"

"Yes. That is to be cherished," Braksis conceded. "Yet the times are changing. The Imperium is being attacked from within increasingly of late. I need to be at my best for my Empress, yet my mind seems to be floating in the clouds and not riding alongside the two of you."

"The clouds, eh?" Solara softly stated as she looked up and saw not a single cloud in the sky. "You must be losing it. There are no clouds."

Braksis turned and gazed at her evilly. "What happened to 'no jests'?"

"That wasn't a jest!"

"Oh no? 'You must be losing it?' Funny, that sounds like an insult to me."

"Well, look up," Solara demanded. "There are no clouds in the sky!"

Looking up, Braksis took in a deep breath. "It's a beautiful day. The sky is clear, the sun is shining, the birds are singing. Not even you could ruin this day for me."

Kai looked to the sky herself. It was a clear shade of blue. But she could feel the changing patterns of the elements. "It's going to rain."

Solara laughed boisterously.

"It can't rain, it's beautiful out," Braksis declared.

"Nevertheless, it will rain soon," Kai adamantly defended her prediction.

"I dare the rain to fall on me today!" Braksis yelled into the air.

"My money is on her. Sorry, boss." Solara giggled.

"Figures," he mumbled.

"You'll look quite good though, drenched without your cloak to cover you. You should have asked Queen Lovey-Dovey for a new one."

"I will be fine. There will be no rain to wash away the feelings that have grown inside of me of late."

"I'll remind you that you said that."

The three rode in silence for a while. Braksis was pleased by the break. It was not that he did not wish to speak, but he desired to sort out his feelings on his own. His life had never been an easy one, and the path he chose led him away from serious matters of the heart. Though many a maiden wished he would pause to give her but a glance and a sense of hope, never before had he felt this way about a woman.

Deciding that this would slow him down, make him a liability to his people and himself, and possibly get others killed, he knew that any further interaction with Zerilla would be impossible. Her long, flowing blonde hair, the intent gaze of her eyes, the beautiful pale skin—all must be extracted from his memory. Somehow, he needed to leave her memory behind and move on.

With this firmly implanted in his mind, his joy seemed to turn to sorrow. He was unhappy with his decision, but logically felt it would be for the best. The only thoughts that he should have now, dealt with the infraction in Dartie. Although the decision was made, Braksis would learn in time that when dealing with matters of the heart, the will of the mind is not always the stronger.

❖ ❖ ❖ ❖ ❖

Several hours later, the storm continued to pound down on the riders. Kai, as it turned out, was right about the approaching storm. The rain seemed to increase in intensity, becoming far more dense as the day dragged on. The winds soon began to howl, and the sky opened up in loud bursts of thunder and blinding lightning jutting across the sky.

Having trouble seeing clearly ahead, Braksis did his best to keep his horse moving straight ahead. His long brown hair was soaked and hung dripping in strands from his head. His whole face looked like the edge of a waterfall as rain flowed down his forehead, nose, and goatee.

Solara nudged her horse twice to advance on Braksis. "You're pouting."

"I am not pouting."

"You certainly are. If only you could see your lips. Kai, look at his lips. Isn't he pouting?"

Kai smiled at Solara. The two seemed to quickly become conspirators in antagonizing Braksis. "That is definitely a pout."

"Bah! I am just wet."

"Just wet? Look at poor Tiot. He is soaked, but is still keeping up and appears in good spirits. I think you're upset that you were wrong. Should have listened to Kai when she said it was about to rain. But did you? No. You dared the rain to come. And did it? Yes."

"Let's make camp for the night. We will cover ground much quicker when it is drier and we have a good night's sleep."

"As you wish. But good luck starting a fire! I'll leave that to you tonight."

The riders dismounted and led their horses to the edge of the forest. Hoping the trees would provide some shelter from the elements, they walked in several yards and tied their horses to an extended branch.

They could still feel the wind and the rain, yet not as violently as out in the open. The three removed small pouches of blankets to arrange sleeping spaces, and set them up as close to the trees as possible for cover.

Braksis gathered as much dry wood as he could find, but most of the kindling lying about was damp and useless. Nonetheless, in under an hour, he managed to find enough to create a small pile and actually start a fire to keep the storm-drenched travelers warm.

He gleamed over at Solara, grinning deviously. "Good thing you left me to the fire or else we would be cold all night!"

"Humph," was her only response, though she was happy he seemed to be snapping out of his lovesick haze and slowly returning to the man she had always known and admired.

"We should get some sleep. Hopefully the storm will pass quickly. You two sleep first and I'll take the first watch."

Solara and Kai did not need to be told twice. They both snuggled deeply into their respective blankets and covered themselves as best they could from the storm above. Although sleep did not come easily, both drifted off in time.

❖ ❖ ❖ ❖ ❖

Soon, Kai began to dream. Ever since coming to this land, her dreams seemed focused on her task and objective. She would always see a small village, then focus in closer to a small cottage. Within the cottage was a young girl, appearing full of innocence, spirit, and a desire to explore new things.

The child was always the same—a young blonde girl with a gleaming smile. Kai knew this could only be the Chosen One she was sent to find and protect. The girl who was prophesied by her people.

In this dream, Kai watched the child running through a field chasing a butterfly with a small net. Not a care in the world other than the task she held at hand. Her laughter and giggling were infectious, and Kai felt like laughing herself.

Yet she also felt a deep sense of regret. This small child seemed so happy. So full of life. If the Triad were to succeed, that lifestyle would be robbed, and in exchange, the child would be faced with pain, suffering, and deeds that potentially could sunder the strongest of wills.

As Kai continued to watch the child play gleefully, she tried to look around and gain a sense of the surroundings. The child was playing in long fields of tall grass. In the background, there were mountains to one side, and the sea to the other. Kai absorbed all of these small details in an attempt to ascertain a direction, for clues in how to locate the child.

The images started to change, and Kai felt a dark sense of foreboding and apprehension. She forced her eyes open and glanced around, reaching for her dagger as she did. The storm had subsided slightly, but the winds and rain still remained.

She saw Braksis standing by the edge of the woods looking out. Tiot was at his side, tense. The Warlord appeared to be speaking to the wolf, though Kai could not hear what was being said through the storm. Solara was still sleeping and nothing else seemed amiss.

Kai stood, placed her cloak back over her head, and approached Braksis.

"You're up early, Kai," he said. "I'm still on watch for another hour."

"A sense of danger has awakened me prematurely," she said as she gazed out across the open land.

"Tiot senses it, too. I have not seen anything yet," Braksis admitted.

Focusing through the storm, the young Madrew elf's enhanced sight could make out riders approaching. "It looks like we have company coming. Riders. A lot of them."

"You can see them?"

"Yes. Madrew have strong eyesight, though this storm is making things more difficult than I would have liked."

"Stay here and keep watching them. I'll wake up Solara." With that, the Warlord turned and returned to the forest for his companion.

Kai watched intently. As the riders got closer, she thought she could count ten in all. They were riding ponies not horses. They also seemed shorter than those she had met thus far in the realm. Several other ponies were also traveling, along with a couple of carriages. Perhaps these riders were not the cause of her restlessness after all.

Braksis returned quickly to Solara, who appeared alert and ready for anything. She had already donned her complete arsenal of weapons and began observing their surroundings for potential battle tactics.

"Anything new to report?" Braksis inquired.

"I see ten riders, yet they are shorter than me. They ride ponies and also have wagons."

Solara looked out but could see nothing. "Can you see their faces? Are they bearded or discolored?"

"They wear cloaks and hoods that hide their features. I can only make out their size."

Looking at Braksis, Solara offered her advice. “No need to take chances. We could pack up and leave, or try to hide here.”

Contemplating the options, Braksis’s curiosity was growing. “No, I wish to see who these travelers are. They are traveling in the dark of night, and perhaps do not wish to be seen. I feel that makes it our job to discover those who wish to remain hidden. We are after all a military presence for the Imperium.”

“We are still outnumbered and have little tactical information. How do you want to do this?” Solara questioned.

“We’ll improvise.” He beamed back at her.

“Improvise? Great,” mumbled Solara.

“Kai, go grab your bow and gear. I want you to take to the trees, but do not attack unless we are attacked first. Solara, you should move as quickly as possible across the way to those small hills. Hide there and watch as well.”

“What will you do?” she inquired with concern.

“I’m going to increase the blaze of the fire, and make sure they know I am here.”

Looking at the smile on his face, she knew he would not change his mind. That didn’t alter the fact that she wished to be closer than a distant hill when ten potential attackers would be coming upon him. “Wonderful. Sounds like a great plan,” she said sarcastically.

“Okay, get moving and be patient. If we don’t need to fight, I don’t want to fight. Not tonight.”

The three quickly separated and went off to their assigned roles for the upcoming confrontation. Tiot, still stiff and looking out toward the approaching riders, turned and went with Braksis as his master whistled for him.

Kai crawled into the tree and looked out from a much better vantage point. She would be well hidden from view on her perch, but also could see the approaching riders more clearly. She saw Solara kneeling down and ready to pounce if Braksis needed her. She also saw Braksis putting some more kindling on the fire to increase its glow and gain the attention of the riders, The riders themselves were gaining. She felt that this would all be resolved within the hour, and until that time, there was nothing more to do than continue to watch and wait.

CHAPTER 10

The riders approached the camp slowly. They took the bait that Braksis offered, but were very cautious as they dismounted and gazed into the forest. From her perch, Kai could make out some voices, but not the language being spoken. The voices were strong, deep, and gruff.

The ten travelers slowly entered the Suspintian Forest and cautiously approached the fire shimmering through the storm. Kai could see the flames reflected off the various weapons those who approached wielded.

She quietly drew her bow and prepared to attack. Her perch truly was a good one, for she had a clear view of Braksis and the camp. She would lose sight of the dismounted riders for only a few moments, as they were shielded by tree or underbrush, but then would be able to strike as they approached her newfound companion.

The storm continued to wail and blow. Ascertaining where everyone was through sound alone would be nearly impossible. Even so, Braksis sat by the fire with his back to the approaching strangers. A risky stratagem based on the attempt to build a sense of security and feeling of control for those approaching. Yet, if they were deadly assailants, with the sounds of the storm, he most likely would never hear his death approach.

Seeing Tiot tensing aside him, but not outwardly displaying signs that others might become aware of, Braksis knew the ten riders were upon him. "If you are wet and cold, I have a roaring flame to warm away your worries."

"Who is it that would invite us without even looking upon us?" Returned a deep and gruff voice spoken in the common tongue.

"I am one who would wish to avoid a confrontation, but also am prepared to offer one. The choice is yours. Friend or foe?" Braksis calmly retorted.

"You are a human. Humans fear those who are different. Full of hate and prejudice. Why should we expect you to be different, when you have not even gazed upon us?"

For the first time, Braksis stood, turned, and drew his sword, which seemed to practically absorb the glow of the fire and emanate. "I am Lord Braksis, Warlord of all of the Imperium. Protector of the Seven Kingdoms and all that falls within the realm." As he announced himself, the riders seemed taken aback slightly. He was bold, full of confidence, and possessed a demeanor that demanded attention and respect.

In her perch, Kai drew her bowstring taut. She could see Braksis confronting the riders, but had yet to see aggression on either side. She wished to be prepared regardless. Focusing on the campsite, she selected her target and determined the order in which she would attack, based on size and weapons selection. All she needed was to perceive threats of violence.

Across the way, Solara gazed out and could see little more than the ponies and carts. One of the riders apparently stayed behind, preventing her from advancing. Still, she thought that in these harsh conditions, she could approach stealthily. Slowly she inched across the ground toward the lone sentry.

Back at the camp, one of the riders stepped forward and pulled his light blue hood back revealing the face of a red-bearded dwarf. His hair was of the same color, and his eyes seemed hardened from many years of violence. "Lord Braksis, you say?"

"That I am. What say you, friend or foe?"

"If you are the same Lord Braksis I have heard many tales of, then I say friend," replied the red-bearded dwarf.

Lowering his sword, Braksis continued the dialogue. "I am curious. What have you heard?"

"Upon a visit from our cousins of Tregador, we were told tale of a king betrayed by his own nephew. Slain in his own bed. The young prince fled into the night, with his cousin quick on his tail. Yet the child would not be slain, he would be rescued by a troll nonetheless, and raised as his own, not to emerge again until he was a great warrior. Are you the young prince?"

"I am he. Braksis, son of Worren, true heir to the throne of Falestia," said Braksis boldly.

"And the troll?"

"Ferceng. He who I call my father now. He who raised me, instructed me, and turned me into the man I am today."

"You are a peculiar human. One with a background unlike many others. I do not think prejudice does flow through your veins as in most. Being as it is, I choose friend over foe, and would be grateful if my companions and I could share a fire with you."

"Very well, come in then. First, allow me to contact my companions. I'd hate to think they would get the wrong idea and attack a newfound friend."

"Companions?" the dwarf repeated in confusion. He had survived many wars and battles with invaders to the Halls of Vorstad, yet he had seen no sign of others present. "Perhaps you were not as vulnerable or outmatched as we had anticipated."

Braksis smiled at his new friend. "At times, I like to be prepared." Looking past the dwarves, Braksis yelled into the storm. "Kai! Solara! Come, meet our new friends!"

Kai undrew her bow and put the arrow back in its quiver. As she began to climb down the tree, a scream pierced the night. The sound came from the mounts, and Kai could see Solara struggling with the sentry.

"We have been betrayed!" one of the dwarves yelled out in their own tongue.

With that, several began to run back toward the ponies. "Olgierd!" They yelled out as they ran past Kai oblivious to her presence.

The red-bearded dwarf looked at Braksis. "If this be betrayal, I had no sense of your deceit. Perhaps the two of us can rectify this with ease and lack of bloodshed."

Braksis nodded and then walked in stride with the dwarf. "I only hope that one of my companions has not harmed one of yours. Truly that would put a strain on us both and on our friendship."

"Yes," said the red-bearded dwarf. "A strain it would be."

As they approached the clearing, Kai dropped from the tree next to the two.

"What is this?" exclaimed the dwarf in shock.

"Nothing to fear; this is one of my companions. We shall hold better introductions soon, for I have yet to hear your name."

"My apologies. I am Thamar of Vorstad, warrior and thrasher of mine enemies," replied Thamar full of pride.

Kai glanced at Braksis and spoke up. "The others ran right past me. It looks like Solara snuck up on the sentry and startled him."

"Olgierd was snuck up upon?" Thamar burst out into a deep, guttural laugh. "If he is unhurt, I will never let him live this down!"

The three stepped out of the forest and could see more clearly. Solara stood holding one of the dwarves with a knife at his throat. The others surrounded her with weapons drawn. She looked up when she heard a bark from Tiot and saw Braksis, Kai, and another dwarf approaching. "Let me guess—friends?"

Braksis nodded and smiled. "Unless you don't let go of their companion there."

Thamar yelled out to his fellow travelers. "Lower your weapons, we are in the company of allies here."

Reluctantly, they agreed, as Solara also lowered her knife and released the dwarf.

"She snuck up on ya, did she, Olgierd?" Thamar questioned with another laugh.

"Did not!" retorted the now-released dwarf. "She tried, but I caught her."

"That is why she had the knife to your throat!" This time, all the dwarves laughed loudly. "Friend Braksis, shall we all escape the elements as best we can and share that fire now?"

"Sounds like a plan to me," replied Braksis.

"Excellent, many stories we shall swap this night! Olgierd, bring the spirits. We shall drink and be merry this cold eve!"

Mumbling to himself, Olgierd started to unpack some supplies from one of the wagons. A couple of other dwarves walked over to assist him. All others returned to the fire and situated themselves around the crackling flames.

Thamar sat next to Braksis, but stood to address his companions. As he stood, Braksis could clearly see Thamar's outfit. Under his blue cloak and hood, he had a long, well-groomed beard and mustache that traveled well down to the middle of his chest. The hair on his back seemed perfectly trimmed at the neckline. He wore a blue short-sleeved shirt, the same tinge as his cloak, with darker blue pants that led into light brown boots extending up just beyond his knees. He also wore light brown leather wristbands, a matching belt that sheathed a dagger, and had two light brown straps crossing his chest. Upon the ground in front of him, he had a large mallet, which if held had to be about half as large as the four-and-a-half-foot dwarf.

"Brave warriors of Vorstad, tonight we share a fire with a human, a peculiar human at that. One raised by a troll, who travels with a wolf, a mystral, and a pink elf like the one whose valiant deeds we heard from Xylona. I am honored, as should we all be, to share a fire with the son of Worren, true king of Falestia, adopted son of Ferceng, mighty Mage Master of the Mage's Council, and he himself, Warlord of the Imperium's armed forces."

The other dwarves in the party rumbled several cheers.

Thamar allowed them to continue for a few moments, and when he saw Olgierd and the others finally approach, he raised his arms and gestured for his people to quiet down. "Here is Olgierd and the young ones now with the spirits. A drink for all, then we shall have better introductions to become more acquainted."

Kai leaned forward. "I beg your pardon, and am hesitant to interrupt, but you mentioned another pink elf, and something about valiant deeds in Xylona. I do not wish to appear impatient, but I would greatly appreciate hearing more of this."

"Fear not, little elf, for I will take none the offense. We are all friends here. A tale you wish before more in-depth introductions, then a tale you shall have!" roared Thamar cheerfully.

Kai smiled at the dwarf and sat down to listen intently. "Thank you."

"This tale is deeply rooted with the purpose for our travels, but many details I shall leave out until deeper into the night, preferably close to morning so as not to give voice to evilness in the darkness of night. Yet some of the tale I must tell, regardless of the bleakness we find ourselves enshrouded within.

"Increasingly of late, the forces of evil seem to be disrupting the land. The orc clan of the east, a massive city with the vile name of 'Severed Head' has been advancing to the west and challenging the Halls of Vorstad. This, as stated, will be a tale for later tonight, yet briefly mentioned to show that something intricate may be in the works with the forces of evil."

Braksis said nothing, but grew interested at the prospect that the increased uprisings within the Seven Kingdoms, like the current one in Dartie, might not be isolated incidents. If other races were also feeling a new darkness sweeping the lands, then perhaps it was time to put aside old injustices, and merge the great and ancient races of good and righteousness to face the threat under one banner. A banner of honor, hope, and peace.

"Tribes of hobgoblins have migrated. There are groups in the South Horwood Forest below the Ardan River. These tribes have tried to cut the dwarven warriors of Vorstad off from our elven allies of Xylona. Other hobgoblin tribes have migrated in above Xylona, pressuring them to always be on the defensive and worry about attack from all sides.

"We ourselves have always lived in peace with the elves of Xylona. We have held many centuries of good relations and trade. Yet the hobgoblins look to separate us and keep us from assisting each other. With the hobgoblins on one side, and the orcs advancing from the other, we may truly be unable to assist our allies in their time of need, for we are in need ourselves.

"Although I have spoke much, and now told you little as to what you inquired, I feel that this information was necessary to set the stage. You must know that the elves of Xylona are a noble race, proud and just. They, however, like us, are bred of a warrior caste. We have always lived with the threats of orcs, goblins, and now hobgoblins as well. The elves live close to the swamps of Tenalong, and many a vile creature seems to be held at bay by their efforts as well. Efforts that now are focused on mere survival and defense."

Thamar paused and picked up a mug of mead before continuing. "Where these hobgoblins originate, I know not. Yet there are several different tribes, and all seem to desire the destruction of both Vorstad and Xylona.

"On one cool morning, a very large and unprecedented attack took place against Xylona. Unprecedented I say, because different hobgoblin tribes usually focus only on their own, and very reluctantly will two tribes strive together with their efforts. Yet here, it was as if five or six tribes all merged into one, with the sole goal of destroying noble Xylona."

Braksis interrupted Thamar. "Perhaps there is some strong power behind them, that all the tribes recognize as a leader?"

"I fear that this may be so, and though I have a name that may go along with your theory, we shall wait to utter it at a more pleasant hour. For now, let us return to Xylona and this assault."

Braksis nodded, then leaned back to contemplate what he was hearing. Although these settlements were devoid of humans, they were still within the Seven Kingdoms, and if the dwarves and elves fell, the creatures could be bold enough to march on the humans. Braksis knew this must be considered, and brought before Empress Karleena quickly. In the back of his mind, he had to also reluctantly admit that he feared for Zerilla, for Xylona was within the borders of Suspinti, and if large tribes of hobgoblins were advancing into her kingdom, then her people may truly have a reason to fear.

"For those of you who have never laid eyes on Xylona, let me tell you about it." Thamar continued. "Xylona cannot be seen from the ground, unless you know where to look. The elves long ago decided to build their homes high in the trees, and have great structures which connect tree to tree with pathways, homes, and audience chambers for meetings.

"From below, as I said, unless you knew where to look, you would see none of this. They crafted their art, and the structures are designed in various shades of the forest itself. Even I, who have been there many a times, still must rub my eyes and focus to see their fair city from below.

"This would seem to be a great defense, for the elves also move swiftly through their habitat, and travel among the trees, though they certainly can come to the ground as well. Yet this camouflage seems to have fooled the hobgoblins naught.

"On the aforementioned cool morning, these tribes marched on Xylona. They used grappling hooks and ladders, and climbed the very trees themselves. They fired flaming arrows at structures in the air, and set aflame the base of the poor trees.

"The elves feared they were lost. Many battles and wars they had fought, but never before had their home been unearthed and assaulted. Many elves died in the initial confusion, though man, woman, and child alike quickly had their wits return, and fought back valiantly.

"Ilias, swiftest of the Xylona elves, leapt through the trees and soon was behind his attackers. He stole a steed, and flew like the wind to the Halls of Vorstad seeking our assistance. His hope was that with all the hobgoblins attacking, he would be able to get to us unencumbered, and we, too, would be able to return without our paths being barred. Still, even if we were as swift as Ilias, the trip from Vorstad to Xylona would take several days, and there was little hope for reinforcements in time.

"The assault continued well into the night, and matters seemed dire in Xylona. Then, something mystical happened. A bright, blinding light illuminated the then dark sky, and when it faded, in its stead, was an elf like none had ever seen before. He had pink skin, a little darker than your shade," he indicated, touching Kai's chin. "He had long hair braided down his back, the shade of purest silver, the sight of which a dwarf would rejoice upon finding in a mine. There were light blue strands trailing back as well, like a comet through the night sky."

"Arifos," Kai whispered.

"Aye, Arifos indeed is his name. You know him?" Thamar inquired.

"Yes. We are both from the same land, far away, beyond what you call the Forbidden Region. The two of us and another make up what is known as the Triad. We are here looking for a savior. The Chosen One," Kai explained.

"Well, it looks like you will have a mighty tale to weave yourself. As for finding a savior, Arifos is a savior. I see no need for another when one as valiant, brave, and skilled as he was already within your midst, yet we shall listen to your full story soon, yes?"

"Yes, I will tell my tale after we finish listening to the story you have begun," Kai replied courteously.

"Story it may be now, but legend it will grow to soon. Many a song will be sung of Arifos and his deeds. Yet I am not one for song, so I shall merely go on with the story as it was told to me.

"When he appeared, the hobgoblins were taken by surprise, and seemed to pause in their assault. This allowed the warriors of Xylona to regroup and push the evil forces back, and in most cases, out of their tree top city as well.

"The hobgoblins were enraged, and saw Arifos as the source of their newfound distress. They seemed to forget the battle that was originally waged, and focused intently on him. Even you, Lord Braksis, I fear would have succumbed to the numbers that quickly faced Arifos. Yet he danced around, leaping, jumping, and making a complete mockery of the invading hobgoblins.

"Hobgoblins slashed and fired arrows, but he was no longer where he was, and their own kin fell victim to their assaults. With every movement, Arifos seemed to release arrows of his own and drop even more of the enemy.

"The hobgoblin ranks completely crumbled, and many fled as the Xylona elves launched death from above, with volleys of arrows into the crowds. Yet all of their arrows combined seemed to fell less of the enemy than Arifos himself, all alone.

"When the final hobgoblin had fled or was slain, the elves of Xylona approached Arifos, and were amazed that nary a scratch was upon him. Not even sweat dared to rest upon his brow. Simply amazing.

"Ilias led myself and two hundred dwarves back to Xylona with him, but we all feared it would be too late. We suspected that we would find the city destroyed and bodies scattered about. Instead, we found that the city was still erect, that the hobgoblins that had fallen had been burned, and their ashes scattered in the winds to warn their surviving tribesmen. The trees that had been burned had already been tended to with magic and potions, and though the blackness of the fires could still be seen, the trees were still vibrant and alive.

"The people themselves were in good spirits, with songs being sung of the feats of Arifos as they continued to work on repairing any damage done to their great city. Amazed was I at what I saw, but no more amazed than Ilias, who hoped for the best but anticipated the worst. Yet, as tale was told shortly after our arrival, if not for Arifos, then Ilias's and my own concerns would have proven to be valid.

"For seven days and seven nights, my dwarves and I remained to assist in a renewed attack. Word came that the hobgoblins were indeed regrouping and reorganizing. We also heard that more tribes had been called to assist in their attacks. We worked side by side with the elves, creating booby traps and erecting obstacles to help keep the hobgoblins at bay.

"Though we came strong and proud to help, many feared that the reason that Xylona had not been attacked again, was because Vorstad had dwindled its defenses. Vorstad itself had recently been besieged for forty days and forty nights, and thoughts that we would not be there if the attack resumed were troubling. This was not a pleasant thought, but we also did not wish to leave our elven allies. We thus split our force in half. One hundred warriors remained, with another hundred returning to the Halls of Vorstad, and not a moment too soon.

"Yet once again, I am dragging on with a tale that goes beyond the query. I shall speak more of what happened upon our return later, if that is acceptable with all of you." Thamar looked intently at Kai to see if he answered her question to her satisfaction.

Kai still had a few questions, but asked only one. "Did Arifos remain in Xylona, or had he gone before you arrived?"

"Arifos remained. Though he had a quest of his own, he knew that in a new land, allies were needed, and that his newfound companions would help him, when the time came and was right to do so. He remains there now, defending Xylona from the evil that seeks to destroy us all."

"Thank you for the news and your tale. I appreciate hearing news of my own kindred."

"Not at all, young one. Now, I have been speaking for some time, and though we all call each other friends, we have yet to share all of our names with each other. Lord Braksis, if you will take over and introduce your ilk first, then I shall rest my voice and have a bite to eat before introducing my own kinsmen."

Braksis placed his arm on Thamar's shoulder. "It would give me great pleasure to introduce ourselves to you and your honorable companions, Thamar. Thank you for the tale, and I am sure that before this storm completely breaks and the night is through, we shall both have told much and learned much the same."

Thamar nodded his assent, then reached his hand out and was given a plate from one of the dwarves that had not yet been introduced.

"As Thamar has announced already, I am Lord Braksis. Apparently tales of my own exploits have reached the Halls of Vorstad, but I am sure that there is much you have not heard as well. For instance, how I have come across my two female companions here."

One of the dwarves laughed. "I merely thought friend Braksis that it was because of those eyes and that smile! Many a heart I am sure you have won with those!"

Thamar threw a bone from his plate at the interrupter. "That is enough of an interruption from you, Graf! I never could fathom how you seemed to attract the unbearded elves, nor why you would want to. If it's because of your eyes and a smile, as you accuse Braksis here, then I truly will be rendered speechless."

"Well, the elves like me, not for a smile and a wink, but because I am extremely well endowed!" Graf jumped up and gestured his hands in the shape of large balls.

Thamar looked behind Graf to one of the other dwarves, who immediately knocked Graf over the head with nothing more than a nonverbal command from Thamar. Thamar nodded to the assailant. "Thank you, Theiler. Perhaps now without his crass commentary, we can continue. Please pardon the intrusion, son of Worren."

Graf rubbed his head where he was hit and looked back at Theiler. Theiler raised his club a second time and Graf retreated with a whimper and no other intrusion.

"No apology necessary, but I thank you for not allowing such talk in front of the ladies. First of which I shall introduce, is my mystral companion, Solara." Solara did not stand, but looked around at all of the dwarves. "She has been with me for many years, and in fact has sworn to protect me with a mystral life debt."

"A mystral life debt?" Thamar echoed. "The introductions can wait. I wish to hear more of this."

"Very well," Braksis thought back to his earlier escapades, then began his tale. "Perhaps a little under two years after first meeting Emperor Conrad and his young daughter Karleena, I was given command of a military unit and went to stop a band of villains who were pillaging various villages in Suspinti.

"The Kingdom of Suspinti itself maintains its own army for defense, but seems to always be enshrouded by fear from the creatures locked within the Suspintian Forest around us." To emphasize, Braksis extended his arm and motioned it around his body toward the many trees. "When they were attacked by the bandits, they cowered down quickly and gave them what they wanted."

"This group was led by a ruthless warlord known as Durgin. It seemed that his only desire in life was to bring pain and terror to others, and he continued that until the very end.

"My men and I tracked Durgin for many days, and found them actually raiding the small town of Bimbadine. Perhaps with the folly of my youth—after all, I had not celebrated my twentieth birthday at the time—I ordered my troops to charge straight into the town and attack."

"Sometimes a frontal assault is best, not necessarily an implication of age," Thamar offered.

"Your words are gracious, Thamar. Still, we were victorious on the day, but I lost many men. We should have assessed the situation a little better than rushing in headfirst."

"I see your point. Wisdom of the ages has made me consider many things. Still, this Durgin was attacking a village. Perhaps if you waited, you would not have the guilt of your men's deaths, which they freely offered to protect the people of Bimbadine, but rather the guilt of dead townsmen. I think you are being too hard on yourself, son of Worren."

"Thank you, Thamar. I do take things deeply and often analyze whether some actions of my own could have saved lives. Perhaps I was taking those early lives personally."

"From the success and reputation you have grown since," Thamar continued, "I think you have learned from your past, if a mistake was indeed made. Internalized. Adapted. You are better off now for those dead soldiers then.

"I am disrupting your thoughts again though, perhaps my brother Theiler should be clubbing me on the head this time. Please continue."

Braksis nodded. "Yes, now where was I? We rushed headlong into the town of Bimbadine. We did manage to surprise Durgin and his men, but they lashed back quickly and viciously. Several took hostages, but I led my troops around and we saved them. As we were rounding up the last of Durgin's men, I saw that the warlord himself was not present.

"Looking for him, I found a trail going off into the forest behind the village. Without waiting for my men, I immediately entered the forest and chased after him. I came out to an opening. A large lake sat below a waterfall off of some cliffs. Standing shallow in the water, was Durgin with two naked women he was trying to restrain."

"Naked women? Now we're talking my kind of story!" Graf yelled out.

Behind him, Theiler clubbed him over the head again, this time without instruction.

"What did I do? I'm just saying that I'm enjoying the story!" Graf pleaded.

Theiler stared down with disgust and clubbed him a second time.

"Lousy, no good, piece of..."

The dwarf next to him cut Graf off. "Keep it up, and Theiler will keep clubbin' you!"

Graf folded his arm and sarcastically smiled at Braksis to signal that he should continue.

"The two women were mystral warriors. The famed warriors who at one time rode the mighty dragons and brought peace to the lands. A proud race torn apart when the dragons fled the realm after dragon hunters challenged their authority. In despair, their mystral counterparts fled into the forests and seclusion, and to my knowledge, have not been seen again by mortal eyes until I saw these two in the lake, held at bay by the Warlord Durgin."

"How did you know they were mystral?" Graf inquired, then ducked quickly in case Theiler went to slug him again.

Braksis stood up and walked to Solara, lightly touching the mark of the dragon above her left eye. "Through Ferceng's teachings, I heard rumors that all the riders of the dragon displayed their symbol across their brow. As you can see, the mark of the green dragon is on Solara's forehead."

"I bet you killed them all dead, and that is why she is indebted to you," Thamar offered.

"If only the tale were that easy. Durgin stood in the water, holding Solara by the throat. Another woman stood nearby trying to get him to release her. Two of his band were standing by the water, enjoying the show until they realized I was there.

"As Durgin saw me, he offered to release the girl if I would let him go. I was confused, for I saw two girls, and he mentioned but one. To emphasize his offer, he plunged his axe deep into the second mystral and began laughing hysterically."

Looking down at Solara, Braksis could see she seemed quite somber and saddened. This tale may have sprung their origins, yet she had lost her mother that day. He sat down behind her and put his arms around her for comfort.

"I screamed that no more innocent blood would be spilt by him as long as I was alive to stop him. He just laughed all the more and sent his two men at me. I dropped both without any effort and was on top of Durgin. He tossed Solara here aside and came at me with his axe. I was determined to avenge the death of the mystral, all the townspeople, and those of the men I lost tracking him."

All of the dwarves edged closer, as if getting closer to the storyteller would help them witness the confrontation.

"He lunged at me and kept on attacking. I found myself fighting a defensive battle very quickly. Durgin was much larger and stronger. Stronger than I am today, much less before my twentieth birthday. Yet I was determined. I fought back valiantly, and the ropes started to turn. Durgin faltered back as we parried through the shallow waters of the lake.

"Off in the distance, I could hear my troops shouting for me. They were coming, looking for me and for Durgin. A moment's distraction was all it took. I yelled to them so that they could find me, but that is when Durgin struck. He brought his axe down and it embedded deep into my right shoulder. Through my armor and all."

"Is it the same suit you wear today?" asked one of the dwarves.

"Yes, though obviously repaired since then. It was forged along with my sword in the molten magma itself by Ferceng."

"Ah, yes. It appeared dwarven. The crafters of Tregador also use this craft. I have heard they are in close proximity. Very strong. I am surprised the armor was pierced."

"Grosskurth, I'm sure Braksis will provide you with details enough. Allow him to continue," Thamar commented.

"My apologies; it seems many of us keep interrupting your tale," Grosskurth said, then bowed in respect and raised his hand, beckoning Braksis to continue.

"As you pointed out–Grosskurth, is it?" Braksis inquired and received a nod of assent from the dwarf. "The armor indeed is strong, and if not for that, the axe thrust most likely would have been a fatal blow. As it was, it was many weeks that I was watched and cared for, and to this day do I have a scar to remind me of the battle and what could happen if distracted.

"Though I could tell you what I know from here, I must admit that I became very disoriented, and my memory is hazy. I remember attempting to get up again. I remember hearing a confrontation, a loud clang, and a scream. I also remember my men trying to get to me, but being warded off. For clarity, I must now turn over the floor to she who maintained her faculties to a greater extent after my wound."

Braksis reached out and embraced Solara in a big hug, then leaned back for her to speak. She took a few deep breaths and wiped her eyes clean of the disturbing thoughts and memories of that fateful day. Then she addressed the audience: "As Braksis fell, Durgin rushed to the horse that Braksis had ridden through the forest in pursuit. He would have escaped Braksis's soldiers with ease, and left behind both Braksis and my mother to die in the lake.

"I desperately wanted to do something, but my own clothes and weapons were atop the waterfall where my mother and I had initially dived in for our daily swim. Seeing him flee, the closest thing I found was a branch from a tree that had fallen. Thick like a log, but able to be lifted with ease. I grabbed the branch and leapt at the departing assailant. I brought the branch down hard upon his armored helmet, and that led to both the clang and scream that Braksis recalls.

"Durgin fell from his horse and was unconscious. I stood above him for another moment to see if he stirred, but he lay motionless. The soldiers were coming, and I quickly returned to the water for Braksis, though I was unaware of who he was at the time.

"Dating back to our time with the dragons, my people have vowed to bind ourselves with protectors, creatures with honor and faith. Even more so, if one of these great souls ever were to defend, or rescue a mystral, then that mystral, and her decedents , were bound to that soul for life as their protector. I viewed the events that happened in those terms, and swore an oath and a life debt to Braksis. No harm shall ever come to him if I can prevent it.

"As the soldiers came through, the rest of what Braksis heard, was me protecting him from them. His wardrobe was not the same, and I was unaware they were together. I began to fight them off, too, until they convinced me they just wanted to help. After that, I would not leave his side. I let none go near him without explaining to me first who they were and what they were intending to do.

"After he recovered, he tried to convince me to leave, but I would hear nothing of it. We have been companions ever since."

Braksis leaned forward again. "Going on ten years now since then."

Thamar smiled. "A most excellent story indeed! Solara, you truly are a warrior to be admired. To hold your beliefs so highly, and follow them through in good times and bad. Impressive. Most impressive. Plus, I am sure there are many more tales you could tell of the past decade."

Braksis stood and returned to his initial seat next to Thamar. "Yes, there are many stories, but if I told them all then we would never finish the introductions."

Thamar laughed boisterously. "Very true, my friend. Though I do have a question I hope you will indulge me with."

"Ask," Braksis replied.

"You mentioned your first meeting of Emperor Conrad and his daughter Karleena. I am very interested in this as well. I know of your flight from the castle when your cousin Rawthorne attacked, and of your ultimate rescue by Ferceng. I have also heard your name as a Warlord for the Imperium, but have no knowledge of how you went from one to the other."

"I see that you wish to fill in some holes in my history. I shall indulge you if it appeases all," Braksis looked around their little circle and saw many eager faces. The dwarves seemed to truly enjoy his last story and were anxious for more. "Very well. Though I will be repeating much of what you already know, to do it justice, this story starts the night my Cousin Rawthorne attacked the house of Worren."

The dwarves intently focused on him, and if any seemed concerned that he was about to recap certain elements that they had heard in legend before, none spoke a word of it.

"That night, I tasted my last meal as a prince and went to bed. I must have been little more than seven years old at the time. A happy childhood I had, and the servants seemed to love my parents dearly.

"On that fateful night, my slumber was disrupted by many screams and sounds of destruction. I was young, and the true events I know not in much detail. Yet one of my father's faithful butlers, a gentle and kindly man named Dobbins rushed into my room to rustle me. He found me, took me in his arms, and ran out at a dash. He was wearing little more than his bathrobe, and I had on only my night garments as well.

"As we ran, he told me that my cousin Rawthorne had returned and sought power. He burst in on my parents in their bedchambers and murdered them both. The servants and guards were trying to defend our home, but Rawthorne came with many men himself.

"Dobbins took us outside of the castle walls and fled into the highland night. Someone must have uncovered our escape, because several of Rawthorne's men were in pursuit. Dobbins managed to get to Lake Senya, which had waterfalls flowing from the oceans and down the mountains themselves.

"He put me in a small raft by the shore, and as he went in to join me, an arrow pierced his chest from behind. The shock on his face will be etched in my brain forevermore. He pushed the raft into the water with pleas that I continue to flee.

"As the raft was caught by the current, I could see Dobbins standing there, and convulsing several times as more arrows pierced his hide."

"A noble servant he must have been," Thamar added.

"Yes. Dobbins was very noble, without a selfish bone in his body." Looking around, Braksis could see that once again he had everyone's attention. "The pursuers came after me in another raft, and I knew they would be stronger and swifter upon the water. I jumped overboard and swam to shore, hoping they would continue after the raft. Unfortunately, they were not fooled.

"I started running down a path on one of the many mountains in Falestia, and as memory serves, I was cold, trembling, shaking, and crying."

"For such a tragic eve, I would expect nothing less," Thamar slowly said as he placed his muscular arm on Braksis's shoulder for support.

"The pursuers continued after me, but never actually hurt me. I fell, and they were on top of me, then mystically were tossed aside. I looked up, and in front of me stood a tall troll. Never before had I seen his like. I have heard of trolls before—of how hideous and dangerous they were. But the creature in front of me was garbed in white and gold, and appeared as if he were my guardian angel."

"Alas, you have met Ferceng!" Thamar yelled out in cheer, which the other dwarves quickly joined in on.

"Yes, indeed it was Ferceng. Though I was unaware of what was happening, I would later learn that Ferceng was a Mage Master, and as such, he had full command of the mystical arts. The attackers went at him, and with little more than a gesture, Ferceng sent them sprawling and flailing through the night sky. The entire time, he seemed to be laughing and joking as if they were nothing more than flies. Mere pests that must be swatted. Indeed, to him, that is all that they were.

"Those who remained conscious quickly fled. The others lay there for hours before their faculties returned. Ferceng was a mighty Mage, and more than a match for several normal human thugs.

"He came to me then expecting me to be afraid. Yet I looked at him with respect in my eyes, and sorrow in my heart for all that had transpired that night. He told me he knew what happened, I must bide my time, and the next time I met my cousin, it would be on my own terms and I would be ready. I said 'okay' in little more than a whimper, and he whisked me up and brought me to the caves that he called his own.

"For the next eleven years, he cared for me as if I were his very own child. He instructed me in the legends of old. Histories both written and rumored. He taught me the code of honor, and the ways of a noble knight. He showed me various arts and forms of fighting, both with a blade, as well as combat techniques when without weapons. He also taught me strategies of many great warriors throughout time. My training was intensive and full, just as his was during his Academy days in the Mage's Council.

"Finally, one day, he told me it was time to go, that my future was at hand and ready to be grasped. He then presented me with the gifts of the armor I wear and the sword I wield. He had spent many nights working on them and handcrafting them to my exact dimensions. He told me that I would follow the emblem of the phoenix, as displayed on both the armor and sword, and that I shall rise from the ashes as the legendary bird had done.

"With those parting gifts, he bade me well, and pointed me in the direction I was to travel. That road brought me to a carriage traveling away from the castle I had once called my own. Though I would not learn this until later, the carriage held the Emperor and his five-year-old daughter. They had just visited my cousin Rawthorne, who claimed the throne those many years before, and recently sought to leave the Imperium.

"As I watched from a nearby peak, I observed what was clearly an ambush. Though the carriage was well guarded, the assailants attacked swiftly and viciously, and many guards fell to their deaths. All that remained of these emerald-clad defenders was one man, who appeared to be painted. I later learned the darkness of his skin was normal and he was none other than Adonis, the famed Captain of the Imperial Guards."

"I have heard of Adonis as well," Thamar exclaimed. "A great and noble warrior."

One of the other dwarves commented, "He's no longer with the Imperial Guard."

"No, he is not. After Conrad's murder, Adonis left the Imperial Guard and began a new group that he calls the Imperial Security and Investigation Authority, or ISIA. He was shattered by the Emperor's death, and decided that he would spend the remainder of his days bringing criminals to justice. His little group has grown immensely over the past year or so. Regardless, this has little to do with my introduction to Emperor Conrad.

"Seeing the futility of the guards and the carriage, I decided to test my new sword and help out these travelers. My assistance was greatly appreciated, and between us, Adonis and I managed to ward off insurmountable odds, and allowed no harm to come to the royal passengers.

"After the battle ended, I still did not know who was in the carriage, but Adonis requested my aid in returning to Trespias, the Imperial City. Thinking back on how Ferceng said that I would find my future, I reluctantly went."

"Reluctantly?" one of the dwarves yet to be introduced asked.

"Yes, reluctantly. For though I had no desire to claim the throne for myself, I also wished to avenge my parents' murder and challenge Rawthorne. Of course, I learned I would be able to do that soon anyway.

"The entire trip to Trespias, Adonis and I spoke at length, but never would he reveal who his passengers were. Then we were in the Imperial City, and still not slowing down. We went right across the bridge and into the palace itself.

"Imagine the surprise and exhilaration of finding myself not only in Trespias, but in the palace! At the time, I was little more than eighteen, and suddenly I had seen something that only a select few had ever gazed upon before. That is when I knew that my life truly would be changing.

"When the carriage doors opened for the first time, I laid my eyes on both Emperor Conrad and his young daughter, the current Empress. I immediately got down on my hands and knees and bowed. This was the man who unified the Seven Kingdoms. Who was I to stand in his presence and look him in the eye? Yet he bid me to stand up and go with him.

"We spoke for many hours. He had me tell him my tale, and was shocked to learn that I was the true heir to the Falestian throne. Then he did a peculiar thing. He declared war on Rawthorne and Falestia, and invited me to ride alongside his General, the fearless Kronos of Danchul."

"Kronos is another name well known by us. His exploits in Danchul were quite noticeable, since Vorstad falls within the Danchul borders," announced Thamar.

"Kronos was wise, and a strategic genius. We spoke at length as we marched back toward Falestia. He took a liking to me, but also watched me closely. We faced Rawthorne and his band of thugs, and with little resistance, captured my dear, sweet cousin. His men were so brave, that rather than fight, they turned and fled when they saw the advancing army. Rawthorne was practically alone, and of course presented little challenge.

"We marched him back to Trespias in irons, and there he stood in judgment before Conrad. The Emperor sentenced him to life imprisonment, where perhaps he could atone for his many sins over years of hard labor. He felt that a death sentence would be too swift, and that Rawthorne should suffer for many long years.

"The Emperor then sent for me again, and we spoke at length. He offered me the crown that was rightfully mine, yet I felt that was not my true path. I declined his offer, and the crown passed instead to my uncle, Lorrents, who is a fair and reasonable ruler, unlike the son he sired.

"Emperor Conrad then asked me what I did wish, and I requested to stay with him. To help the Imperium and fight under his banner. He seemed pleased by this. Conrad stated that I was young, but that both Kronos and Adonis spoke very highly of me and my abilities, and that he was certain I would rise through the ranks quickly.

"He made me a Captain that day, though I never had a command of my own until I tracked down Durgin a little under two years later. From there, I did indeed rise through the ranks quickly, and soon I was designated as a Warlord and placed in command of the entire Imperial armed forces.

"Though Conrad is now gone, his daughter has advanced as Empress. Many factions seem to feel that with a female leader, the Imperium is at its weakest since its inception almost fifty years prior. I have sworn my sword in her name, and will fight to my dying breath to keep the Imperium secure, and to shield her from as much pain and suffering as possible. Before any can get to the Empress, they will have to conquer me and my forces, and that is no easy task."

"Ha, ha! I am sure that it would be quite a difficult task indeed! I pity anyone who is foolish enough to try!" Thamar roared. "Thank you for indulging an old warrior. Please, introduce your last companion."

"Not quite the last, for Tiot, my faithful timber wolf travels with me as well," Braksis declared, to which Tiot sprung up and barked several times before lying down again.

"Ah, yes, how could we forget the wolf? Please continue," Thamar apologized.

"Not much to tell here. One time traveling home to Falestia for a visit, I heard the yelping of an animal. Poor Tiot here had been caught in a hunter's trap. I set him free, and he has traveled with me ever since."

"Indeed that was a short tale, yet one of loyalty. May a curse be placed on those who would hunt for reasons other than consumption or survival," declared Thamar.

"Finally, allow me to introduce Kai. As you learned already, she is from the same people as Arifos, who you have already met. I'm sure she shall indulge us with more of her own background later on. For now, I shall say that perhaps all Madrew elves are saviors, for she mystically appeared when Solara and I were fighting for our lives against a giant three-headed tragon!"

"A tragon? Never before have I heard of such a beast," commented Thamar.

"In all honesty, none of us have. It was an enormous three-headed reptilian beast. We were told that it was a dragon, but clearly it was not. The battle was long, tense, and at times seemed doomed to failure. The creature walked right through a wall and started to attack Comonor, capital of Suspinti. A pair of famed hunters, the Suspintian Guards, Solara, and I all fought valiantly, yet nothing seemed to slow this thing down.

"Suddenly, just like in your tale of Arifos, a blinding light appeared and Kai was in its place, launching arrows into one of the creatures heads, and quickly rendering it lifeless. Before the day was done, she also managed to perform an amazing aerial stunt that saved the life of Solara. If Arifos was your savior, then Kai most certainly was ours. I wonder what fares the third member of the Triad?"

"As do I, Lord Braksis. News of Rulysta would bring me great pleasure," said Kai.

"Well, it pleases me to meet you all, and now with my voice rested, I can give proper introductions to all of my kinsmen as well," began Thamar. "You know my name and where I am from, yet that is all. I am Thamar, son of Thron. I have been a warrior in the Halls of Vorstad going on three hundred years now. During that time, many orcs and goblins have I slain."

"Next I would like to introduce my younger brother, Theiler."

The dwarf who kept clubbing Graf over the head stood up and bowed. When fully erect, he was a little shorter than his brother. Like Thamar, he, too, had a full red beard and head of hair. His eyes appeared hard and stern. A man who had seen much pain and suffering, but also strength and wisdom. He donned a lime-green tunic, with beige shirt and pants. He, too ,wore light brown boots that traveled above his knees, and a belt of matching shade. Attached to his belt were several large pouches, what appeared to be a giant eagle's claw, and a sheathed sword. He also wore gloves the same shade as his boots, and these extended down his arm to his elbows. He still held the club that he used to hit Graf.

"It looks like red beards run in your family," observed Braksis.

"Aye, we have the red beards, as does our father before us. Some times I think even our sister at home could be blessed with a red beard! Though if I see you eyeing her as Graf suggested, our friendship may come to an end quickly!" joked Thamar.

"But I find a beard so attractive on a woman," rebutted Braksis.

Thamar let out a low guttural growl, but quickly returned to his introductions. "Theiler would introduce himself, for he truly has an eloquent tongue. Though fate took away his gift for gab nearly a hundred years ago.

"As I mentioned earlier in the evening, Vorstad and Xylona have been neighbors and allies for many centuries. Our two cities would often enter into exchange and trade, sometimes even just exchange of stories."

"On one such trade mission, Theiler led an expedition to Xylona. Twenty ponies were packed full of supplies for our elven neighbors, and Theiler led his group out. During their journey he spotted a lone Danchul mare. No owner or other steeds in sight."

"If anyone knows anything about Danchul prior to the Great Wars, one of the reasons they had such a formidable army, was because of the steeds that they bred. A horse from Danchul was larger, faster, stronger, and more beautiful than a horse from anywhere else within the Seven Kingdoms. This horse was no exception. A tint of silver, with eyes that shone like gold. Theiler immediately fell in love with the beast.

"Though a dwarf, and not often will you see a dwarf mounted on a horse, Theiler wished to have the steed as his own. He approached, and oddly enough, the beast seemed to welcome him, though it jumped and thrashed at any others who went near it. He named the horse Shimmering Jewel, for its coloring glistened in the light.

"He rode Shimmering Jewel all the way to Xylona, and instantly felt pride as the elves there were fascinated by what they called the most magnificent steed they had ever set their eyes upon. Trade went well, and the dwarves stayed as guests in Xylona for several months. The peace and tranquility there seemed to absorb time, and make the setting sun meaningless to those within Xylona's borders.

"Finally, the dwarves felt that it was time to say good bye to our elven neighbors, and bid them a fond farewell. Theiler proudly mounted Shimmering Jewel, who now had been given many gifts from the elves, and truly seemed to sparkle with every step.

"On the return journey, a hungry griffin spied the small band, and came looking for some food. If you don't know, griffins' desired cuisine is horsemeat, and a Danchul steed was far tastier than most horses!

"The griffin swept down, and was confronted by Theiler and his drawn sword. The half eagle, half lion kept swooping down trying to get past Theiler's sword, but he was an excellent fighter and well trained.

"The other dwarves in the party set several of the ponies loose hoping that if the griffin could see easier prey, it would leave Theiler and Shimmering Jewel alone. Alas, a griffin can be mighty single-minded when it wants something, and it ignored the fleeing ponies.

"As it came down at Theiler and his horse again, this time the griffin shifted and tried to attack Theiler himself. He managed to save his head, but the mighty talons of its claws grasped part of his throat and shred his vocal cords nearly in two."

Solara shuddered and looked away.

Braksis continued to watch Theiler, his attention flowing back to what appeared to be an eagle's claw attached to his belt. Could it be a griffin's claw instead?

"Theiler fell over, his life blood seeping out of him. Shimmering Jewel realized its master was hurt, and started running like the light itself to escape the griffin. The griffin had large wings that spanned over twenty-five feet, and it would not allow its desired dinner to escape.

"The griffin flew down at Shimmering Jewel one last time, grasped the horse by its sides, and lifted the horse and dying rider into the air. Theiler was not as dead as the griffin thought, and he thrust his sword straight up with all of his remaining might. The blade pierced the griffin's furry hide, and dug into its heart, killing it almost instantly.

"Fortunately, they were not too high off the ground. Shimmering Jewel managed to land safely, and kept Theiler juggled on its back. The griffin fell forward lifeless. Turning, Shimmering Jewel rushed Theiler back to Xylona, where the elves tended to his wounds and saved his life, though he will never be able to speak again.

"After leaving Xylona the second time, Theiler and Shimmering Jewel were inseparable. The first thing they did was return to the crash site, where Theiler removed the claw that severed his vocal cords, and made it into an ornament and keepsake of besting the beast and protecting his beloved steed."

"What happened to Shimmering Jewel?" Kai inquired.

"The two lived for many years, shocking many dwarves that he rode a horse. For a while, he returned to Xylona with Shimmering Jewel and spent many years riding his horse with no concerns other than for his steed. Soon, he was called home when a group of goblins attacked, and his sword was needed once more.

"He indicated that he wished a cave to be dug large enough for Shimmering Jewel to go underground with him. Many thought this ludicrous but some helped. In the end, the help was wise indeed, for Theiler marched atop of Shimmering Jewel and slew many goblin raiders. The dwarf and mount became heroes. Because of his injuries, many called Theiler the 'Silent Death.' An avenger who rode in on his valiant steed, and left none standing in his wake.

"The years took their toll, and Shimmering Jewel joined the brave spirits of Vorstad in the afterlife. Theiler was saddened, but knows that his steed will be waiting for him when he, too, falls into the endless slumber of death."

"A tragic tale you tell of your brother, Thamar," Braksis allowed.

"That which does not slay us, makes us stronger. Do I wish my brother could still speak? Certainly. Yet he has become a champion of all of Vorstad after incurring his injuries. We do not look back with regret, only at the results of unfortunate circumstances."

"Champion of Vorstad? Bah! Champion of clubbing your comrades would be better!" Graf mumbled under his breath.

Theiler rewarded him by clubbing him again as he sat down.

"Hey! I've just about had enough of you!" Graf shouted at Theiler.

Thamar stood and walked over to the disruptive dwarf. "Perhaps we should introduce Graf so that we will have finally heard enough out of him!"

"Oh, sure. Typical. Pick on the little guy!" Graf mumbled again. At about four feet, he was shorter than either Thamar or Theiler. His beard was mostly black, though strands of gray were scattered throughout. He wore a brown hood and cloak, with chainmail armor clinking beneath. He, too, had a dark brown strap slung across his shoulder with a dagger clipped onto it. A single-bladed battle-axe rested by his black-booted feet.

"As you've heard many times in interruption, this is Graf," Thamar began. "He likes to think of himself as a romantic, yet no dwarf will have him!" To this remark many of the dwarves laughed boisterously.

"Though Graf so rudely remarked earlier, remarkably, the elven females are fond of him."

"Hey, Kai, want me to show you why?" Graf grinned until Theiler clubbed him over the head again. "I was just joking!"

"His crassness aside, Graf is a masterful fighter. Though his brain may not match his blade."

"Hey! You didn't insult your brother. Why are you insulting me?" Graf demanded.

Thamar just shook his head several times. "Anyway, he had this grand scheme where he would put a notch in his belt for every orc he slayed. He killed so many, he wore his belt down to next to nothing! One night at dinner, it burst open and his pants fell to his knees!"

All present began to laugh, much to Graf's dismay. "Why did you have to tell that part?" His objections could barely be heard over the boisterous laughter.

One of the other dwarves stood up and chimed in. "Says he's well endowed, does he? Then he must have meant his stomach, because he had nothing to be proud of that night!"

All present erupted in laughter once more. Frustrated, Graf stood up and walked away from the camp. "Bah, who needs any of you?"

Thamar tried to control his giggle, then addressed Braksis. "As promised, we have finally heard enough of Graf!"

"I heard that!" Graf yelled out from where the ponies were resting. The only effect was more laughter from all around.

Thamar raised his hands and looked to the sky. "The storm is breaking, and soon shall the morning sun also brighten this somber sky. We shall speed up our introductions, for we still have much to discuss before this night is over."

Braksis nodded at the dwarven leader, and Thamar approached another dwarf to introduce him.

"This is Detroz, the famed destroyer of orcs!" As Detroz stood and bowed, he appeared a formidable foe. Standing slightly taller than Thamar, with a long whitish-gray beard flowing down his chest, his bushy eyebrows flowed above eyes that appeared to be able to burn through someone with but a gaze. He wore a charcoal gray cloak and hood, but also had a horned helmet atop his brow. His wardrobe was black—shirt, pants, boots, and gloves—with chainmail on top of his chest. On his belt was attached both a small dagger and a sword. In both hands, he was twirling for emphasis two leather-handled battle-axes.

"Detroz has fought beside me in many campaigns and wars against the orcs, and I still marvel at how the beasts tremble in fear when they see him," continued Thamar.

"When an enemy fears, they are already slain without realizing it," declared Detroz in a deep, booming voice.

"Psychological warfare," offered Braksis with a nod.

"Next we have good old Olgierd! The dwarf who prides himself on never being snuck up on." Thamar started to laugh as he was speaking. "And was not only snuck up on, but captured by our new mystral friend!"

Olgierd jumped up to his defense. "I saw her, I did!" He was slightly shorter than Thamar, with a full gray beard flowing down his chest. The ends of his mustache weaved into braids that flowed just as long. Unlike the others, his colors were more decorative and bright. His cloak and hood were a vibrant aquamarine blue. His tunic was a fiery red, with a dark brown belt tucking it in at the waist, that flowed below the belt in tails. Attached to his belt was a sheathed sword on his right and a quiver of small arrows on his left. His pants were a light blue that flowed into dark brown boots with leather straps circling upward to keep the boots tightly on his feet. Strapped across his shoulder was a crossbow, which hung loosely by his hip.

"All joking aside," continued Thamar, "Olgierd is a famed sentry of the Halls of Vorstad. He has the vision and senses of an elf. He can see nearly a mile in the distance and can ascertain the slightest shift or movement. He has been invaluable to our mighty city in warning our troops to assemble, long before the invaders reach our hollowed caves."

"Humph. That's more like it," said Olgierd. "Give a dwarf the respect he deserves!"

"Easy, my friend, easy. We all know your true value." Then winking to Solara he added, "Even if this female bested you!" Laughter erupted once more, and Olgierd lowered his head in defeat and sulked for several minutes.

"Next I shall introduce two, rather than one. Bassi and Logier." As Thamar announced each, he extended his arm toward the name he spoke. Both were similarly garbed in what looked like a greenish-yellow reptilian skin outfit. They wore this completely from head to toe, with boots made of the same substance. Their cloaks both were a shade of grass green and were the only article of clothing that did not appear to be made of the reptilian hide. Bassi had dark brown hair and beard, whereas Logier had a black head of hair and beard. Both dwarves held a polearm, with another weapon strapped to their backs. For Bassi, it was an elongated battle-axe, and for Logier it was a scimitar.

"The reason I introduce both together is for they share a tale that I find myself wanting to tell."

"Please, feel free," responded Braksis.

"Excellent. As you may know, the swamps of Tenalong have a great many creatures and beasts that would boggle the senses and drive a sane man mad. Yet full details of what was actually in the swamps was little and far between. Rumors however came forth of a massive orc city, far larger than any ever seen before. This is something that both our elven friends in Xylona, and the dwarves of Vorstad felt must be solidified in our minds as to the validity. After all, a massive orc city could pose a huge threat if they wished to march on our cities.

"A call went forth through both Xylona and Vorstad. Ten volunteers from each were sought. This combined force of elves and dwarves would enter the swamps on an expedition, seeking the truth of the orc city, and other terrors that may cause concern.

"Bassi and Logier here were two of the ten Vorstad volunteers. While in the swamps, things started to go wrong, and the expedition was segmented. Bassi and Logier found themselves in a small grouping of five, with another dwarf and two elves. This smaller group stumbled across a raspler den.

"Raspler?" Braksis inquired. "Forgive me, for I have never traveled within the borders of Tenalong and am not familiar with these creatures."

"Bassi, Logier? Would either of you care to explain?" queried Thamar.

The brown-bearded dwarf, Bassi, stood. "I would be honored to fill you in on our tale and the creatures we faced. A raspler is a reptilian creature that dwells in the swamps of Tenalong. Typically a pack hunter, about three to five go out searching for meals for the entire den. Carnivorous, so humanoid flesh would satisfy their culinary needs.

"When we stumbled on the den, we did not realize what we had found. The hunters were out foraging for food, but we found their nests. It would have been wise to flee quickly, for when the hunters returned, they found us within their den and attacked viciously. Brave Rali, my dearest brother, was the first to fall at their claws and thunderous tails.

"We fought hard, and Logier and I managed to survive. Our remaining companions did not." Bassi lowered his head in regret as he remembered the tragic day he lost his brother.

"I see you are wearing reptilian skins for attire," observed Braksis.

"Yes, for we saw it a waste to have killed the beasts and leave them to rot. Our clothing was in tatters, and Logier and I made a makeshift replacement from their skin. Upon returning to Xylona, the elves thanked us for returning with their fallen ilk, and rewarded us by crafting the skins into well-fitting garments."

"Was there an orc city?" Solara chimed in.

Thamar nodded. "Aye, there was. 'Murky Death' they called it. It fits for the murkiness of the swamps. Only a handful of the twenty returned, with only one who had actually seen the city. An elf he was, who claimed that the city looked as if it could hold well over a hundred thousand orcs! Whether it was filled or not we will never know. With those numbers, Xylona and Vorstad would quickly fall if they attacked. Fortunately, that was decades ago, and no orc has been spotted exiting the Tenalong swamplands."

Pausing for a moment, Thamar glanced at Grosskurth and grinned. "Next we have Grosskurth, the master of stealth and observation." Grosskurth wore a light tan cloak, with matching off-white pants and shirt. His belt and boots were also tinted the same as his cloak. His beard was a light brown that flowed off of his chin. He had two darker leather straps, which crossed over his chest and each strung a sheathed scimitar to his back.

"Grosskurth here traveled east completely by himself when the orcs first started to advance westward, and returned with invaluable tactical information. He seems to be like your Solara, he can sneak up on anyone if he were to try. His mind also seems to be able to absorb details at a glance that would take me hours of study to even notice. Though stealth is his game, he is also quite formidable with his blades.

"Finally, we are down to the last two. Culverwell and Grevesse. Both are young and have yet to reach their one-hundredth year. They have fought valiantly of late and were selected to gain experience from the rest of us on this mission."

Culverwell and Grevesse appeared younger than the others. Both beards were only slightly longer than their chins, with a shade of dusty brown for the former and a deep black for the latter. Each of the two younger dwarves were almost identically clad as well. They had light green cloaks, with chainmail armor underneath to protect them. Below the armor, they were garbed in lighter colors, with beige shirts and light brown pants. Boots were also brown and extended above the knee. Both wore a dagger clipped on their belts, and carried an axe.

"Well, now that our introductions are finally complete, we truly are all friends now!" Thamar declared.

"I am curious, Thamar, you have mentioned earlier and again now that the orcs are advancing west, toward Vorstad. I would like to hear more of this," Braksis remarked as he poured himself another drink.

"Excellent! Then a tale shall be told that will make you quake in your seat, my friend!" Thamar bellowed. "I told you before of the hobgoblins' raid, and mentioned briefly the orcs in the east. The east will indeed be the primary point of my story now.

"For centuries, the warriors of Vorstad were aware of the Severed Head clan located in the Carrion Mountains of the east. Many settlements bred warriors, such as Vorstad, Xylona, and even the human Danchul soldiers to defend against the orcish threat. Many wars there were, and always, the orcs faltered and succumbed to our combined might.

"During the Great Wars, the orcs played no role. This, as you know, was mostly a human war, and the people of Danchul turned their backs on the races that inhabited the mountains, caves, and forests of their southern border. Now don't get me wrong, the Severed Head clan is actually within the borders of Frocomon, but it was Danchul who fought the wars, not the fishermen and farmers who lived closest to the threat.

"Miraculously, or perhaps ominously, the orcs did not take advantage of the warring nations, and bided their time. The elves of Xylona and dwarves of Vorstad had anticipated an orcish uprising, and we prepared ourselves well, fortifying our defenses and training our young, but the battles never came.

"After the Great Wars ended, and the Imperium was first established, we lowered our guard slightly. Though nonhumans were not part of the Imperium as it was established, the realm was at peace, and tales of woe were few and far between.

"About a year ago, while deep within the caverns below Vorstad, several dwarves found themselves nearly mauled as creatures of the deep fled the east in a frantic stampede. When this was reported, Chaddrick, the mighty and wise King of all of Vorstad, feared that it was a sign of bad things to come."

Braksis listened intently to the time line. It was just about a year before that Conrad had been murdered and the uprisings soon followed. Was it a mere coincidence? Or a more sinister design at work here?

"Many of the warriors of old were summoned to consider this sign, and they all agreed Vorstad should prepare for war once more, even though peace had reigned for over fifty years. As they met, the stealthy Grosskurth, who I introduced recently, was dispatched to ascertain as much as he could." Thamar paused and looked at his companion. "Grosskurth, perhaps you should pick up the tale here."

"Yes Thamar, I shall do so." Grosskurth rose and walked to the center of the circle, as close to the fire as possible. "I set out immediately hoping to bring back word for my King and the assembled warriors of old. The signs I saw early on were not very promising.

"To the East, I saw large blackbirds encircling the sky. I knew I must be careful, for something surely was amiss. As I got closer, and time was not that long, for the birds approached me as well, I saw other signs that worried me. Locusts, maggots, and the like.

"I searched the mountains, the caves, and even the dark passages deep under the mountains. What I found truly was frightening. During the day, orcs slept within the caves. Thousands of them bunched together. At night, they traveled freely among the mountains and at the base of the mountains, moving west, laying claim to all in their wake. The dark passages and tunnels, these were putrid to the senses, with signs of large groups of orcs traveling through there.

"Not only the orcish warrior caste, but also thousands of goblin slaves. The goblins were being forced to travel in the lead, and uncover any dangers before the orcs themselves would be injured.

"Seeing this advancing army, I returned as swiftly as I could manage to the Halls of Vorstad. King Chaddrick anticipated my news but was dismayed by the numbers. Fortunately, they had already begun preparations and fortified the defenses of Vorstad. The entrances to the caves and tunnels below the city were filled in and blocked to prevent orcish attack. For them to reach us, they would either come straight at us from the dark tunnels we left unbarred, or through the passages that led to the surface.

"I believe Thamar can weave a tale far more eloquently than I. A gift that the house of Thron has always possessed. I shall yield the floor for him to tell the rest of the tale." Grosskurth nodded to his companion and friend, then returned to his original seat in the circle.

"Thank you, friend." Thamar bowed in return. "As Grosskurth indicated, Chaddrick ordered the tunnels and caves below the city to be filled. Many a dwarf rushed into the depths at his command and began looking to bar the way. Ceilings collapsed. Other areas were mined to bring debris to fill the cracks. It was a long and tiring process, but we knew that we needed to control how the orcs could oppose us.

"Riders were dispatched to Xylona seeking assistance against the orcs, but by then, the hobgoblins had also migrated in, and passage was difficult and dangerous. It was as if the orcs and hobgoblins were in tandem, looking to cut us off from each other and squeeze us until we could do nothing more than burst.

"Sentries, like Olgierd here, maintained a constant vigil, and finally, the enemy was upon us. For forty days and forty nights, the orcs attacked. By being underground, not even the rising sun would bring us a daily reprieve. With their goblin slaves on the front lines, we had difficulty getting past them to try to tackle the orcs themselves. It was as if their forces were endless. Spirits were down, and the warriors of Vorstad weary. Then one night, the attacks ceased.

"All night long, the warriors of Vorstad remained at their posts awaiting the assault, but it never came. A trick it certainly must have been, for why would they stop attacking? Every night, for over a week, the warriors of Vorstad waited, with little sleep, for we all feared that it was a plot to take us unawares. Yet the orcs refrained from attacking again."

"Do you know why?" inquired Braksis.

"We do not know for certain, but the orcs were chanting when they attacked. Speaking out a name they were fighting for. A name we were not familiar with. Many debates began, and some, including myself, felt that this individual somehow prevented them from attacking."

"What is the name?" Braksis questioned, curious to see if it was the same name of Zoldex that he had been hearing increasingly of late on the battlefields opposing him.

Thamar looked toward the eastern horizon where the sun would soon be rising. "We shall wait a little longer before uttering the name, just in case darkness, too, is the servant of this one."

"I understand. Please continue."

"After not being attacked for nearly a week, we gradually sent scouts out searching for the orcs. They found them, but farther away than we had anticipated. Not completely withdrawn to their home in Frocomon, but several days' journey away from us. The scouts reported that the orcs were eating, drinking, and being disruptive. Typical orcish behavior.

"We found this very curious, and were uncertain how to proceed. Did we stay and wait? Did we pursue and attack? Had we worn them down and claimed a victory? Were they just waiting for reinforcements? Or was this all part of a grander scheme?

"The questions were many, and the answers few. However, that is when noble Ilias arrived and pleaded with Chaddrick to send help immediately to Xylona. Very weary was Chaddrick, and with the assaults we endured and the enemy so near he was pensive and hesitant. Yet, he finally decided that if we could help clear the path to Xylona of hobgoblins, then the next time we sent for reinforcements, our elvish allies would be able to arrive.

"Two hundred dwarves were dispatched that very evening, and this story you already know. So I shall pick it up again where I left off much earlier this evening. In Xylona, many of the dwarves who went to assist wished to get back to the Halls of Vorstad in case the orcs were to attack again, something that we all felt was inevitable. Yet Xylona also needed our assistance. Thus, we split our forces in two, and one hundred dwarves began their travels back home.

"In Vorstad, the goblins and orcs began to attack again. This time more ruthlessly and determined than ever. Though two hundred dwarves sounds like much, it is not really a large force when considering the warriors within the Halls of Vorstad. Yet, when we returned—for remember, I was part of the group sent to Xylona—we arrived just in time as the orcs were breaking through the defenses.

"It was a sight that I never thought I would have to bear to see. The walls of our great city had been forced open and the wretched orcs had entered our towering halls. I ordered my hundred proud to attack to their final breaths if need be, and attack we did. The element of surprise was ours, and the orcs crumbled at our might. Those who could flee, once more went into the dark caverns toward the east. Those who could not, found themselves trapped between my returning troops, and the warriors who remained within Vorstad. They met their end swiftly.

"When we reentered the Halls of Vorstad, grateful were the people for our timely intervention. We were greeted as heroes with much fanfare, yet we could also see weariness about our proud people. Though we represented a gleam of hope, the attacks, and even worse, the anticipation of attacks was getting to everyone.

"I immediately went to Chaddrick and told him of the events that unfolded and the miraculous victory in Xylona. He was pleased that our elvish allies were still counted among the living, but was disheartened to learn that half of our forces remained in Xylona, and that the threat of more hobgoblin attacks would most likely prevent them, and certainly elven reinforcements, from coming to our aid.

"Both cities continued to be under siege, and the battles in the south soon seemed to be turning against both Xylona and Vorstad. Ultimately, Chaddrick saw the wisdom of searching for other allies in this time of need. Allies that this small band before you was dispatched to acquire."

"What about the avarians?" Braksis inquired. "The hovering city of Estonis is in the south and closest to your aid. Have you attempted to contact them?"

"May the avarians be damned!" Thamar spit out. "They and their floating city in the sky. They feel that the problems of the world are beneath them, and none of their concern. May their city fall and see what happens when the forces of evil are upon them!"

"I have heard that the avarians prefer to remain isolated and to themselves. However, if approached, I feel that they may still be able to offer some kind of assistance."

"Even if we wished to seek their assistance, friend Braksis, how would we get their attention? Dwarves cannot fly!" Thamar said sarcastically. Clearly, the avarians were a topic that he was passionate about in his distaste.

"A valid point you make," conceded Braksis. "Tell me what has happened since you began your mission for assistance."

"We left the Halls of Vorstad going on a month now. We seek our cousins in the Northern Mountains, the dwarves of Tregador. They may not be as akin to battle as we are, but as we discussed earlier, they are far more effective with the design of weapons and armor. Both of which, under the care of a true Vorstad warrior, would fell many foes. If they could provide us with some reinforcements as well, it would be invaluable."

Shaking his head in the affirmative, Braksis agreed this would help.

"Our travels have been long. In secret we must ride, for the humans still dislike those who are different, and not many friends have we met on this journey. This brings you up-to-date, my friend," finished Thamar.

"Thamar," Braksis began. "Xylona is also in trouble. Have you considered seeking out the elves in the Suspintian Forest? To the best of my knowledge, there are two great cities—Wild Wood and Turning Leaf."

"You are accurate in your knowledge, though I would not really refer to Wild Wood as a city, but more of a tribal community," Solara confirmed. "Wild Wood would only be a slight deviation from your path, if your band would risk entering the forests on the way to Tregador. Turning Leaf would be a bit out of your way, but is also the largest elvish city in the entire realm. If they would assist you, you could also save much time with elven guides bringing you through the Suspintian Forest. It would cut many days off of your journey, though you would arrive at Xylona traveling this way before returning to Vorstad."

"Hmm, an interesting suggestion. Something that must be contemplated seriously. The more, the merrier, I say!" Thamar considered.

Braksis glanced to the East and could see the orange glow of the rising sun on the horizon. The new allies had talked the night through, and now he desired to know if both of their plights were indeed related. "Thamar, with morning upon us, and our time together coming close to an end, I must ask a question."

Thamar nodded, offering his full attention to the warlord.

"As I have listened to you, I have contemplated much. You say that the Severed Head orcs began their march a year ago. Hobgoblins also began migrating into your area separating you from your longtime allies of Xylona around the same time. About a year ago, Emperor Conrad was murdered, throwing much of the Imperium into disarray. I have felt that the recent uprisings since that time were a direct challenge to the young Empress, but now I am not so certain. Timing seems too convenient and a grander scheme I fear is in the works."

Pondering his statement, Thamar rubbed his bearded chin and could see the parallels.

"You have mentioned in several tales a name that you did not wish to speak in the dead of the night. This sparked a response from me as well. Those who I have been confronted with have recently been swearing their allegiance to someone by the name of Zoldex."

Thamar's eyes widened in shock at the news. "Lord Braksis! The orcs serve this Zoldex as well!"

Kai also appeared startled and spoke up. "If Zoldex is in your land, then there is much more at stake than any of us previously imagined." With this statement, all present, with the exception of Graf who could be heard snoring in the background, immediately set their gaze on Kai for explanation. "Where I come from, Zoldex is known as well.

"His name has long been embedded with our legends as one who is evil, cunning, and ruthless. We even hear tales that Zoldex and his ilk first brought magic to my land, though we do not know whether this is true or not."

"Is he some kind of god?" Thamar asked slowly.

"No. He lives longer than the written word has been created, but those like him have perished over the years." As Kai was speaking, she seemed very solemn, and trembled slightly. "If he is here, then he must have fled my land just as my people did. I prayed I would never hear that name again."

"A plot he must have formed!" roared Thamar. "Lord Braksis, it appears that this night has proved quite fortuitous and prosperous for both of our people. Perhaps it is indeed time to reunite the species rather than allow this slime to rip us asunder individually."

"I agree, Thamar, and I personally will guarantee that the humans will help you with those reinforcement needs as soon as I can pull the army away from the battlefields in the Dartian plains."

"Very warming is your statement, and sincere I know it is," stated Thamar. Before their conversation could be completed, both Olgierd and Kai jumped up at once looking out of the trees toward the east. "What is it, Olgierd?"

"Trouble."

"Trouble? What kind of trouble?" Thamar demanded.

Braksis looked over at Kai, and she nodded her assent that trouble indeed was coming.

"It looks like close to fifty humans, and they look mighty angry!" relayed Olgierd.

"I told you Olgierd had the senses and sight of an elf!" boasted Thamar. "Are these assailants after you, son of Worren?"

Braksis strained but could see nothing coming. "I fear so. News of our feats in Suspinti could have been heard, and this must be some of the Dartian hunters sent to give us a nice little welcoming party before rejoining the army."

"Ha!" Thamar laughed. "Then pick up your sword and prepare yourself. We will show them Braksis fights not alone! That the races have united, and any servant of Zoldex should beware!" He raised his hammer above his head and yelled out. "Prepare yourselves! My hammer will fight alongside Braksis! May the enemy quiver in their boots!" Glancing back at the snoring Graf, Thamar signaled Theiler. "And wake up Graf! I do not wish to listen to his whining if he slept through a glorious battle and was forced to endure our song of victory!"

CHAPTER 11

As the Dartians approached the Suspintian Forest where Braksis and his newfound friends spent the night, loud yells and taunts were released threatening the warlord. Though they could not see within the forest, and had no true clue as to how many traveled with Braksis, they felt confident that the fifty hunters sent to intercept him would be more than enough to eliminate the Imperial leader.

Out of the trees in unison appeared Lord Braksis, Solara, Kai, Thamar, and Tiot. The five entered into the clearing and defiantly approached the forces amassed against them. About twenty paces away from the forest, and still from their foes, they stopped and stood staring at their adversaries.

A few of the hunters laughed out loud and yelled obscenities. They found it ludicrous that five would face fifty. But the small group stood, unmoving, and sent a ripple of intimidation through the foes before them.

Thamar yelled aloud to those before him, "I stand beside Braksis, Warlord of the Imperium. Leave peacefully now or feel our wrath!"

His words led to much laughter from the hunters. One man stepped forward. "Little man, you can leave Lord Braksis now or feel our wrath."

"You intend to insult and demean me. You fail to do both. For the fact that I am not a man, but a dwarf, I realize that you are too ignorant to know what you speak of, and should be ignored like the flea you are! I am Thamar, the thrasher of mine enemies, son of Thron, and noble champion of Vorstad! My hammer belongs to Braksis, and I vow that not one of you will lay a hand on him!"

His challenge sent ripples through the Dartians, and for a moment, several stepped back as if they needed more room between the two groups to feel safe. But humans often find comfort in numbers, and fifty still outnumbered five. The hunters regained their composure and continued their taunts.

Solara did not take her eyes off of the foes before her; yet spoke softly so only her group could hear her words. "So much for having them flee in terror at your words, Thamar."

Thamar turned to look at Solara with a look of demonic possession in his eyes. A desire for bloodlust that would not be satiated until this battle was complete. "Flee or stay, many will feel my hammer and then feel no more!"

"Prepare yourselves, they are about to attack," Braksis advised.

At this, Kai pulled an arrow from its quiver and drew her bow. Solara unsheathed her elongated lightweight blade that gained its fame from the tales of the mystrals' days as dragon riders. Braksis placed his hand on the hilt of the Phoenix but waited before drawing it himself. Thamar smiled and let out a deep guttural laugh. His mouth seemed to be watering in anticipation.

One of the hunters bellowed out the order to charge, and quickly fifty Dartians were in motion charging the twenty remaining paces toward the five heroes. Their orders were simple in that they were not to allow Braksis to return to the battlefield. They believed fifty was a bit excessive, but his reputation preceded him and the hunters agreed there was safety in numbers. Safety that they would quickly learn was nothing more than a false perception.

Kai was the first to spring into action. Her hand moved so swiftly that it appeared to be a blur to her companions beside her. Arrows launched from her bow, and hunters continued to fall as they charged.

About five feet from the quintet, Braksis finally drew the Phoenix. The sunlight reflected off of the blade as he held it high in the air for all to see. Then he brought the blade down in a swishing arch, slicing the first hunter to reach him from right shoulder to lower left stomach. The man fell to his death, and Braksis brought his sword up moving on to his next target.

Kai dropped back behind her friends who formed a pocket for her where she could continue to launch arrows in safety, whereas they battered anyone who came upon them.

Thamar held his position while swinging his hammer. Facing the first wave of hunters he dropped four with one turning swing. Those behind seemed to back off slightly as the battle-starved dwarf roared in cheer as hunters fell around him.

Solara was the first to break the pocket. Her greatest strength in a battle had always been her agility and athleticism, so she dodged under one blow and came up behind the hunter and started dancing around, attacking all in her vicinity.

Tiot jumped and dug his teeth into the throat of one hunter who tried to attack Braksis from behind. The timber wolf did not release his grip until he could sense that the hunter's heart stopped pumping. Though many would question this, Tiot seemed overly aggressive, as if he knew these were the hunters that at one time entrapped him.

The large Dartian numbers continued to advance, and as they did so, they found themselves having to crawl over the dead to get to their targets. This left them open for Braksis, Solara, and Thamar to strike, leaving those in the distance for Kai to fell with her arrows.

During a momentary reprieve with no hunters to swing his mighty mallet at, Thamar raised his hammer in the air and screamed out. "Warned you were; now a lesson in futility you shall have!" As his hammer lowered, his nine companions charged from the trees, and this time, the Dartian hunters seemed to see the error of their ways.

The dwarves were upon them quickly. Detroz was the first to enter the fray with both of his axes swinging as he ran. A pile of bodies quickly paved the path he took, and Dartian hunters fled before him. Detroz marched through their ranks, humming a dwarvan battle hymn.

Olgierd stopped next to Kai, and assisted her with assaulting those in the distance. Though his crossbow could not shoot as far as her bow, he continued to prime his weapon and release a volley of arrows, striking whomever he aimed at.

Grosskurth unsheathed both scimitars and slowly cut his way through the hunters toward Solara so that she would not have to fight alone. His expression was serious for he liked to observe all, and very rarely had he ever showed joy or sorrow in the face of an enemy. Yet he easily observed in the hunters that those remaining wore the deep signs of defeat clearly across their brow.

Theiler and Graf came up to Thamar, who was laughing at the futility and ignorance of the human hunters. Theiler stuck his club in his belt and unsheathed the sword that had felled the griffin those many years ago. Graf held his battle-axe loosely and scanned the disorganized foes for targets with deep anticipation.

Braksis stabbed one hunter, then spun around slashing another one who was coming at him from the side. Seeing no other enemies directly near him, he watched as Grosskurth carved his way to Solara. One hunter brought his sword thrusting down at the dwarf, who raised both scimitars in a cross to block the attack. He then lowered both arms slightly, and pushed up quickly throwing the hunter's blade back up. In one fluid motion, Grosskurth then brought the blades down and cleaved into the hunter on both sides of his stomach, cleanly cutting him in half as his body crumpled to the ground.

All around, the sights were the same. The dwarves had charged in quickly and ruthlessly. Though Thamar, Solara, Kai, Tiot, and Braksis were holding their own, ultimately, numbers would have taken their toll. With the surprise of the added dwarves, the human hunters were falling quicker than the eye could see.

Bassi and Logier seemed to be sticking close to the younger dwarves, Culverwell and Grevesse, as if to protect them. Yet all four were quickly bringing down any hunters in their vicinity, and not once did any seem to be in jeopardy.

Looking for a target, Braksis could find none. All the hunters fell before the wrath of the dwarves, just as Thamar had promised.

Thamar walked over with his brother Theiler and Graf at his side. "Warned them I did. Never take a warrior of Vorstad for granted! We have been born and bred for generations to be fighters. Perhaps these 'hunters' learned that before they fell."

Braksis resheathed the Phoenix and smiled at his newfound friend. "Yes, Thamar, I think they learned their lesson. And let me just add this as well, I am glad that we decided on friend over foe last night."

Thamar erupted in laughter, then watched as the dwarves returned to his side. "May all the forces of Zoldex fall so easily."

"If we could only be so fortunate," agreed Braksis.

"With this battle complete, I fear that it is time to go our separate ways. You have a war to win, and I have reinforcements to recruit." Thamar glanced back at his dwarves. "Prepare the ponies. We leave immediately."

The dwarves all nodded their assent and began preparing for departure.

"Thamar," Braksis spoke out. "There is something I wish to say."

"No need for formalities, my friend. We have bonded in tale and now deed," Thamar replied. "Speak your mind."

"Upon the close of the battle in the Dartian plains, I will send troops to Danchul to assist your people as promised. On this you have my word. I will then return to Trespias, inform the Empress of what we have learned, and plead for her attempt to reunite all of our noble races as they once were in the days of old."

"For this I am grateful, son of Worren. You do your people proud. I am honored to be your friend," Thamar said, placing his hand on Braksis's shoulder.

"It is I who am proud, Thamar. One more thing I feel must be said. Whether it is an old myth or mother's tale to scare children, I have heard of a threat that I fear may hinder your journey."

"Tale or no, tell me of this so we will be prepared," requested the dwarf.

"The tale as I remember it is that in the Blackstock Mountains, which you must pass to get to Tregador, there is an ancient evil that plagues the night. Creatures known as kriverlings travel in the dark of the night and search for weary travelers or townspeople they can capture for food."

"Kriverlings, eh? I have heard rumors of these beasts as well, yet have never laid eyes on one," Thamar said.

"Nor have I, and I must admit, I often thought it was a story simply to keep the young home and in bed at night. Yet since becoming a warlord, we have received some reports of travelers disappearing, and some of the towns of Suspinti, close to the Blackstock Mountains, claim these creatures have been so bold as to enter their borders and make off with citizens quietly in the night. Whether an old myth, or a deadly threat, be prepared and ready."

"Thank you, my friend. Prepared we shall be. Let these kriverlings attack! They will find my hammer is not as forgiving as a child's toy!" Thamar focused on Kai and Solara. "I bid you both find what you seek. Solara, to protect and honor your ways well. Kai, to find the child who is the Chosen One and protect her so that she truly can be a savior. If ever you find yourselves near the Halls of Vorstad, I will make sure we have week long feasts and celebrations in any of your honors!"

With his parting remarks, Thamar turned and joined his fellow dwarves for the remainder of his quest north and into the mountains.

CHAPTER 12

The journey through the rest of Suspinti was uneventful. The dwarves had quickly prepared their supplies, and began traveling north once more. Braksis bid them a fond farewell, then broke his own camp as well. Within another day's journey, they arrived at the borders of Suspinti and Dartie.

The Drynan River originated in the Falestian Mountains, and flowed down into many smaller streams and rivers that ran through the realm. This particular river was actually used as the border of Suspinti and Dartie, with nothing more than a small bridge joining the two kingdoms.

Solara was on guard and her senses were focused on the surroundings. The area on both sides of the bridge was open, with the closest cover being the Dartian Woods, which was on the Dartian side of the river, but well over several hours' journey. Regardless, after the attack just the day before, she felt certain this small bridge provided little cover and another threat could spring out at them.

With the years they spent together, Braksis felt he knew what his mystral companion was considering. "I thought the same thing myself."

Startled by his words when no conversation was being spoken, Solara looked at Braksis. "What?"

"That this is an open area, and we could be vulnerable," Braksis concluded.

"I was just thinking that where we were attacked seemed to put us at the advantage. With the cover of the trees and all."

"Yes, that allowed the dwarves to play a surprising role that the hunters did not anticipate," Braksis concurred.

"Here seems like a much better site. They would not really be able to sneak up on us unless they were in the water, but they would also know our numbers."

"Whoever said that our opponents considered strategy or logic? Besides, from their perspective, there were only two of us. Two against fifty is not really a big concern for them."

"I still don't like it. We should be cautious," Solara pointed out.

"Kai, do you see anything?" Braksis deferred to the young elf, who had the keenest eyesight of the three.

"No. I see no signs of trouble at all."

"Thank you. Shall we cross then?" With his last statement, the three riders, Tiot, and their pony with supplies walked across the bridge and entered Dartie. "See, nothing to worry about. In another couple of days, we will be reunited with our forces, then we will see what has been transpiring in our absence."

Kai gazed to her right, and seemed drawn to go there. As if something was calling her, or signaling her that her true path was not east with her new friends, but south.

Noticing her focused gaze, Solara looked south as well. "Do you see something in the distant forest? Is there anything we should be concerned about?"

"No, yet I feel as if I am at an impasse. I wish to continue on with you, yet I feel drawn by something to the south." Her words were slowly spoken, and full of indecision.

Listening to the brief exchange, Braksis looked at his elven companion. "We have always known that our paths would lead us in different directions one day. Solara and I must journey on to the battlefield, yet you are on a quest that may hold the fate of the future in your hands. If you are drawn to the south, then I implore you to travel south."

"Your words are very wise, and I feel that we truly are at a point where we shall part ways. I wish you well with the battle that awaits you, and even more fortune with future skirmishes against Zoldex and his aligned forces of evil, for I fear your trials are only beginning."

"Perhaps our paths will cross again one day. It sounds as if Zoldex is your enemy as well, and if this child is the savior of all, undoubtedly, we will fight side by side in the future."

"With the exception of peace, nothing would please me more than to stand aside you in battle once more. If our paths were to cross again, I would find much satisfaction in that," finished Kai.

"Then go, find this child who will save us all, then do not be a stranger. May fortune ride with you, and hardships trouble you naught," Braksis concluded. He reached out his hand and touched her arm. Then he turned his horse and resumed his travels to the Dartian plains. Tiot in stride jogged alongside him.

Solara embraced Kai's arm as well, and parted with a few words of warning. "As the dwarves moved slowly, so should you. Centuries ago, the prejudices of humans were so great, that Race Wars erupted, and those races that survived, fled into seclusion. To wander the lands alone is a dangerous task indeed. Be cautious, and avoid the humans whenever you can."

"I thank you for this warning. I picked up some of what you say from Comonor and our evening with the dwarves. Yet to know details and a reason is always prudent when one journeys. I will heed your words, and avoid humans whenever possible."

"Good. Then I bid you a fond farewell and a good journey," Solara concluded.

"To you as well. I wish you every success in the upcoming battle. As I said, with Zoldex at work here in your world, caution you must exert. There is more at work here than what has been uncovered thus far. Orcs, goblins, hobgoblins, humans, they may all be rising up against the forces of good, but there is a far more intricate scheme that has not yet been unfolded. This is merely the outlying sign. If for this alone, I wish that our paths remained together, but alas, my mission must come first."

"I understand, and as Braksis stated, if you need us, you only must seek us out. We will help you, in any way that we can. With the power of the Imperium behind us, that help is often far more than one would anticipate."

"I shall remember your gracious offer, and may look you up after all. For now, I must depart, for the pull to travel south is strong, and I wish to begin."

Solara and Kai quickly went through the provisions so Kai would have enough supplies to last her a few days on her own and to still leave enough for Braksis and Solara to arrive at the encampment. With that, the two bid their final farewells and both were off. Kai toward the sensation that she must travel south, and Solara east to catch up to her master.

❖ ❖ ❖ ❖ ❖

The remainder of the trip through Dartie seemed slow moving, and tension was building. Braksis felt they had been away for far too long and wished to be with his troops once more. Even conversation did not help to sway his drive for the final hours.

Rather than camp in Dartie, Braksis pushed his group as quickly as he could. They did not rest for an entire night, but stopped for an hour here or there to rest the horses. The feeling that they needed to be with the army continued to grow, and delays seemed to infuriate the warlord.

Braksis and Solara spoke at length about all they had heard on their trip. All about the orc, goblin, and hobgoblin attacks in the south, as well as the human attacks in the north. The name Zoldex, and the implications Kai brought forth, were troubling. Something clearly was being planned, but what was still unknown.

Knowing that after the battle Braksis would return to Trespias, he wondered how to approach the Empress. He must implore her to consider this threat more seriously, but she was raised like many humans, to think only of their own kind, and not the other races within the realm. Regardless, that was a bridge to be crossed another day. For now, he only wished to be back in his own encampment with his generals and forces to command.

As if on cue, Braksis spotted riders in the distance. They were approaching quickly and, it appeared, in vast numbers. "Riders are approaching."

Solara watched them as they approached but did not seem alarmed. "I think they are ours." She strained to see better. "Yes, they are wearing white and black armor. They are ours."

"Then let's increase our speed and meet them sooner. News of the battle I crave to hear." The two rode hard, with the pony losing ground behind them. Tiot stayed close by the horses' feet.

The riders were soon upon them. A full battalion of twenty cavalry riders. Each wore a full body suit of black leather from neck to toe, with a white armored breastplate, coat of mail, and skirt to protect the body. Arms and legs also had white armor protection, though the joints were unencumbered by armor and only had the black leather. An armored gauntlet for each of the hands, with armored boots for the feet. With the exception of the officer, all of the riders wore a white helmet that had an opening at the eyes and a slit trailing down to reveal their nose and mouth. They all held an elongated triangular white shield with a black border.

Each rider also held a spear, with swords sheathed and attached to the saddle of each horse.

The officer of the group rode forward to meet Braksis. "My lord, we have been searching for you in anticipation of your return. Rumors of a hunting party sent to intercept you reached our spies too late. We were afraid, and we have been riding looking for sign of you since."

"The hunters did reach us, but met an untimely demise."

"You two bested a whole party of hunters?" the rider asked incredulously. "Most impressive."

"Yes, Captain. Though we had assistance from allies met upon the road. Now, speak to me your name so I can address you with more than your rank and give me any news you may have."

"Apologies, my lord, I am Travers, Captain of this small cavalry unit." Travers was garbed identically as the riders but had no helmet. He had long brown hair, and a day's growth of stubble on his face. His dark blue eyes seemed to portray genuine relief that they had found the warlord and his companion safe. "As for news, there is not much to report."

"Not much to report?" Braksis asked in disbelief. "We have been gone for over two weeks. Nothing has happened?"

"No, sir. No battles or confrontations. The hunters kept withdrawing, and we kept following. It was as if they were determined to fight, but also as if they were waiting for something. When news came that they sent a party out to ambush you, we feared all they waited for was your death to provide a swift blow to the Imperium's morale. As I said, it gives me great pleasure to know you have survived, and I am sure this will not bode well for our adversaries," surmised Travers.

"Yes, well, we have talked long enough. I desire to return to camp. Will you lead the way?"

"Certainly, my lord. This will bring much relief to the generals and the men," replied Travers.

"Also, could you send a man farther back? We left our pony behind to meet you, but he should be tended to," Braksis requested.

"As you wish, my lord." Travers raised two fingers and beckoned away in the distance. Two of the riders broke ranks and went off toward the weary pony. All others turned and began the journey back to the camp. Braksis, Solara, and Travers rode in the lead, with Tiot by their side.

CHAPTER 13

At almost the exact instant Braksis and Solara first sighted Travers and the riders, Kai, too, came across her first sign of human life. Remembering Solara's warning about the humans, she decided to enter the woods that she was traveling alongside rather than allowing her existence to become known by the humans.

Traveling in secrecy was one thing she certainly understood from her days before coming to this world. Blending into her surroundings and appearing practically invisible to those around her, was a stealth like art that fate deemed necessary for her to master.

As she entered the trees, she dismounted her steed and walked ahead leading the horse by the reins. The foliage was thick at times, but with some effort and her dagger, she managed to create an opening to pass.

For several hours she traveled in the thick of the trees, glad to be away from the humans, but constantly alert to all signs of life around her. After all, this was a new world, with many new creatures and experiences of which she had no knowledge.

She could see birds perched on trees. Large reptilian creatures slithering or crawling around. Various other animals scampering across the ground. As each distinctive sound drew her attention, she soon found herself growing more comfortable with her surroundings and fascinated by all that the forest had to offer.

"We'll rest here for a little while," she announced to her steed as she removed her gear from his back. She leaned down with her back to a tree, and slowly ate a small pastry that had been baked in Comonor for their travels. It was round in shape with a chocolate filling in the middle. As she took a bite out of it, it was sweet to the taste and quite good. Never before had she had something of this nature, but she suddenly found herself hoping that morsels of this sort would be plentiful in the days to come.

After her snack, she closed her eyes and allowed herself to simply absorb the world around her. Opening herself to nature like this, she could hear the voices of the wild. Not comprehending what she heard, she could still distinguish the various creatures scurrying about speaking to one another. The pitter-patter of feet also was clearly apparent, and every time she opened her eyes to see if an animal was indeed where she thought it was, she smiled with triumph at being right.

Finally, her little game grew tiresome, and her eyes did not open so freely anymore. Soon she was sound asleep, and pleasantly so. As she slept, images flowed into her mind once more.

She could see the open fields of tall grass. Mountains towering into the blue sky off in the distance. Hills off to one side that overlooked oceans spread as far as the eye could see and beyond. Indeed, the view appeared breathtaking.

The young girl was there again. She was weaving in and out of the tall grasses with her arms widespread, giggling as she did so. Playing as if there were not a care in the world. Happy in the perceived tranquility of the world.

As the child played, the scene in the distance changed slightly. Darkness crept in. Kai tried to focus on the mountains and see what was causing this subtle change. Dark birds circled the mountains, as if waiting for some kind of ancient evil to provide them with carrion to feast upon.

The scene continued to focus in on the mountains, as if Kai were flying toward them. The entire time, she could still hear the laughter of the child playing. Then she was upon the mountains, and the birds were flying overhead. Kai stared up at them, puzzled at what they represented, yet feeling somehow she knew.

Then something touched the child's shoulder, and she turned with a gasp as an orc grasped her and growled in triumph. The playing child suddenly screamed in the distance. Moving quickly to try to escape the orc, Kai's eyes flew open and the dream was nothing more than a memory.

Taking a moment to reorient herself, Kai looked around. Still deep within the woods. Her horse tied to a nearby branch. Her skin was drenched with cold sweat. From the look of the leaves around where she was sleeping, she had been thrashing around in her sleep as well.

Reflecting back upon the dream, she remembered what Grosskurth had said about the birds flying in the sky above the Carrion Mountains of the east, most likely sensing evil intentions and hoping to be present after any battles to devour the fallen warriors.

The sight of an orc troubled her, for she had never seen one before, yet his image now burned deep within her soul. The creature was vile and crude. It was a grayish-green creature, with large, almost canine-like teeth that clearly preferred the ripping and gnawing of flesh to any other method of devouring its meals. Its ears were erect and pointed, yet the most fearsome and memorable feature were the reddish eyes that bore into her soul.

She cringed at the memory of the creature from her dream and wondered if this was indeed what an orc looked like, or whether all of these visions were merely aspects of her imagination running wild. Either way, the dwarves mentioned that the orcs had come from the mountains at the southern borders of Frocomon, and that is where she felt she was being drawn. Not to the mountains themselves, but to the fields of tall grass, close to the hills that overlooked the oceans. That was where her destination would be. Whether the orcs were a threat, or simply a guide to help her find her destination, she did not know.

In case it was indeed a threat, she wished to delay no longer, and began to repack her belongings. Travel through the trees was much slower than going in the open, though she did not wish to risk discovery.

Taking the reins of her horse, she began to cut her way through the dense foliage once more. Slowly heading south toward her destiny. Lost in thought as she continued on her journey, she attempted to make sense out of her dreams and visions. She truly believed they were signs, and must be a gift from Eldiir to help guide her way.

So lost in thought she was that she began to walk into a small village before she realized what she had done. Stopping suddenly at the realization, she looked around. She spied several small huts with grass roofs held up by tall poles made of wood. The huts themselves had no walls other than the poles for support, but each had clearings where small possessions were kept, including what appeared to be necklaces, wooden spears, and other nature-constructed weapons, and arranged grasses that resembled beds.

No signs of life were visible, and Kai did not wish to uncover them. She had violated this sanctuary, and she was mentally chastising herself for foolishly traveling without concentrating on the task at hand.

Turning to leave, she heard almost a feline growl above her. "Going so soon, pretty?" The language was choppy, though clearly spoken in the common tongue most species seemed to comprehend.

Kai looked up, but saw nothing. "I did not wish to intrude. It was an accident."

Then two brownish red arms with darker brown slashes on them reached out, lifted her from the ground, and tossed her farther into the trees. There, two more arms, a little more yellow in nature, though also with slanted markings caught her and tossed her onto the ground. "Accident? We think not."

Kai continued to look up for sign of her attackers, but she could see nothing. "I swear to you, it was an accident. I wished to avoid the humans and stumbled across your village quite by chance."

"Avoid the humans? You stink of a human. As does your horse!" roared one voice. "You expect us to believe you, little pretty?"

"I can only tell you that which is true. Whether you believe me or not is up to you. Either believe me or kill me. I leave the choice to you and shall not struggle." As she uttered these words, Kai prayed that if her time was truly up, Arifos or Rulysta would have better luck finding and protecting the child than she.

To her surprise, several creatures dropped down from the trees. They were cat-like with furred coats that seemed to vary in color from light yellow to a much darker shade of brownish red. Tall and slender, they all ranged between five and six feet tall and clearly had good strength since they were able to fling her through the sky with little effort. Their eyes glowed with a tinge of lime green. On both hands and feet, they had claws that could retract and extend when they flexed. Each also had a long tail, which wove patterns in the air behind them. All of them were female, yet none wore apparel of any kind, which shocked Kai since these feline beasts clearly seemed sentient.

"I say we eat the pretty," one offered as she bared her fangs in a hiss.

One of the lighter tinted ones stepped forward. "No. I believe this one. Besides, we do not eat other sentients." She then turned her gaze upon Kai. "If you prove me wrong, I will track and slay you myself."

Kai gazed into the glowing lime-green eyes and nodded. "No deception intended. I merely wish for safe passage as I travel south on a mission of much importance."

"That being the case, you shall be our guest and rest here. Then we will lead you to the edge of the forest where no human eyes will spy you. For they are our enemies, too, as they desire our pelts for clothing and decoration."

At the words, Kai considered the furry hides of the feline creatures for the first time and admitted to herself that they were quite attractive and appealing.

"I am Hr'Sheesh, you shall be my guest, and my responsibility. Those about you are known as the tigrel, and that is all that you must know for now," Hr'Sheesh commented.

"My name is Kai, and I am what is known as a Madrew elf," she offered as cryptically and with as little information as was offered to her.

Hr'Sheesh regarded her for a moment. "These women are the rest of my clan's hunting caste. My sister Hr'Tesh, Ez'Lang, Br'Tanh, her sister Br'Lesk, and finally Az'Horth."

Kai glanced around at each, and with the exception of slightly varied shades and designs of their pelts, she knew that she would never be able to tell two tigrel apart.

"Come. We shall have a feast, for the hunt has proven good. Then we will be on our way after the next moon goes down," Hr'Sheesh commented.

Kai set in stride with the tigrel and followed her back to the small village. To her amazement, several male tigrel and young children now occupied the village, and began preparing the food for a feast. "I don't understand. This was empty before."

"Very good are tigrel senses. Very hard to sneak up on us. We heard you long before you came close to our village. We prepared," Hr'Sheesh said matter-of-factly.

"Only females are in your hunting party?" Kai surmised as she watched the men cook.

"Yes, the women do the hunting, though the men are strong and will protect us if we are invaded." Hr'Sheesh grabbed Kai by the arm and forced her down. "Sit, we will be having warthog tonight. You will be well fed, well rested, then we shall be off. I will lead you myself."

"Thank you for your gracious hospitality," Kai replied sincerely. As she watched the tigrel working, she could see how organized and efficient they were. The entire clan was working together, and before long, all were gathered around a feast fit for kings.

The warthog was in the middle of their dining area as promised. It had been slowly roasted, and was the main coarse for all to eat. They also had wines, which the children had helped to make by crushing berries. Large platters were also displayed, some with fruits and vegetables, and others with a wide variety of smaller meat products. Included throughout the entire display of dining materials were torches to illuminate the quickly darkening sky.

The tigrel spoke for several minutes and thanked all those involved in the hunt and all who helped with the preparations. They also greeted and welcomed Kai to their small village and spoke for several minutes about the changing times when a non-tigrel would be welcomed at their table as a friend. They wondered if it was sign that perhaps the tigrel could once more journey into the land they had once populated in large numbers without fear.

After the discussions and blessings were completed, all began to eat and thoroughly enjoy the spoils of their labor. Kai herself admitted that all she ate was quite good, and she surprised herself by having multiple servings when offered.

After the feast was concluded, all of the tigrel just leaned back where they were seated and started talking to one another as they lay by the table. Jokes were told. Tales of old relayed to the younger members of the clan. The hunters also spoke of some of their more dangerous hunts. All was quite peaceful and pleasant.

Kai fell asleep at the table listening to their voices. Though they did not all speak the common tongue well, they had all made the attempt rather than speaking in their own tigrel dialect, merely for her comfort and benefit.

For the first time since arriving in the Seven Kingdoms, Kai did not dream of the child. Instead, her sleep was deep and full, and not plagued by visions of orcs or other threats. A deep sleep that did her well, and would allow her to travel long and face many hardships. Such was the gift of the tigrel wine.

❖ ❖ ❖ ❖ ❖

When she awoke, Hr'Sheesh was kneeling beside her head and looking down at her. "Rise and shine, pretty. Time to lead you to the end of the Dimmu and set you back on your journey."

Kai rested on her elbow and looked around. Once again, the village was deserted. Only Hr'Sheesh and one other, which Kai swore was Hr'Tesh, though they all resembled each other far too much to know for certain, was present. "Dimmu?"

"The Dimmu Forest. Hr'Tesh and I will guide you. We will move swiftly now. You need not worry."

Kai looked around for her horse, but could not see the mare. "Where is my horse?"

"No need to worry. The steed could not make it on the path you go. We brought it to a friend who can travel in the open. He will leave your horse where we will exit. Fear not."

"A friend? A human? I thought you did not trust or like them?" Determined to know what happened to her horse, Kai pressed her host.

"A human but not. Questions you need not ask, and worries you need not have. Come, we shall leave now."

To her words, Kai jumped up and stretched her body to remove any last signs of fatigue. Her bow and arrows were with her horse, leaving her with only her dagger. This did not entirely please her, but her tigrel guides seemed not to be worried in the least. They themselves carried no weapons, but were confident that with tooth and nail, they could best any creature within the woods.

As soon as they were off, Kai was amazed at how quickly they traveled. The forest did not inhibit the tigrel at all. They moved quickly, and always seemed to land on their feet no matter how far they leapt. Kai herself was much slower than her two guides, but they slowed down for her and did not allow her to fall too far behind.

She could see now why they sent the horse along a different path. If the faithful steed were here, they would not be able to travel as quickly, and the terrain itself seemed to grow more rough and unsteady which could break a leg if one were not careful. She was glad that her horse was not still with her.

For hours they traveled without word, only pausing when Kai faltered behind them and needed rest. She was truly amazed, for she was one of the swiftest and most agile of all the Madrew, yet these tigrel put her to shame.

"We should stop and let her rest for a while," she overheard Hr'Sheesh commenting to her sister.

"Rest? Let the pretty keep moving. She slows us down enough," spat Hr'Tesh.

After this brief exchange, Kai found energy within herself to push onward, and from that moment on, stayed much closer to her tigrel guides.

As daylight soon began to vanish, the trio continued to fly through the forest. Hr'Sheesh slowed down to speak with Kai. Hr'Tesh continued onward. "We will be with your horse soon. The forest is almost at its end."

Ahead of them where Hr'Tesh had continued on, they heard a swooshing noise, followed by loud bells clanging. Hr'Sheesh tensed and began after her sister much swifter than she had traveled thus far that day. Kai followed her as quickly as she could.

When they reached Hr'Tesh, she was dangling from the air upside down in a trap, carrying on in her own tongue without pause.

Hr'Sheesh tried to calm her down with soothing words and looked around. The trap had been covered by the debris along the ground, and was sprung when Hr'Tesh stepped within its grasp. The bells clearly were a signal so that the hunters could come claim their prize. They most likely would be nearby.

Indeed the hunters were. Hr'Sheesh heard them first. She tensed, then gazed off in the distance. "They are coming."

"Get me down then!" spat Hr'Tesh.

Following the rope, Kai found an edge strung to a tree for support. She looked up at Hr'Tesh, and cautioned her. "This may hurt." Without any further delay, she unsheathed her dagger and brought it crashing down on the rope, severing it in two.

Hr'Tesh fell quickly, but managed to twist and land on her hands and feet. The bells clanged louder as she hurtled through the air and landed.

Kai and Hr'Sheesh began to cut the untangled wire from their snared ally. By now, Kai, too, could hear the hunters coming. They were almost upon them. "We must hurry."

"We are hurrying–you are the slow one!" Hr'Tesh growled.

"You're welcome," she said sarcastically.

Finally the last tangle was cut free, and without a second's pause, Hr'Tesh was up and running again toward their original destination. Hr'Sheesh and Kai joined her and fled the approaching hunters.

She could imagine their faces when they came upon their trap and found nothing there. This thought brought a small smile to Kai's face. One that Hr'Sheesh was able to read.

"Do not be too proud, little one. They are hunters and they desire our pelts for sale. They will follow our tracks."

"Will they catch you?"

"Humph! Never!" Hr'Tesh responded from ahead. "Unless you keep slowing us down."

Hr'Sheesh patted Kai on the shoulder. "Fear not, you will be with your horse and off soon. Then they will have no chance against a tigrel's own stealthy nature. We will be fine."

For the remainder of their journey, the sounds of the hunters could be heard in the distance. Kai now realized what she must have sounded like when the tigrel first confronted her. Loud and out of place with the rest of nature.

Then, a clearing was upon them, and her horse was tied in wait of her. "Amazing," Kai remarked.

"Yes, we have cut several days off your journey. If not for our friend, your horse, too, would be days behind."

"Who is your friend, Hr'Sheesh?"

"One that will remain a friend to us, but also may befriend you again in time of need. Worry not, and more knowledge need you not." Pointing toward the bundles on the horse, Hr'Sheesh continued. "We have added more provisions, as well as tigrel wine. Only drink that if you have time and are in need of sound sleep."

"Thank you. I do not know what more I can say."

"How about goodbye?" Hr'Tesh sarcastically commented. "Time for pretty and us to part. They grow near."

"Yes, my sister is right. We wish you well on your journey, wherever that may lead. Now we must be off or off we never will be."

Kai waived goodbye as she watched the two return to the trees and vanish as if they never were. "Thank you again. Thank you." Hearing the hunters still approach, she untied her horse and mounted quickly. She was now several days closer to the Chosen One, and with the fates, several days could mean much. With that realization, she was off leaving the trees of the Dimmu Forest and the kingdom of Dartie behind her.

CHAPTER 14

As Braksis and his fellow riders arrived back at the camp, he witnessed many exiting their tents and cheering his name as they rode in. The tale of his battle with the tragon apparently had reached friend and foe alike. The fact that they survived the ambush sent for them also led to much rejoicing.

Morale was good for the troops, and Braksis did not discourage this reaction. He rode proudly and triumphantly through the camp.

When they reached the command tent, Travers spoke up. "The generals should be inside waiting to brief you, sir."

"Thank you, Captain." Braksis dismounted and approached the tent. Solara, too, dismounted and was merely a step behind him. Tiot approached the opening of the tent and sat down to rest.

As he walked in, Braksis could see his command staff diligently reviewing the maps and tactical data for the Dartian plains. As each looked up and acknowledged his presence, they seemed gladdened and relieved he had survived his journey.

Kronos stepped forward and addressed the Warlord. "My lord, we welcome you back and will rest easier knowing you have survived your ordeals and returned to us where you belong."

"Thank you, Kronos. I would have been back sooner, but the roads were long and delays seemed unavoidable. I wish an update. The Captain who sought me out stated that the hunters seemed to withdraw and not attack. Can we end their hostilities peacefully?"

Letting out a small sigh, Kronos returned to the map. "If only that were so. Alas, I am afraid we shall not be so fortunate."

"Explain," ordered Braksis as he approached the maps himself.

"The enemy has indeed withdrawn as if in waiting. And waiting they were. Only last night, they were joined by another party that has seemingly doubled their forces."

"Doubled?" Braksis asked in awe. "How many are we facing?"

In response, Sevlow spoke up. "My scouts have estimated, with this new addition, between eight and ten thousand men."

All of the leaders were quiet for a moment. Braksis paused in disbelief that so many could be involved in this uprising. Indeed, the reach of Zoldex was far and quite dangerous. "How many men do we have?"

"We sent for reinforcements from Trespias ourselves and nearly doubled their numbers. This battle still should be one-sided," responded Kronos.

"Do not be so certain, old friend. Solara, Tiot, an elf, ten dwarves, and myself brought a force of fifty to their knees with little trouble. These warriors believe what they are fighting for and feel just. I fear that this will not be as one-sided as we may like to think."

"That is very possible," conceded Hinbar. "However, they wear skins of animals and are a disgruntled band of thugs. We are armored and trained to be the best fighting force in all the Imperium. Many will be lost, but still an Imperium victory this day will bring."

"I am gladdened by your optimism. What are our options?" Braksis requested.

Kronos stepped back and raised an open palm out to Hinbar.

Hinbar nodded. "In our last meeting, we stressed a strategy of getting the cavalry behind them. With their backs to the Ordell Mountains and the Olbrus Rapids flowing from Falestia, this is no longer an option. I suggest a frontal assault with our foot soldiers and heavy spear. Archers will remain behind and barrage our foes and help to dwindle their numbers. The cavalry and crossbow units can come in as relief and deliver a final blow to the enemy."

"Thank you, Hinbar," Kronos added. "General Lowred, your recommendation."

Lowred took a deep breath and let it out slowly. "A frontal attack I am wary of, though in this battle, there may be no other alternative. Yet, with about a day's ride, we could send part of our cavalry farther east and have them travel in the cover of the trees, then along the outskirts of the Olbrus Rapids. They would not be completely behind the enemy, but would be able to surprise them. Other than that, I shall concur with Hinbar."

"Thank you, Lowred. Sevlow?" Kronos continued.

"Lowred looks to give us an advantage, yet my scouts have also considered that path and feel that it is being watched. We would only weaken our own efforts to send troops that way. I feel that the line should be established as Hinbar suggested, and utilize the archers. However, where my proposal differs, is the holding back of the cavalry and crossbow units. The archers can fire from a distance, yet the crossbow units must be somewhat closer. I suggest they should line up directly behind the foot soldiers and heavy spear units, then send volleys of their own into the enemy. They could fire with precision even after we have engaged the hunters. As for the cavalry, I feel they should move in quickly—a burst straight down the middle in a charge to split the enemy forces. If they are successful, our cavalry would indeed be behind the enemy, and split between our forces."

Braksis considered the options before commenting. "Are we certain they will attack?"

"Yes," Kronos said. "From our last scouting report, they were fully arming themselves and preparing for battle."

"Very well. Prepare the men. General Lowred, I like your suggestion of sending horses a day's ride to surprise our enemies. Though if the scouts feel that this is not feasible, I do not wish to lose members of the cavalry, yet I would like to implement that portion of the plan."

"How can we do both if you will not send the cavalry?" Lowred inquired.

"General Sevlow, I wish for you to depart immediately. Take all of your scouts and arm yourselves well. Hopefully when the battle begins, you can enter the fray and assist us in attacking from behind. If not, then hopefully you will at least split the enemy and delay them."

Sevlow bowed. "I understand, my lord. My men shall be prepared to depart within the hour."

"Excellent. The remainder of the plan we shall proceed as Sevlow suggested. Those in the cavalry will have a dangerous mission, and will most likely have the heaviest toll taken upon them. I shall lead this force personally, and hopefully my name will inspire our troops, and send the enemy scurrying."

"Is this wise, my lord?" Kronos inquired.

"I would not ask a lesser officer to submit to this plan if I would not lead the charge myself. General Hinbar, you shall lead the foot soldiers, heavy spear and crossbow units. General Lowred, you shall command the archers, and in this, I desperately hope that during our charge, your men are swift and accurate."

"We shall not fail you, my lord," Lowred said.

"General Kronos will maintain tactical command and will issue orders to all units. Are there any questions?"

All the generals stood at attention and no questions were asked. "Excellent. Then we shall attack this time tomorrow. That should give you just enough time to get your men into position, wouldn't you say, General Sevlow?"

"More than enough time, sir," Sevlow returned.

"Excellent. Then everyone prepare your troops. Try to get some rest tonight, for tomorrow will be a long day," Braksis concluded, and one by one, his generals exited the tent to issue orders to their men.

"Very daring to lead this charge through ten thousand men. Suicidal?" Solara inquired.

"No. I have a good feeling about this plan. It will be successful."

"Either way, I will ride at your side."

"I cannot ask that of you for this mission," Braksis stated with a serious expression on his face.

"Who is asking? I would not leave your side if you so ordered it."

"Thank you." He took a deep breath and looked around. "Now if only I could find another cloak to replace the one I lost, everything would be the way it should be."

Solara considered him for a moment as he searched for a replacement cloak, and had to laugh. Facing insurmountable odds and almost certain death with the route he selected, his largest concern was for a cloak. If they both lived one hundred years, she didn't think she would ever truly understand him completely.

CHAPTER 15

The following day brought a cool foggy mist that enshrouded the would-be battlefield. Rows upon rows of black-and-white clad Imperial troops lined up and prepared for the upcoming skirmish. The aligned forces were quite impressive and rather intimidating.

Braksis rested upon his horse, with his newly replaced red cloak gently blowing in the wind. He looked out at his troops and the visible plains in front of them. He did not see his foes clearly yet, but he could hear them approaching in the distance.

Walking up behind him, Kronos pondered the weather. "This does not seem natural. I fear something mystical may be at play here."

Braksis regarded the elderly General and remembered the words he heard of Zoldex on his journey. Something mystical indeed. "Be prepared for anything. I have heard much recently of one that is manipulating many, and caution I would advise."

"Can you tell me more, my lord?"

"Not now, Kronos. We must survive the day before continuing the war. After this day has ended, you will be called upon to do and learn much of our plight."

"You speak in riddles, though I agree we must pay attention to the here and now. I shall return to my post and begin issuing orders. May your horse be swift and your sword be true." Turning after his prayer, Kronos returned to his station where he would command the combined forces.

Braksis glanced back at Solara. "Unless my ears deceive me, it sounds as if they are almost on top of us already."

She strained her eyes to see, but was as blind as him. "I know not how we would be able to determine this."

"I do." He dug his heels into Blaze's side and was off at a gallop. Not a minute later, he was upon his foes. Turning quickly, he began back toward his troops, unsheathing the Phoenix as he did so. Light pierced the fog and focused on his blade. The area around him cleared, and his forces could see not only him, but the rapidly approaching hunters as well.

General Lowred was farthest away. He rested atop his horse and positioned himself in front of his assembled archers, who were ten rows deep and a hundred men across. Seeing the fog lift where Braksis rode, he could tell that the enemy was upon them. He raised his cane straight up in the air, then sliced it down, signaling his troops to begin their barrage.

Arrows filled the air in a shower of death for the hunters. Those who had shields did their best to protect themselves, but far more screamed out in pain as they were hit, and even more fell to their deaths. The volley continued, and rows of hunters fell before the onslaught.

The fog that covered the field completely dissipated, and the day was clear once more. Both armies could see each other clearly for the first time, and the Imperium forces let out a cheer when they saw so many injured and dead hunters sprawled out upon the ground as Lowred's attack continued.

Kronos watched the fog dissipate before him. "Mystical indeed," he whispered to himself, and suddenly felt a sense of foreboding.

Braksis returned to the cavalry and twirled the Phoenix above his head. "We now ride into numbers far greater. We seek to create a wedge between the forces, destroy their supplies, and attack from behind. It will not be an easy task, but if you ride true and stay close, we will triumph!"

His speech led to many cheers, for him, for the Imperium, and for victory. Then all riders charged out in a near stampede toward the enemy's forces. As they hit their foes, many fell before their charge. The various cavalry troops were armed with spears and lances. All also had short swords and shields. They used their elongated blades to strike as many as possible, and switched to swords if their primary weapon was lost.

Row upon row of the enemy they pierced before finding themselves slowing down. Soon, hunters surrounded them on all sides, and the cavalry found themselves hacking down at their foes just to try to move.

Braksis swung the mighty Phoenix many times, bringing numerous foes to their untimely demise. Solara was close to him, bringing her fair share of foes down as well. He looked around and saw many falter, but knew they must continue.

Another volley of arrows came in, just missing Braksis and his company. In fact, one arrow sliced through his new cloak, and was embedded into the head of one of his attackers. Hundreds of hunters fell around them, and Braksis issued the command to push forward.

More and more hunters were coming at them, though some seemed to pause and flee when they saw the rider clad in black armor and a red cloak. For they knew Braksis well and of his deeds. Though they were promised much by Zoldex, fear for their own lives would win out in the end.

Hundreds of men dropped their weapons and turned to flee. Braksis took advantage of this and drove his remaining men on even farther. Behind them, a path had been created where dead bodies lay in their wake.

Finally reaching the end of their opponent's forces, Braksis turned and looked at the battle ensuing in front of him. He had made it through, though if not for the sharp-sightedness of Lowred's men and the cowardice of some of their foes, they would have fallen almost halfway through their appointed rounds.

Captain Travers rode up next to the Warlord. His sword was doused in red, and his armor also shared the same crimson color of death. "My lord, what are your orders now?"

"Captain, take your men and find their supplies. If we destroy those, then morale will falter. I will take the rest of the men and continue to attack."

"Understood." Travers beckoned with his hand, and his remaining forces fell in line behind him. They rode out in search for the enemies storehouses.

Braksis looked at his remaining men. Many had been battered and bruised. All were bloodied, either from their own wounds or from their enemies'. Some were out of breath and ready to collapse, yet when he had them regroup, all fatigue and weariness seemed to vanish. The men were ready to fight once more.

"We have fought hard to break through their forces. Now that we are here, we can try to separate their ranks once more. We are tired, weary, and desire rest. Yet until the last hunter has fallen or fled, the Imperium is in danger and we are needed. Who will ride with me?"

All cheered once more, then they were off, back into the thick of their enemies, resuming the battle.

❖ ❖ ❖ ❖ ❖

On the front lines, General Hinbar watched as Braksis and his troops cut a line through the enemy. The forces were cut in half, but would soon regroup unless he pressed the attack himself. He sent out the command that five units were to advance. In all, five units were not much. Each unit contained only one hundred men, though he felt that the five units could help to keep the forces divided as they attacked the remainder of his troops.

The units marched out in an awl formation. This triangular battle technique would force the foes to split around them if they continued to charge, and create an even deeper wedge between the forces.

The three units in the lead were heavy spear units, with two units of foot soldiers behind them. The foot soldiers were better in defense than the heavy spears, and they would try to protect their attacking companions.

As the units set forth, Hinbar saw that the hunters' forces were splitting into two sides as they had hoped. Divide and conquer. An age-old strategy that thus far was working quite well against the hunters.

As the hunters came within range, the crossbow units unleashed a volley of their own. Those who survived the volley of arrows came across lines upon lines of soldiers waiting for them. As they reached the line, the Imperial troops, waiting until the last possible moment, struck and brought the hunters down quickly.

Hinbar was proud of the early stages thus far. His infantry was fighting admirably, hundreds of the enemy had fallen, and his lines still held.

❖ ❖ ❖ ❖ ❖

General Lowred continued his volley, directing his men to fire at specific clusters of troops. Their accuracy was astounding; he was amazed that not one Imperial cavalryman fell when they fired in close proximity.

He watched as the five units advanced and continued to attack any that tried to return to the middle of the battlefield. All others separated and attacked from either the right or left side of the lines.

Lowred commanded half of his troops to fire on one side and half to fire on the other. Arrows continued to pierce the sky and find their mark in the thick of the enemy forces. Then, one volley halted and remained immobile in the air. It was as if the arrows had struck an invisible wall.

"What devilry is this?" Lowred growled.

The levitated arrows then slowly fell to the ground harmlessly. More enemy forces approached from that area toward the lines set up by Hinbar. Suddenly, Imperial troops were flung backward and the lines crumbled.

Lowred stared in disbelief as hunters pressed the attack and entered the front lines, attacking all in their path. Behind them, Lowred could see a figure clad in white garments, a robe with golden designs stenciled into the fabric. "A Mage," he whispered to himself. Yelling for all to hear, he sounded an alarm. "They have a Mage!"

CHAPTER 16

Seeing the Mage sweep his way through the Imperial forces with nothing more than a wave of his hand or a gesture, Kronos knew this must have been the cause of his foreboding. The Mage must have been responsible for the misty fog that enshrouded the battlefield. Clearly, he had designed it to allow surprise to be on the side of the Dartian hunters.

The battle had been going smoothly. Braksis had separated the forces, and Hinbar had advanced and driven an even greater wedge between them. Lowred continued his barrage, and enemies were faltering before they even got close to the front lines. Yet those who did quickly met their own demise.

The enemy had been in shambles, yet Kronos was amazed at how quickly the tide could be turned. One Mage entered the fray, and suddenly the hunters seemed reinvigorated and pressed their assault once more.

Contemplating how to take down a Mage, Kronos was at a loss. They were part of an ancient order, usually secluded, but formidable and beyond the means of men when they attacked. Numbers would no longer matter, he feared. This one man may have just turned the tide and single-handedly brought ruin to the Imperium.

❖ ❖ ❖ ❖ ❖

General Hinbar directed his troops to reposition themselves and attempt to hold the lines where the hunters and the Mage were breaking through. Facing the hunters was one thing, but the Mage would just sweep his arm, and dozens of men in close proximity would suddenly find themselves hurtling away from him.

To fight a Mage, one needed a Mage—either that, or a miracle. Some kind of mystically gifted individual or item perhaps. Then Hinbar remembered the beginning of the attack. The fog had enshrouded them until Braksis unsheathed his mighty blade, the Phoenix. A sword forged from the molten magma of the planet itself, by none other than a Mage Master.

Hinbar looked out across the plains and prayed that Braksis would return soon. His sword and skills were needed, or else all hope may be lost.

❖ ❖ ❖ ❖ ❖

It did not take long for Travers and his men to find the supplies. Three large structures were built to hold enough food and drink to last a month for the forces amassed against the Imperium. The buildings were guarded by only a dozen hunters, and they were no match for Travers and his men.

They moved swiftly and set fire to the storehouses. The flames ignited quickly, and the dark smoke of waste could be seen trailing into the clear sky.

Travers looked out at the hunters still engaged in battle. "Let's see how their morale continues now. No food or supplies, this battle can only last the day." In response to his comments, he did see many hunters drop their weapons and flee as others had before them. "It is time to rejoin the battle. For honor!"

His men all replied with "for honor" and they charged back to the battle, leaving the burning storehouses in their wake.

❖ ❖ ❖ ❖ ❖

Braksis and Solara advanced their troops into the battle, and were deeply entrenched with foes that they swung at swiftly as they rode through the enemy's ranks. Many men continued to flee before them, and signs that the battle would soon be over were undeniable as the hunters continued to fall or flee.

Searching for the progress of others, Braksis could see that the storehouses were aflame, and that Travers was returning to the battle with his men. Braksis was becoming quite impressed with the Captain, and plans for his future were growing.

No sign of General Sevlow was to be seen, though much could have happened to slow down the General's advance; some obstacle could have been in the way. He trusted that the general would appear in time, though his efforts may not prove necessary.

His own remaining cavalry troops were faring quite well. The enemy was in such disarray, very few sought to attack them, although those who did fell before the noble riders. Since the initial charge, few cavalry members had fallen in battle.

The only area of concern was the front lines. Though he could not make it out clearly, he saw they seemed to be crumbling in spots, and the volley of arrows, a huge tactical advantage for the Imperium, had halted. Most curious.

A horn blew out from the command center, and Braksis knew something was amiss. He was needed, with as many of his troops as he could afford. Their multi-pronged assault tactics may have been working, but the front lines and primary forces were in jeopardy.

Just then, Braksis saw General Sevlow and his men entering the fray with their swords brandished high. Their numbers had dwindled significantly from when they had departed the day before, so clearly they had met some kind of resistance or problem. Alas, they had joined the battle and that was all that mattered for now.

Braksis yelled out for all who could hear, "The horn signals that we are needed! Ride with me again, and we will blaze yet another path straight back to our own front lines!"

With this, he began a charge again and all of the cavalry fell in line behind him. General Sevlow and Captain Travers advanced with them as well, though slightly behind their assault.

Hunters fled from their path, looking to escape the fate that befell their comrades during the last charge. Any foolish enough to remain in their way felt the blades of Braksis and his men, leaving another wake of bodies behind them.

As they approached their own front lines, Braksis could see the cause of distress. A Mage was on the side of the Dartian hunters. From the designs on his robe, he appeared to be of lower status than Ferceng, which Braksis presumed made him a Paladin, one that entered the world in order to find himself and to grow through discovery and exploration.

The Mage picked up a spear from one of the fallen soldiers and used the weapon to attack his foes. With each thrust, far more than just the one he struck faltered.

Braksis knew that this Mage must be stopped, and the hunters would fall quickly without him. He charged straight for the Mage and leapt from his horse with his sword aimed directly for the Mage's chest.

The Mage spun around and with a wave knocked Braksis from the sky. For the first time, Braksis could see the Mage's features and was amazed that it was not human as he had thought. Under the robes of the ancient order, the Mage garnished the face of a decaying skeleton. The hands that held so much mystical power were likewise decayed, and looked almost as if holding the spear would cause them to crumble and blow away in the wind.

Within the two black openings where human eyes would be, Braksis could see a faint red glow that held his gaze. The white and gold robe blended before his eyes, and a dark green garment remained. Was this an actual Mage from the Mage's Council, or something else?

The Mage opened its bony mouth and released a hiss at Braksis. Though no words were spoken, he suddenly seemed to understand. This creature was indeed a Mage, though like none they had ever known. Cursed to serve the rest of his days in the darkness and shadows as a minion for Zoldex. Pitiful, yet deadly.

The Mage approached Braksis and raised his spear. Braksis lay there in wait, preparing to dodge and strike. As the spear came down, a sword hurtled through the sky and pierced the Shadow Mage's chest, sending it backward several steps.

Braksis looked out and saw Captain Travers, now disarmed, approaching quickly to assist him. He flung his sword with accuracy and struck the Shadow Mage.

The Mage looked down at the blade impaling his chest and pulled it out with no signs of pain or weakness. As he held the blade, it started smoking and crumbled in his hands. With another hiss, he threw the hilt aside and stepped toward Braksis once more.

Braksis jumped up onto his feet and brought the Phoenix around, though deflected by the spear. He quickly spun around and brought the blade at the Mage's other side, but was parried there as well.

Solara watched the exchange, but knew that her master would desire her to take over in his stead rather than interfere in a battle where she would have little impact. Travers's intervention pointed that out to her. She rallied the men and continued to attack the hunters, who seemed stunned that the Mage that fought alongside of them was a hideous creature, and not a human like them.

With the newfound shock, many more fled, and those who remained quickly fell under the combined might of the Imperium without a Mage's intervention.

Travers wished to help further, but could see no way for the time being. He picked up another weapon that had fallen on the battlefield, and bided his time in case the Warlord would need his assistance again.

Though the Shadow Mage was parrying and blocking all attacks, Braksis clearly was the better swordsman. His attack was swift and brutal, and the Mage seemed to forget he could attack with mystical abilities as well.

With the spear held high to block a thrusting blow, the Phoenix cleaved the spear in two, and sliced down into the Mage's shoulder. Braksis quickly took his advantage, and swung his blade again high toward the Shadow Mage's head, severing it from the body with one swing.

As the head rolled to the ground, the body itself turned to dust, leaving only a cloak and a pile of ashes behind. Braksis looked down at the skull as it rolled along the ground, and watched as the eerie red glow of the eyes slowly flickered out, then the head, too, turned to dust.

Travers stepped up behind him and placed his hand on his shoulder. "The tide has turned, sir. The hunters have faltered. This battle will be over within the hour." He saw that Braksis still stared at the pile of dust, which now blew in the wind, and wondered if the Warlord was injured. "Are you okay, sir?"

"Yes, Captain. I am fine." Taking his gaze from the remains of the fallen Mage, he focused on Travers. "Thank you for your assistance. I will remember all that you have done today."

"Certainly is nice to hear, but this day isn't over yet. Shall we end it?"

"Yes, let's do that." Travers handed Braksis the reins to his horse, and both men mounted their steeds. Braksis looked at the Captain one last time. "The battle should be just about over now."

The two rode off and attacked any that still managed to fight. Indeed, the battle was soon over. With the death of the Shadow Mage, those who remained quickly faltered, and the Imperium seized the day in victory.

CHAPTER 17

Hours after the final soldier was slain, troops still searched the plains for wounded and survivors. All would receive proper burials, friend and foe alike. Braksis wished to show those who remained that the Imperium did not dishonor the dead, and if the people would return to the order, all would be forgiven. Besides, he deduced that Zoldex had manipulated them, which he hoped could wear off.

The sight of the Shadow Mage concerned him; never before had he heard of such a thing. He desired the council of a Mage Master himself, though he knew he could not get to Ferceng to discuss what had happened. Perhaps he would seek an audience with the Council itself and ask his questions. It was a thought he would have to consider further upon returning to Trespias.

His staff was assembled in the command tent, and this time he invited Travers. The two had searched the plains together for any cavalry troops that may have survived. Only a couple of injured soldiers were uncovered.

"Gentleman, I would like to commend you all on the battle. We fared quite well considering. Now, I feel that much must be discussed that has been revealed to me of late." Braksis looked around the room at the expressionless faces of his staff. They all awaited his report. Only Solara knew details of what he wished to discuss.

"In recent days, I have heard the name of Zoldex repeated by our foes many times. Even by many on the battlefield we just left." The command staff all nodded, for they, too, had heard the name of late. "It has also been brought to my attention that this same Zoldex is aligning the orcs, goblins, and hobgoblins in the south."

The officers stood stunned for a moment. These vile creatures had not been seen or heard from since the Race Wars, hundreds of years before. Now, not only to have returned, but also to be organized boggled the mind.

Kronos considered this deeply and feared for his home in Danchul. "Have they attacked Danchul yet?"

"No. For now, they have focused on the Halls of Vorstad and Xylona."

"Vorstad and Xylona?" inquired Hinbar. "Let them fight and resume their ancient wars then. What concern is it of ours?"

Glaring at his General, Braksis continued. "If Vorstad and Xylona fall, then Danchul and Frocomon will be next. Remember, the same foe who has manipulated the Dartian hunters and other revolts this past year, is also playing a hand with our ancient enemies. We would be foolish to ignore the threat."

"Sir, begging your pardon, but we are being attacked by our own humans. Is that not our priority?" Hinbar pressed.

"Yes, General, although I feel it will soon be time to reunite the species against a common foe." Braksis looked around and took in all of their expressions. Some seemed disgusted, others were harder to read. "We need more information, and I will attempt to acquire that. In the meantime, whether an attack be from orc or human, we must be prepared."

"What will you have us do?" Travers stood proud and inquired. "Where you lead, my men shall follow."

"I was hoping you would feel that way, Captain. I have an important mission for you. One that you must not fail at, though it will be difficult."

"Declare it, and my men and I shall perform admirably." Travers beamed with pride and confidence.

"Various clans of hobgoblins have been assaulting Xylona. That proud city of the elves almost fell, though the fates played their own hand by bringing a savior. As we speak, they could be fighting. Dwarves have also gone to assist them, though they still will be trapped and outnumbered." Braksis paused to make sure that the information was getting through to the Captain. "I would like you to take one hundred riders and go to their aid. Hunt the hobgoblins. Strengthen Xylona's defenses. Destroy any forces of evil that appear in your path. Do you feel up to this, Captain?"

"Yes, my lord, I would be honored to do so," replied Travers. "We shall leave immediately."

"Not so fast. Let the men rest for the night, then be on your way in the morning," Braksis advised.

"Understood, sir."

"General Kronos, how would you like to return to Danchul?" Braksis inquired.

"Ah, to see the land of my home once more would be a dream come true, my lord."

"I am glad you feel that way. I want you to take five thousand men and march to southern Danchul. Offer your assistance to Vorstad, for they are understaffed and have been sieged now for many months. Any orcs, goblins, or hobgoblins you see are fair game. Leave none standing and show them the might of men."

"A truly inspiring mission, my lord. I feel like a youth again just thinking about it." In fact, looking at Kronos, he appeared almost twenty years younger after being given his orders.

Hinbar shook his head. "Five thousand men–you cut our surviving forces in half. What if we are attacked again?"

"Not half General, but more than that. General Sevlow, I wish for you to remain here with a garrison of two thousand men. Just a precaution in case any of those who fled desire to band together again."

"Yes, my lord." Sevlow bowed in obedience.

"As for you, Hinbar–you and Lowred will return with the rest of the men to Trespias with me. From there, I want you to actively recruit and train as many men as possible. I fear that our numbers will need to more than triple if we are to survive the impending storm."

"Triple? Impossible!" bellowed Hinbar. "There are not enough men left to enlarge our forces that much."

"Then take women," Braksis curtly replied.

"Women?" he sneered.

"Yes, look at Solara here. She fought beside me and defeated men who were larger and stronger. Her size is irrelevant, but her training and skill are exceptional." He watched his steaming General, who clearly preferred the old days when only men fought in battles, and the women remained behind to tend to home and family. "General, these women can be trained with bows, swords, and spears. They can carry crossbows and add their numbers to the cavalry. At least try. Let the women decide if they can fight or not."

Clearly displeased, Hinbar bowed without further argument.

"General Sevlow, I have a few questions for you." Braksis turned to change the topic.

"Yes, my lord?"

"You spent much of your youth in Tenalong, and even worked there as a spy in your early days. Have you ever heard of a clan of orcs in a large city known as Murky Death?"

Sevlow seemed to shudder with the thought. "All in Tenalong have heard of the Murky Death clan, though none have lived who have sought it. Rumor has it deep beyond the swamps near the Bloody River and the Forbidden Forest. It's hidden and secluded. Larger than any orc city has a right to be."

"Thank you, General. Captain Travers, you must be cautious to watch your back as well. If this clan migrates out of the swamps, we will not be able to stop them from swarming the lands."

"Yes, sir. I will keep a constant vigil for new enemies," Travers replied.

"Gentlemen, our lives are about to change. Everything we thought we knew must now be questioned. Be cautious, but be bold. We must not allow the forces of evil to spread. This is our realm, and we must protect it."

All present nodded and agreed with the Warlord.

"Further, any news, no matter how small, about this Zoldex, I want riders dispatched to Trespias with it immediately. I must know all that he is considering and scheming if I am to uncover his plot."

"What about the Shadow Mage?" Lowred brought up. "If there are more of them, can our attempts survive?"

Braksis considered for a minute. "The Shadow Mage is indeed something that must be considered. If more of them are out there, and I fear that they will be, then we could all be in much graver danger unless we get the support of the Mage's Council behind us. I will speak of this with the Empress."

Sitting there contemplating what was discussed and what he knew, he felt he had done all he could at this juncture. Seeing he was finished, the command staff departed one by one to prepare the troops and begin their assigned tasks. Many hardships would fall on them all after this day, and as Braksis sat there, he hoped his decisions were wise and his course of action true.

CHAPTER 18

The kingdom of Frocomon was one faced with a deep history of regret and consequences that seemed impossible to overcome. Located south of Trespias, the Imperial City, Frocomon was a water-faring kingdom that lost most of its land after the Great Wars to its western neighbor, Danchul.

During the Great Wars, Frocomon boasted a powerful armada that could best any opponent, and lashed out at any who dared venture onto the seas. Their survival depended heavily on their naval prowess, as well as the farmers who cultivated the rich soil in their kingdom. Unlike their neighbors in Danchul, they had no military skill for land forces and relied heavily on their neighbors for support if attack ever came. To repay Sarlec, King of Danchul, they split the provisions from their agricultural exploits.

When Conrad began his endeavors to unify the people and bring an end to the hostilities, he and Morex started their conquest in the sea. Morex was a tactical genius and with new innovations designed by their allies, he was able to design naval battle tactics never seen before. These tactics were used against Frocomon's armada and reined supreme.

After conquering the seas, Conrad sought new alliances and found a valuable one in King Sarlec, who pledged his entire army to the man who would become Emperor. Very few could match Danchul on the ground, and Morex controlled the sea. This brought an end to the Great Wars and introduced a new era, uniting the Seven Kingdoms under Conrad's rule as the Imperium.

To thank King Sarlec for his support and punish Frocomon for its resistance, Emperor Conrad gave much of Frocomon's land to Danchul.

This lost territory held almost all of the fertile land they had cultivated for centuries.

Unhappy with this arrangement, the people of Frocomon found life increasingly difficult. Farmers could work their old land as employees to new landowners in Danchul. As a result, Danchul increased its wealth and output, and Frocomon became enslaved to low rates and starving citizens.

A new industry needed to be explored to help revitalize the kingdom, and the people turned to the seas they once conquered. Fishing villages sprung up throughout the costal areas and people swarmed to learn this new trade. However, this, too, was no easy endeavor.

With large masses of people entering the fishing trade, too many fish were caught early on, and the seas now needed to be scoured far and wide to find decent catches. What seemed at first like an ideal solution, quickly faltered, creating more poverty and unrest within the kingdom.

To make matters worse, in southern Frocomon, a clan of orcs known as the Severed Head clan, as well as scattered clans of goblins, roamed the mountains and called them home. With the people looking to migrate closer to the coasts, many increased their proximity to these creatures, and lives were lost to raids and battles. Fishing vessels would return to find their harbors destroyed, homes looted, and families slain.

Those who lived close to these clans and tribes soon moved once more, overpopulating the coastal towns farthest away from the Carrion Mountains. Hardship and poverty followed them wherever they went.

In the small coastal town of Arkham, these hardships plagued the people who wished to do nothing more than feed their families and enjoy their lives. From the town, one could see the Carrion Mountains in the distance, with the Green Mountains much closer. Many feared the orcs and goblins would use this closer mountain range to attack them unawares. Closer to Arkham, fields of tall grasses surrounded the town, and hills directly blocked the town itself from the sea. The population was overcrowded and disease often spread quickly.

Kyria, a young girl with long blonde hair, knew none of this and acted as if she lived in a world full of riches. She ran through the fields giggling; her only concerns focused around having a joyous time. Though young, she had a spirit about her, an indomitable will, and a determination to be more than what people expected of her. Even at the age of twelve, many admired her as an attractive child, and several frequently said that with time, when she developed further, she would be a real heartbreaker. Endowed with natural beauty, as well as her spirit and ideals, she was a unique child who cherished each moment and saw joy and love in most situations.

At the edges of the tall grass she stopped and stared at the mountains in the distance. For the first time, she stopped laughing and gazed intently, as if she could feel the presence of evil. Acting as if she did not wish to risk being seen, she slowly back stepped into the tall grasses, and when safely inside, she turned and ran back to the town once more.

Reaching the town, Kyria noticed her best friend Nezbith jogging toward the path leading to the docks. Though they shared the same age, Nezbith was considerably smaller, at least a foot shorter than Kyria. He also did not share her playfulness but often tried to act serious, as if he were an adult already. His fiery red hair matched the young girl's demeanor far more than it did his.

Playfully deciding to sneak up on Nezbith, Kyria sprinted to the hills to watch him below. From her perch, she saw Nezbith approaching his father and several other fishermen from the town returning from the seas. Kyria shuddered, knowing how badly Nezbith feared him. He only wished to make his father happy, but far more often seemed to incur his wrath.

She was unable to hear what Nezbith and his father Guldan were saying, but could hear the other crew members laughing. Then without warning, Guldan backhanded his son across the face and sent Nezbith sprawling along the ground. Guldan, too, laughed, then they left the crying boy lying in the dust on the road.

When the fishermen were out of sight, Kyria ran down the hill quickly to see if Nezbith was all right. She could hear his crying as she approached, and her heart sank. "Nezbith? Are you okay?"

The small boy looked at her, then turned away quickly. Blood was flowing from his nose and right cheek. "Go away!"

"No, Nezbith, you need that tended to." She sat down next to him and reached slowly for his face.

"I said leave!" he screamed as he slapped her hand away.

"Okay, but you still need that tended to." Standing up, she looked down at him and was uncertain what exactly to do if he refused her help.

"Just leave," he mumbled. "I should have known better than to leave the town. Should have known better."

Tears slowly ran from Kyria's eyes as well as she watched her friend in such turmoil. "Let's go, Nezbith, we need to have that looked at." She reached her hand out and held it there. This time, he did not slap it away, but took it in his and slowly stood up.

The two friends returned to the town of Arkham without saying another word. This was not the first time that Nezbith had been hit by his father, and most likely would not be the last. Guldan always seemed so angry that he could find hardly any fish. After giving in to his anger, he and his friends would get drunk and start talking of the days when they were feared and had a powerful armada. Nezbith would often hide during these bouts, but even then his father would find him and take out some of his aggression on the child.

The assaults were traumatic, and Nezbith seemed to grow up very quickly as a result. When together, Kyria often tried to be playful and help him find an avenue of escape, but he never could snap out of his internal despair.

When they returned to the town, Kyria led Nezbith to the side of one of the buildings. "Sit down so I can look at that." This time Nezbith did as he was told without objection.

Tearing part of the hem of her dress, Kyria gently dabbed at her friends face. His cheek was already swelling and grew into a bubble. After tending to his injuries for several minutes, constantly speaking in soft gentle tones, she studied his cheek and nose and saw that the bulk of the bleeding had stopped. "Hold this on your cheek."

He looked into her light blue eyes with gratitude. Tears flowed down both children's cheeks once more.

"It's okay, Nezbith. You're going to be fine. We'll get you home and you're going to be fine."

"Will you walk me there?" His words seemed little more than a whimper.

"Of course, silly boy. I'll tuck you into bed and all!" Grinning wildly, she attempted to lighten the mood and his spirits a little.

"That would be most improper," he retorted.

"Improper? Humph. It would be improper of me not to make sure that you got home safe and sound."

"We should hurry before my father returns from the pub." A look of sheer panic crept over his face with the thought.

"Don't worry. I'll have you home before you know it!" She reached her hand out and helped him up again. "Let's go."

The two quickly headed to Nezbith's cottage. His family did not live too far into the town, which made things easier since he seemed to be wincing with each step.

As they arrived by the door, Kyria held up her hand. "Let me look first." She then crept to the living room window and peered inside.

All was quiet. Nezbith's father and three older brothers must all be at the pub drinking. He never knew his mother, for she had not survived his birth, another reason that Guldan seemed to take out his aggression on his youngest son.

"It's all clear. Let's go."

Nezbith released a sigh of relief. He had been holding his breath since she first went to the window. "Okay, but we should still hurry."

They opened the front door and went straight to Nezbith's room. Kyria pulled the covers of his bed down a little so that he could get in easily. "See, I told you I would tuck you in."

Nezbith saw her smile and returned one for the first time that night. "Thank you, Kyria." He then got into bed, and she pulled the covers back up and tucked him in.

"Good night, Nezbith. I'll check on you in the morning."

"Thanks," he mumbled, then closed his eyes to allow slumber to remove his pain.

Kyria started to leave, but heard Guldan returning, swearing drunkenly. She quickly dove under the kitchen table and stared at the door.

The door burst open as Guldan almost fell inside his cottage. "Damned door!" He punched it, then slammed it closed as hard as he could. Stumbling inside, he stopped at the table.

Kyria's eyes widened. What would happen if he found her? She thought he could certainly hear her breathing. He had to know that she was there. Standing right in front of her. The tension was growing, and she feared she would join Nezbith with scars from this vile man.

With a belch, he stumbled away again and picked up his axe, which hung on the mantle above the fireplace. It was a double-bladed battle-axe that had been in his family since the Race Wars. An elder of his family line had fought and bested a dwarf, and claimed the fallen weapon of his foe as his own. The battle-axe served him well, killing many foes, and leading to the name Carnage, which he hoped would instill fear in his enemies.

He twirled the ancient weapon and laughed sinisterly. "Well, Carnage, perhaps we can wreak some carnage again!"

Afraid to move, Kyria listened, almost passing out from shock when another voice, one that sent chills through her body, spoke with a dark air of evil. The voice did not come from another person—for she knew that it held no physical substance in the room—but sounded as if it was coming from the shadows themselves.

"Guldan, your blade shall perform its namesake once more."

Guldan laughed again and roared into the air. "They shall pay for taking our land! They shall all pay!"

"That is right, Guldan. Only you can make them pay. Those pompous fools in Danchul. Growing fat and lazy off of your people's struggles. They betrayed your ancestors, and now deserve to be betrayed!"

Not able to comprehend what was happening, Kyria listened with a great sense of foreboding and fear, yet also a slight exhilaration since she was doing something she clearly should not.

"You are right, Zoldex! We must reclaim our land! Let the blood of those who would deny us what is rightfully ours flow! All that face Guldan shall tremble with fear!"

"Yes, Guldan. First you shall reclaim your land. Then you shall reclaim your birthright. Frocomon will indeed become powerful once more."

Guldan erupted in laughter. "Then I personally will deal with that bitch who calls herself Empress! I, Guldan, will rule!"

"Yes, Guldan, first reclaim your land, then all things you desire will come your way."

As she listened, Kyria instinctively knew this voice; this Zoldex, as Guldan called him, could not be trusted. He seemed to be telling Guldan what he wanted to hear. To instigate him and leave him clinging to false promises. Manipulation.

"Yes. Come my way. Oh yes."

As Guldan started laughing again, Kyria felt she had to leave. She watched him as he stumbled toward the mantelpiece. Slowly she crawled toward the door. As she reached it, she looked over and saw that Guldan still had his head turned away from her. She took the chance and slowly turned the knob on the door.

The knob made no sound. Kyria kept watching the intoxicated Guldan, wondering whether he or this strange voice of Zoldex would notice her first. With the knob fully turned, she began to slowly open the door, but it creaked. She froze and saw Guldan was turning toward her.

Kyria pulled the door open and slammed it quickly again as she ran from the cottage. She heard a loud cracking sound when she first closed the door, and turned to see that Carnage had been hurtled toward the door, one of its heads jutting through the wooden obstacle where she had just stood.

Not looking back, she fled quickly into the night hoping that Guldan would not know it was her, and even more so, that he would not take out his frustrations on Nezbith. Thinking of her friend again, tears flowed once more. Not for her own ordeals, but for the pain and suffering he was certain to be in for.

CHAPTER 19

The return to Trespias was an arduous one and very draining for Lord Braksis. He desperately wished to understand more about what was going on with Zoldex, the Shadow Mages, and the forces that were attacking on all fronts. Time was of the essence and he felt a great uneasiness.

His next task would not be an easy one. He must confront the Empress and her ministers to convince them of the peril at hand. He knew that the Empress would be open to seeing his arguments, and with the help of Admiral Morex, they would be able to address the impending dark times in the manner that they should be dealt with. The ministers, however, held their own agendas, and would not wish to decrease their own perceived value by opening dialogue with the races once more.

A rider approached from the walls of Trespias. He was a messenger sent ahead by Braksis to inform the Empress they were successful, but that upon his return more pressing matters must be brought to her attention.

The rider rode up to the front of the lines where Braksis, Solara, Hinbar, and Lowred were lined up together, leading the army who either marched in formation or were upon horseback behind them. "Lord Braksis, welcome back to Trespias, sir."

"Yes. Did you deliver my message to the Empress?"

"Alas, I was unable to, sir. She has been deep in conference with the ministers, and I was unable to see her."

"I see." Looking to General Hinbar, Braksis issued his orders. "General, take the men and return to the barracks. They deserve food and rest. Solara and I shall go to the palace personally."

"As you command, sir." Hinbar nodded in assent.

"Begging your pardon, sir, but that would not be the best idea," the rider said.

"And why exactly is that?"

"Well, sir, I was unable to see the Empress, but word has spread to the people. They are aligned around the streets to celebrate your approach."

"I see." He paused. "These matters cannot be delayed, although I must go through the streets to reach the bridge to the palace. It will be good for the men to receive a royal homecoming. Fall in line, soldier, and let us be on our way."

"Yes, sir." The rider smiled, then rode back to join his colleagues.

The troops were quickly upon the gates to the city, which remained open to them. The walls encompassed all of Trespias, and in themselves, were impressive by their size and scope. When the Imperial City was initially designed, Conrad was opposed to the walls. He felt that for the Seven Kingdoms to become one, the great city must be open to all. His advisors strongly opposed that plan, and ultimately a compromise was reached. The wall would be built, but the gates would remain open for all time unless war sullied the lands once more.

Architects from all around the Seven Kingdoms journeyed to the site that would become Trespias, and construction began. Rumors over the years hinted that dwarves also assisted in the construction due to the sheer magnificence and beauty of the city and walls, but those rumors were never substantiated.

The wall itself was composed of stone and brick that towered twenty feet into the sky. Guard towers were built every twenty feet and stood thirty feet high. The wall was also designed to be wide and sturdy. Ten men could stand side by side with the two men on each end barely touching both sides of the wall. This design was made to protect the city and those within from potential invasion, with the thickness also being a deterrent to toppling or smashing through the walls. With the guard towers constantly manned, early warnings of an attack would be sounded. Many soldiers could then stand atop the walls and defend with arrows, heavy stones, and cauldrons of searing oil.

As they marched through the gates, the guards on the two towers waved and whistled in cheer. Braksis kept his men in line and continued marching his troops into the city. He could see that something as simple as a cheer had quickly sparked life back into his men. This day would be good for them, especially if they would soon be going to war with unknown masses of evil.

The city lay before them in rows of finely sculpted buildings. Some were larger than others, but the smallest of buildings rose four to six stories high. Each structure was an off-white color with elaborate pillars designed at the base. Windows in the shape of arches encompassed all levels above the ground floor. The tops of the structures were highly detailed domes that were golden, with shimmering jewels along the foundations.

The main streets of the city had well-tended gardens that were lush and colorful. Hybrid flowers were designed by botanists to make the gardens of Trespias more beautiful than any other in the realm. Hundreds of botanists tended the gardens to ensure that the beauty would never fade away, grow old, or perish.

Separating various portions of the city was a groined vault, which like the domes, was golden and jeweled. This multi-arched structure led travelers either into the main streets leading to the palace, down a path toward the Mage's Council, toward the Colosseum, or back toward the gates of the city.

Heading straight through the groined vault, Braksis led his men down the main roads toward the palace. As they came through the giant arch, the sides of the street had double rows of city guards, known as Guardsmen. With fewer threats of outright hand-to-hand hostilities than the army faced, the Guardsmen wore much simpler attire, fashioned more on function and style than combat readiness, yet they were well-trained and capable defenders. They wore turquoise shirts with loose-fitting shorts of the same color. Atop their shirts was a golden breastplate etched with the design of a hawk. Their helmets were also golden, with strands of turquoise fabric feathered back. On their wrists were golden bracers, and on their feet sandals that laced up just under the knees.

Each Guardsman held a rectangular shield with a turquoise background and a golden hawk with its wings spread in the middle. The other hand held a spear, and a short sword was sheathed on a belt across the waist. For every ten Guardsmen, an officer stood in front of his unit. The officers were similarly garbed, though they lacked the spear and shield, and also had a turquoise cape loosely clipped below the neck and hanging over the shoulders and down the back.

Behind the Guardsmen were rows upon rows of the citizens of Trespias who had flooded out to see the returning army and cheer for their victory, waving streamers. Flower petals had been distributed and were tossed into the air, raining down on the troops. People reached out of windows of buildings along the road yelling and offering their support to the returning soldiers. Musicians played joyful melodies as the soldiers marched through the crowds. A celebration like this had not been seen for many years in the Imperium. Many rejoiced when the Imperium was first established, but then life continued. Without threats and the burdens of war, the ideals of peace, prosperity, and freedom seemed to become minute details. Yet when one's way of life is threatened, all that you have suddenly seems so much more important, and you begin to cling to and cherish the little things more freely. This celebration reminded the people of what they could lose if the uprisings were successful, and they were determined to show their appreciation, admiration, and respect to those who fought in their names.

Marching through the city took the army a good half hour before they reached the bridge to the palace. Braksis nodded to Hinbar and continued ahead, whereas Hinbar led the troops off toward the barracks and army encampment, located at the southern borders of Trespias.

Before the entrance to the palace, a row of large statues had been erected in full detail of Emperor Conrad, Admiral Morex, King Sarlec, Mage Master Jeffa, and several other heroes who helped bring about the formation of the Imperium. These figures stood proud and seemed to demand admiration from all that would behold them.

The entrance to the palace was a large circular building known as the Chamber. This structure was where most diplomatic activity within Trespias transpired. It held a variety of rooms and halls in which to meet. When walking into this building, the duties of the Guardsmen ended, and those of the palace guards began.

The palace guards, known as the Imperial Guards, were hand-selected by the Captain of the Guards, currently Centain, and Adonis before him. They were chosen for their unswerving loyalty, dedication to the Imperium, the royal family, and willingness to selflessly sacrifice themselves in order to protect those within the palaces walls.

The guards were garbed in an emerald green color. The color was selected after Karleena's birth, when Conrad looked into her emerald eyes for the first time and wished to forevermore cherish the memory by surrounding himself with reminders. These guards wore full body armor, hidden by emerald cloaks. Long, loose sleeves covered their arms, and emerald gloves their hands. Helmets completely encased their heads and rested upon their cloaked shoulders. A small cross of shaded glass was located from the eyes down to their mouths so that visitors would be unable to see what the guards were looking at.

For those who did not belong in the palace, these armored guards often instilled fear and paranoia, with their identities concealed. Many visitors felt they were constantly being watched, which was one of the purposes for the design.

The only visible weapon the palace guards held were halberds. Though these were displayed for all to see, weapons of other varieties were easily hidden within their cloaks.

Braksis and Solara, with Tiot by their side, walked straight through the Chamber. Very little activity was transpiring, for most of the people who normally would fill these halls were in the courtyard or street cheering for the returning militia.

At the end of the Chamber, two Imperial Guards stood at attention guarding the opening to a bridge that led into the actual palace. Braksis nodded at the guards, who stood aside and allowed them to pass.

The bridge itself was retractable so that if invaders entered the Chamber, the guards could raise the bridge and prevent access to the palace. It extended close to thirty feet long and ten feet wide. The palace was built on a small island close to Trespias, so below the bridge was a large ravine with a deadly drop onto rocky shores.

On the other side of the bridge, two more guards stood at attention to block entry into the palace. They, too, moved aside for the well-known Warlord.

Inside the palace, every step one took was full of ornamentation, detail, and beauty. The floor was paved in gold with ornate designs. The walls held murals and images that transcended beauty. The ceiling was covered with lush vegetation known as Harlocten plants. These plants had no end as they covered every inch of the ceiling with leaves, vines, and shimmering flowers that changed colors throughout the spectrum to match the moods of those closest.

Braksis led Solara toward the audience chamber where he anticipated he would find Karleena. As they walked through the halls, they passed many pairs of palace guards manning their posts. When arriving at the audience chamber, Braksis saw Centain, the Captain of the Guards, along with several of his men.

Centain was a proud and dedicated man. Braksis had always known him to push himself to his limits, then to train even harder to enhance those boundaries. Whenever not on duty, he spent many hours honing his skills with all forms of weaponry, as well as placing himself through a rigorous athletic program. Braksis had never known another man to be so determined and driven as Centain.

Centain also took great pride in his appearance. He had a perfectly groomed black beard and mustache, with hair pulled back into a ponytail. Unlike his guards, he did not wear armor covered by a cloak, though he did wear the same colors. His shirt had double-breasted buttons and a collar fastened halfway up his neck. The sleeves tucked into shadowy black gloves. His pants shared the same tint as his shirt, and tucked into shiny knee-high black boots.

At his waist, a black belt separated his shirt from his pants, and held his sword, the Nocplest, an elvish blade forged generations ago by an uncommon ancestor in a time when the species were at war. The hilt was jeweled with words carved in the elvish tongue. All in Centain's family knew the words of their ancestor and could read the ancient text. It said, "When hopes and dreams overcome nightmares, and two become one, all injustices can be vanquished. In love, the circle will be closed."

Braksis noticed that Centain had his eyes closed and was lightly stroking his chest. Before he could say a word, Centain spoke first. "Welcome back, Lord Braksis." He then opened his eyes for the first time and looked at the newcomers.

"Centain," Braksis said with a nod.

Solara smiled politely in greeting.

"Can we see the Empress? It is very important," Braksis requested.

"Yes, but perhaps it is best to wait a few minutes before announcing yourselves. She is in heavy discussions right now," Centain replied.

"With whom? I may wish to speak to them as well."

"Prime Minister Torscen and his cabinet of ministers. Fortunately for the Empress, Admiral Morex and King Sarlec are also with her."

"That bad, huh?"

"That bad. Come, we'll enter quietly."

Braksis wondered to himself how Centain always seemed to know exactly what was transpiring and being said within these walls. As they silently entered the audience chamber, as usual, Centain was right.

The Empress was looking out a window listening to her ministers. From her expression, Braksis could see she was troubled. The tension in the room itself was rather thick.

The audience chamber was a vast domed hall with windows encircling the perimeter. Harlocten plants filled the foundations with their shimmering flowers. Scattered every few feet, Imperial Guards observed the meeting and watched for any signs of threat against Karleena. At the far end of the chamber, a throne was prominent. Sitting next to the throne were two white tigers, pets of the Empress.

Prime Minister Torscen was walking around the chamber as he spoke. His words filled the room with bureaucratic double-talk and innuendo. He even at times was bold enough to insult the Empress, daring much with the heroes that stood by her side.

Karleena turned around. As she did so, her expression changed dramatically, and all concern and troubles vanished. Though only seventeen, she was well poised and held an air of authority. Her long brown hair was currently braided and wrapped ornamentally in a sparkling, jeweled, lavender headpiece. Her gown was ruffled at the shoulders, leaving them bare. It puffed out at her hips like a bell and streamed to the ground. The color was light lavender, ornamented with streamers and ribbons of darker purple. Around her neck she wore a finely detailed necklace with a large emerald stone that matched the tinge of her eyes. The necklace was a gift from the parents she cherished.

"I am listening to your arguments, Torscen, but I must question the authenticity of your words." Her reply was calm and steady.

"Authenticity? You would doubt your own Prime Minister?" Torscen snapped back.

"I do not doubt your sincerity. I only question your advice. You state that the people are happy, yet they revolt. This is a contradiction, Minister Torscen."

"This is getting us nowhere. If your father were here, these revolts would never have happened. It's because you are but a child and know nothing of the ways of grown men."

King Sarlec stepped forward and confronted Torscen. "If Conrad were here, he would strike you dead where you stand for speaking to his daughter as you just have."

Sarlec was one of the strongest supporters of the Imperium since its inception. He had been a young king during the Great Wars, controlling the most powerful army in all of the Seven Kingdoms. When he first met Conrad, he knew the man had vision and a plan, and he immediately agreed to support the efforts to unite the realm. Since then, he had always put the needs and wishes of the Empire first, proving time and again his devotion and dedication.

Though time was catching up with him, Sarlec still portrayed strength and vitality. Where once he had flowing golden hair, Sarlec was now balding with a handful of gray strands remaining, although he still had a full gray beard that hung to his chest. Without the wars that plagued the land during his childhood, he had grown in bulk as he aged.

His gaze seemed to burn through the Prime Minister. Imposing and intimidating, Torscen took a step back as Sarlec challenged him. To question the Imperium in Sarlec's presence would often lead to an argument and a fight. The thought of an Imperium official being the one to disrespect all that he believed in was too much to bear.

"I meant no disrespect," Torscen said in an attempt to appease King Sarlec.

"I'm sure you did not, Prime Minister Torscen," Admiral Morex calmly stated as he placed a hand on Sarlec's shoulder. "Let us continue our discussion without resorting to insults or violence."

Like Sarlec, Morex showed signs of aging. His hair had turned gray long ago and wrinkles were beginning to appear around his eyes. His entire body was thin but not frail. Unlike Sarlec, Morex was a tactical genius without equal, and very rarely revealed any signs of emotion. He would never confront an opponent with brute force, but would contemplate strategy and analyze the situation in mere moments with a plan that often proved to be infallible. More so than any other, Karleena found his counsel to be invaluable.

Admiral Morex would never be found without his Imperial uniform. He considered himself always on duty, and therefore dressed the part. The uniform was dark gray and composed of pants, shirt, and jacket. The jacket was fastened together, and had five small metallic bars upon his shoulders to represent his rank. His hands and feet were covered with black gloves and boots. In his right hand he held a small rod, which he often would tap in his left hand as he was thinking.

"Thank you, Admiral," Karleena stated as she reentered the conversation. "Minister Torscen, I do not wish to reject your advice or ignore it. However, I feel it is time to hear what the people truly say. Not what the wealthy families are telling you, but the commoners themselves. I intend to make some changes, Minister, then I will hear what both the wealthy and common man have to say. Only then will I feel that I am running the Seven Kingdoms appropriately."

"This is madness. Letting the people have a say? What you are thinking will destroy everything your father has built!" Fury fueled his words.

Sarlec took a step closer again to intervene, but Karleena waved him off. "Prime Minister, if you and your cabinet will excuse me, I see that Lord Braksis has returned. I wish to hear news of the recent uprising. We shall continue this discussion another time."

Torscen narrowed his eyes as he glared at the Empress. "I can see that this barbarian is worth more than your loyal advisors. We shall leave, but know this, we shall also fight you on this idea of yours." With those closing remarks, he turned and walked out with his cabinet of ministers close behind him.

"And good riddance!" Sarlec boomed.

"Calm down, my old friend. Torscen carries much weight with the wealthy families," Morex advised.

"The hell with the wealthy families. If their Empress, kings, and queens so decree, then they are honor-bound to oblige." Sarlec looked up at Braksis. "What news have you, lord?"

"Wait," Karleena said. "I wish to leave this hall. We shall talk in my father's old office." It was not far. Conrad had placed his office close to the audience chamber so he could work up until the time he had to appear.

Inside the office, Karleena walked straight to a display case resting on the wall. Inside the case was her father's sword, the Ochroid. The hilt was gold with emeralds at each end. The center of the blade was shaped like a golden dagger that stretched almost the entire distance of the sword. This blade was wielded by her father during the Great Wars, and modified slightly after her birth at his request. She often would look at it for inspiration and memory of her departed father.

"Gentlemen, I wish to see times change. All of you have existed in a world of violence. I wish to rule a world that lacks it, so we can all live in harmony. Why do the ministers oppose me so?"

"My lady, though the Great Wars were long ago, and indeed we fought valiantly in them to bring forth this nation we find ourselves in now, there are still many who are distrustful and hold on to old grudges." Admiral Morex watched the Empress for signs. He admired her determination, and hoped she would stand by her beliefs.

"We must somehow overcome these old grudges. Only by allowing me to truly hear what the people are saying and thinking, do I feel this can be accomplished."

"My Empress," Braksis spoke slowly. "Your goals are just, but I fear we must be so bold as to take them even further than you currently envision."

Karleena turned around to face those she had known since her youth. These men had helped her father, and over the years, had taught her so much. Their comments and opinions meant more to her than any number of ministers. "Explain."

"Though we were victorious on the field of battle, it has come to my attention that far more is going on than we ever dreamed possible." Braksis paused to look at the people in the room. He knew that he must present his arguments in an organized fashion. He must lead them to his recommended course of action, not request it outright.

"I have learned that the uprising was manipulated by someone known as Zoldex. Some who fought even referred to him as a god."

"A god? Bah! There is no such thing. Superstition by those who wish not to take responsibility for their own actions." Sarlec shook his head in disbelief that people still clung to what he considered false ideals.

"I am not claiming that this Zoldex is a god, only that others feel he is," Braksis clarified.

Admiral Morex said nothing, but watched Braksis intently, absorbing his words and analyzing the possibilities.

"On the field of battle, I also fought a Shadow Mage."

Karleena looked puzzled. "A Shadow Mage?"

"By appearance, he was a Mage. He wore the robes and colors of the Mage's Council, yet that was just an illusion. It was really some kind of creature of darkness, but with all the powers of a Mage. Many of my men perished fighting him. Only my own weapon, the Phoenix, forged by a Mage Master, had any effect at all."

"You killed this creature?" Karleena asked.

"Yes, my Empress. Though the battle was a hard one."

"Shadow Mages and gods. I say we march down to the Mage's Council and demand some answers!" Sarlec offered.

"There is more," Braksis declared.

"Continue, lord," Admiral Morex said calmly.

"During our travels, I have come across a few new friends. Friends who have warned me of grave days ahead."

"What are these warnings?" Karleena spoke softly.

"Orcs, goblins, and hobgoblins are being organized."

"Organized?" Surprise was clear in Morex's voice, not a typical reaction.

"Yes, Admiral. Organized. They have begun their raids and attacks in the south."

"The south? My beloved Danchul? If this were so, I would know of it. No human has been attacked in the south! Your newfound friends lie!" Sarlec barked.

"You assume, King Sarlec, that I speak of human friends. I do not." Braksis watched Sarlec as he sat down. "The Halls of Vorstad are being overrun. Xylona is also being barraged."

"You speak of dwarves and elves. We have not concerned ourselves with their affairs in hundreds of years. Not since the Race Wars. If they go to war, what affair is it of ours?" Sarlec asked.

"A name. A name connects us together." Braksis regarded the room again. Morex was unreadable as usual. Karleena seemed troubled. Sarlec struggled to see the relevance to the Imperium. Centain and Solara were both simply listening intently.

Admiral Morex broke the silence. "Zoldex."

"Yes, Admiral. Zoldex. Whoever he is, he is causing unrest not only with the humans; he is also organizing some of our ancient foes. For what purpose, I know not."

"What are you suggesting, lord?" Karleena said softly.

"He is suggesting that we unite the races to face a common foe," Morex interrupted. "Am I correct?"

"Yes, Admiral."

"I'm still not convinced." Sarlec stood up again. "Why risk human lives for dwarves and elves?"

"What happens to Danchul if Vorstad and Xylona fall? Where would the conquerors turn next, King Sarlec? To Danchul perhaps?" Braksis needled.

"They will find us ready."

Admiral Morex walked over to King Sarlec. "Unless I am reading him wrong, I think that Lord Braksis has already taken steps to prove your statement right, my friend."

"Steps?" Karleena asked.

"Yes, Admiral Morex is correct. I have sent troops to both Vorstad and Xylona," Braksis admitted.

"Without my approval?" inquired Karleena.

"My Empress, this is the earliest I could have arrived to bring this matter to your attention. We could still withdraw our forces, although I plead with you not to. Vorstad and Xylona are full of strong and noble races. If they fall, it would be a great loss to us, especially if this Zoldex is really scheming something darker for all of our futures."

"A wise decision, Lord Braksis. I would have taken the same measures myself," indicated Morex. "My lady, if my counsel means anything, I feel Braksis is right in his recommendation."

"The ministers opposed granting the people a voice in an open forum to me. They clearly would balk at uniting the races." Karleena returned her gaze to the Ochroid.

"There are times when a leader must make a decision that may be unpopular, but is right," Morex advised.

"Yes, you are right. I will not order you to recall your forces. Though I desire much more information. Who is this Zoldex? What is his plan? Are there more of these Shadow Mages?"

"My Empress, I thank you for seeing why I have acted as I have. There is one more thing."

"You have my undivided attention, Braksis. Might as well continue." Karleena turned to look at him again.

"The dwarves I met had heard rumors of an orc city in Tenalong, known as the Murky Death clan. They claimed that an expedition of elves and dwarves went into Tenalong to ascertain the validity of this city. Many perished. The few survivors estimated that one hundred thousand orcs lived there."

"One hundred thousand?" Sarlec said softly.

"One hundred thousand. This Zoldex could be building an invasion force. Just waiting for the elves and dwarves to fall before this vast army advances," Braksis theorized.

"How do our forces compare?" Karleena seemed to plead for good news.

"We currently would not stand a chance. I have already ordered recruitment and training to increase, and have authorized a new light-foot regiment that will accept female volunteers."

"You still will not have enough if these reports are true," Morex stated. "We must validate the information ourselves. If they are true, then unifying the races may be our only hope."

"I spoke with General Sevlow, who told me that when he was growing up in Tenalong, there were rumors of a vast orc clan beyond the swamps. I can send scouts into Tenalong to validate both stories," Braksis offered.

"No," Karleena returned. "If I am truly going to attempt to unite the races, I will need support from all the royal families. I will not send troops into Tenalong without King Garum first being given the opportunity to investigate."

"Bah! Garum is a puppet of the Hidden Empire. Lady Salaman pulls his strings," Sarlec sneered.

"That may be so. Regardless, he is a king. Send Geist, my personal messenger. If Garum does nothing, then I shall leave the matter up to you, Braksis."

"Thank you." Braksis glanced around the room again. "One last thing that may be of import..."

"Oh, don't hold back on me now, Warlord," Karleena snickered in disbelief.

"I also came across an elf from beyond the Forbidden Regions. She claims to know of Zoldex and alludes to him as being quite evil and sinister. A man not to be trusted, but at least a man."

"I told you he was no god!" Sarlec beamed.

"Yes. She also said that she was on a sacred mission. Looking for the Chosen One. The one who has been prophesied to save us all."

"Prophecy now? More nonsense," Sarlec grumbled.

"Perhaps. But this elf saved both Solara's life and mine. She was honorable, just, and valiant. If what she says is true, then the child she seeks should also receive Imperial protection if we can."

"You speak of conspiracies, plots, plans, and a child will be our savior," Sarlec barked. "Bah! We shall have to defend the Imperium like never before! The Great Wars may be upon us once more."

"I truly hope you are wrong, King Sarlec. I truly do," Karleena whispered.

Two quick knocks preceded the opening of a back door. An older woman, Sharnesta, peered inside. "Time to get ready, my lady." Sharnesta had been personally responsible for Karleena since birth. In fact, she had been a young servant who first began taking care of Karleena's mother. As the one who raised two generations, she took great pride in all that Karleena did, and wished to see her always prosper.

"Thank you, Sharnesta. I shall be with you shortly," Karleena responded. "Lord Braksis, tonight is the Lumnia championships. I trust that you will be able to attend?"

"Do you feel that wise, Empress?" Braksis inquired.

"Yes. I do not wish to create panic. The Imperium shall see us continue, in spite of what was discussed today. We shall contemplate how to proceed more after the game."

"Ha, ha! Yes! When Danchul reigns victorious over Dartie!" Sarlec beamed.

"That is a possibility, Sarlec, though I myself hope Dartie claims victory tonight," Karleena said.

"What? May I ask why?" Sarlec screamed incredulously.

"I wish for Dartie to see that even with the revolts in their land, life goes on, and the Imperium will not make matters worse for them. We must bring them back into the fold. If that means their winning and having a sense of pride, then I am in complete favor."

"Well, Empress, I would do anything for the Imperium, but I will not vote against my boys!" Sarlec declared.

"I shall see you all at the Colosseum this evening." Without further ado, Karleena exited the room to prepare for the game.

The remaining occupants had several parting words then went about their own business. Braksis felt the meeting had gone well. Sending military aid was approved, and that was but the first step. The aid would make it easier to meet with the elves and dwarves, and begin forging bonds for an alliance in the days certain to come. Things definitely were progressing quite nicely.

CHAPTER 20

Leaving the palace, Braksis led Solara and Tiot toward the barracks. He hoped to have a little personal time to unwind and get cleaned up before the championship game that night. All the thoughts that had been plaguing his mind flowed out of him with relief that the Empress had been so receptive. He finally allowed his weariness to become outwardly apparent.

Unseen by Braksis and his party, a young woman had observed them leave the palace and had been following them surreptitiously ever since. If the group could have seen her eyes, they would easily have been able to ascertain the cunning and trickery in her intentions.

"You look exhausted," Solara commented.

"I feel exhausted," Braksis quickly retorted. "A few hours' sleep before getting up for the game will do me well." Looking deviously at Solara, he added a taunt of his own. "I've seen better looking barn animals than you. Smelled better, too. I'd seriously consider some beauty sleep and a bath."

"Ha, ha. Very funny." In her peripheral vision, Solara spotted the woman with her hands gently removing Braksis's money pouch. She bent over to look at the girl. "Excuse me. Do you know who you are trying to steal from?"

Braksis stopped and spun around to see the girl. He shook off his fatigue and was instantly prepared for action. Tiot also turned, but surprisingly did not growl or show any sign that this girl was a threat.

The woman appeared to be in her early twenties. She had long dark brown hair that was knotted and hung in strands. Her brown eyes stared at Solara as if defying her discovery of the attempted theft. Her face was slightly dirty and hardened as if she had been through harsh ordeals. Her dark shirt was tight fitting and revealing, cut just above her waist. A black tattoo with thorns jutting out of slashes encircled her left arm. Her pants were a dark murky gray and also were tight fitting and revealing. The girl clearly was well endowed and physically fit.

As he looked at her, he could see the defiance and anger. Yet he sensed something else. Something beneath her dirty exterior. Tiot's lack of concern also befuddled him. That typically meant that the girl was not a threat, yet she tried to steal from him. Perhaps she was simply hungry and forced into this lot in life.

The girl suddenly smiled at the two. "Steal? You think I was trying to steal?"

Solara cracked a smile in disbelief. "I caught you red-handed."

The girl held out her two hands to display them. "They don't look red to me. But I'll bite, who did I allegedly try to steal from?"

"This is Lord Braksis, Warlord of all the Imperium," Solara boasted.

"Let's hear a big whoop for you. Is your ego as big as your title?"

Braksis stifled a laugh.

Solara stared at him incredulously. "What's so funny? You're the one she tried to steal from."

"Actually, Braxy baby, I'm the one who did steal from you." She pulled the pouch out from behind her back and tossed it up in the air and caught it again.

Braksis reached back and was amazed to discover his currency pouch indeed had been removed. "I'll take that back now."

"As if, big boy." The girl smiled deviously, then her face changed into horror as she stumbled backward. A member of ISIA was walking past them, and the girl bumped into him. She turned and looked up at him with desperation in her eyes. "Help me, please. They are trying to attack me."

The Authority agent could sense the panic and immediately was determined to defend her. "I'll protect you, young lady." He stepped in front of her and looked up at Braksis for the first time. As soon as he saw who he was facing, confusion and doubt crept in.

"Thanks for the distraction, officer." The girl reached over and unsheathed his sword. The weight of the blade was too much for her to handle, and it clanged to the ground. "Damn, how do you wield one of these things?"

"Hey!" the guard yelled out as he spun around toward the girl.

She smiled again and pushed him with all of her might. The red-uniformed guard fell backward into Braksis and Solara. "I hate to steal and run, but I'll make an exception this time."

Turning, she started to run, but came up short as two Guardsmen looked down at her. "I do believe this girl just admitted to being a thief."

"Yes, I believe I also heard that," the second Guardsman replied.

"You better come with us, ma'am."

The girl leapt into the air and performed a spinning back kick. Her foot connected with both Guardsmen's heads, sending them toppling over. "Not this time, gentlemen. A lady is never escorted by a stranger." With the road clear, she ran off again.

One of the Guardsmen pulled out a whistle and blew it. Out of random streets and buildings, city guards poured into the street looking for the disturbance. "Thief, after her!" The guards quickly dashed in pursuit.

Solara watched the Guardsmen begin the chase. "She won't elude them all."

Braksis smiled. "I'll lay odds she will."

"You seem pleased by this."

"Hey, I think the girl has spunk. I like her."

"This from the man who was just robbed by her. I don't think I'll ever truly understand you."

"Well, Solara, I truly like to be unique. Keep you guessing."

She looked at his unreadable face and shook her head. Sometimes she could tell exactly what he was thinking, and other times she was completely at a loss.

Braksis stood up and reached down to help the Authority agent up as well. "No hard feelings, right?"

"No, sir. I mean, yes, sir," the agent stumbled with his words.

Braksis glanced at Solara. "Come on. I want to see this."

"Oh, I assure you, I do, too."

❖ ❖ ❖ ❖ ❖

The girl darted down the street and spotted several Guardsmen as they gathered to chase her. She ran, scanning her surroundings and trying to absorb every detail as she passed. Each minute detail could be important, and any one of them could be invaluable to saving her life.

Five Guardsmen ran around a corner and appeared directly in front of her. The girl's eyes grew in shock when she first spotted them, but then she smiled at them. "All of you against little old me?"

One of the Guardsmen stepped forward. "Cease your flight. We have you cornered."

The girl looked behind her and saw that the Guardsmen who were pursuing her had finally caught up. The turquoise-and-gold-garbed city defenders surrounded her. "Well, it certainly does look like you pulled out all the stops to capture me. I should be flattered. Instead, I think I'll just leave now."

The Guardsmen all chuckled at the statement, and a couple approached to apprehend her. Instead, she jumped up and grasped on to the second story of a building with her hands. Though she barely made it with the jump, she as able to pull herself up very quickly, and the Guardsmen were left behind trying to grab her feet.

"Better luck next time, boys." She ducked into an open window and vanished.

"Inside! After her!" The lead Guardsmen yelled. "She won't escape!"

The girl ran through the room and spotted a couple of people who were shocked to see her. "Excuse me. Coming through."

She found the stairs and could hear the troops rushing up to capture her. Looking up, she quickly ascended the staircase to the upper levels. The stairs led all the way to the roof. She glanced around and devised a plan.

Someone had his clothes hanging on a stretched line. She ran over and pulled the rope down and dragged it toward the door. She wrapped the rope around a small ventilation tube on one side, and tautly pulled it across the door's opening. On the other side, she wrapped it around the hook where the line was originally fastened to the wall.

She quickly ran toward the pole that held the rope in the first place and pulled it from the ground. The pole was a little taller than she was, designed that way so the clothes would not fall and get dirty, though now they were scattered all across the roof.

She stood several feet from the doorway and waited. As the first couple of Guardsmen ran up, she waived to them. "Hey, boys, catch me if you can."

The Guardsmen increased their speed and ran toward the roof. As they hit the door, both men failed to see the rope strung across the bottom of the doorway and tripped.

"Hope that didn't hurt. Too much." The girl then took a running jump, and with the pole, vaulted herself over the alleyway and onto the roof of the neighboring building. "It's been fun, boys. Not too much fun."

As more Guardsmen reached the roof, whistles were blown again and she could see a few troops running around the street. One of the men leapt across the roof and continued the pursuit.

"Humph. Show off." She sprinted across the roof and jumped cleanly onto another one.

The pursuing Guardsman continued onto the next roof as well.

The girl leapt onto another roof and quickly hid behind a few boxes stacked in the middle. As the Guardsman landed on the roof, she spun out and startled him. A punch connected with his jaw and he fell back and knocked himself out hitting his head on the ledge.

The girl walked over and checked to make sure he was still breathing and then darted off again. She saw a ladder and descended back toward the ground.

A couple of Guardsmen saw her and yelled out. She held onto the ends of the ladder and slid the rest of the way down. "Persistent, aren't you?"

A Guardsman jumped out in front of her, and she ducked down and crawled through his legs. She then used her legs to kick herself off in another sprint away, leaving an embarrassed Guardsman staring in disbelief.

She began to use this tactic with the rest of the Guardsmen. She kept dodging and dancing around them as they tried to grab her. She was fast and agile, and able to move around quickly. A crowd grew, finding immense humor in the pitiful efforts of the frustrated Guardsmen.

The entire time, the girl taunted and laughed at them. She could see they were becoming enraged and lunging without thinking. A jump here, a sidestep there. Each time she managed to get out of the way.

Growing weary of the chase, she decided to put an end to it. She saw several barrels of ale stacked up next to the city wall where the owner of the nearby pub had stored them.

The girl ran toward the barrels and began climbing them. The remaining Guardsmen went up after her. As she reached the top, she clung onto the wall and wiggled back and forth. The top drum of ale swayed and, as it fell, caused a chain reaction as many barrels toppled. Splintered wood and ale burst all over the pursuing Guardsmen and the streets below.

The pub owner ran out screaming curses at his lost product.

The girl looked down at them all and bellowed deeply. As she turned, she was shocked to see Solara standing there with both arms crossed at her shoulders, a sword in each hand. Before the girl could move, Solara slashed both blades forward and drove them into the wall, crossed snugly at the girl's throat.

"Um, hi," the girl said.

Braksis stepped forward and looked at the girl. "I'm impressed. The way you danced around trained troops. You made them look like amateurs."

"You mean fools." The girl beamed.

Solara gazed at her icily. "You are the one pinned to the wall. Who is the fool now?"

Several Guardsmen came running toward them. "We'll take it from here."

Braksis turned and looked at the guards. Their tunics were covered with red ale, dirt, grime, and sweat. "No, I don't think so. You should go get cleaned up. I'll take it from here."

"But, sir..."

"No buts. I said I would take it from here. Do you wish to challenge the words of Warlord Braksis?"

"No, sir. You can take it from here."

Braksis watched as the men turned and walked away in defeat. Glancing at the girl, he could see her smiling again. "You don't have anything to smile about. I may have a worse fate in mind for you than anything they would be authorized to do."

"I'm sure, Braxy baby."

Reaching behind her back, Braksis recovered his money pouch. "What is your name anyway?"

"Angel."

Solara snorted. "I know you're no angel."

"That's my name. Really it's Angelica, but everyone calls me Angel."

"I would like to have a conversation with you, Angelica. Would you be willing to do that?"

"I'm not under arrest?" Angel asked.

"No."

"And she'll take her swords away?" With this, Angel looked down at the two mystral drantanas pinching the skin of her neck.

"Yes," Braksis declared. "Will you come?"

"It doesn't look like I have much of a choice."

With a nod from Braksis, Solara withdrew her swords and sheathed them both in the cases strapped to her back.

"Come. We'll talk now. I'll even buy you lunch."

"Well, you should have said that in the first place, Braxy baby. I'm all over that deal."

"It's Braksis," he corrected.

"Sure thing, Brax. Whatever you say," returned Angel.

They walked down the stairs of the guard tower and returned to the pub. Braksis paid the owner several gold pieces for the damage, and with little nudging, Angel apologized for the damage. The three then sat down at a table inside for lunch. Tiot crawled under the table and waited for any scraps sent his way.

"How did you know to go up to the roof?" Angel inquired.

Braksis smiled at her. "We watched you since you left. I saw it as an obvious escape route for you. Sooner or later, I knew you would climb the drums to the top of the wall."

"In other words, you guessed."

Solara stared at the girl. "Braksis is not a warlord for nothing. He watches and learns his opponents. He has training and tactical acuity. He did not guess."

"Ooh, excuse me. He anticipated my move. Better?" Angel stared back at Solara and then smiled at her. "Like I said, he guessed."

"Ladies," Braksis slowly said under his breath. Both women quieted down.

A waitress walked over with food and drink. Watching Angel, Braksis could see she was ravenous. As soon as the waitress walked away, she quickly dug in and practically inhaled the food.

"So, Angelica, what brings you here?" Braksis inquired.

"Please, just call me Angel."

"Then I assume that you will just call me Braksis?"

Angel smiled innocently. "Would I call you anything else?"

"Mm-hm. That's what I thought."

Angel took a drink to clear her throat. "Well, I'm ashamed to say it, but I am here because of a man."

"A man?" Solara chimed in.

"Yup. One genuine athlete. Handsome, gifted in many ways if you know what I mean." She smiled deviously at Solara and winked. "Oh yes, and of course a complete prick."

Angel broke off a bone of meat from her plate and reached under the table to give it to Tiot. "Okay, I dated a Lumnia player from Falestia. Of course, we didn't make the championships, so he wanted to come and watch the final game."

"Sounds reasonable so far," Braksis commented.

"Well, yes. Once we got here, he found this floozy who was all over him. I'm sure you know the type. Bleached blonde hair, too much makeup, breasts the size of watermelons, and a waist the size of your sword's hilt."

"I'm sure you exaggerate," Solara said doubtfully.

"I don't care. I'm painting a picture of this bimbo. You have a general idea of what I'm talking about, right?"

"Yes, please continue," Braksis said.

"Well, he jumped into bed with her, and took all of my money with him. Suddenly, I'm in a strange city, I know no one, I have no money, and no way to eat or get home again."

"Where did you learn to fight like that?" Braksis asked.

"I have eight brothers. I'm the only girl. You learn how to fight." Angel grinned cockily.

"I have a proposition for you," Braksis began.

"I'm listening Braxy baby, um, I mean, Braksis."

"I am looking to begin an Imperial regiment with women. The reasoning I will not get into right now, but this is very important. I am impressed by you, and think you could help me a lot in establishing this unit."

"You want me to be a warrior? As if. Fighting a bunch of sweaty bad guys isn't my idea of a good time."

"If that is your opinion, I will provide you with funds to return home, and we'll call it quits right now. However, I assure you this is something that needs to happen. It is imperative that this unit starts up. After what I saw today, I can think of nobody better to take charge of it. I'll let you command. Ranking officer. You'll have a hand in recruiting, training, and running the unit."

"Brax, I have to admit, becoming an officer would be pretty nice. I'd be in a better position than my eight bully brothers. But you saw me with the Authority agent's sword. I couldn't even lift it."

Solara reached back and pulled out one of her swords. She rotated it around and held it out handle-first to Angel. "This is a drantana. Extremely lightweight and easy to handle, yet strong and able to exchange blows with a normal blade."

Angel took the blade and was amazed at how light it really was. "This thing can really stand up to a broad sword or bastard sword?"

"Battle-axe and more," Solara returned.

"And you can make me replicas of these?"

Solara closed her eyes in contemplation. "These blades are mystral weapons only. Though with what we have learned, I fear that I must share the technology, or the Imperium may be lost. So, yes."

"Hey, Brax, she doesn't even like me, but she makes a compelling argument. If you'll have me, I'm in."

"Excellent," Braksis smiled.

Solara grinned deviously at Braksis then looked at Angel. "First things first; I've seen better looking barn animals than you. Smelled better, too. I'd seriously consider some beauty sleep and a bath."

Braksis chortled. "Now where have I heard that before?"

Solara laughed and for the first time, genuinely smiled at Angel. This was the beginning of a beautiful friendship.

CHAPTER 21

After several hours of much needed rest and relaxation, a refreshed Braksis led Solara and Angel to the Colosseum. Tiot remained behind at the barracks rather than being subjected to a stadium full of screaming fans in the championship Lumnia game.

Angel seemed to go through a remarkable transformation herself. After bathing, she managed to comb out the locks in her hair so it flowed in waves down her shoulders and onto her back. She also modified a uniform and was clothed from neck to toe in the skintight black leather garb that the troops wore under their armor.

As they approached the Colosseum, many heads turned to look at both Solara, who wore her traditional skimpy red mystral outfit, and Angel with her modified uniform. Braksis could tell that Angel enjoyed the attention. The occasional whistle and cheer he knew must be inspiring and ego boosting especially after having been tossed aside for another woman. How someone could do so was something he could not understand. She was spirited, lively, personable, had a great sense of humor, and though he struggled not to admit it, she was quite pleasant to look at.

"Did you have to make it skintight?" he asked casually.

"Hey, Brax, I could only do so much with what you gave me. It was either this or walk around half naked."

"I'm glad you chose this," he conceded.

"Hey, does that mean you disapprove of the way I dress?" Solara jokingly asked.

"I can't win, can I?"

"Braxy baby, you don't even know the half of it." Angel laughed.

"You had trouble dealing with me alone. You're sunk if you expect to match wits with two of us," Solara said in a challenging tone.

Wincing, Braksis took a few steps back. "I know when to quit. I'll just follow you two lovely ladies from a discreet distance."

Angel looked at Solara with a devilish grin. "The man knows his place in the world. Have to give him credit."

Both women laughed as they entered the concourse of the Colosseum. Braksis walked in about ten feet behind them.

Angel smiled as she walked out and saw the field. "I never can get over how breathtaking this is."

The Colosseum was a large stadium with tiered seats raising thirty rows high. The seats completely encompassed the Lumnia field down below. A little over one hundred thousand people could fit within the stadium comfortably, and during the championship games, even more than that attended with the hope of seeing as much of the contest as they could by standing in the back.

Solara shook her head. "I never can understand what the attraction to this game is."

"Stick with me, Sister Sol, and I'll teach you more than you want to know."

"Sister Sol?" questioned Solara. "Where do you come up with these names?"

"Oh, come on, you need to get into the spirit. Live a little. Have fun. Be a kid again." With a giggle, she started down the aisleway to find a seat.

From behind, a masculine voice yelled out. "Is that Angelica?"

Angel stopped short. Cold shivers shuddered throughout her spine. Slowly she pivoted around and came face-to-face with her ex-boyfriend. In a monotone sneer, she responded. "Hello Lantro."

Solara watched the exchange and prepared for any problems. She saw that Lantro was arm in arm with a blonde who actually fit the exaggerated description Angel had given. Extremely thin, bleach blonde hair, way too much makeup, and with breasts so large that Solara was amazed the woman could actually stand up straight.

"Whoa, bitch cleans up." Lantro smiled deviously at her.

"I see you are still with the bimbo," Angel deduced in an icy tone.

"Bimbo? Are you going to let her talk to me that way, Sugar Bear?"

Solara shuddered at the voice. It was a high-pitched screech that played on the nerves.

"Don't listen to what that bitch says, baby." Lantro reached over and madly began kissing the blonde while openly fondling her breasts. Finishing that, he turned and smiled at Angel. "Bitch is just jealous."

Lantro spun around quickly as he felt a heavy hand land on his shoulder.

Braksis stood there holding him. "I think the lady deserves an apology."

"Apology? Bitch got what she deserves. Who the hell are you to tell me what to do?"

Braksis smiled. "I'm the man who is telling you how it is. You'll apologize all nice and sincere-like, then you'll give Angel enough money to get home whenever she so chooses."

"I think not. You clearly don't know who I am. I am Lantro, defensiveback of the Falestian Lumnia team!"

"I'm just shaking in my boots," Braksis rebutted as he stared into Lantro's eyes.

"The hell with this. I'll show you who is boss!" Lantro threw a punch at Braksis, who merely caught his fist and squeezed. Lantro shuddered in pain as he looked up and saw Braksis smiling down at him. "You broke my hand!"

"Hey, Braxy baby, I've got this one covered," Angel offered. "Let him go."

Braksis released Lantro's hand and nodded to Angel.

Lantro immediately clutched it in pain. He spun around to face Angel. "Bitch, your new plaything may have cost me next season!"

A look of mock sorrow filled her face. "Oh, poor baby. I'll cost you a bit more." She then rammed her foot up, kicking Lantro directly in his genitals.

Lantro fell down coughing and wheezing. His eyesight blurred and lost focus. Tears flowed from his eyes as he bellowed in high-pitched agony.

The blonde immediately fell to her knees and started stroking Lantro in the groin, which caused him to scream out even more. "Sugar Bear, I want to help."

Angel reached down and removed Lantro's money pouch. "I'd say that makes us just about even now. He's all yours, Blondie."

Angel spun around and resumed her search for a seat, a smile on her face from ear to ear.

Solara grinned up at Braksis. "And when we first met, I didn't think we'd get along."

Braksis chuckled. "I never had a doubt."

The two caught up with Angel who found three open seats and sat down. "Hey, Sister Sol, I promised to tell you the rules."

Solara looked at her and giggled. "How about talking about what happened?"

"Nah, that bastard stole enough of my life. Let's leave him crawling in agony where he belongs." Angel leaned out and looked at Braksis. "Thanks for the assist. It's rare for a man to stand up for me."

"I look after those I care about," Braksis replied.

"Braxy baby, you care about me?"

"Not if you keep calling him Braxy baby," Solara joked.

"Seriously," Angel said.

Braksis did not say another word. However, Solara leaned in close and said, "He chooses his friends cautiously, but when he makes one, he would give his life for them. You should feel honored."

"That says a lot. I'll make sure I live up to his expectations."

"He has no expectations. You could walk away and not work on this project another day, and he'd still consider you a friend," Solara declared.

A Guardsman approached their row and leaned over. "Excuse me, miss, you will have to come with me."

Angel looked up and laughed when she saw it was the same Guardsman who tried to arrest her earlier. "I see that you got all of the ale out of your hair. How much of it did you drink?"

Realizing who she was, the Guardsman became infuriated. "Why I ought to..."

"Do nothing, soldier," Braksis said as he stood up. "Just as I commanded earlier. What seems to be the problem?"

"She is the problem!" he spat. "She keeps creating a scene and endangering the public. She assaulted a man back there."

"He provoked her, and truth to tell, I assaulted him first. Are you going to try to arrest me?"

"Lord Braksis, I would never..."

"Then you shall leave us alone. Besides, look at her collar. She outranks you. You'd try to arrest a superior officer?"

The Guardsman looked over in shock. Angel raised her neck to reveal the two gold bars displaying the rank insignia of a captain in the Imperial Army. "She was just street trash this morning."

"And a captain now. Imagine that? Must have been the way I made you look like a fool. Why don't you go and get me something to drink?

An ale perhaps? Maybe you can still ring some out of your hair," said Angel.

The Guardsman clearly was frustrated and his temper was close to the boiling point.

Braksis stood up and looked him in the eye. "All jokes from my officer aside, you should leave now."

The Guardsman stared hard at Braksis and seemed close to growling.

"That was not a suggestion," Braksis clarified.

Enraged, the Guardsman spun around and stormed off without another word to the trio.

"That was just too precious." The smile on Angel's face somehow grew even larger than it was when she kicked Lantro.

"You must learn to control your tongue. You will not be able to lead troops anywhere but into trouble unless you can curb it."

"Don't worry, Braxy baby, I may have a style of my own, but it's all good. The unit I assemble will be the best unit of women warriors in all of the Seven Kingdoms."

"That doesn't say much since it will be the only unit of women warriors," Braksis pointed out.

"Are you forgetting my people, the mystral?" Solara jumped into the conversation.

"I meant woman soldiers," Braksis corrected himself.

"That's better. Now, if you don't mind, our new officer was about to tell me the rules of the game."

"Whatever. Pretend I'm not here," Braksis said.

"That's what we intend, Braxy baby." Angel smiled at him.

"Wonderful," Braksis sneered under his breath.

"Anyway, Lumnia is a game of strength, skill, and endurance. Eleven men take the field with the simple goal of winning."

"How do you win?" Solara asked.

"A team needs to score fifteen goals," Angel replied.

"So fifteen points will end the game?"

"Not so fast. Whoever gets to fifteen first will win a round. A team needs to win three rounds to actually claim a victory."

Solara's shoulders slumped. "How come I get the feeling that we are going to be here for a while?"

"Because we will be, Sister Sol." Angel beamed back.

"Don't the players get tired?"

"Tired. Battered. Brutalized. Oh yes. That's why they have a twenty-five-man roster. Though they can only substitute a player when one of three things happens. The ball goes out of bounds, someone scores, or there is an injury on the field."

"What happens the rest of the time?"

"All is fair. The players actively attempt to gain control of the ball and score a goal. They can pass it, kick it, or run with it. If someone gets in the way, they just plow through them."

"Barbaric. People find this entertaining?"

"Oh yeah. I myself find Lumnia players very attractive," Angel admitted.

"Like our crying friend up there?"

"Well, not him anymore. I would love to get to meet Dozzer."

"Dozzer?" Solara asked.

"He's only the best Lumnia player in all of the Seven Kingdoms. He is the only player who never substitutes out. He is a middleback, but leads all of Dartie in scoring. A god to the game." Angel leaned back and closed her eyes with a brief fantasy of the professional player.

Solara watched her and laughed. "For your sake, I hope he didn't see what you did just a few minutes ago."

"No worries. I treat that area with extra care when a guy treats me right. If you catch my drift."

Solara watched Angel and could see so many facets of this girl before her. She was so open and straightforward. Very different from the company she usually held. "I think I know exactly what you mean."

"Oh yeah, I'm sure you get to practice with Braxy baby, right?"

"Did I hear my name?" Braksis leaned forward.

Both women giggled.

Braksis looked from face-to-face and realized that it was a conversation that he wasn't meant to be a part of. "I must have been mistaken. This is me going back to being invisible."

Angel looked Solara in the eye. "Well?"

Solara shook her head negative. "We've never had a relationship like that."

"So he's free, eh? Interesting."

"Oh, no." Solara shook her head wondering what Angel was contemplating.

Angel glanced at Braksis, then smiled cunningly to Solara.

"What?" Solara asked.

"I just would have sworn that you two were closer than mere companions. That's all."

Solara lowered her head in contemplation, remembering her anger at Queen Zerilla when she received Braksis's affection.

"I knew it!" Angel beamed.

As Solara looked up, she spotted Braksis's profile and knew that Angel was correct. She did have feelings for him. She wasn't certain when they developed, but they were indeed there.

Looking at each other as if they shared an intimate secret, both started giggling.

Trumpets blared into the Colosseum and the three turned and watched as the Empress entered and was escorted to her private box, which was placed at the fifty-yard line of the stadium. She walked through a row of Imperial Guards who stretched the entire thirty rows of the stadium. Centain and six other guards walked directly behind her as an escort.

Waiting in the private box, Braksis saw King Sarlec and his son Winton of Danchul, King Palenial and his wife Queen Celenia of Dartie, and Admiral Morex. He would have to make his way to their box and extend his greeting to them at some point during the game.

Leaning back, he heard Solara and Angel resume giggling, and he wondered whether he should just go and get the pleasantries taken care of now.

Trumpets blared a second time, and twenty-two athletes took the field. Eleven men rushed to their positions on each side. Five forwards, two middlebacks, three defensivebacks, and a goalie. Four referees jogged onto the field, and the battle of spirit and prowess began.

❖ ❖ ❖ ❖ ❖

As Karleena was escorted to her private box, she was glad to see that everyone was already seated and seemed to be enjoying themselves. She had worried briefly that the events in Dartie of late would cause strain and tension between King Palenial and the rest of the guests in her box. Her concerns did not appear to be justified.

Moving through the rows, many of the fans stood and cheered as she descended to her box. The Imperial Guards stood by the rows so nobody could get through to her. Centain handled security with his usual thoroughness and exceptional attention to detail.

For this event, Karleena wore an outfit with the combined colors of both kingdoms. She wished to honor the championship kingdoms while not displaying a favorite on either side. She had on the traditional white silk blouse and short skirt of a Danchul woman, along with a yellow fur cloak with orange spots as a sign of the Dartian aristocracy. Her feet were covered with sandals laced up past her ankles, with similarly laced bracelets upon her wrists and arms. The only symbol she wore of her own stature was her emerald necklace.

As she entered the private box, all who were awaiting her arrival stood and bowed in greeting. Karleena returned a curt nod and then beckoned for all to sit and prepare for the game. Karleena sat between Sarlec and Palenial, with Winton next to his father on the right, and Celenia next to her husband on the left. In the second row, Centain and Morex sat in the two seats behind the Empress, with the six Imperial Guards stationed around the edges and behind them.

King Palenial leaned over and spoke softly to Karleena. "I regret not being able to see you earlier. I was told that you were in conference and were not to be disturbed."

"My apologies, King Palenial. I was not informed of your arrival or I would have issued a recess to greet you."

"Not necessary, my Empress. I did not wish to disturb you, especially with all the strain I am sure my kingdom has placed upon you."

Karleena turned to regard Palenial. He was a proud man who sought to right the wrongs of the past. After the Great Wars ended, Conrad had awarded added land to Dartie's neighbor, Dartais. Dartais, however, did not desire the extra land, and Palenial, the young king, worked hard to maintain the peace and reunite the two kingdoms that once were one.

Palenial himself made many sacrifices to support the new Imperium, even though his father had fought viciously against it. In time, his determination and efforts impacted his people, and Dartie soon grasped the Imperium with open arms. The Dartians were a pivotal part of the new Imperium, and it was distressing that recent revolts could be stirring trouble up for them again.

"Palenial, I assure you that whatever strain these revolts have brought, the fault is not yours."

"The fault must be in leadership, and I am the leader of Dartie."

"We have learned that not all is as it seems. Please trust my words and do not add blame of this onto your conscience."

Palenial leaned back and thought for a moment. He knew what blame already tormented his soul, and what Karleena was hinting at. Many years ago, while on a family picnic, a lupan surprised them and killed his daughter. He broke into a berserker rage and attacked the mighty creature with nothing more than his bare hands. His face and much of his body were still scarred to remind him of that day. His loss was something he had never forgotten, nor forgiven himself for.

Other than his scarred reminders, he took pride in his appearance. His face had a full black beard, and hair pulled into a ponytail extended far down his back. His eyes were a light blue hue, and were filled with sympathy and compassion. The scars upon his face were troubling at first, but people quickly grew used to them. Many admired how he managed to fight a lupan with his bare hands and survive.

Similar to the cloak that Karleena was wearing, Palenial wore fur and leather garments for his entire outfit. Contrary to hers, he wore the white pelt of a lupan, as he had decreed that all lupans who entered his land were to be exterminated. The outfit was another reminder to him of his failure to his daughter. Closing his eyes, he envisioned her briefly, then turned to Karleena again. "I still feel that I have a shortcoming here, but I shall accept that I may not have been entirely responsible. I thank you for this generosity."

"I am glad your people can come to the capital today and cheer on their team. A sign that the actions of a few will not return the Great Wars and send the Imperium sprawling back into Civil War."

"I, too, feel this way."

King Sarlec leaned forward and smiled at his counterpart. "Of course, my boys are going to slaughter you on the field, so don't expect another respite."

"Ah, King Sarlec, as usual, you underestimate the Kingdom of Dartie. We will be more than ready to take this game and reign victorious."

"Bah! If you take Dozzer out of your lineup, your team is done!"

Palenial pointed down to the Dartie sideline. "If you can see there, I am losing Dozzer after this game. Perhaps you are right Sarlec, and next year we will not even be able to compete."

Karleena followed his finger and saw a familiar face. "Adonis?"

"Yes. Adonis has convinced Dozzer to join his growing cadre of ISIA agents. It is a sad day for Lumnia, but a great day for the Imperium. Dozzer will serve well."

The trumpets blared a second time to signal that the players were taking the field. As the twenty-two athletes rushed to their positions, they all stopped in synchronous order and saluted the private box.

Karleena stood up and waved to each of the players as they passed by. Seeing the acknowledgment, the referees took the field, ready to begin. Sitting back down, Karleena noticed that Queen Celenia seemed to have an oblivious gaze, as if she were in a world of her own and not cognizant of the events around her. She seemed sad and somber, fragile and incomplete. Karleena had met Celenia once before her daughter had been killed. She had been so strong and determined. She worked just as hard as her husband to bring Dartie into the Imperium and have the kingdom thrive. Now, she was merely a shell of the woman she had once been.

One referee approached the middle of the field. He took a position directly next to the two center forwards, one from each team. They stood in a small circle where only the three of them were allowed to enter to start the game. The referee tossed the ball in the air, and the championship series officially began.

The center forward for Dartie, a man named Makkas, was much taller than his counterpart, and managed to leap higher and capture the spherical ball for his team. In his leap, he grabbed it and tossed the ball back toward his middleback, Dozzer.

When Dozzer acquired the ball, the stadium erupted in cheer. Many were joyous that Dartie had acquired the ball and Dozzer specifically was in possession. Many others were upset that Danchul must begin the series on the defense.

Dozzer made the most of getting the ball and charged straight ahead. This was a role that brought him success as the best middleback in the entire league. He was far larger, and surprisingly more agile than any of his competitors. A pair of Danchul forwards attempted to block his charge into their territory, but Dozzer lowered his shoulder and barreled his way right through them.

Yelling, screaming, taunts, and cheers erupted again as the two Danchul players fell backward and Dozzer continued his advance toward the end zone. The players on the field had learned to block this out and remain focused only on the play on the field. Dozzer heard nothing as he plowed through several other defenders, dropped the ball, and kicked it past the goalie to put Dartie up by one within the first few seconds of the game.

Karleena leaned over to Palenial. "I see why Adonis would chose him. He is spectacular."

Sarlec bellowed. "Yes, spectacular! You better take advantage of him this year, Palenial, because without him next season, you'll be in dead last!"

Palenial smiled at Sarlec and leaned back to enjoy the game.

The goalie recovered the ball from the net and quickly underhand-tossed it to one of his defensivebacks. Dowling, the defensiveback then threw the ball sixty yards to one of the Danchul forwards, putting Dartie on the defensive for the first time in the game.

Sarlec leaned over to taunt Palenial. "See what I mean? Are there any players with an arm as strong as Dowling? I think not, my friend."

Palenial smiled, struggling to hear above the roaring of the crowd.

The Danchul forward found himself surrounded by Dartie defensemen.

"Pass the damned ball!" one fan screamed.

"Nail him!" bellowed another.

The forward stopped and looked around. Naudus was wide open and was beckoning for him to pass the ball. Tossing the ball, one of the defenders tipped it and sent it scurrying along the ground.

Naudus ran in to try to recover it for Danchul, but the swift rookie Pravin managed to kick the ball away from Naudus and took it downfield again.

Palenial leaned forward to return Sarlec's taunt right back to him. "See what I mean? Are there any players with such fancy footwork as Pravin? I think not, my obese friend."

Karleena had to stifle a laugh as Palenial on one side was beaming and Sarlec on the other was growling.

Pravin continued to use his feet and kick the ball as he weaved in and out of Danchul players. This was a gifted talent that Pravin exploited. Too many players desired to have the ball in their hands to feel like they had better control of the game. Pravin realized he didn't need to hold the ball to be swift and cunning. He also had pinpoint accuracy and could pass without missing a step.

A pair of defenders charged Pravin. He stepped in front of the ball and kicked it backward with his heel. Though he had not been looking, the ball landed chest-high in the arms of Makkas for a perfect pass.

The crowds erupted again. Chants of "Makkas, Makkas, Makkas!"

Makkas ran with the ball and approached the end zone. Dowling dove at him to try to knock the ball away. Makkas leapt into the air and sailed over Dowling's dive. While in midair, Makkas hurled the ball past a very frustrated goalie making it a two-to-nothing game.

Sarlec grumbled and looked over at his son Winton. He noticed the boy kept glancing over at Karleena, and moving back again so that she would not see him. This shocked Sarlec who was so bold and outgoing, that his son would appear cowardly and hide from an apparent attraction.

Like Sarlec during his youth, Winton could turn the heads of women just by walking into a room. Spending most of his time in the sun, his consequent dark complexion was quite becoming. In fact, a permanent tan seemed to be painted on him from the day of his birth. His long black hair was tied into a ponytail and swung down to the midsection of his back. By being of royal blood, he had been waited on hand and foot, however he sought the best trainers he could find and kept himself physically fit. Muscular and athletic. No matter where you looked, you would not see any fat or fatigue on his body. All of this paled to the angelic face that could win a heart with nothing more than a smile.

Sarlec elbowed his son in the ribs. "She's a mighty attractive woman, isn't she, my boy?"

Shocked, Winton looked at his father as if he noticed him for the first time. "What?"

"The Empress. You are attracted to her. I think you two would make a handsome couple. You just need to let your feelings be known more."

Winton glanced over at Karleena and saw that she heard what the two were discussing. He blushed instantly, leading to a roaring laugh from his father.

"Father, please. If I desire the Empress, then I shall do so in my own manner."

"I see. Well boy, perhaps we are not so alike after all." Sarlec leaned over to Karleena. "If I were his age, I would make my intentions known."

Karleena merely smiled back to Sarlec. "Perhaps we should discuss this later."

Palenial leaned forward. "Yes, you pompous idiot. You are embarrassing your son. What, if you aren't winning, you need to find other ways to make people's lives miserable? Watch the game! I'm winning if you haven't noticed."

"I've noticed," Sarlec grumbled.

Palenial leaned back and continued to smile. Karleena gently squeezed his hand to thank him for the intrusion.

As the game continued, early indication seemed that Dartie would be the clear victor. Whenever the team fell behind, they got the ball to Dozzer and he practically carried the whole team on his back. Regardless, they had some definite up-and-coming stars who would most likely bring Dartie back to the championships even after Dozzer left.

Dartie dominated the first two rounds, then Danchul came back and claimed close victories in the next two. As they approached the final match of the championships, weary players could hear the crowd still had a lot of energy left.

For the last two defeats, many fans criticized the Dartian players. Vulgarities were being spewed, as well as insults and base anger for the apparent reduction in playing skill.

A new chant escaped the lips of many fans in the Colosseum: "Dozzer, you suck!"

Even with the hostile crowd, Dartie took the field for the final match and came on strong. This last match was taken much more personally, and the players put their fatigue aside. Hits were a little harder, runs a little swifter, and passes a little more accurate. The team really pulled together and began to reclaim their dominance in the final and decisive match.

Karleena watched intently and thoroughly enjoyed the competitiveness of the sport. Both teams fared well, and she saw Sarlec go through an extreme of emotions. From taunts, to frustration, to brimming pride, to teeth-clenching moments as he watched the events unfold. On her other side, Palenial took it all in stride and thoroughly enjoyed the event. Though the two did engage in occasional shots at each other, Palenial did not seem overly upset at the changing tides in the game. He was merely glad to be there and to be experiencing the championship.

The series was coming close to an end. Dartie was up eleven to eight in the final round. The first team to reach fifteen would win the championships. Who the victor would be, was something that Karleena would have to learn later, for she would not be present to witness the final results herself.

A messenger approached the private box and whispered to Centain. Centain leaned over and spoke briefly to Admiral Morex before gaining Karleena's attention. "My Empress, apologies for the intrusion at such an exciting climax, but I fear there is dreadful news."

Karleena looked back at the Captain. Without saying a word, her eyes beckoned him to continue.

"I fear there have been further raids. A small farming village in Danchul has been destroyed."

"Destroyed?"

King Sarlec turned to listen, his eyes practically bulging from his head hearing that a village in Danchul was attacked. His kingdom was a utopia now. Who would attack them?

"Yes, my Empress. The report I was given indicated that all who lived there have been slaughtered. The bodies were displayed as a warning for all to see."

"Displayed?" Karleena feared what this would mean but had to know.

"I wish to spare you the gruesome details," Centain stated, his eyes pleading with her.

"I must know, Captain. How can I rule if I am spared the atrocities that plague my kingdom?"

Sarlec spoke for the first time. "It is my kingdom, Karleena. Please, spare yourself this memory. I shall look upon the destruction myself."

"I appreciate the sentiment, Sarlec. You are like an uncle to me. I value your opinions and advice more than most. However, I must at least know."

Sarlec nodded to Centain to continue.

"The people were nailed to wooden posts in the ground, then the attackers set them aflame. Men. Women. Children. Even babies. None was spared this onslaught."

The anger in Sarlec boiled over. "Who would dare do such a thing?"

Behind them, Palenial did not speak, but prayed that those involved in the recent uprisings in Dartie had not migrated south and attacked their neighbors.

"Credit was taken by a merchant town in Frocomon. A town known as Arkham," Centain informed.

"Credit was taken?" Karleena spoke in a low whisper.

Admiral Morex leaned forward. "May I recommend that we retire to the palace? The Colosseum is no place to be discussing such matters, my lady."

"Yes, yes. Of course you are right, Admiral. We should leave." Standing up she looked at Palenial and Celenia. "If you would please excuse us."

"Of course, your majesty. If you need anything, please do not hesitate to ask," Palenial replied with a nod.

As Sarlec stood up, Winton glanced up at him. "You will miss the end, father. Where are you going?"

"Business, boy. I must go," Sarlec roared back.

"Imperial business you mean?" Winton pouted.

"Grow a backbone, boy. One day you will rule, and you, too, will know what it means to have responsibility. For now, enjoy the game. I will see you back home."

"Yes, father." As Sarlec walked away, Winton looked back at him with a glare of hatred. He despised the fact that his father continued to put the Imperium before his own family. When he was king, he promised that he would only care about himself and those who mattered to him. Not the needs of strangers and people from other kingdoms.

As Karleena began ascending the stairway to the exit, she looked around for Braksis. She knew he was here and hoped that he, too, received the message of the attack. At the top of the stairs, she saw him standing there along with Solara and a uniformed woman she was unfamiliar with. He clearly had already received the message.

Centain led the way back up the stairs with Karleena, Admiral Morex, King Sarlec, and the Imperial Guards following him. As they reached the top, the crowd erupted in cheers as Dozzer scored again.

Karleena lowered her head in sorrow. All of these people were so happy and excited. Yet the world around them was changing for the worse. It was time to stop worrying about the ministers, the aristocracy, or what people would think of her in general. These raids must stop. From this moment on, she vowed that she would take a more direct role and follow her own heart and instincts. It was time not just to rule, but to lead.

CHAPTER 22

Such a beautiful day. The sky above was a bright blue, violated only by the purity and whiteness of the clouds. The ground was green as far as the eye could see. Even the trees, bushes, and shrubs seemed to breathe life and harmony into the air.

For Kai, days like this were far from her norm. Perhaps that was why she spent extra time enjoying her surroundings. Taking it all in. For today was a beautiful day. No thoughts and images of her past or her mission would be allowed to dampen her appreciation.

As she slowly walked through the tall grasslands, she allowed her hands to skim the blades. She wondered how the world could hold such majesty, but also so many tragedies. No. She was not going to think, just exist in the here and now.

Since leaving the tigrel, she had no longer been plagued by the dreams and sense of foreboding. The tigrel wine must have had a lingering effect on her. She still instinctively knew that she must hurry, but the beauty of her surroundings was intoxicating.

As she continued to walk slowly, an expression of pure glee and happiness appeared on her elven face. This was exactly what she needed, after traveling so long and so far. After being run out of her home and venturing into the unknown. After being given the task of looking to reunite her people. Some time to relax and reflect was invaluable.

Kai could hear the gentle flow of a stream somewhere off to the side. As the trickling of water against rocks clarified, she realized how thirsty she was. Her mouth was positively watering with the sensation and need for a sampling of the stream.

She started a quick jog looking for the stream. Pure delight and laughter erupted from her mouth. Suddenly she paused, ducked down, and grabbed her bow. Scanning her surroundings, her senses completely alert, she called out, "Is someone here?"

With no reply or sense that anything was out of place, she begin to think of the laughter, and realized that it was not another, but herself who had laughed. The shock over the absurdity of her actions filled her head. How long had it been since she laughed? Truly laughed? But to think that her own laughter was another person? That thought alone made her laugh again.

Kai quickly found the stream, and dropped to her knees looking into the water below. The water was very clear. Amazed once again at how peaceful and beautiful everything was, Kai just stared at her reflection and smiled.

As she watched her reflection, she noticed a sparkle in her greenish-blue eyes. Something she had never noticed before. Could a smile truly change you so much?

Her reflection smiled back at her, but was soon dispersed as she reached in with both hands and took a drink. After satisfying this sudden desire for fluid nourishment, she leaned back and stared up at the sky once more.

Where her people were now, they would never see a sky so blue. Clouds so white. Where they were now, there was a constant haze and fog. Raging storms that made ship navigation a near impossibility were frequent and constant. Yet that is where her people now resided with fear–fear of discovery–in their hearts.

If only her people, her family, friends could see her now. How long since any of them had truly smiled? Ever since being forced out of their homeland years ago, happiness and joy were nothing but memories. Yet here she was, smiling and enjoying herself. If only this could last forever.

Weapons certainly were uncomfortable when relaxing, but had become like a second skin to Kai. Yet they seemed out of place in the surrounding atmosphere. Even she herself seemed out of place here. With that thought, Kai took off her weapons and laid them aside. Even with her visions of the orcs, there was no danger here now.

Her bow was her most trusted of weapons. She had made it when she was a child. The bow was perfectly crafted to her grip, and had stencils of her accomplishments etched onto the wooden stalk. The casing of arrows was also hand-designed. When needed, she was quite proficient with arming her bow quickly, and sending an arrow, or multiple arrows at a target with accuracy and precision. Taking them off seemed odd, but not as odd as wearing them here.

She also had wrapped a small elastic grip around her leg and now she untied it. The grip held several pouch openings, with blades she could throw. These blades were indeed small and would do little damage to a large opponent, but as with the bow, Kai mastered their use and never missed her mark.

Her final weapon was the dagger that she kept located in the boot on her left leg. This was the one weapon she was not entirely comfortable with. Her height was smaller than most, even most of her fellow elves. If she could not win a conflict from afar, she knew that she could be in trouble.

Height was not necessarily the issue. She had amazing speed and reflexes. Her acrobatic abilities were unparalleled in her home village. However, from a young age, her parents had focused on long-range tactics. Hand-to-hand combat and the use of a dagger or sword were foreign to her. She could do it, but she preferred not to. At the same time, without the dagger, she would not have been able to release Hr'Tesh from the hunter's trap.

After removing her weapons, Kai carefully attached them to her horse's saddle. With them removed, it was like a weight lifted from her. She felt lighter than air, as if she could truly float off the ground and touch the clouds herself. All instruments of death and destruction were gone, and her history along with them. All that was left was the moment. A moment that she wished to cherish and have last forever.

With thoughts of her surroundings and a feeling of comfort and protection encompassing her, Kai drifted off into slumber, and dreamed of a world where she and her people could all be as comfortable as she was right here and now. Tranquility, however, was not meant for one with such a dire mission.

❖ ❖ ❖ ❖ ❖

In the midst of her dream, images of a storm appeared. Odd she thought, that there was a storm on such a calm and peaceful afternoon. A face also. The face of the young human girl came to her again. The child was smiling at her, beckoning her to come. Then, just as quickly, she faltered. Blood streamed down the young girl's face. What could this mean? Is this vision a reality? A prophecy? Are the two somehow bonded? Or is this truly just another dream? A large man brandishing an axe jumped out, startling her. Kai awakened with a start and was brought back to the real world.

Disturbed by the images in her dream, she found herself in a cold sweat and shaking. She looked around and noticed that night had fallen. The stars shone brightly in the sky. Everything seemed just as calm as before she fell asleep, but the vision she feared was a sign that things were getting worse, and that by even slowing down slightly, the Chosen One could be in jeopardy.

Angry with herself for surrendering to the tranquil landscape, Kai jumped up and prepared to depart in search of the young girl once more. The time had come for them to be together. She knew this instinctively, and feared that if she did not arrive quickly, it would be too late. With so much riding on this mission, she could not fail.

With one last drink of water, a sense of regret at the disturbance to her tranquility flooded through her. Kai approached her horse, which seemed on edge, and once again donned her weapons. As she attached the blades, she realized that this was the life she truly existed in. The world she actually belonged to.

As she slung her bow across her back, she gently stroked her horse, noting for the first time the mare's agitation. "What is it? What has you riled up so? Have you, too, started to have visions?"

Without an answer, she looked off to the south where she knew her destiny awaited. So pretty from here. She could see the mountains in the distance. This far out, you would hardly know that something disastrous was happening, and without her visions, she would be blinded to the danger as well.

Mounting her horse, she pulled the reins and resumed her journey toward the girl in her visions. The horse she could see was well rested and rejuvenated. Though still slightly restless, he traveled swiftly and with strength.

Suddenly, the horse stopped and stood up on its two hind legs neighing to the night sky. A sudden uneasiness grew in Kai. Something was clearly wrong. Danger. In one quick motion, she leapt to the ground, removing her bow and an arrow before landing. She studied her surroundings and listened for whatever set her and the horse on edge in the background.

A deer ran out of the bushes and dashed toward the woods. Kai let out a little sigh of relief. Just a deer. A little confused that a deer caused such a warning sign of danger, Kai looked down at her bow. Her instincts were normally infallible. Perhaps the recent visions had a larger impact upon her than she would have even deemed possible.

She slowly stood back up and approached her horse. The steed still was stamping the ground and she became alert. Then she heard rustling in the grass behind her.

Not the deer. If not for that brief instant's warning, she would have been killed instantly. A large feline-like animal jumped out of the bushes and landed right where she had been planted. If she hadn't rolled with the sound, she wouldn't have stood a chance.

Startled by the attack, the horse kicked out with its back legs at the beast and hit it in the head, then ran off into the depths of the night.

As the creature stumbled back momentarily, Kai tried to absorb all of its details. Never before had she seen the like. It had a long mane of silver hair flowing from its head down the majority of its back. Its mouth had two large protruding teeth, accompanied by a full set of teeth that made the creature appear carnivorous. Its paws all had long nails that looked like they had the ability to clasp onto something and not let go. Kai immediately got the impression that like her feline tigrel friends, this beast could climb trees with ease. From head to foot, this thing was well over six feet, and was easily three times her size in bulk weight.

With a savage growl, the creature turned and lunged at Kai. Her agility truly was an asset. She braced herself until the last instant and dodged the lunge once again. Kai could see splashes of blood where the horse had kicked the beast.

Close attacks were not her idea of fighting, especially with a large and formidable foe. Just like when she had faced the tragon, her assaults were mostly made from a distance with her bow. Distance that she needed to add between her and this creature as quickly as possible.

Kai quickly searched her short-term memory for an analysis of her surroundings. The entire time, she kept her gaze on the beast before her. It turned and lunged again. This time, Kai leapt backward leaving the creature short, and ready to pounce again. With a back flip, Kai landed in the bushes that the deer had previously hidden in.

Her entire life to this point had trained her. Constantly challenged her. The world she had come from, although far from here, had always been one of conflict and battle. Of course there were the occasional times when people were at peace. But experience taught her that was usually just enemies lulling her people into a false sense of security. The danger quickly came; the horde quickly came. Unlike many of Kai's fellow elves, she refused to lower her guard or surrender—the main reason she volunteered for this mission. She was always calm, cool, and collected when it came to danger. Allowing her instincts and ability to analyze the situation and to quickly take over.

With this unknown beast three times her size and weight looking to make her its dinner, she was not afraid. She did not look back and regret the events that brought her here. This was her life. This was what she trained for since she was a child. The creature's larger size mattered not. She would find a way to claim victory this day.

The beast lunged at her again, and had several branches stabbing it in the face as it did so. Already sensitive from the horse's kick, it flinched with the shock of the impact. Kai took advantage of the few precious seconds to get some distance between her and the creature.

She heard the growl again and knew that she wouldn't get far enough away. She reached down to her leg and removed four of the small throwing blades. In mid-step, she spun around launching herself in the air and released all four blades at the deadly predator. All impacted its head, sending the beast roaring in anger and shock.

Kai picked up two arrows and opted for a short-range assault. She definitely would not have the safety of distance, but she also did not want to wind up as a meal. Facing this thing with the dagger alone sent shudders up her spine. But that would not hinder her. Even if she was forced to face this thing on its own terms, she would do what needed to be done. Ashamed of the shudders, she took several quick breaths to regain her calm and composure.

As the beast began its pursuit of her once more, she dropped, knelt, turned, and released both arrows at the pursuing creature. One arrow impacted it on its chest, whereas the other pierced its right eye.

The creature roared with pain and anger. This particular prey was beginning to cause it grief. No snack would ever cause it this much agony and go anywhere but in its gullet. Shaking its head desperately to try to dislodge the arrow, the predator's anger continued to swell. With another earsplitting growl, it took one more lunge at the intended meal before it.

This time Kai knew she was trapped. Her back was to several stones, and the beast was leaping right toward her. She had hoped the creature would be delayed longer when it was hit, but unfortunately it recovered quicker than anticipated. Rather than being on top of the rocks and having the strategic advantage akin to that of a sniper, she was now trapped at the bottom of the rocky crevice.

As she watched the creature soaring toward her, her mind cleared. Details became painfully apparent. She could feel the drips of sweat pouring off of her head. In fluid motion, she quickly fired arrows at the hurtling beast, each hitting its mark. Unhindered, the feline beast was almost on top of her, its mouth opened and ready to bite, saliva dripping as it flew through the air.

Reluctantly, but with pure desperation and survival on her mind, she grabbed the dagger and held it ready for the oncoming beast. Its head arrived first with its mouth ready to snap down on her neck. Kai could feel the warmth of the saliva dripping onto her body as she dropped to the ground and the beast plunged headfirst into the rock behind her. Dazed, its body went slightly limp, landing on top of her and pinning her down. The brunt of the hit seemed to impact her arm, instantly shooting stabs of pain into her shoulder. Kai took advantage of the momentary lapse of assault, and rammed the dagger up into the attacker's belly.

She quickly removed the dagger and kept stabbing. The weight of the creature on top of her was immense. However, survival was all that mattered. The tables turned, predator now becoming prey, the beast attempted to defend itself, clawing weakly at Kai. Even without much strength left, its razor-sharp claws managed to rip her tunic and cloak to shreds in seconds.

She kept stabbing and stabbing again. A feeling of warmth and wetness completely enveloped Kai. Blood was everywhere, and she was unable to distinguish between hers and the creature's. All that mattered was survival. A newfound strength blossomed inside of her, and she kept her arm moving and stabbing as long as she could. Even after the creature appeared to stop breathing, she kept thrusting the blade into it to make certain it was dead.

Kai struggled to get out from under the beast. Its weight was immense. Even more so now that it was dead. She could feel the pain in her chest and arms. There was more hindering her than just the weight of this creature. She was losing blood, and with it, strength. With that realization, Kai knew she had to get out from under the beast quickly before she were trapped and no longer had the ability to free herself.

She could feel the cold edges of the rocks above her head when she reached, and knew that this was her best bet. She struggled to move toward the rocks. The beast had crashed into them when the confrontation began, but its head weighed far less than the rest of its body. Kai stabbed her dagger into the ground and used it to push with her good arm farther up toward the rocks behind her.

Slowly, she managed to move slightly, the weight of the beast continuing to threaten to crush her, as well as any hopes for survival. Every movement was filled with agony. Every inch threatened to have her black out and risk suffocation, or possibly even drown in the blood of the creature atop of her. Refusing to give in to the darkness, Kai kept pushing at the dagger through the pain. Finally, she could feel the rocks behind her. Kai managed to push herself up into a sitting position.

She could see the eyes of the beast in front of her now. The lifeless eyes. The eyes she stole the shine from. Her arrow had blinded one eye earlier. She could see the piercing and cloudiness that already filled it from below. The arrow must have been dislodged when it crashed into the rocks that knocked it senseless.

The other eye was still clear. Staring at her. Looking through her. How she hated that she was forced to kill a life form that was just trying to survive. Still, it was either her or this creature, and that was a debate she would always look to win.

What she earlier saw as being trapped actually became her salvation. Without the feline beast slamming headfirst into the rocks, she would have been lost for certain. Not just in pain, but eviscerated, consumed.

Kai bent her knees and tried to bring her legs up. As she did so, the mass of the animal's body slid off and settled on the ground. She was almost free. Almost. Using the rocks as a brace, she pushed on the beast with all of her remaining strength. She only managed to move it slightly, but that would be enough.

With the bulk of the weight off of her, Kai managed to roll over and completely free herself. She took a sigh of relief at her freedom, but the pain shooting through her body would not allow her to relax for long.

She looked down at her clothes in tatters, and her skin underneath was not in much better shape. She had claw marks piercing her breasts and right arm. A lot of blood, but most of it was from the dead animal.

Disbelief came over her quickly. When did the beast manage to slice into her arm? She remembered falling on it and feeling the shooting pain, but actually being pierced? The adrenaline rush must have numbed her senses. This realization was frightening. If she didn't feel something as deep and threatening as the injuries to her breasts and right arm, then perhaps something else was seriously wrong as well. Could she be in shock?

Brushing off her worries and allowing instinct to take over, she took off the remains of her top and did her best to wrap it around her wounds. With that secure, Kai tried to listen for the flow of the stream. The same stream she had found earlier that day. She knew that it was long and winding, so it should be near her here as well.

The pain was increasing. The need to close her eyes was overwhelming. Concentration was all but impossible. But concentrate she must. Falling asleep now would only lead to the forever sleep. "I'm not going to join the beastie just yet," she thought.

Kai knelt down and tried to ease her breathing. Regulate it. Her heart was still racing. Deep breathes in and out. She could feel the dizziness starting to overcome her, but she managed to stay awake and focused. Then she could hear it. The stream trickling on rocks.

Listening, she thought that perhaps the stream was close to the rocks where the final struggle with the beast transpired. She stood back up and approached them slowly. The trickling of water was close, very close. Kai stumbled slightly as she walked, but managed to climb over the rocky obstacle and peer down at the water below. The sight was akin to a shining light, the light at the end of the tunnel.

Sliding down the remainder of the rocks, Kai landed in the stream, and sat watching as blood polluted the water around her. Removing the remaining slashed clothes and revealing her wounds, Kai could feel her lifeblood seeping out of her. A stream of its own.

Kai soaked her tattered clothes and washed her wounds. Surprisingly, the wounds were superficial, not as deep as expected. The beast had already been close to death and making a last ditch effort to lash out. Successful in some regard, but not enough to prove fatal. The bulk of the blood in the stream must have belonged to the creature, and simply washed off of her while she sat in the water.

Washing the wounds, Kai ripped her clothes a little more to create layers of bandages. She applied wet cloths to the wound, then tied them on with dry strands to apply pressure. The dizziness was beginning to fade slightly, but a feeling of nausea overcame her. Rather than fight it, Kai gave in and allowed herself to be sick.

After several minutes of vomiting and pain, which fluttered through her body with each heave, Kai washed herself off in the stream before returning to the beast.

As she started back toward the deceased animal, Kai contemplated her condition. She was weak, slow, stumbling, her clothes were completely in ruins, and her horse had run off. Though the creature had failed to kill her, it certainly did its fair share of damage.

As she stood and looked down at it, tears of sympathy streamed down her cheek. In life, you don't always choose your enemies or your battles. Sometimes they chose you. Thinking of battles and potential dangers, she looked out toward the mountains. So far away. In her current state, without her horse, she doubted she would be able to make it to the child without rest. Perhaps it was better to be late, than not to arrive to help the child at all.

With that thought, Kai slowly gathered some kindling from broken branches and created a fire. She slumped down and rested. While sitting there, she realized how hungry she was, and that all of her food was packed on the horse.

Considering the fallen feline creature, a small smile pierced her pained face. No use allowing this beast to go to waste, she decided. As she gazed at it once more, multiple options entered her head. Not only could she use this beast for sustenance, but also as replacement wardrobe. Even more so, a symbol of her victory this evening. Though the victory had come at a high price, and deep down, she blamed herself for taking time to enjoy her surroundings rather than fulfilling her mission. Now, she only hoped that her actions here did not lead to the destruction of all. The Chosen One must be protected.

Feeling the pressures of her mission and time once more, she moved to the beast and explored how she would transform the creature into an outfit. The thought of wearing another life form bothered her, but this thing left her little choice. She certainly could not continue her quest in nothing more than some scraps and bandages.

With that, Kai studied the mane of silvery hair, the ferocious looking mouth, and knew exactly what she was going to do. Thoughts of how to proceed danced through her head as she finally gave in and allowed herself to drift off into a state of unconsciousness.

CHAPTER 23

Kyria opened her eyes and looked around. She was puzzled. The last thing she remembered was her mother tucking her into bed. Now, as she opened her eyes, she was out in an open field. The sun was shining. It was a beautiful day.

Confused, Kyria started walking. No—she was riding a horse through the tall grasses. A sound startled her. What was it? Could Guldan have come for her knowing that she had been listening to his conversation that one night last month?

She dropped to her knees and had a bow at the ready with an arrow already nocked. Confusion set in again. This couldn't be right. She had never even fired a bow before. These sensations, these images, they seemed so clear. The carrier of the bow was well trained and experienced. Instinctively she knew she wasn't looking through her own eyes, but then whose?

In her haze, Kyria tried to study the images further. Suddenly she no longer was looking through eyes, but the scene changed as if she were now watching the event unfold. Who was it? It looked like an elf, but like no elf she had ever seen. The woman's skin was a pinkish pigmentation. Her hair flowed behind her in strands of crimson. She did not know who the elf was, but at the same time, the image appeared strangely familiar.

She instinctively knew she had never met the elf she now could see, feel, and smell in whatever this was she was experiencing. Yet, she also knew this elf, whoever it was, was somehow linked to her. As if their fates were somehow intertwined. How could this be possible?

The images continued to flow. Suddenly, a large koxlen, a dangerous feline predator, launched out at the pink elf, and a battle ensued. To Kyria, the battle was intense. Never-ending. The pressure, the fear, the dread was all-encompassing. How could she feel these sensations when they were not even happening to her?

She watched as the pink elf was injured. Clawed in the arm and breasts. It looked like it was all over. The koxlen was going to win. The elf sent a barrage of arrows, but it still pounced on top of her, clawing desperately at its prey below. Odd, she was so certain that this elf had something to do with her. How could she be so wrong?

Wait a second. Just wait a second. The koxlen went limp. Could it be? The pink-pigmented elf won. Bruised and battered, the pink elf actually won. A sense of accomplishment, of pride crept into Kyria. A sense that quickly ended. Just as quickly as she had seemed to be experiencing these images, she was back in her own present. Her own reality.

Nezbith's father was laughing again as he slammed through the door. Kyria felt terrified. She looked around and found herself under the kitchen table again. He stood right next to her. She could smell the alcohol that permeated his body. This time, he must have heard her.

Guldan's axe splintered the table in two. Kyria's eyes bulged as she looked up at him. Guldan's features were altered, more insane than even his normal cruelty. His eyes glowed in an eerie red that would haunt her forever. He raised his axe, and with a maniacal laugh, he brought Carnage down toward her.

Kyria screamed out and sat up. Her whole body was covered in sweat. As she looked around, she was sitting in her own house, safe in her own bed. It was just a dream. Everything had seemed so real to her.

She could still hear the people outside celebrating. She did not know why they were so happy, but the adults had left for a couple of weeks, and now returned. They all seemed changed. As if possessed. She was frightened.

A lingering moment of her dream was like a whisper on the wind. She closed her eyes and could see the pink elf clearly in her mind. The elf looked straight at her and spoke. "Hold on, I am coming."

CHAPTER 24

Kai awoke the following morning to the sounds of birds screeching overhead. Slowly, she opened her eyes and allowed them to adjust to the sunlight. It was blinding at first, and she was unable to see. She could only feel the pain from her chest and arm, as well as aches all over her body. It took her several moments to adjust and remember where she was and what had happened.

The predator lay beneath her, falling the night before to its prey. She used it through the night as a pillow, and found herself completely exposed to the elements with no clothes to call her own but the scraps she used as bandages. Although Kai did not recall removing her boots and pants, she saw them bundled up with her weapons by the tail of the creature.

The vultures that had awakened her were circling in the sky above the fallen beast. A few had even landed and were on the rocks above. Life truly had its own methods and design. A great beast, a predator had fallen in its hunt, and suddenly it became the prey of the other creatures looking to survive yet another day. But this was her beast. Her conquest. They could only have what she left behind.

Kai jumped up and threw small stones at the blackbirds. Nothing that could hurt them, but coupled with her screams and yells to leave, they did opt to bide their time and try again later.

Kai slumped back down looking at the source of her current predicament. So large and ferocious, it was amazing she had actually survived the experience. With a slight sigh, Kai stood back up and walked over to the remains of her clothes.

Under close evaluation, all that could be saved were her pants and boots. Not entirely the best wardrobe for her to go seeking out answers to her recent visions.

While she slept, she'd had another vision. It was the same girl, though this time she was fully grown. The details were hazy, but Kai knew that the face, albeit older than when she saw the child in the first vision, was the same girl she was seeking. This young woman was nearly encased in a shiny skintight suit of silver armor. She also wielded a blade that glimmered and released an aura of purity, a blinding white light burning on the blade itself.

Never before had Kai's visions displayed an older woman or symbols such as this. However, she was certain that the image in her mind was reality. She found this slightly comforting, since most of her other images seemed to place the younger version of the girl in peril and danger.

Kai picked up her dagger and walked over to the beast. As she looked down at it, she shook her head and sighed once more. "Funny calling you a beast or creature." With a long pause, Kai chuckled and spoke to the corpse once again. "I think I'll call you Lucky."

With a smile, Kai approached her newly named corpse. "Well, perhaps not lucky for you, but I certainly was lucky facing you. You might just be my new lucky charm."

Realizing the absurdity of speaking to a dead animal, Kai got to work. She had a few things to do before she could resume the journey toward her final destination. First, she had to eat and drink. She lost a lot of blood last night, and though she felt stronger already, she needed to make sure she regained her strength. Although eating Lucky turned her stomach, she did need to survive, and leaving its carcass for the birds to return was not logical.

Second, replacement clothing definitely needed to be crafted. Walking around in pants and boots certainly wouldn't help her out in terms of dignity. It's bad enough that with the exception of the band of dwarves and the tigrel, she found little traces of nonhuman species on this continent, but to suddenly be stripped of her clothes, she'd feel less than sentient. Fortunately, Lucky could help there as well. He was far larger than her after all, and could provide her with plenty of material to design a new outfit.

Third, she was still in pain and not up to par. With her horse gone, riding to her destination certainly was no longer an option. She would have to walk, or try to jog if she could bear the pain.

Her injured arm could be used, but still sent excruciating pain when she moved it too quickly. As for her chest, the more she moved, the more she felt like she would be moving no further. Also, when she had bent her knees and pushed Lucky the night before, something must have pulled, because her legs had a burning sensation and were killing her. She needed to find something to help her along her journey.

At least she specialized in long-range combat. If something attacked or even injured her, she was formidable at a distance. If they attempted to get in close, as Lucky had the night before, she wouldn't even have the strength to run this time. This thought weighed very heavily. Learning to fight in close quarters was something she must master. She vowed that she would find some way to train herself in the skills she lacked. This was the attitude of a survivor. She was determined and would learn to adapt and improve. Feeling confident was one thing, but only mastering her warrior skills from a distance made her cocky, and that cockiness almost got her killed. Not all threats can be handled from afar.

The fire from the night before was still burning, but the kindling was running out. Kai tossed a few more branches onto the fire to bring it raging back to life. Then she went to work on Lucky. She started off grabbing a large branch and using it as a lever. With its assistance, she managed to put her weight into it and turn Lucky from his belly to his side.

From there, Kai removed the dagger from where she slammed it into the ground the night before and carefully dug into Lucky's underside. After removing a substantial portion of meat from Lucky, she speared it with one of her arrows and placed it above the fire.

As the meat cooked, she looked back at Lucky and made plans for her new wardrobe. The silvery mane was beautiful. Definitely she wanted to use that. Also, Lucky had been proud, strong, and determined. He should not be forgotten for what he was, as well as a reminder of her conquest of him. His head would have to be preserved somehow.

Kai grabbed the lever again, then stopped to study it. This particular branch might be exactly what she needed for her third dilemma. She was having pain in her legs; perhaps this sturdy branch could be forged into a walking staff. The size was right; it could touch the ground and still come up to her head. She definitely would have no problem using it to brace herself.

Possibly, with time and practice, she could also learn to adapt to it. Perhaps use it for jumping, leaping, and covering larger distances when needed. Those thoughts were practically laughable. She needed the pole to help her walk because of injuries. If they healed, why would she ever need to keep the tool after that? After serving its purpose, she would be done with it. And while she was injured, she certainly would be in no shape to be doing aerial acrobatics with a staff.

Still, for now, this piece of wood, which she used as a lever, was akin to a godsend. It was precisely what she needed. To make sure it didn't break or wind up in the fire, Kai tossed it aside by her pants, boots, and remaining weapons.

She turned back to face Lucky again, and suddenly smiled. Inspiration had hit. She knew precisely what she was going to do.

She very carefully carved the outer layers of fur from Lucky's head and mane. This was the most important part of her outfit. About halfway through the process, she could smell that the meat over the fire was ready.

Kai walked over, took the arrow away, and picked up one of her throwing knives to cut the meat into manageable bites. For someone who did not often eat meats, Kai found Lucky to be quite tasty.

This revelation caused a stir of emotions within her. To find pleasure in the sustenance of another living creature seemed to be the greatest betrayal to her sense of belonging in the world. Even more so the sense of serenity and peace she had experienced just the day before. How long ago that now seemed.

Still, the meal was quite good. There was no denying that. She certainly would not make a habit of fighting these creatures for food, but she also would not waste the meal she currently had in front of her.

Surprisingly, Kai found herself stuffed quite quickly. The meal was great, and she devoured what she had cooked, but she was amazed by how much she had eaten and how quickly.

She stood up and headed back toward the little stream. A drink to wash down her feast, followed perhaps by a soothing bath.

She looked into the stream at her reflection and was not pleased by the sight. Compared to the prior day, it was as if she had been through a war. In a manner of speaking, she had been. Her face was worn and tired. The smile and joy that she saw yesterday, as well as the glint in her eyes were nothing more than memories. As she looked at her naked body, she realized the bandages had held the bleeding at bay. Blood only slightly seeped through and had clearly stopped at some point during the night.

Slowly removing her bandages to examine her wounds, Kai once again felt fortunate to be kneeling here at all, whether it was in pain or not. She lightly dabbed the wounds to wash the dried-up blood away. She would definitely be left with scars, but that did not bother her. What did concern her was that she needed her right arm to fire her bow. With her arm torn up like this, she was uncertain whether she would still be able to handle her trusted weapon.

Leaving her worries behind, Kai walked into the water heading toward a portion near the middle that was deep enough for her to bathe in. The water felt wonderful on her body. Cool, but calm and gentle. After the night she had, calm and gentle was the best remedy she could think of.

As she lay in the water relaxing, she thought once more of the young blonde in her visions. At first she was desperate to get to her. Eldiir had indicated to the Triad that it was imperative to find the Chosen One, and that timing was of the essence. The frequent visions of her in danger were overwhelming. However, seeing the last vision, Kai's sense of urgency seemed to fade. After all, perhaps if she were not rushing so badly the night before, she would not be in her current predicament.

As one with a sense of duty, honor, and responsibility, relaxing like this when someone could be in trouble appalled her. How could she just be sitting here like this? Though she had no desire to leave the water, Kai got back out and returned to Lucky to finish her work.

With some food in her and a quick dip in the water, Kai was amazed at how quickly she was progressing after resuming her work on Lucky. She quickly had the bulk of her new outfit completed, and only had some minor adjustments to take care of. All in all, it took her a little over three hours to complete her task.

This time when Kai returned to the stream to look at her reflection, she was fully garbed in her new outfit. An outfit fitting of a warrior. Well, at least a hunter if not a warrior, but is a hunter not a form of warrior?

Kai had Lucky's head encompassing her upper body. He really was much larger than her, even his head. His forehead was just below her neck, having its eyes and upper portion of its face covering her injured breasts. His carnivorous mouth fit directly under her breasts and fit quite snugly with the rest of her features. While molding the features into a wardrobe, Kai made certain Lucky would always have his mouth opened in a roar of defiance, baring his fangs, as long as she was wearing it. Below Lucky's chin, Kai opted to leave her belly uncovered, revealing her fit and trim torso. The beautiful silvery mane covered her shoulders and hung down her back. Underneath, she also had fur from Lucky's hide covering her back as far down as she was covered on the front.

Kai used part of the skin to create a padded sleeve on her injured right arm. The fur protector was attached at the shoulder to the rest of the outfit, and trailed all the way down to her wrist. She hoped this would allow her to still fire her bow without the string rubbing against her injuries. Her left arm remained bare.

Visualizing the orcs from her visions, Kai opted to create some added melee weapons. She used the razor-sharp claws and created gloves that covered her hands, but not her fingers. Four claws on each hand were attached to the top of the gloves, so that if she were throwing a punch, the tips of the claws would extend and strike her opponent. The remaining claws she collected and put in a pouch that she made and hung over her waist. After all, if she ever were to lose or damage one, she wanted a replacement handy.

With the new portions of her outfit, her pants and boots no longer matched. She cut her pants down slightly and used portions as replacement bandages before she got dressed again. What she had left were shorts that she complemented by lacing leather from Lucky's hide onto the top, and had a streak trailing down the sides of her shorts.

Her elastic holder with throwing knives still went around her left leg, but now was against bare skin rather than fabric.

On her boots, she had cut some of the silvery mane and used it to add frill around the top of the boots. Purely decorative, but she wished for everything to flow together. She slid her dagger back into its casing on the inside of her left boot.

To finish off her new garb, she slung her pouch of arrows and bow over her shoulder and across her back. Finally ready, she picked up her new staff to help her walk along the journey. As she stared at her image in the water, she was amazed at how many changes one person could go through so quickly.

Before resuming her journey, Kai packed several more helpings of meat from Lucky for later consumption. She was finally ready. Physically weaker than she was a day before, but far stronger mentally. She looked out at the mountains in the south again, and whispered into the air, "Hold on, I am coming."

CHAPTER 25

"Come on, Nezbith!" Kyria dashed ahead of her friend up the hillside. She glanced back at Nezbith with a sinister smile and an overall feeling of freedom and excitement. A feeling that she seemed to have lacked since the night she had brought Nezbith home.

"Kyria, stop!" Nezbith reluctantly pursued Kyria. He really shouldn't be going up the hill. His father had always warned him never to leave the village. Yet, how could he let Kyria see him stay behind in fear of reprisal? Besides, his father often was away from home. He had to prove to himself that he was the equal of any man, and could do anything anyone else could do. Even if it was Kyria that he needed to best.

Kyria stopped and turned around to see Nezbith reluctantly climbing the hill again. In a burst of laughter, she goaded him. "Come on, Nezbith! Are you twelve or two? You're not going to let a girl beat you, are you?"

After she made the comment, she instantly regretted it. The bruise and scar where Guldan had hit his son still shone on Nezbith's right cheek. She knew, more than anyone, how bruised and battered Nezbith really was. She hoped that in the context of playfulness, he would not continue to despair.

That comment was the last straw. Nezbith sprinted after Kyria with anger in his eyes and blood boiling in his veins.

Seeing him charge after her, Kyria grinned and began her ascent once again as well. As she got to the top, she glanced around for a suitable hiding place, and quickly devised a plan for ambushing her friend.

The hills of Arkham consisted of steep slopes heading away from the main town toward the sea. The hills were covered with various obstacles that children enjoyed playing with, including fallen trees, ditches, large rocks, and grasses that easily came to a child's waist. The other side of the hill had far less of an incline, dropping off into the rocky shores and the waters beyond.

Due to the danger of the landscape, many parents scolded and chastised their children for wandering off and playing in the hills. There were numerous ways children could hurt themselves playing here, but that only increased the allure and desire to ascend to the top.

By the time Nezbith managed to reach the highest point of the hills, his lungs were gasping for breath. He quickly scanned the area, noting the view. From here, the small village looked like nothing more than a collection of toys. With the sight of the town, Nezbith again considered his father's reaction to his disobedient presence here. He wanted to find Kyria and convince her to return to the village with him. Where was she? If anything happened to her, he knew he would be in trouble. He was the man, the responsible one after all. He wondered why he always had to listen to her. "Kyria?"

Without warning, Kyria jumped from behind the boulder she had chosen as a hiding spot and tackled Nezbith. He fell screaming as she pinned him to the ground. He squirmed, trying to get her to let him go. Laughter was the only reaction he induced from Kyria.

"Stop it!"

"I can't help it. You look so hopeless. You're trying everything you can think of. It won't work," Kyria boasted triumphantly. "That's it. When we get older, I'll go out and do the manly things. You can stay home, cook, clean, and raise the kids!"

Nezbith kept struggling with his laughing friend. His anger was beginning to grow for the shots at his birthright. Defiantly, he screamed inside his own head. No girl could be superior to him. He was the boy. Nobody. Not Kyria, not anyone!

As quickly as her attack began, it ended. She stood up and looked down at him. Though she was acting playful, deep down, she hoped to have this time alone to talk to her friend.

With the onslaught ended, Nezbith dusted himself off and glared over at her in amazement that a girl bested him. His father would be most displeased. "I can't believe..."

"Come here. We have to talk."

Nezbith felt close to tears. Kyria was his best friend, but sometimes he felt like she walked all over him. At times, they'd play castle and pretend games. Kyria was always good at being the queen. She may not have been born to royalty, but she commanded others like people were destined to listen to only her.

At her beckoning, Nezbith crawled over to where she was sitting. He looked up at her desperately trying to control his emotions.

Kyria gazed down at their village and Nezbith was shocked to see a tear flowing down her cheek.

"What is it? What's wrong?" he inquired compassionately.

"I've been so frightened lately."

Nezbith just watched her intently. She had always been so strong for him, been there and seemed to know just what to do. He hoped he could return the favor and help her out now.

"I don't understand things that are happening."

"Like what?"

"Haven't you noticed strange things lately?" Kyria turned and watched his reaction.

Nezbith shook his head back and forth.

"No, of course not. You're too focused on trying to keep your father happy."

Nezbith turned away for a moment, thinking again of how much trouble he would be in for being up here. It didn't matter. He looked back at Kyria. "Why don't you tell me what has been strange then?"

Kyria stood up and pointed toward the mountains. "Can you feel the darkness?"

Nezbith studied her but wasn't certain how to reply. How could one feel darkness? It was either light or dark. You couldn't feel it. "I don't understand."

"That place, it is evil. I can feel it. I have felt it. It's spreading."

"Spreading?"

Kyria then returned her gaze to the village below. "Yes. Spreading. To our own village."

"Arkham?" Nezbith gasped.

"The night I tucked you in, I heard your father speaking to a man who wasn't there. His voice sent shivers up my spine. I have never been so terrified in my life."

Nezbith pondered this for a minute. How could his father be speaking to someone who wasn't there? "Perhaps you imagined it."

"No," Kyria declared. She turned and stared at Nezbith. "Something was there, but it wasn't. The voice, it was pure evil. Since then, the entire town seems to have changed. Even my own parents."

"I still don't understand. What do you mean by changed?"

"Where did they go a few weeks ago? All the adults vanished, leaving us alone to fend for ourselves. When they came back, they seemed mad. Some were covered in blood. Everyone wanted to celebrate and get drunk. Doesn't that seem odd?"

Nezbith agreed the behavior was odd. His father often went out fishing for days at a time with his older brothers and other members of the crew. Yet, never had he seen all the adults leave before. He also had never seen the entire town consume as much alcohol as they did last night. He truly feared that his father would come in and beat him senseless, but he did not return home.

In quiet contemplation, Kyria walked to the edge and sat on a large rock to look out at the sea. What she saw shocked her. The bay was full of ships, large warships. "Nezbith, come here."

Nezbith walked over to see what caught her attention this time. When he saw the ships, he froze. Alarmed, he looked at his friend for insight and guidance. "What are they doing there?"

With a sigh, she turned and shrugged her shoulders.

There were twelve warships in all, Imperial Gallies. They all displayed a white flag with black slashes and two emerald eyes in the middle. The flags were the symbol the Empress used.

Kyria had never even seen Imperial troops before. As they navigated the harbor and dropped smaller rafts with troops and equipment, she was impressed with the speed and efficiency of the coming party.

"I don't like this" Nezbith whined. "Let's go home and forget we even saw anything."

Kyria shook her head. "A little longer. What can they do to us from down there?" The answer was rather simple, even Nezbith knew that. On the peak of the hills, they were lying down in the grass behind some rocks, and it certainly hid them sufficiently. In fact, even if somebody was on the hill with them, they could hide for hours without being found. Several children had learned of this when they were scolded and hoped to avoid further punishment.

Watching the troops reach the shores, Kyria knew this arrival did not bode well for the people of Arkham. She was certain the disappearance and strange behavior of the adults was the direct cause of their arrival.

As the troops disembarked, Nezbith's eyes bulged out. "We need to leave. Now!" The desperation and fear in his voice were clearly evident to Kyria.

Kyria finally agreed. Even though people were acting oddly, they were still her friends and family. She hoped to rush down the hills and warn them. "Okay, let's go warn everyone."

Both children stood up and sprinted back toward the village. To her surprise, Nezbith was in the lead this time and continued to increase his pace all the way back home.

CHAPTER 26

As the lead boat approached the shore, Lord Braksis glanced at his forces with admiration and approval. After hearing of the destruction of Loveskia, his forces had to move quickly to organize for this operation. Even after recently returning from the Dartian plains, his men were well organized and in good spirits. They truly were professional and in his opinion, the best troops he could ever hope for.

The boat dug into the ground at the beachfront and Braksis allowed his momentum to carry him out of the boat and onto the ground in front of him. He carefully scanned and methodically searched the land for any sign of life that could hinder his forces' ascent. He and Admiral Morex specifically chose the bay rather than the harbor so that they might be able to hide their forces and surprise their foes. The element of surprise could often be the decisive factor in a battle.

At the top of the hill, a brief reflection of light caught his eye. Somebody had seen them. No use masking their approach. Surprise was no longer on their side. He was disappointed, but knew that it wouldn't matter once the barrage commenced.

The next out of the boat was Solara. She walked up beside him and followed his gaze to the hillside. "You saw it, too?"

Without so much as a glance back or reply, Braksis let out two low whistles, and was joined by his faithful timber wolf. Tiot, too, scanned the beachfront with his heightened lupine senses, looking for signs of life.

As the remaining transports came to shore, Braksis raised his right hand and waived with two fingers. Pauslo, a representative of the Empress stepped forward upon his beckon. Though Braksis, Morex, and Sarlec pleaded with Karleena to remain behind, she was adamant about coming in person and seeing the events firsthand. As such, her representative would be the first to go to Arkham and try to settle this matter without unnecessary violence or destruction. Perhaps the guilty parties would surrender and this would all end quickly. Braksis sincerely doubted that. This day would not end without bloodshed.

"Karleena hopes to avoid a battle. Go forth and offer them the chance to surrender. Let them know that they face Lord Braksis and the entire might of her Majesties forces. Bring me their response."

Pauslo nodded. He knew the Empress's wishes in this regard. The people of Arkham had attacked and slaughtered a nearby farming village without cause or reprieve. The few survivors said the men had their way with the women and young children before crucifying everyone and burning both the people and village. The Empress was outraged, and demanded swift justice, though she did not wish for more innocents to suffer. Actions like this would no longer transpire in her Imperium. However, the name Braksis often could dispel opponents without an ounce of bloodshed spilt. A public reckoning would be just as acceptable as raising the village, yet there would be no further property damage. Enough had been destroyed already.

Pauslo headed over to one of the transports that carried the horses and mounted up. Before he left, he scanned the forces that were amassed disembarking and regrouping on the shore. The sea of troops flowing toward the shores with thoughts on justice and retribution in their minds. An example would be set, but who would be foolish enough to resist the Imperial forces led by Lord Braksis?

As Pauslo trotted off, Braksis approached the raft that carried the artillery. "The catapults should be set up over there." As he pointed, the troops acknowledged his orders and brought out the equipment to set up. From the spot he indicated, they could fire into Arkham itself. He paused for one last moment and hoped these weapons of destruction would not need to be deployed.

❖ ❖ ❖ ❖ ❖

Aboard the Imperial flagship, *Reliance,* Admiral Morex observed the troops disembarking through his optical enhancers, a device he designed years ago during the Great Wars. The enhancers utilized glass and light to enlarge objects that one was viewing and make it appear closer. Morex always prided himself with the magnificence of his armada and the troops of the Imperium. Times had certainly changed since he first met a young man named Conrad and they dreamt of ways to change the world.

He heard the creaking of the boards on deck, and spoke without so much as a backward glance. "It will all be over soon, my lady."

Empress Karleena walked over to stand next to Morex. To oversee these events, she opted to wear a simpler outfit than she normally would be seen in. She had on a light gray blouse with slightly darker pants. To cover that, she also donned a black cloak to symbolize remorse at the losses that the Imperium had felt, and those they were about to feel. Even without her normal royal attire, she still maintained a poise and air of leadership about her. "I was unaware you knew I came on deck, Admiral."

Standing on his bridge, Morex looked so old to her. She would always remember him as he was when she had been younger, but the years were beginning to take their toll. For as long as she knew him, he always wore his Imperial uniform with pride. "My lady, I have commanded this fleet for you and your father before you. I have designed most of the ships in the fleet, and handpicked all of my officers. I know every squeak and shudder, every whisper and curse that occurs on these ships. I do, and always will, know where you are while you are aboard any of my vessels."

Karleena smiled at the man and his sentiment. She always felt protected when he was around. Lowering her eyes, she spoke of matters of more relevance. "Morex, shall we claim victory today?" Instinctively, she knew the answer to her question without stating the words out loud. Very few could hope to confront the Imperium and claim victory. The forces that were amassed against them were immense. This thought constantly troubled her since so many seemed to be rebelling of late.

With a small shrug, Morex looked his Empress in the eye. "Aye, we shall claim victory today." With that Morex went back to the optical enhancers, then slowly spoke. "Of course, it would be best if Pauslo is successful. It will not be easy to return to Trespias and claim to be the champion of the people if you have just slaughtered them."

Karleena allowed the words to sink in. They made sense. She was still so young. Perhaps she was being impetuous with her order of justice for this raid. Yet, the people of Arkham attacked without warning. The atrocities they committed could not be excused. Though King Sarlec personally went to Loveskia to see the damage, Karleena shuddered at the images he would be confronted with. She may be young, but she would not sway in her path. “I understand what you are saying, Admiral, and respect your thoughts. Your guidance has always been appreciated. Still, I feel that swift retribution would be required so that other nations do not continue to revolt as well.”

“To sway a revolt, my lady, is admirable. However, you are facing many large issues yourself of late. You fought to bring the voice of the people to Trespias. Now, you may begin to fight to bring the voice of the races to Trespias. Both plans will be opposed. You must choose your battles and allies well.”

“Do you feel I am trying to change too much too soon?”

“It is not how I regard your decisions. After all, I fought to change the whole world with your father. Still, it would behoove you to be cautious. You will have much opposition, then incidents like today may increase.”

Karleena breathed deeply before responding. “Are you telling me not to proceed? To try to gain the support of others rather than making executive decisions?”

“If what Lord Braksis said is true, time is a luxury we may not have. I am merely helping you to see the road you are about to embark upon.”

Karleena contemplated his words, and knew that she would have to walk this dangerous path. Things were changing rapidly, and she needed to make sure they changed in a way that would protect her people the most. If that meant placing her in danger, or making decisions that were unfavorable, then she would sacrifice herself for the greater good.

CHAPTER 27

Pauslo approached the village of Arkham slowly with anticipation. The closer he got the more armed villagers he observed. A whole army was lying in wait in this village instead of mere fishermen. This may not be as one-sided as they all felt. There was definitely something more going on here than a border dispute or a brutal raid. Yet, he knew the might that opposed this ragtag group, and remained confident that the Imperium's forces would reign supreme.

A tall muscular man stepped out of a small building and glared at Pauslo. He was wearing only leather pants, with no shirt to cover his bulging muscles. In his hand was a double-sided battle-axe. "Halt where you are."

Pauslo obeyed without question. He was already treading in dangerous waters as it was. No use antagonizing the people he was about to inform of their death sentence. "I am a representative of Her Majesty Empress Karleena's Imperial forces. I am speaking on behalf–"

"Enough!" roared the warrior. "I am Guldan, and I say that we don't acknowledge any empire that is led by a wee babe!"

Sweat flowed from Pauslo's bald scalp. He timidly searched the faces of the villagers around him, and once again offered the terms of surrender. "We are here under the command of Lord Braksis and will offer you this one chance to surrender."

Guldan erupted with laughter. "Surrender?"

Pauslo slowly backed up to leave. "Yes, surrender. If you do not, Lord Braksis will march on your village and leave none standing, as you yourselves have recently done to Loveskia." He made an emphasis of defiance on the last part of his offer. "At least consider the women and children."

Guldan allowed a smile to cross his lips. "If none shall remain standing, at least you will not be here to see it."

Fear instantly rushed into Pauslo's eyes. He turned his mare around and kicked her sides to escape. Guldan whirled his axe over his head and sent it hurling through the air at the messenger. The blow knocked him right off of his horse and he landed on the ground in agony.

Pauslo tried to move; he felt tired and wet. He tried to open his eyes, but everything was black. He knew that he must get up and warn Braksis of the army lying in wait. That he must complete his mission. Pauslo continued to try to move but was overwhelmed by the darkness, then came the cold. Chills deep to the core. A shining light pierced the darkness, and Pauslo unexpectedly felt warm again, a sense of hope. He opened his eyes one last time, and was engulfed by light.

Guldan walked over to the lifeless body and retrieved his axe. "Terms of the agreement denied." He raised the bloody axe into the air and screamed out for all to hear. "First blood is ours. Prepare for the onslaught." With that, Guldan returned to the building he had emerged from, as all present whooped and cheered.

❖ ❖ ❖ ❖ ❖

Nezbith and Kyria arrived back in the village just in time to see Guldan kill Pauslo. Nezbith couldn't believe what he saw. How could this be his father? So relentless and without honor? He attacked the rider from behind! Then again, these strangers were coming here. He convinced himself his father was probably just protecting the village. No use informing them of the fleet. Obviously they already knew. Why risk getting into any more trouble than need be?

As Nezbith slowed to a halt, Kyria frowned and looked at him. "Come on, Nezbith, we need to warn everyone."

"They already know. My father repelled the attack. We don't need to let them know we were playing in the hills."

Kyria glared at her friend, turned around, and ran into the village. Nezbith didn't understand these things, but she did. She must warn everyone of the scope of the attacking forces.

❖ ❖ ❖ ❖ ❖

Tiot let out a low growl and his hair stood on end. Lord Braksis looked down at the wolf and knew that something had gone wrong. Braksis focused on where Tiot was gazing and soon saw Pauslo's mount returning without him. He waited for one of his troops to rein in the horse before he said anything, but he already knew what choice the people of Arkham had made. This onslaught would go forth as planned.

As the soldier who collected the horse was tying it up, he spotted blotches of dark red blood. Pauslo would not be returning to them this campaign. "Lord Braksis, blood."

Braksis nodded to this report, then for the first time turned around to address his command staff. He only had two of his generals along with him for this battle. General Hinbar would command the infantry and oversee the majority of the land forces. General Lowred would be responsible for the catapults and archers. That would leave Braksis to personally command the cavalry.

Even without the rest of his command staff or forces, Braksis was confident they would be victorious this day. With everything that was transpiring of late, his forces would continue to dwindle in size and have to focus on various uprisings. This was the main reason he hoped Angel would be successful in her efforts to create a light-foot infantry. Though she desired to travel with him to Arkham, he ordered her to begin her travels and recruitment.

"Generals," Braksis addressed his men. "Options."

General Hinbar spoke up first. "Lord Braksis, this is my plan. We have lost the element of surprise that we had hoped for, but our adversary still does not know our true numbers. We could send the foot soldiers and heavy spear troops down the path to confront them, while the archers and crossbow troops scale the hills and attack from above. Your cavalry could travel down the beach and circle around the village, attacking when the time is right."

Braksis nodded to Hinbar, then turned to General Lowred.

"I believe that General Hinbar forgets the catapults my men are constructing. We have a decisive advantage by being able to barrage the village before sending in a single troop. The artillery shall be ready within the hour. Upon completion, I suggest the artillery send a constant barrage. My archers and crossbow units could ascend the hill as suggested, and attack from above. I agree with Hinbar in the deployment of the foot soldiers, heavy spear and cavalry. However, they should time their attack to coincide with the conclusion of the bombardment."

Braksis slowly stroked his goatee. "Very well. We shall go with your plan, General Lowred. Prepare for the bombardment. I hoped to spare the village and innocents, but reports did indicate the involvement of women on the raiding party. They did not surrender; therefore, we must show them the might of the Imperium."

Lowred nodded his assent. "Understood, my lord."

"General Hinbar, upon the cessation of the bombardment, you will advance the infantry. However, do not advance until you see the cavalry begin our attack."

Hinbar put his hand on Braksis's shoulder and then looked over to Lowred. "Just make sure that when we go in, you shoot the right troops."

Both Hinbar and Lowred shared a slight laugh. Lowred had always been efficient and precise. He facilitated that in his troops as well.

"Prepare your troops and move out. The bombardment shall begin within the hour when you are ready, Lowred." With that, Lord Braksis stood up and headed to prepare his mount for the upcoming assault. Solara and Tiot were mere steps behind him. Soon they would be in battle. Soon they would be home.

CHAPTER 28

Guldan returned to his home in a rage. "Zoldex! Show yourself!"

As if in response, next to Guldan, an image appeared. The figure was almost transparent. He could look right through the cloaked apparition and see the wall behind him. Obviously an image, and not a physical presence. Dressed in long gray robes and a cloak, the apparition revealed nothing about his true identity.

"Zoldex, you fool! You told us that we would have your protection. That the Empress would not be able to retaliate! What is this? Where is our protection?"

The image flickered slightly, then spoke. "The Empress's involvement was inevitable. I offered my assistance and guidance and you have it. You should not have raped and butchered women and children."

"What? You hold me responsible for the indiscretions of a few of my men?"

"A leader is always responsible for his men, Guldan." This transparent figure of the one called Zoldex revealed little, but obviously maintained command of the situation. Guldan was loud, angry, and reckless. Zoldex was calm, cool, and collected.

Guldan was increasing in his agitation. "I did as you ordered, now protect me!"

The image of Zoldex dimmed for a second, then he nodded. "Very well. Although you brought the Empress's wrath upon yourself, even this is as I have foreseen. I shall help you." Zoldex gestured with his right hand, and although he was not physically there, Guldan's axe brightened into a blinding light. Guldan was forced to look away from the illumination, then it gradually dimmed back as if nothing happened. "Your axe has been augmented. It is now unbreakable and can carve any substance with ease."

Although Guldan did not understand all that Zoldex was saying about this impending battle being foreseen, he was appeased by his weapon's newfound invulnerability. This would be a great battle indeed. Bring on Lord Braksis. With the indestructible Carnage by his side, he felt nobody could stop him now.

❖ ❖ ❖ ❖ ❖

As Kyria ran through the streets looking for her parents, she was shocked by all of the weapons being prepared. She had warned the village of the ships, and they entrenched themselves for the impending assault. Yet, why would anybody want to attack a peaceful village? Even after Kyria thought this, she glanced around and began to question it. If their village was so peaceful, why were there so many weapons? Once again she questioned where everyone had gone a few weeks earlier and the sense of darkness she could feel encompassing them all.

Nezbith jogged up to her all out of breath. "Kyria, we need to get inside!" he frantically pleaded with her.

Kyria frowned and looked back at Nezbith. "Coward. You'll probably run at the first sign of trouble. Like the little coward you are." Even with her quick jab, she noticed that all of the people had suddenly disappeared. They were hidden in little underground tunnels and trenches that recently had been devised. Perhaps her small village was anticipating this confrontation. That revelation sent a shiver through her spine. Who would purposefully want to oppose the Imperium? Perhaps her people were not the angels she saw through the innocent eyes of a child.

Nezbith had had enough. Why in times like this did Kyria always find it necessary to goad him? In his brief moment of anger, he shoved her aside. As she fell, dirt and trees erupted around him. What was that?

Nezbith wiped some blood off of his cheek and nose. Some of the shrapnel had slashed his face. Where was Kyria? Did he cause this? Where was she?

More explosions erupted around the streets and buildings. Trees splintered and structures caught ablaze. Nezbith could not grasp how this was happening. Large spheres of flaming death roared overhead. Those who had not found shelter were screaming in panic and chaos in the streets.

Focusing again, Nezbith spied his friend Kyria. Her body was lying still by a crater, right where he pushed her!

The screams and confusion increased. Kyria was dead. It's all my fault; Nezbith repeated in his head. The blame was easily taken. He felt responsible for everything. He didn't warn his father of the ships. He gave in to his anger and pushed Kyria to her death. This was entirely his fault.

The barrage continued while tears flowed down Nezbith's cheeks. As he looked around, life began to slow down. The people running for cover seemed to be moving at a turtle's pace. Even the debris flying through the sky slowed to a near halt as they continued to impact structures. Buildings were ablaze. Villagers lying dead in the street. Others screaming with limbs violently severed from their bodies.

Nezbith couldn't take the screaming and death any longer. Guilt was overpowering him. He turned and sprinted out of the village, never looking back, his thoughts plagued by remorse and regret. He could only visualize the blood and death. No matter how far or fast he ran, the images stayed with him. Then the guilt set in, knowing that he refrained from warning the villagers, and also how he pushed Kyria. Guilt that threatened to overwhelm and consume him.

❖ ❖ ❖ ❖ ❖

Lord Braksis quietly watched the onslaught of the village. Seeing so much death and destruction, all at his hands, he plotted the next portion of the assault devoid of emotion. At one time, he was born to royalty, and the activities commencing below him would be atrocious. Now, he was numb to the devilry of the world, and accepted its many faces. This cold brutality made him both respected and feared throughout the Seven Kingdoms.

The artillery was continuing the barrage with cold efficiency. The air quickly became swarmed with arrows. Soon, it would be time to advance. To move in and stop watching death from above, and actually bring the cold grasp of the ever after to people personally. Looking into their eyes, and watching the light dim. His job was so much more personal.

Braksis looked at his troops. This mounted cavalry would be more than sufficient to handle whatever was left behind in the village of Arkham. However, the infantry would also be marching on the small village. Upon their ascent, there truly would be no chance for the rebels left behind. Braksis hoped to avoid prolonging this day and finish things personally.

Suddenly, the barrage of arrows ceased, and a single flaming arrow pierced the sky. The time had come. The people below would know what it means to attack the Imperium, and feel the wrath of its greatest warlord.

❖ ❖ ❖ ❖ ❖

On board the *Reliance,* Admiral Morex scanned the eyes of the young Empress. In them, he saw the strength and vitality of his old friend, as well as innocence. An innocence that was quickly being stolen from her. This he regretted immensely. Old leaders and warriors like himself, and even the empire's fist, Lord Braksis, were more than enough to handle affairs such as the uprising of Arkham. To actually have Karleena here was something he hoped would not scar her permanently.

"Admiral," Karleena softly addressed her trusted advisor while watching the glitter on the horizon where flames dashed toward the stars. "It's a pity."

Without commenting, Morex continued to watch the Empress, allowing her to state whatever she was thinking. Patience, after all, was a virtue.

"From here, it is so lovely. The fire illuminating the night sky. The reflections in the water." Karleena paused as she continued to study the view. "A pity that on the other side, all there is, is death and destruction."

"Perhaps it is time to leave, my lady." Morex headed toward the bridge to help save his Empress from witnessing any more. It was enough to know there was death and destruction. There was no need to witness it any further.

Sternly, Karleena objected. "No, Admiral." Shaking her head, as a single tear formed in her right eye, Karleena stood and approached Morex. "If I do not witness, I will not see. If I do not see, then this is destined to happen again in the future. I will not allow that to happen."

Morex nodded his assent and understanding. To keep her innocent would be preferable, but she was right. Those who do not learn from history are destined to repeat it.

"Admiral."

"Yes, my lady?"

"Upon our return to the palace, I wish to seek an audience with the Council of Elders."

Admiral Morex found himself intrigued, and a little shocked as well. The Council of Elders were the inner voices of the Mage's Council. This organization had been designed thousands of years ago in an attempt to bring magic to the world. Any who had mystical potential were separated at birth and brought within the walls of the tower for tutoring in the ways of the mystical arts. However, after years of offering to assist the land as advisors, consultants, or arbitrators, they declared they would never again become involved with politics external to their own beliefs.

"I wish to seek their divine guidance to help assure that something like this will not happen again. Also, I see no way to bring the races back together without their help. The races will not trust us." Karleena stopped watching the illuminated shores for the first time to search for a reaction in Morex. She could not glean much from the pure professionalism he constantly displayed as his outer armor. "What say you of this, Admiral?"

A slight sigh, a momentary pause, then Morex addressed her concerns. "My lady, it is true the races do not trust humans, and with good reason. The Race Wars were difficult, and humans were cruel. As I have advised before, this is a necessary step, you will be met with much resistance."

"All the more reason to have a neutral party that is respected by all. Upon our return, please contact Mage Master Jeffa. He fought alongside you and my father, and I feel would be our best contact to get me in to address the Council."

"As you wish, my lady. I certainly could contact Jeffa for you. Though he alone may not be able to gain that which you desire."

"Yes, Admiral. I know that I must convince the Council of Elders themselves. I am desperate to do so. I shall not fail." The conviction in her voice was quite convincing to Morex.

"I shall support whatever decision you make, my lady, as always." In his peripheral vision, Morex saw the single flaming arrow pierce the sky. The signal for Braksis to advance. He turned and walked toward the edge of the bridge. "It will be all over soon, my lady. You should prepare yourself to disembark."

CHAPTER 29

At the sign of the flaming arrow, the cavalry stormed out of the hills down toward the burning village below. Bodies could be seen in the glimmering of the fire, lying throughout the village. This indeed was truly a tragic campaign.

As the horses galloped through the bodies, the troops had little to do. The charge had ended with no resistance. Lord Braksis signaled for everyone to spread out and search for survivors. He doubted the battle would conclude itself only with the initial volley. There had to be warriors somewhere, lying in wait, hoping to lull the Imperial forces into a false sense of security.

Braksis dismounted and approached the body of a young girl. This was the greatest tragedy. The death of an innocent. One who was so young, fragile, and vulnerable. He noticed the crater where the shrapnel had landed, sending iron death to those in the vicinity, including this young girl lying face down in the dirt. As Braksis leaned down to turn her over, screams pierced the quiet of the night. The battle was not yet won.

❖ ❖ ❖ ❖ ❖

Guldan led his men out of the trenches and charged the unsuspecting cavalry. He knew he had them. They had been taken in by the slaughter at their own hands and were weakened by it. His own men simply grew angrier while looking around. He grinned as he realized the potential of this information. His fellow villagers would fight with passion, not despair. They would each be worth several Imperial troops. He spotted Braksis in the distance and smiled, thinking this would be a night that would be written throughout history. The night when one man managed to bring down an empire.

Guldan raised his axe high, and roared a piercing wail as he approached the closest soldier. The soldier, who had blood smeared on his outfit as he was trying to find survivors, quickly pulled his sword and stood in a defensive posture.

Guldan grasped the axe with both hands and swung down with the mighty blade. The soldier, well experienced in his own right, quickly raised his blade to block the assault. Guldan savored the look of terror in the soldier's eyes as the axe cut through the sword like butter, and met little resistance as it ripped the life out of the soldier.

Smiling triumphantly, Guldan let out another piercing wail. Zoldex had told the truth. His blade was all-powerful. Let all beware. Guldan would have his share of kills across his blade this day.

Two soldiers approached him as he cheered in triumph. Guldan glared at them and offered a smirk. Challenge offered and accepted. Both fell with one swing of the mystically altered Carnage.

Guldan twirled his axe above his head and screamed to his neighbors. "Leave none standing!"

CHAPTER 30

The warriors of Arkham began the assault, taking the cavalry by surprise. This angered Lord Braksis, and also made him realize he, too, had faltered this day. Something he must contemplate when it was over.

"To your horses!" The command was given, but he watched as villagers poured out of the ground and burning buildings. The cavalry would have to fight this battle on the ground. Braksis only hoped that his dismounted troops could hold out until Hinbar arrived with the ground forces.

Braksis rushed forward toward the bulk of his troops and tried to restore order as they were attacked. The villagers' assault was brutal and unrelenting. "Form a defensive perimeter!"

A woman jumped up onto Braksis and knocked him backward. As they fell, she held onto his neck with one hand, then tried to gouge his eyes out with the other. Dropping his sword, he held onto her arms.

The woman released her grip and tried to claw his face with both hands. He was amazed at her strength. Her fingers were getting closer to his skin. A deranged smile upon her face.

Braksis raised his legs and wrapped them around her shoulders, then kicked as hard as he could, sending her spiraling off of him. Grabbing the Phoenix, he stood up and prepared to defend himself, but the woman had already run off to find a potentially easier adversary.

Looking to regain his bearings, he witnessed a larger group approaching him. Glancing sideways, he knew he was separated and alone. He found it odd that he was facing large numbers of attackers, and for the first time in years, Solara was not by his side.

Quickly counting and sizing up his opponents he deduced that he was facing at least nine warriors. A challenge indeed, but one he should be able to handle. He mentally selected the order that he wished to tackle them, determining which ones seemed to be more dangerous.

As the first opponent approached, Braksis had to laugh. To gang up on him was strategically smart. But to then separate and face him one at a time? A foolish endeavor.

His first opponent was slightly larger than Braksis in height, and wielded a mace. No subtlety at all in his approach. Overconfident in his size and the group's numbers, he merely charged Braksis.

Braksis raised his sword, and stood ready for the oncoming confrontation. The warrior ran in as Braksis, with lightning-like reflexes, sidestepped and tripped him. The warrior ended up with a face full of dirt and blood, which was flowing like a stream throughout the village by now. He roared in rage as he got up, and noticed that Braksis had already moved on to another foe.

The second attacker moved in to the side with a sideswipe of his sword. Braksis easily parried and landed a fist on his face, sending him reeling away with a broken nose.

To his left, a third warrior announced his assault with the crack of a whip. Braksis turned as the whip came dangerously close to his face. Braksis reacted by grabbing the whip, and quickly yanking the attacker toward him. The unbalanced attacker stumbled into Braksis, who used him as a shield against another attacker who had thrown a knife chest high. The whip bearer showed an expression of shock as the blade pierced his back, and slowly slid down the Warlord to the ground.

Braksis responded by removing the knife from the dead man and sending it back toward the man who threw it. Still shocked by the fact that he killed his friend instead of his target, the knife thrower did nothing to defend himself, allowing the blade to pierce his chest and slowly seep the life out of him. Two down, seven to go.

The original attacker jumped up and hoped to catch Braksis off guard. Braksis twirled his sword and faced another attacker, who wielded a sword himself. Without even looking, Braksis stopped twirling his blade, and jutted it back between his body and arm, surprising the original attacker with a stomach wound. Braksis then pulled the blade up, and immediately sent it spinning around, blocking an attack from the swordsman. A quick slice up, then down, and he had the swordsman disarmed, with a wound sliced across his chest. Four down, five to go.

The remaining attackers were amazed at how quickly their numbers were falling. They realized who their opponent was, but to see him so quickly take the life out of their friends and neighbors' eyes was uncanny. The sense of safety in numbers was quickly abandoning them.

As for Lord Braksis, a small smile crept onto his face. This battle reminded him of a game with young children. How they always broke up and never fought in unison. He could just keep circling around, keeping them off balance, then taking them out of the fight one at a time.

The last five decided to be a little more cautious. They did not barge right in, but attempted to anticipate Lord Braksis's next move. However, Braksis would not give in. He stared them down with a cold glare of the fate they knew would soon come. As soon as that thought was realized, their own fear and dread at facing this opponent would be their undoing. This, too, added to Braksis's advantage.

Impatience crept in, and two of the attackers decided to advance in unison. Braksis dropped to his knees spinning, and severed both men's legs at the knees. As they collapsed to the ground, their shrieks of pain took the fight out of their three remaining comrades. The newly crippled warriors lay there on the ground, and the remaining three turned and fled.

As Braksis watched the final three flee, he glimpsed Solara in battle with a few opponents of her own. She was attempting to advance, slowly but surely, toward the roaring Guldan, who single-handedly was cutting down the forces under Braksis's command. Braksis took a deep breath, put the two fallen warriors out of their misery with one sword stroke to each, then advanced to face Guldan.

❖ ❖ ❖ ❖ ❖

Separated from Braksis when the initial attack commenced, Solara quickly attacked on her own. Tiot, too, had been separated and stayed close to her. She desperately wished to be by Braksis's side, but knew he was more than capable of handling himself.

The attack initially left the cavalry unorganized and on the defensive. However, their superior training quickly gave them the upper hand. When General Hinbar arrived with his troops, the Arkham rebels were quickly crumbling before the Imperium.

Solara paused as a triumphant roar pierced the night. She looked for the source and saw a warrior wielding an axe. In a berserker rage, he stormed through the Imperial troops swinging his axe at any who got close. All that were unfortunate enough to come near him fell to their deaths.

Knowing this man was the most dangerous one on the battlefield, Solara slowly made her way toward him. Several villagers had other ideas, but her speed, reflexes, and mystral training allowed her to dance around their attempts and dispel them quickly.

Only two villagers stood in her way as the man with the axe spun around and killed several of the Imperial troops in a circular motion. The two before Solara charged. She took two steps and jumped into the air. She closed her legs and arms tightly to her body and sailed between them, extending her two mystral drantanas and severing their heads before landing behind them.

Solara looked up and saw her foe before her. He had not yet realized that she was there as he plunged his axe into another Imperial troop. Removing one of her small throwing blades, she sent it toward the warrior's head, where it slashed his left cheek.

Guldan roared in pain and fury, and instantly sought to return the favor in kind to the thrower of the blade. Before him stood a woman. As Guldan stared at her, he instantly decided not to kill her. This female would be his prize. After slaughtering his foes, he would bed her and make her his slave.

Guldan's mouth nearly watered as he looked her over. "You think you have what it takes to best me, whore?"

Solara defiantly looked back at Guldan, and broadened her smile. She was going to enjoy this.

"You like the idea of being my whore. When this is all done, I will show you what it means to be my whore!"

With what hardly seemed like motion at all, Solara unlatched four more blades from the holster on her right leg and sent them hurtling toward Guldan. As his eyes widened with disbelief, he motioned his axe to attempt to block them. The blades, however, were only decoys as Solara jump-kicked and brought her foot down with immense force on Guldan's unprotected torso.

Guldan faltered in pain. The kick, as well as two of the blades, landed accurately, and his vision of invincibility waned. As he looked up, he had mere seconds before Solara was upon him again and attempting to end this confrontation with one quick slice of her blade.

As he rolled out of the way, Solara's sword dug into the ground where Guldan's head was. As a warrior born and bred, she immediately anticipated his move, spun around on her blade, and planted another kick into Guldan's side as he was desperately attempting to flee.

Guldan collapsed with the pain, and cursed Zoldex for making his axe invulnerable and not him.

Solara saw the advantage and lunged at Guldan once more. This time, the side of her hand connected with Guldan's windpipe, causing him to wheeze and gasp. As Guldan fell, he attempted to swipe her legs out from under her, but she jumped out of the way and landed another kick into his manhood.

Blood flowed out of Guldan's mouth. Agony was the only sensation he could feel, until he heard his attacker mock him. "How do you like your whore now, eh?" The fury began to build in Guldan. He would not be bested by a woman.

With this newfound strength and anger, Guldan grabbed his axe and swung viciously at Solara. As he did so, she kept retreating back step-by-step.

She had seen what he did to the troops earlier. The axe had some kind of strange abilities. It appeared to be able to cut through anything. Solara was not certain that even with her advanced prowess, she would be able to dodge his blows forever. That is why she attempted to keep him off balance and end things quickly. Then for the first time in this confrontation, fear crept into her eyes. Fear and doubt. Both elements instantly appearing as she fell backward, tripping over a fallen horse from the initial raid.

As she lay there on the ground, in a completely indefensible posture, Guldan let out a light bellow and went to end this confrontation and move on. She succeeded in hurting him, and though he wanted her for his bed, he craved the satisfaction of the kill even more.

Solara stared into his eyes waiting for the entry into oblivion, defying it until the end. Then she heard her master, and knew her course in life was far from over.

CHAPTER 31

Kai found traveling to be much slower now, but she could see that she was making definite progress. Her new staff was quite handy, and she quickly found herself adapting to it. She had seen the smoke trailing into the sky and knew her destination was close. By all estimations, at her current rate of progress, Kai would make it there just before nightfall. Odds of finding the girl from her vision were not in her favor, but Kai remained optimistic.

Her senses alert, she saw some rustling in the grasses ahead. Something was definitely coming. By the sounds of it, whatever it was certainly was not predatory or feral. This time she had no warning signs or indications of danger. Rather, she received the distinct impression that whatever was approaching her, was crying.

A few minor adjustments and Kai put herself directly in the path of whatever was rushing toward her. All she had to do now was wait. As the rustling gradually approached, she braced herself and prepared to move quickly if need be.

True to her senses, what was approaching was not anything adversarial, but rather a young redheaded boy. A boy who clearly showed signs of extensive crying and fatigue.

As the boy came upon Kai, his eyes widened in sudden shock and terror of what was facing him. His tears released into a short scream, and he attempted to run in the opposite direction from the waiting Kai. Perhaps, Kai considered, it wasn't her that frightened him, but rather the suit of the creature she was garbed in.

As the boy turned to run, Kai quickly jabbed her new staff out and tripped him. He looked up at her with sudden dread in his eyes, and she could see he did not expect to survive this encounter.

Attempting to lose any appearance of intimidation, Kai crouched down and moved her staff away from his legs. "My name is Kai." Watching the boy closely, constantly gazing into his eyes, she looked for some sign that he understood. "I will not hurt you."

The boy slitted his eyes in a dubious glare. Was this creature truly no threat? Fatigue hit him. His lungs ready to burst, his only response was filled with gasping and desperate attempts to fill his lungs with air.

Kai continued to watch him, then decided that perhaps a little distance would make the boy feel more at ease. Allow him to let his guard down. At the worst, all he could do was run away again. She knew he had no weapons. If he did run, what did she lose other than a few minutes of her journey?

She stood up and walked away. Pausing after several steps, still keeping her back to him, she spoke softly. "What is your name, young one?"

Not truly expecting an answer, she listened intently to his breathing. Although her back was to him, she knew precisely where he was and what he was doing. She even heard him pick up a rock, and would know the instant he decided that she was indeed a threat.

Without moving, she continued to try to get the young redheaded boy to speak. "Not much for talking, are you? That's okay. You've been running. Why not catch your breath? We can talk soon."

Still not moving, Kai could hear that the boy dropped the rock. He must have somehow determined she was not the threat that he anticipated. She also noted his breathing eased a little.

"Nezbith," he wheezed.

Kai turned around to look at the boy. "What was that?"

"Nezbith. That's my name." The words came slowly. Nezbith still had not caught his breath, but Kai managed to understand him.

"Well, Nezbith, what made you run so fast?" Nezbith turned his head away. Apparently he was not yet ready to answer all of her questions.

Kai reached into her pouch and pulled out some of the meat remaining from her encounter with Lucky. "Nezbith, are you hungry?"

To this, Nezbith's eyes widened, and without any formality, he lunged at the food in her hand, grabbed it, and quickly inhaled the leftover meat.

"I guess that means you are hungry, eh, young one?" Kai smiled as she watched the boy eating as if he had not touched food in days. "Would you like some more?"

Nezbith slowed his chewing and looked her straight in the face. "You have more?"

Kai let out a low chuckle and smiled right back at him. "I wouldn't have offered if I didn't."

"Yes, please."

"Well then, why not find some kindling and we'll heat some up—have a real meal?"

Nezbith jumped up looking like all fatigue was suddenly gone. "You bet!" With his quick reply, he was jogging around with his head to the ground looking for loose branches. As he did so, Kai removed a larger portion of the remaining meat and placed it on another arrow. It had been a few hours since she rested and ate. Perhaps she could get some information from this boy to help her on her quest.

By the time she finished preparing the meat, she noticed that Nezbith was back with an armful of small branches and logs. "Will these do, ma'am?"

Kai nodded an affirmative. "Put them right over there. I'll light it." Nezbith quickly complied, and Kai had the fire raging in a matter of minutes.

With the thought of food on his mind, Nezbith became much friendlier and open-mouthed. Rather than having to force information out of him, he became a well filled with information. He also asked a fair share of questions himself.

"I've never seen a pink lady before."

Kai continued to turn the meat over the fire as she replied. "Where I come from, all of my people are pink."

"Really? You must be from far away then."

Kai stared down for a minute, remembering her home and her people. Yes, she was far away from home. She nodded slightly. "Yes. I am." A tone of sorrow entered her voice, but if Nezbith picked up on it, he showed no signs of comprehension.

The young boy was an enigma. In one minute, he was frightened and timid. The next he seemed like he had betrayed the world. When calmed down, he was pleasant, polite, well mannered, and full of life. Something must have happened to make him so timid so quickly. The bruise on his right cheek also caught her attention. Determined to learn more about the girl in her vision, Kai opted to try to confront Nezbith about her.

"Nezbith?"

Chewing happily on his meal, Nezbith answered with his mouth full. "Yes, ma'am?"

Looking at him and wondering how to best ask the question without frightening him, she took a long breath and let out a sigh. The truth was always the best approach. "I have been having dreams." Pausing to confirm that she had his attention, she watched his eyes closely. "Dreams about a young girl. A girl your age."

Although he did not hear any more than that, he seemed to become a little more anxious. Suddenly he appeared uneasy and started fidgeting. It was as if he did not want to be there anymore. She wondered what he could be hiding that would agitate him this badly?

"The young girl has beautiful blonde hair and is full of life."

Nezbith stood up. The look across his face was filled with a contradiction of sorrow and shock. It was as if he saw a ghost before him, but also felt like his accusers were facing him. Kai suddenly had become that accuser.

"Nezbith. Are you okay?"

He backed up slowly. Step by step. No answer was forthcoming.

Kai watched in silent disbelief. Something was seriously bothering this boy, but she felt she would not learn any answers this day. She obviously had approached him wrong, and any action to restrain him would set back any progress she had made toward gaining his trust and cooperation. "Do you know this girl?"

That was the final question that she could ask. As soon as she did, Nezbith turned and ran away again. The boy was clearly troubled. A pity she could not have done more for him than fill his belly. However, this had all taken her away from her true quest. Her reason for being here. It was not a small redheaded boy, but rather a small blonde-haired girl.

Kai recovered her belongings. With one last look in the direction that Nezbith ran, she shook her head and resumed her journey toward the smoke-filled sky in the south.

❖ ❖ ❖ ❖ ❖

As Nezbith ran away, he could not believe what he had heard. Who was this Kai? She seemed to befriend him, to help him, to garner his trust. Yet she was his nemesis.

How could she know about Kyria? Oh sweet Kyria. His ultimate betrayal by allowing harm to come to her. Allowing her to fall to her death.

Death? Could that be who this Kai is? If not Death herself, then a messenger of the end of all that there is? That would explain the outfit she wore. The ferociousness of it. A defiant cry from a beast she had sent to her master. A warning to all others that their time, too, would come all too quickly.

As he ran, Nezbith started to convince himself that he just eluded the grasp of Death's thrall. If so, how much time did he really gain? Was it his time to die alongside his friend Kyria? Should he be sitting in the pit of blood and grime alongside her? Or was this agent of Death supposed to claim him?

Perhaps she did! Poison. She could have poisoned me! The horror of this realization brought tears back to his eyes. The certainty and power of his beliefs were overwhelming. He was going to die. It was fated. You cannot elude death.

How did she know about Kyria? Why did she not just come out and accuse him of killing Kyria? Of not helping her? Why be so cryptic about it? Crypt? Is that where the word is from? Could it be another term of the almighty Death?

With his imagination running away with him, Nezbith lost complete track of reality. Everything that was truly happening in the real world was gone. In his eyes, he was still running. Running far and fast. Running to escape the clutches of Death.

This was all in his imagination. In reality, the carriage slowly inched down the road. Nezbith was oblivious to his true surroundings. Too far lost in his own delusions, fantasy, and guilt, his true location was in a cage attached to the back of this cart. The man directing the horses didn't seem to notice or mind the cries coming from Nezbith. Perhaps he, too, was trapped in a world of his own.

CHAPTER 32

Braksis continued his way toward Guldan and Solara. He fought his way to them, constantly focusing on their battle and her progress. As he saw her fall, he was afraid he still wasn't close enough. From the deepest pits of his being, he let out a roar that demanded to be heard. "Guldan!"

As he did so, he noticed Guldan stop short of ending Solara's life and turn to face his new foe. "I challenge you, Guldan. A challenge, leader to leader."

Guldan looked back at Solara and sent his foot into her face rendering her unconscious. "I'll be back for you. Perhaps I'll bed you yet, whore." As he turned to face Lord Braksis again, he realized that he was foolish to turn his back. Braksis was already on top of him, and a sword thrust was barely dodged, nicking his back slightly.

Guldan twirled out of the way and attempted to raise his axe to bear on Braksis, but the swiftness of the dark warrior kept him stumbling backward and off balance. Braksis kept slashing, thrusting, lunging. With each attempt, Guldan was forced back another step, away from Solara.

As he continued backward, Guldan could see his eventual demise. The tides must be turned, and he needed to be back in control of his own destiny. His axe was all-powerful. Why not use that to his advantage?

With the next lunge by Lord Braksis, Guldan deflected the attack, and the mystically charged axe severed Braksis's blade in two.

Braksis stumbled to the ground in a state of shock and disbelief. The handcrafted Phoenix served him well in battle after battle. Campaign after campaign. And now, in one parry, it lay in pieces.

Guldan saw his advantage had finally come, and he lifted the axe high above his head, intending to bring it down, slicing Braksis in two. At the same time, Braksis kept his focus on his opponents' eyes. He knew they would reveal all.

As Guldan began his downward swing, Braksis slid to the left, and thrust his leg into Guldan's knee, sending him down on the ground. As he fell, Braksis quickly got up and looked for a replacement weapon. There were bodies and weapons all around, but the closest option would be the tip of his shattered sword.

As he moved toward the portion of his blade, Guldan was back up and coming to eliminate Braksis once and for all. Close, so close, but not close enough, he realized. The blade was an arm's reach out of the way. Braksis could hear the wind as the axe was being plunged down at him. He stared up at Guldan in defiance, refusing to even give him the satisfaction of seeing weakness. Then the blade stopped swinging and Guldan screamed.

Braksis grabbed the portion of the sword and turned to see Tiot viciously ripping into Guldan's calf. With a kick, Guldan knocked Tiot off then raised his axe one final time to strike Braksis. This time however, the Warlord did not give him the chance. He jabbed up with the blade sliver and plunged it deeply into Guldan's heart.

As Braksis watched his opponent falter, he could see the disbelief flowing through his eyes. "But... Zoldex...promised." The words were nothing more than a wheezing whisper, but the sense of betrayal was evident.

Guldan dropped to his knees, looked down at the blade piercing his chest, then collapsed as the light in his eyes flowed away forevermore.

Braksis checked Guldan's pulse to confirm that he was truly dead, then motioned for Tiot to come to him. The timber wolf shook off the pain from Guldan's kick and walked to Braksis, who patted his head. "Good boy, Tiot. Good boy."

Standing up, he walked over to Solara and checked to make sure she would be okay. Relief flooded through him as he realized that his mystral protector would be fine, and only needed some rest.

❖ ❖ ❖ ❖ ❖

Many miles and lands away from the battle at Arkham, Zoldex leaned back watching the image that he created of the events as they unfolded. He was surrounded by images of the battle, as if he truly were there, a part of it all. As Guldan fell, and Braksis rose triumphant once again, a low laugh grew into a roar.

Zoldex continued to watch the images as Braksis picked up the axe of his fallen adversary. As Empress Karleena was escorted to shore and saw the death and destruction firsthand. As all reboarded the ships and sailed away. All except for Lord Braksis and Solara who remained behind with a small complement of soldiers.

Watching the events as they occurred, Zoldex smiled deviously. "Everything is proceeding as I have foreseen." If anyone else were around to hear, all that they would recognize was the sinister laugh as the Mage Master continued to bask in his triumph long into the night.

CHAPTER 33

In what seemed like an eternity to the small elf, Kai finally saw and approached the burnt remains of the town once known as Arkham. Everywhere she looked, signs of battle were scattered about. Slain townspeople and soldiers, blood, fire, and debris clustered the ground. Nothing could survive here.

She closed her eyes and concentrated. She attempted to reclaim the vision of the girl and gain some insight as to how to find her. Kai only hoped she was not too late.

Beginning her search of the remains as if she had been here previously, Kai quickly moved around to where the vision showed the young girl had fallen. With each step, her certainty that the girl would be alive increased.

In the distance, Kai heard voices. The sound of them at first shocked her as she looked at the bodies scattered around. Her instincts immediately on alert, she realized that it was futile to assume that she was alone here. After facing Lucky, she silently vowed to herself never to be taken by surprise again. Her search for the girl would have to be put on hold once more.

Moving as quickly as she could with her injuries, she stealthily approached the voices. Pausing behind some rubble, Kai began to gain a grasp of what was going on. These voices came from the attackers. The ones responsible for destroying this small village in the first place.

Kai advanced cautiously to better hear what the men were saying. She soon discovered that these people were part of the Imperium. Images of the man she had traveled with when first arriving here danced through her mind. She trusted her instincts implicitly, and they told her that Braksis was an honorable and trustworthy man. Yet glancing around, she also surmised that this Imperium he served was evil. What else could something be that ruled with an iron fist? Ruled through fear, intimidation, and destruction?

The men she was spying on were soldiers garbed in black and white, though blood and dirt encompassed most of their armor. They were checking the bodies, looking for any survivors or those in need of medical attention. Others were carrying the dead away and lining them up for burial.

The sight of the Imperial soldiers acting so compassionately shocked Kai again. She truly did not understand what was going on, but from experience, she knew that true barbarians would have no care for those they left behind brutalized on the field of battle. To return and bury the dead of one's enemies was most unusual. She would have to learn more about this Imperium before judging them completely. That was only fair.

Silently backing away from her perch, Kai resumed a search of her own—the search for the young girl. Closing her eyes again, she could see clearly the explosion when the girl was hit. Saw her fall. Saw the crater that would be her final resting place if she did not hurry.

As she looked around, she could visualize what the town looked like before the bombardment. This enhanced sense of perception allowed her to hone in on the landmarks where she saw the young girl in her dreams.

Stepping over bodies and crumbling debris, she finally found a sign right across the street that she recalled from her vision of the explosion. She hoped this meant that she was close to the girl.

As Kai turned slowly around, she spotted the crater. She felt the explosion as if she were experiencing it personally. The pure certainty that she was in the right place overwhelmed her. She quickly moved over to the crater and found herself speechless as she saw Lord Braksis kneeling down by the girl.

Hearing movement behind him, Braksis looked up and likewise found himself stunned to see Kai standing there. "Kai?"

Without saying a word, Kai moved into the pit and quickly searched the girl for signs of life. She was not conscious. Her face was caked with dried blood. A head injury could prove to be fatal. However, Kai could feel the small girl's heart beating. The slow, yet rhythmic sound of inhaling and exhaling. She was alive. Still alive.

Braksis watched and saw signs of desperation on the face of the elf who had been so calm under pressure when he first met her. He also glanced at her new outfit and absorbed the signs of severe injury. Clearly, Kai had been through quite an ordeal since he had seen her last.

"She's alive," Kai whispered at first, then more joyously smiled and looked up at Braksis. "She's alive."

"Yes," Braksis confirmed. "I saw her during the battle and decided to check on her. I admit, I feared the worst when I came down here."

Kai closed her eyes and silently thanked the fates for allowing the child to survive. Though she was still hurt, she would get stronger and better.

Regarding her, Braksis leaned over and lightly touched one of Kai's scars. "Why don't we have a medic take a look at both of you?"

Opening her eyes again, Kai shook her head. "We must not delay. I fear for the child's safety if we remain."

"Surely the child would be better off with medical attention," Braksis surmised. "I will not allow anything to happen to you while you are under my care."

Sighing, Kai regarded Braksis as if probing for any ulterior motives. "Why was this village attacked?"

Braksis removed his fingers from Kai's wounds and leaned back. "You don't trust me anymore." The words were not a question, but a bold declaration.

Kai shook her head again. "It's not that. I do trust you. You know that. I just am uncertain about why everything has happened. So much destruction. Where I come from, I am faced with destruction all the time. That did not seem to be the norm here, yet I look around and cannot help but feel like I am back home."

"I understand what you are saying. I, too, look around and am appalled at all of this. I wish that things could have worked out differently. Some way we could have captured these people rather than killed them. However, things don't always work out as we would like."

"This place feels cold. Evil. I thought it was the Imperium, but I cannot envision you that way."

Braksis considered her words. "The man who led this assault mentioned the name Zoldex. Perhaps his influence is this evil you feel."

Her eyes immediately widened. "Zoldex?"

Braksis nodded.

Kai ignored the pain searing through her body as she lifted the small girl and carried her out of the crater. She wished that she could take

Braksis up on the offer of medical attention and help the child here, but hearing the name Zoldex sent chills pulsating down her spine. Like a trapped animal, she hoped only to get away.

"Let me help," Braksis offered.

"I cannot allow Zoldex to find us. We must leave." The determination in her voice was evident.

Braksis stepped out of the small crater and offered his hand to help Kai and the unconscious child up. After they were all out of the crater, he spoke once again. "You probably would be safest in Trespias. Allow some of my men to escort and protect you."

Kai would not hear of it. "I fear that Zoldex has his clutches in your city as well as on the battlefield. We would be safer moving along."

"Then come with Solara and me down south. We will travel to Vorstad to check on how the dwarves are faring. I have five thousand troops there. The child will not be in any danger."

Kai glanced south at the mountains, and though the sun was shining, they seemed to darken considerably with a murky aspect as she looked at them. "There is danger in the south. We will head north."

"At least allow me to give you some medical supplies," Braksis urged.

Approaching quietly, Solara was suddenly standing beside Braksis. Her left eye was bloodshot, and the redness matched her swollen cheek where Guldan had stomped on her face. "You've looked better."

Kai looked over at Solara and smiled briefly. "You shouldn't talk."

"What's going on?" Solara asked openly.

"This child is the Chosen One. It is my destiny to protect and guide her. She will save us all," Kai declared.

Solara nodded with interest. "Intriguing. I guess you need to get her some medical attention then."

Braksis shot her a smile, and she winked back. She had heard some of their conversation and was also trying to convince Kai to seek medical attention.

"We must leave. Immediately."

Solara held Kai's gaze for a long moment, then nodded her consent. "I understand."

"You understand?" Braksis asked incredulously. "I don't. Why not take medical supplies? I see no threat right now."

"It's not the threat that you can see that is troubling her. Let her go," advised Solara.

"Thank you, my friends," returned Kai.

"Let me make a suggestion," Solara said. "If you are indeed heading north, then I would recommend returning to Suspinti. In the northwestern Suspintian Forest, you will find a small pool where the fairies roam, known as Shimendyn. Those in the forest know the waters from this pool have healing powers. It could help both you and the girl."

"Yes," Kai agreed. "This sounds like a viable destination. We shall head there. Thank you again."

Solara nodded. "Oh yeah, one more thing."

Kai stood motionless waiting for Solara. The child remained unconscious in her arms, and her staff was tightly gripped to provide steady support for both of them.

"Might as well take this." Solara stepped over to Kai and placed a small package on the child. "The medics gave it to me for my own injuries, but it will serve you better."

Kai smiled sincerely. "Thank you, my friend. I owe you once more."

"Think nothing of it. You saved me from the tragon. If I wasn't already sworn to Braksis, I would be indebted to you," Solara replied modestly.

"Then may we meet again soon, under less trying times."

Braksis reached over and gently caressed her wounds once more. "Yes, we would like that."

Slowly, Kai turned around and walked back the way she had come. Braksis and Solara stood watching her as she vanished in the distance.

Looking at his companion, Braksis broke the silence. "Were we foolish to let her go?"

"We had no choice. She has her own path to follow."

"Yes," Braksis agreed. "Well, we have our own path to follow as well." He gently touched the hilt of his sword in its sheath. "We will head south and check in with General Kronos. See how things truly are in Vorstad and Xylona. Then work our way back up north."

"To see Ferceng?" Solara inquired.

"Yes. Though any forger could make me a sword, I prefer one like that which I have lost. My father will craft me a new one."

"We have a lot to do, and I don't think you really want to be away from Karleena for too long. So why don't we pack up and begin our journey?"

Braksis agreed. They had wasted too much time already, and there was no telling when Zoldex or his forces would strike again. He only hoped that Karleena would not be in danger or need him until he returned.

Whistling for Tiot, Braksis walked back to his horse, mounted up, then he, too, slowly left the destruction of Arkham behind him.

CHAPTER 34

Returning home to Larcridge, the Danchul village that housed the royal family, Winton knew precisely where he was going and who he wanted to see. A visitor who had come to him many nights before when he was angry that his father left him to go help Karleena and the Imperium. This visitor could peer into the depths of Winton's soul and know exactly what he needed to continue.

As he stormed toward the castle, several people approached to greet him. The women especially always hoped to gain Winton's attention. Not only was he a prince, but he also was a very handsome man.

They were mostly wearing thin, loose-fitting white garments. The outfits were revealing and left little to the imagination. Yet Winton stormed past the hopeful females without even giving them a second glance.

Winton walked through the castle gates and then toward a staircase that wound down into the depths of the basement below. He allowed the visitor to live in the basement without the knowledge of his father. Though his father would be angry if he discovered that Winton had done this, he was not worried for it had been a long time since Sarlec noticed anything on the home front.

As he descended the winding stairwell, Winton could hear voices below him. He paused, and his blood froze as if turning to ice. He had only heard his visitor speak like this on occasion, but when he did, it terrified him.

The sinister voice barked out in impatience. "I am a busy many, Krug. Stop delaying and report."

"I be begging your pardon, my humble master."

This second voice, the one Winton presumed was Krug, was unknown to him. It was deep and choppy as if the speaker struggled to speak the common language. He very much doubted this individual was a human. That thought alone sent Winton into an internal debate. Should he leave and return with a weapon, or confront the uninvited guest and demand to know what was happening. Without truly deciding, he decreased his pace and continued down into the darkness below.

Krug continued. "Unprepared we were. Most unprepared. Humans have come. Many, many humans. Retreat we were forced to do."

"Retreat? I am most displeased, Krug. You assured me the Halls of Vorstad would fall under your might."

"Fall they would if the humans did not come. More help we need."

"More help? I have already helped you considerably." Silence ensued, until a sinister laugh erupted from the visitor's lips.

"I be begging your pardon, my humble master, but what is so funny?" Krug inquired.

"Your ineptitude may work out to our benefit, Krug. I will send you assistance. A warrior to lead your forces into battle."

"More battle?"

"Yes, Krug. More battle. One more battle to be precise."

"We are to take Vorstad in one final assault? A very powerful leader this warrior must be," Krug replied.

"You are no longer required to conquer Vorstad. The human involvement has changed things considerably. You will make one large, final, and brutal attack. You will strike swiftly, then return to your home and await further instructions. The warrior I send will direct you so you pull back at the right time."

"We will not fail you again, my master," Krug promised.

"I have little faith in the sincerity of your words, Krug. Just know this: If this last attack does not meet with my satisfaction, you will not be around long enough to know the full extent of my fury."

"I understand, my master," Krug whispered.

The silence disturbed Winton. He did not understand what happened to the second speaker, but suddenly it was as if the basement was barren once more. An eerie flickering glow also vanished when Krug stopped speaking. Winton was perplexed as to what was happening.

Rather than letting anyone know he had been eavesdropping, Winton yelled out into the darkness as he increased his pace down the stairway. "Zoldex, are you down there?"

From the darkness, an answer sang out almost joyfully. "Winton, my lad. Come hither."

Winton was amazed at how different Zoldex's voice could be when he was speaking. To him, he perceived Zoldex as a friendly and joyous man who acted more like a father than his own. Yet the crisp, cold, chilling voice he heard moments before also belonged to the same man.

Now that Zoldex knew he was there, Winton jogged down the steps and jumped the last three onto the basement floor. He looked around at the dark-infested room. The only illumination was that from three candles placed in a triangle on the floor. He knew that something more than just these small candles had caused the flickering lights during the conversation with Krug, though he could not determine from where the added source of light originated.

Winton looked around the basement, scanning quickly for any signs of Krug. There were not many places one could hide down here, yet Krug was nowhere to be seen.

In the center of the triangle, he could see the form of Zoldex illuminated. It never ceased to amaze him just how fitting Zoldex seemed to be in the darkness. As if his life was truly dictated by the shadows. As if he belonged nowhere else but in the depths and embrace of darkness.

"You seem to be distracted, lad. Is everything all right?"

Slightly timid about revealing that he had overheard Zoldex speaking, Winton also did not wish to lie. "I must have been imagining things, but I could swear that I heard voices speaking."

"Oh?"

Winton paused at the reply. He was uncertain what to say or how to continue. He wondered whether he really had imagined the discussion with Krug. Clearly there was nobody else here. "My ears must have been playing tricks on me. I don't see anyone else here, and nobody passed me on the steps."

"Well, my lad, these old castles sometimes have the ability to play tricks on a person. Nothing to worry about."

"That must be it," Winton admitted, actually believing now that he had imagined the conversation.

"You still seem troubled; what is wrong?" Zoldex asked in a concerned tone.

Remembering why he had originally come here, the anger toward his father refueled him. Deep down, he resented and despised his father.

Not outwardly of course. Sarlec was a great man and leader. If not for Sarlec's joining forces with Conrad and Morex so many years ago, the way of life that Winton enjoyed would never have been feasible. Still, people looked at him and expected to see a tad of his father in him. So many people looked at him, but all he felt was emptiness.

He was not his father. Not a great man. Not a hero. Even if the Great Wars were still transpiring, he doubted that he would have the resolve to lead his people in battle to help the greater good. He would never want to risk his own existence for the ideals of others.

Yet the ideals of his father were exactly the point of contention between them. He only wished for some compassion, time, and understanding from Sarlec, but instead, the respected King was off on another emergency for the Imperium.

Perhaps his own feeling of worthlessness, as well as the ever-increasing resentment toward his father and the Imperium, was why he, too, felt comfortable in the darkness here with Zoldex. He was never looked down upon. Never judged. He felt comfortable here. Comfortable in the shadows and the cold embrace of the basement's depths.

Tragic as this may be, Winton had his whole life ahead of him. His father had groomed him since infancy to succeed him in time. No matter how he perceived the outcome, others looked up to him, sought his companionship and idealism. Yet he still felt empty inside, like the praise and acceptance were unwarranted. As if his life had been wasted.

Winton was truly a looker, and he knew that. He used that to his advantage. To date, he had never been rebutted. Even the women he passed on his way to see Zoldex he knew would jump at the chance to spend a single evening with him. Sure, he was royalty and perhaps people just wanted to sleep with the future king, but in his eyes, it was his charm, wit, and abilities.

Those were the skills he had developed and was proud of. In his own right, he knew he would go far. However, that was the extent of his being. Was that not shallow? He knew how to fight, but had not found a cause worth trying his sword for. He knew diplomacy, but found the act useless and bothersome. He knew the expectations of his father, and that drove him insane.

His father had always put the Imperium first. Winton had always played second fiddle in his father's heart. Nothing more than a distraction from what Sarlec truly cared about. First Conrad, then Karleena.

How could he possibly compete with those who brought the world to its knees and rebuilt it in their own image? With a charming smile? No.

His conquests of women were a distraction. Something to take his mind off of his feelings of inadequacy and disappointment in his father's eyes. Something he was truly good at, but that was of no consequence.

Winton was unable to confide in these many women. How could he? Distractions. Thrills. Enjoyment. Nothing serious enough to require revealing his own deep insecurities and worries to the world. No. Those will remain a mystery to all. For others, he must always maintain the charade of the perfect son and future ruler. His true feeling must be repressed. Repressed everywhere but here. Here with Zoldex.

Seeing that Winton was lost in his own world, Zoldex tried to ascertain what was bothering the heir to the throne now. "You are troubled, my lad. Let me help you."

Winton came over to the triangle of lights and strained to see his friend. His mentor. His guide. Through the darkness, it was hard to see Zoldex's true features. The dark robe and cloak he wore only helped to enshroud him further. The most outstanding feature that Winton could see was his eyes. Full of concern now, but he had seen the fire burning inside of them when Zoldex spoke passionately of things.

With a sigh, Winton let out his recent woes. He spoke of how his father had embarrassed him at the Lumnia championships, and though he was sitting next to him, Sarlec still acted distant. Then a messenger came, and without any explanation, he ran off to matters of the Imperium once more with little concern for the feelings of his own son. Winton concluded by commenting how he felt he could die and his father would still go to the Empress and offer his support without batting an eye.

Listening intently, Zoldex said nothing as Winton revealed what was on his mind. Thinking and plotting to himself, a sinister grin pierced his veil of concern.

Just as quickly as he began, Winton stopped speaking, puzzled by the grin, and he asked Zoldex directly about it. "What are you smiling about?"

Feeling humbled by this boy, Zoldex removed the smile from his face. How long had it been since he lost his focus like that? Hundreds of years at least. Thinking quickly, Zoldex responded as if this were his true thought: "Winton, my lad. Perhaps you should go along with your father. Show more interest in the Imperium."

Stunned disbelief creasing his brow, Winton was struck speechless.

Zoldex merely shook his head. "I am serious. Your father is old. Frail. He will not be with us much longer."

"Ha." Winton's sarcastic laugh displayed his disbelief of the words he heard. "Clearly you have not seen my father recently. It's like he was still as young and vibrant as he was in the Great Wars. Old? Frail? Ha!"

Zoldex smiled once again. "Perhaps then, when the time is right, you should do something about this."

"Do something? What on terra are you speaking of?"

Zoldex paused, allowing Winton to think for a minute before continuing. "Let me tell you of a vision I have just had. In this vision, you go to the palace alongside your father. As equals. The Empress is in a state of distress because her champion, Lord Braksis, has fallen to his doom."

Winton listened to Zoldex speaking, but couldn't believe what he was hearing. "Fallen to his doom? Braksis is quite alive, old man."

"Ah, yes, but we can work on that, too. Hire assassins. Be secretive about it. They can bring Braksis down. Even if they do not, they can distract him while you go to the Empress."

Winton shook his head, still unable to grasp what Zoldex was hinting at.

"In my vision, you will help a sorrowful Karleena. Help her in her time of need. Then it will be your turn to get help."

"Why would I need help?" Impatience emphasized every word. Winton practically demanded to know what Zoldex was hinting at.

"You would need help because of your grief." Another pause to allow his words to sink in before continuing. "Your grief over the death of your father."

"My father?"

"Yes. After you plot and murder him."

"Murder my father?"

Zoldex stood for the first time since Winton arrived. He was not a tall man by any means, but those eyes were like a raging inferno searing through Winton. Every word he spoke grew with intensity. "I have foreseen it. Your father has always put the Imperium before you. You will then become the Imperium. With Lord Braksis and your father out of the way, Karleena will be helpless. Add to that your sorrow for the untimely demise of your father, and she will gain sympathy for you. Sympathy that will grow. Sympathy, which added with your natural wit, charm, and good looks, will gain you her hand in marriage. Then you, you, my boy, will become the next Emperor of the Imperium. A new Imperium that you can build in your own image."

Winton turned away, unwilling to look into Zoldex's eyes any further. He wondered whether these words could truly be a prophecy. If Zoldex had foreseen this, then perhaps it was fated to be. Destiny. Still, to send assassins after Lord Braksis? Many had tried to kill him and failed. To make an enemy out of him would be unwise. It would also be contrary to everything his father stood for.

Suddenly thinking of his father again, Winton wondered whether such a bold move would inspire him. Would finally gain his attention. With that in mind, the feasibility of doing as Zoldex suggested suddenly seemed much more probable. The Hidden Empire had assassins he could contract. If they couldn't track it back to him, then it couldn't hurt to try.

That took care of going after Braksis. What about his father? He truly wished for his father's love and respect. Could he really take his own father's life? The answer came surprisingly quick. Yes. He had felt nothing but loathing for his father for far too long now. All he had wanted was even a portion of the love, the time, the intensity he devoted to the Imperium, but he did not even get that. Yes. He could kill his father.

He wondered about marrying Karleena. She was a lovely girl. She also saw no suitors. That would take a little more time than the other two acts, but he had not yet failed in any of his conquests. Besides, with Sarlec gone, he would be King. Was it not a king's role to rule? Why not expand that to Emperor? Yes. He could do it all. Would do it all. Failure was not an option. Success was the only path open to him.

The emptiness was suddenly gone. No longer did he need fulfillment. An Emperor needed nothing. They were the beginning and ending of all. Their vision would sweep the land as no other ideal could. With a jolt of elation, Winton felt he finally found his true destiny. All that was left was to take the steps to get there. "Thank you, wise one. I will keep you apprised."

With that, Zoldex watched as Winton ascended back into the world of light. A world that would soon have far more darkness than it had known in centuries. A world where people were puppets, and only he was the puppet master.

CHAPTER 35

As the *Reliance* split the ocean and crashed through the waves, a somber Empress stared down at the waters below. Although the actions at Arkham the prior day seemed to be just and appropriate in her eyes, a feeling of failure permeated her thoughts. A true leader should not have to resort to violence. This was something she would address immediately.

Turning her head to look around the ship, she could see that life continued as it always had. Admiral Morex was standing proud on the bridge along with Harnell, the ship's Captain, surveying their fleet, sailors content to go about their daily chores on the warship. Even her honor guard stood vigilant to make certain that no harm came to her.

Looking back into the crashing waters below, she became lost in thought. She already knew what she wanted to do; now she just needed to do it. To help bring the voice of the people out, she wished to create a form of government where the people selected delegates to represent their needs and wishes. A senate or council that would report their wishes to her so that she could make decisions that would help the majority, not just the privileged few.

Yet to form this body of government, she still had to consider the needs of the ruling council. The kings, queens, and other ruling families. Those who had the most power and influence across the Seven Kingdoms. Regardless of the people's wishes, these were the ones that could cause havoc for the people. Therefore, they, too, must be represented. A ruling class council, or rather a House of Lords.

The two would need to be able to have the impression they were making a difference to be successful. Therefore, she needed to have trusted representatives to lead both houses and report to her. This was the most difficult step. How could she sit on both councils and maintain that both branches of her new government were content and satisfied with the fairness? Yet if she showed favoritism to one over the other, there could be further revolts.

The only viable solution in her eyes was to have both bodies elected. One elected by the people, the other by the ruling class. She personally would then select the leadership of each house from those selected. Those representatives would report directly to her, and she would make final decisions based on that.

Her selection of the House of Lords would be an easy one. If King Sarlec of Danchul would serve, he would be her representative. He was well respected throughout the Seven Kingdoms for his actions during the Great Wars, and there was none more dedicated to the ideals of the Imperium. She could think of nobody better to serve as the head of the House.

These thoughts also could turn against her. The Great Wars were long and harsh. All kingdoms revolted and fought for their own rights. Only when a young Conrad intervened with his theories of unification did things begin to settle down. The work of a few great men, and those willing to die for ideals were what led to the formation of the Imperium. By creating a new government, could this be the downfall of the world that she knew? Yet with the revolts and uprisings, something needed to change.

These times were full of change. The biggest probably being her leadership style over that of her father's. Unlike Conrad, she had not fought any wars nor proved herself. People obeyed the laws of the Imperium, but she had not yet earned their respect. Respect was very important when only one voice led such a large realm.

Regardless, she was now Empress, and her thoughts and decisions would be the ones that would bring the empire into the future. If she felt that a new body of law and government would be imperative to the Imperium's survival, then it would be established immediately. Any objections would be listened to, but would also be addressed quickly as to put out any fires before they did too much damage.

Mere days ago, these thoughts were the most important things on her mind. Now she knew some outside influence had been stirring up much of this trouble. Of course, the people must be unhappy, otherwise they would not be so easily swayed. This thought only confirmed her decision to alter the structure of the Imperium. However, Braksis's words that it perhaps was time to reach out to the other races and try to unite against a common foe were quite unsettling.

She was already receiving much opposition for her plan to bring in the voice of the people. The ministers were avidly fighting her, and they represented many of the affluent families in the Seven Kingdoms. If she then also tried to bring elves and dwarves into the government and daily society, she feared that revolts and dissent would only increase.

Though she had been looking to make changes for a while, she understood Morex's advice that she may only be able to choose one option or the other. To alter the structure of the government, or to reunite the races. At least for the time being. That being the case, it seemed more logical to pursue the unification, even if that were the less enticing alternative to her subjects.

After all, if there were added bodies of government, then the possibility of bringing the other races into the Imperium as allies would fall before a democratic council. This process could be debated and discussed, and the races may never be accepted. With the pressing time frame that Braksis had indicated, something needed to be done immediately, and not left open to committee.

Knowing instinctively that this was true, and that as a result, all she had hoped to achieve in the near future would be delayed, Karleena contemplated how to go about contacting these potential allies. She knew the initial contact and discussions must be done delicately. The races mistrusted humans, and after the Race Wars, this lack of trust was certainly warranted. Still, it was imperative for them to listen to what she had to say.

The only solution she could think of was the Mages. Everything kept returning to them and their aid. If Mage Master Jeffa could not help her to convince the Council of Elders of the importance of their assistance, all could be lost before it had truly even begun. With their help, she hoped she could gain the trust of the races to at least be willing to meet with her. Matters would be up to her after that to convince them that they could not survive the turbulent times that were coming individually.

In the distance, Karleena could see the Mage's Tower stretching toward the clouds. The home of the Mages was mystical and impressive. A symbol that stood the test of time, and she hoped would soon be one recognized and respected by many in the Imperium. Realizing they would soon be entering the palace, she was determined to act quickly before the ministers could object to her plans.

To her left, Karleena could see the shipyards a slight distance away from Trespias. The design was established so that the fleet could be mobilized and provide a defense against a sea assault before an invading force got close to the palace.

With the exception of the *Reliance,* all the ships would dock in the shipyards. Barracks were also provided for all of the sailors. Admiral Morex designed his navy so that the sailors would remain on site and ready to travel at a moment's notice. The on-site navy was about two thirds of the actual size that was available, allowing a rotation of sailors to spend time at their own homes and with family. A three-way rotation was set up on an annual basis, with sailors on site for eight months at a time before being eligible to return home.

The soldiers who traveled with the navy would disembark here and march to the main headquarters in Trespias. From there, they would be dispersed to other locations throughout the Seven Kingdoms, or be placed on standby until needed again.

As the *Reliance* made its final approach to the palace, she turned slowly and was backed into the structure. When designed, a cavern was included underneath the palace allowing the flagship to rest within the walls themselves. This would allow Empress Karleena to flee quickly if needed. Unlike the majority of the Imperial Navy, the crew of the *Reliance* lived in barracks by their ship within the walls of the palace.

Karleena gazed back toward the bridge and watched as Morex directed his crew. Pure professionalism and confidence were demonstrated even when he wasn't aware of doing so. A very humbling and comforting presence in her own little inner circle of people she trusted and relied upon.

On the dock she could see Centain along with a full contingent of Imperial Guards awaiting their arrival.

As the ship docked, her honor guard came to attention and was ready to disembark with their Empress. Admiral Morex hopped down from the bridge and approached her. With a gentlemanly nod, he said, "This ends our journey, my lady. I wish you best fortune in the course you have plotted. Call upon me if you have need of me."

Karleena bowed her head in appreciation. "Thank you, Admiral. Your counsel is always appreciated. As for our prior discussion, I trust that you will contact Jeffa for me?"

Admiral Morex nodded. "I shall inform him of your request immediately."

"Thank you. Please keep me apprised." She then pivoted around and led her guards down the ramp to the docks below. "Captain," she said in greeting as she approached Centain.

Centain nodded as well. "Empress. I trust the campaign was a successful one?"

As Karleena reached him, he pivoted and walked alongside her. Imperial Guards were lined up at attention on both sides of the docks. They walked between the rows, and the honor guard that had traveled with Karleena followed in two equal lines of three.

"The campaign was indeed successful if you consider needless slaughter a success, Captain." A sigh indicated her regret and frustration in the matter. "Has Geist returned from Tenalong yet?"

"He returned this morning, Empress."

"Excellent. Was his mission a success?"

"Scouts will be dispatched to ascertain the validity of the orc city," Centain reported.

Closing her eyes, Karleena breathed a sigh of relief. She hoped the reports were exaggerated as to the size of the orc clan, but she would know soon enough. She also was glad she did not have to circumvent King Garum and try to send her own scouts.

With these thoughts behind her, she decided to pursue her plan quickly before the ministers had a chance to try to influence or delay her. "Have Geist dispatch a summons to all of the kings and queens of the Seven Kingdoms. We shall be convening for a meeting as soon as they all arrive."

"As you wish, Empress."

"I also seek an audience with the Council of Elders."

"The Council of Elders, Empress?"

"Yes. Morex will be sending word to the Mage's Council that the daughter of Conrad wishes to speak to Jeffa. He shall make arrangements for my meeting with the Council."

Centain absorbed the information and immediately posed various scenarios and threats. "If you were to go within the walls of the Council,

I would be unable to protect you. I must insist that the meeting either take place within the palace, or that I personally shall attend this meeting with you."

"First things first, Captain. Morex must schedule the meeting. Let's not get ahead of ourselves. We shall face security needs as we get closer to the event." She stopped walking to look directly at her captain. "I see this does not sit well with you. I assure you that you will be heavily involved in the upcoming meetings. That is all for now, Captain."

"Yes, Empress. I shall inform Ceist to dispatch riders with summonses immediately." With that, he clapped both boots together, pivoted, and returned to the docks to dismiss his troops.

Watching him walk away, Karleena headed toward her chambers once more, her honor guard close behind her. Thoughts of the new government structure and her meetings ahead slowly were fading away. All she wanted now was to get back home and to bed. She could face her tasks and plans in a few hours much more competently than she could right now.

As she approached her chambers, two of the guards entered ahead of her to make sure the room was secure. When they confirmed her room was not compromised, they came back out into the hallway where they would remain until relieved, allowing her to go in to sleep. She briefly nodded her thanks to one of the guards, and went into her chambers to try to allow slumber to remove her burdens for the time being.

Being completely alone, she slowly paced toward her bed, dropping clothing on the floor behind her as she went. In privacy, there was no need for vanity or appropriateness. She shook her long brown hair free of its harness, and it lightly cascaded onto her shoulders and down her now naked back Her entire body was smooth and soft. Not a mark or scar could be found anywhere. As an Empress by age seventeen, she had a lot of growing to do. Experience to be gained. As a young girl developing into fruition, she embodied pure perfection.

Reaching her bed, Karleena pulled the covers up and stared at her hands as they hugged one of the pillows. Although clean, she could still clearly see the blood of the prior day's actions as if it would never wash away. Blood she felt personally responsible for. Blood she hoped to never see spilled again. Watching her hands, she soon drifted off into nightmarish sleep filled with wrong decisions and tragedies. Visions of death and destruction all brought about in her name.

CHAPTER 36

Kai gently lowered the injured girl to the ground. She used the medicine Solara provided to clean the child's wounds and bandage her up. Kyria still remained unconscious, which troubled the pink elf.

She hoped the child would have awakened hours ago, but that had not happened. The young girl was alive, but if she remained in a coma, Kai was uncertain how to proceed.

Her own injuries also were beginning to trouble her. Walking on her own was a slight struggle, but manageable. Traveling while also carrying an unconscious child was pushing her beyond her limits. Realizing this, Kai sincerely wished her horse had not run off when Lucky attacked.

Looking down at the defenseless form, Kai gently stroked her hair. "You rest now, little one. You need your strength, for soon you will be running and playing again."

As she said the words, she hoped they were true, although remembering Eldiir and the prophecy, she seriously doubted this child would ever be truly happy again. Remembering her visions of the child acting so joyously, a single tear trickled down Kai's cheek.

"No more of that," she whispered to herself.

Looking around at the open plains, Kai suddenly felt exposed and vulnerable. She would be much more content when they reached the Suspintian Forest and could hide in the cover of the trees. In the open like this, anything could come across them, and she doubted she could put up much resistance in her current state.

Pumping her fist, she felt waves of pain pulsate through her body. Realizing the state she was in, she wondered whether she had been foolish to reject Braksis's offer of an escort back to the Imperial City. Though she wished to protect the child in her own way, she sensed this was not the best way to be going about that.

The thoughts of "what if" flowed through her. What if she had arrived in time to whisk the child away from the battlefield? What if she had not been injured by Lucky? What if the horse had not run away? What if she went with Braksis? What if she went with soldiers back to Trespias? These questions could be never-ending and maddening.

Looking up at the clear night sky, she watched as a star fell. "Is this another sign? Are we destined to fall?"

Assessing her situation, Kai leaned back and found her eyelids very heavy. Before giving in, she wished deeply that something positive would happen. She had found the child. Why then would she be in a situation where she would be unable to protect her? "Please," she whispered. "Please send us some help."

With those last words trailing off in slumber, Kai fell asleep. Though it was a deep and restful sleep, she suddenly felt alert—as if something were out of place. She opened her eyes and quickly reached for her dagger, though what she saw posed no real danger.

Sitting next to her and staring at her intently, was a pack mule. The mule had supplies strapped to its back, including food, water, medical supplies, and blankets.

Kai stood up and looked around for the owner of the mule, but could see little sign of any other people on the open plains. They were still alone, except for this mule joining them.

Rubbing her eyes to make certain that she was not dreaming, Kai realized she was indeed awake.

"Where is your master?" She asked the mule as she checked the pack of supplies.

With no indication or sign of ownership, Kai decided not to question how or why this had happened, but to only be grateful that it did. She looked up at the stars one last time, and mouthed two short words. "Thank you."

CHAPTER 37

Sleep never lasted long for those with burdens and weight on their shoulders. Karleena awoke with her handmaidens kneeling down beside the bed waiting for her to awaken. Five in all, these young women were responsible for her appearance and presentation. With her recent requests and decisions, these five servants would be challenged immensely in the days to come.

Standing up, Sharnesta clapped her hands twice. The other four women quickly sprang into action. A bath was being readied. Clothing selected and laid out. Materials being arranged for styling of hair, nails, eyes, and lips. Everything arranged for convenience when tending to their Empress. Sharnesta clapped her hands a second time, and the girls returned to the bed to assist Karleena. "Time for your bath, my lady."

Wishing that sleep had been more peaceful than it had, not to mention longer, Karleena sighed as she sat up. "Thank you, Sharnesta."

As Karleena stood up, her nakedness was revealed. Sharnesta shook her head slowly. "My lady, we have discussed this before. A lady of stature should not sleep in such a state."

"Relax, Sharnesta, I was tired and dirty, and nobody was here."

"That is beside the point, my lady," Sharnesta scolded. "It is inappropriate and unladylike."

Realizing Sharnesta would not back down, even though she preferred to sleep in the nude, Karleena nodded her assent without another word. This was an age-old argument the two had regularly over the years. It would not be resolved on this particular morning.

As Karleena approached the bath, two of the other girls disrobed and walked into the tub first. She slowly walked down the steps of the tub allowing warm water to overcome her body. In the middle of the tub was a small stool underneath the water. She went directly to this and sat down, leaving all but her head submerged.

The first two girls in the tub stood behind her. One scrubbed her back while the other washed her hair. Two other girls disrobed and followed Karleena into the tub. One scrubbed her chest and legs while the other focused on her face and mouth. Sharnesta stood outside of the tub supervising and instructing when necessary.

Karleena enjoyed these morning baths. The girls were quite talented and helped her to relax. When the actual bathing was done, they massaged her muscles to help her calm down and rest. When their treatment was completed, Karleena would lie in the warm water for several minutes allowing the heat and steam to overcome her senses.

The entire process lasted around an hour. When done, Karleena was well rested, calm, clean, and ready to face her daily tasks. Standing up, she walked back up the steps and out of the tub. Two of the girls who had vacated the bath earlier were standing by with towels to dry her off. The other two were at a station arranged to perform the rigorous efforts of fashion and style. This is where she would go next and spend another chunk of her time while the four attendants worked relentlessly at the art of beauty. Manicure, pedicure, eyelashes, hair, and makeup—all would be carefully and methodically addressed while Sharnesta circled the group making small comments and remarks. Recommendations and critiques.

When completed here, Karleena finally donned her attire for the day. Her meeting with the Council of Elders had her fashionably garbed in an exquisitely designed dress in the white shade of the Mages themselves. The back of the dress was open in a slit down to the small of her back, where the dress puffed slightly and hung to her ankles. Curving light gray designs laced through the dress, with a larger concentration of patterns around her waist. Lace netting in the same color was woven through her hair and down her otherwise exposed back. Around her neck, as always, she wore her emerald necklace.

Overseeing the final touches to the outfit personally, Sharnesta smiled into the mirror allowing Karleena to see her satisfaction in the reflection. She clapped her hands twice and the handmaidens vacated the room into an adjoining chamber where they would prepare themselves for the day in colors similar to those worn by the Empress.

Karleena looked up at Sharnesta in the mirror. Though not voiced, her eyes spoke volumes.

"Go with your heart, my lady. Trust your instincts. They shall not lead you astray," Sharnesta offered with a comforting smile as if reading Karleena's mind.

"Thank you, Sharnesta." Karleena smiled back. "Time to get started."

Sharnesta nodded and then silently followed the handmaidens into the adjoining room.

After completing her morning rituals of preparing for the new day as Empress of the realm, Karleena approached the doors to her room as they were opened by two of the guards outside. In the hallway, she saw Centain standing and awaiting her arrival. On both sides of the hall, Imperial Guards stood vigilantly at their posts.

"Good morning, Captain."

"To you as well, Empress. Might I say, you look quite exquisite this morning. I take it you slept well." With the statement, both walked down the hallway, with two guards leading the way, two following, and two remaining at her chambers.

Closing her eyes for a brief moment, Karleena wished she truly could speak her mind. Let Centain know of the nightmares that plagued her the night before. The constant repetition of the onslaught that she witnessed at Arkham. However, in matters of decorum, she must always hold her own thoughts internally, and not allow others to perceive a potential weakness. "Quite well, thank you, Captain."

Noticing the delayed pause with her response, Centain wished to inquire further. He knew she had witnessed something tragic, and that it most likely would be bothering her. Yet with her passion, he also knew she needed to see the tragedies in life in order to work even harder to assure they never transpired again. "As requested, riders have been dispatched to all Seven Kingdoms. We should hear back from them soon."

Karleena closed her eyes momentarily and nodded. "Things will progress rapidly from here. I must be ready. Has Morex successfully arranged a meeting with Jeffa for me?"

"This was a rather difficult request. Never before has an individual without a mystical affinity requested to enter the halls of the Mage's Council, much less visit the Council of Elders. However, Jeffa was saved by Morex and your father in the Great Wars, and promised that he will gain you entrance, if not assistance."

"Not assistance? I do not understand."

"Jeffa indicated that the Council of Elders is split and fragmented. Some may be willing to assist you, whereas others would clearly be against it. At the same time, some may be willing to assist you, but vote against you just because someone they disagree with votes for you."

Shaking her head in disbelief, she stopped to consider this statement. "Not a very productive or efficient system."

"Yet you wish to make a similar system yourself in our very own government."

"Captain, I sense much negativity in you," Karleena shot back quickly.

"Empress, I wish you no disrespect. If you wish to enter into a more bureaucratic society, then that is what we shall do. I will remain by your side protecting you and the occupants of this palace regardless of the established government. That is my job. However, I feel I must overstep my bounds and remind you that history was not kind to the Seven Kingdoms. We suffered through the Race Wars and then the Great Wars. Your father put an end to that, and designed the current system. Yet you want the people to have a voice, the disagreements of which led to the Great Wars. You also want to unite the races, the differences of which led to the Race Wars. I would not jump too quickly to eliminate what was worked so hard to achieve."

"I appreciate your candor on the matter. I understand the implications. I do not wish to lose the efforts or memory of my father. However, times are changing and the Imperium must be flexible to change with it."

Just then, Morex rounded the corner. "I could not agree with you more. Things that are unwilling to change in time, will fail to advance with the times."

"Admiral Morex." Karleena greeted him with a smile. "Centain informs me that Jeffa will grant me a meeting with the Council of Elders."

"Yes, though did he also inform you that Jeffa fears swaying the Council will be a difficult ordeal?"

"Yes. This troubles me. What do you suggest?"

Morex stroked his chin a few times in contemplation. "Though Jeffa is an old ally, I would not trust him to vote your way today."

Centain could not contain his surprise at the statement. "Why is that?"

"Jeffa has no power on the Council. From what I understand, he has the reputation of voting identically to the Council's leader, Pierce."

"He would not support the Empress?" Centain questioned.

"If Pierce supports the Empress, though that I would doubt as well," Morex surmised.

"What is your recommendation then?" inquired Karleena.

Morex regarded her for a moment. "Ilfanti."

"Ilfanti?" she repeated.

"Yes. He is well respected and has a lot of influence on the Council. If you can convince him, you will most likely win the vote."

"Thank you, Admiral. I appreciate the insight." Taking a deep breath, Karleena's thoughts flowed over the long battle that lay ahead with the changes she wished to make. "When will I be granted a meeting?"

"I will escort you there personally within the hour," Centain replied. "Just be prepared to go into the Council of Elders and argue as passionately as you have this morning with me. If you do, victory is assured."

As Karleena looked at Centain, she could see a smile and respect written on his face. Was their prior argument just a test to prepare her for the impending meeting? If so, that would be something she would expect far more from Admiral Morex than her Captain of the Guards. Still, she was grateful that so many of her trusted advisors and aids looked after her well-being and continuously tested her resolve. She would indeed visit the Council, and she would procure their assistance. She was certain of that.

❖ ❖ ❖ ❖ ❖

The next hour moved very quickly. Time flew by in a blur. Centain organized a near parade of security officers to march through the streets of the Imperial City toward the Mage's Council. He was a very thorough man and took his duties very seriously. Those in the streets witnessed the gates to the palace opening, and row upon row of Imperial Guards marching past them.

Some guards rode atop horses, but most were marching on foot. Karleena herself was on board one of five enclosed and heavily guarded carriages so that none would know which truly held the Empress of the realm. She had objected to being hidden, but Centain and Morex both expressed concern based on recent hostilities. Ultimately, she conceded and allowed herself to be concealed.

The carriages were exorbitant and highly decorated with exquisite gold designs. Inside, the walls and floor were plush and full of red pillows to maximize her comfort when traveling. Due to the attempted security measures, drapes, which normally would be open for her to wave to the people, were tied down to keep them from blowing in the wind.

Without these measures, Karleena enjoyed watching her surroundings as she traveled. Ever since she was a little girl traveling with her father, she never could get enough of the world around her. To watch the passing scenery and imagine all kinds of stories and adventures she could have if she were out there and part of it. Even now, the invisible dragons of her youth were dispelled, but there was still a world just brimming with curiosity that she would love to explore. To be able to see the people she ruled. To look into their faces and show them that things would improve. That the violence and outbreaks of recent months were being dealt with, and they could resume their lives once more.

The carriage came to a halt, and after a short delay, the door opened with Centain standing with his hand extended to help her down. As she stepped out of the carriage, she saw the Imperial Guards had completely blocked off this section of the city. Even so, out of each of the other four carriages, she saw exquisitely dressed women who had been selected with similar appearance to her as decoys.

Centain raised his hand to beckon her to approach the Mage's Tower. "Jeffa will come to greet you and bring you inside personally. He should be arriving momentarily."

"Thank you, Captain," Karleena replied. As she looked up, she had to admit the Tower was breathtaking. Eclipsing the structure was a pressurized blast of water that danced in the sky and continued to change color. Behind the wall of water, the Tower itself was a tinge of light ivory that reflected in the sun.

Centain reached behind his back and withdrew a small dagger. "It would make me feel better if you went in with some form of protection, Empress."

Karleena smiled at the gesture, but nodded negatively. "I'm sorry, Captain, but if my goal is peace, I must first demonstrate my own resolve. I will not bring a weapon of violence in with me."

Before Centain could rebut her words, the water surrounding the tower began to flow more rapidly, and a circular opening gradually appeared before the Empress. On the other side, a lone figure stepped through the aperture and toward the waiting guards.

The man walked right up to the proper Karleena and smiled. "So good to see you again, little Karlie."

Karleena knew that the word "see" was not quite accurate. Jeffa had been severely injured during the Great Wars, and he lost his eyesight as a result. Now, he wore a solid gold mask from his forehead down to his nose and cheeks. Below the mask, a long white beard flowed in disarray down his chest.

Like all Mages, Jeffa was garbed in white robes. As a Council of Elders member, he had his robes decorated with large portions of gold. All Mages were allowed to decorate their robes in gold however they desired as they advanced in rank and skill. Jeffa's designs all portrayed animals, which played an integral role in his life.

On his shoulder, a small furry klatia was perched. A full-grown klatia could fit in the palm of one's hand, and often attracted small children with the harmonics of its voice. It had little paws with claws that allowed it to climb trees, or in this case cling to the Master's robes. It also had a small pink face and nose that was bobbing up and down as it was looking at all of the people surrounding Jeffa.

This particular creature was more than a pet to Jeffa. Since the loss of his eyesight, he found he was able to use his mystical abilities to see through the eyes of others. In this instance, the klatia was acting as his eyes.

"I haven't been called Karlie in a very long time." Karleena smiled back at the Mage Master.

"Just another thing that has been too long in the waiting. Never lose your youth. You'll miss it when you are my age!" Jeffa joked. "Are you ready?"

Karleena nodded her acknowledgment and looked at Centain for support. He smiled back at her, and she advanced to follow Jeffa into the Mage's Council.

As they approached the flowing water, Jeffa raised a hand in caution. "Be careful not to touch the water. Beautiful though it may be, the pressure if enough to sever a limb."

Considering his words, she watched as he walked through the tunnel of flowing water. Slowly, she followed him in. The sight was truly impressive. All around her water way spraying at an immense speed. It sparkled and glowed as it swirled like a whirlpool. Yet, not a single drop touched her skin. No mist or spray clouded the tunnel either.

Reaching the other side of the opening, Karleena looked back as the tube returned to vertical pillars of flowing water. An interesting barrier to separate the Mages from the rest of the world, she decided.

"You are the first person without an affinity for magic to ever step within the Mage's domain," Jeffa informed her.

"I am honored then to be the first," Karleena replied sincerely. As she looked around, the grounds were enormous. Her senses felt betrayed. From the streets beyond the barrier, the Tower seemed so close. When inside, it appeared miles away with gardens more beautiful than the mind can imagine between where she stood and the giant structure.

"You are shocked at the size of the land," Jeffa said.

"Yes. This place is breathtaking. How can the perceptions be so different from what is seen on the outside?"

"You will quickly see that here, nothing is as it seems." His smile widened as he walked toward the Tower.

Karleena felt joyous as she looked around. Small children garbed in white robes were playing on the grounds. Older Mages were sitting around and talking. Others just lay there and enjoyed the smell of the flowers or the sun in the sky. Things seemed so peaceful and tranquil here. As if these Mage's lived in an ideal society. "Is everyone happy here?"

Jeffa continued to walk toward the Tower. A small raspler no more than eight years old bumped into him. Jeffa glanced down and smiled. "What do you say, Volkmer?"

Volkmer's reptilian hide turned a purplish tinge and he lowered his head. "I'sss sssorry, Masssster Jeffa."

"That's quite all right, Volkmer. Go back and play," Jeffa added with a devious smile. "Ghiggi is hiding in the tree over there. Go get her!"

"Thanksss, masssster!" Volkmer yelled as his tinge returned to its normal green. He joyously darted off toward the tree.

Jeffa turned to regard Karleena. "As with all things in life, not everyone is always happy, but we live a gifted life here. You can see that in the eyes of the children."

Thinking briefly again of how a blind man speaks of seeing happiness in the eyes of children, she watched as the raspler approached the tree, then jumped up and grabbed the tail of another child in the tree. A feline creature, which she presumed was Ghiggi, dropped from the tree and the two rolled around laughing.

Seeing two children of such diverse races playing, she was inspired that the unification of the races could be attainable.

Catching her sight, she watched as several avarians flew threw the sky. Once again she was amazed that to the outside world, none of this was visible. How could they miss a flying Mage?

Jeffa smiled at her as he walked toward the Tower again. "It's magic."

"What is?" Karleena asked, surprised that he seemed to know what she was thinking.

"This whole place, Karlie. It's all magic. Don't try to understand it, just accept it."

Though she wished to know more, she followed the Mage Master and simply observed those she passed. Perhaps she could not understand or explain how the things she saw were happening, but she certainly could enjoy the sight.

When they arrived at the base of the Tower, Karleena was slightly perplexed. There were no doors. The Tower just stretched from the ground straight up into the air. "How do we get in?"

Jeffa reached out his hand to her. "You must take a leap of faith. Do you trust me, Karlie?"

Karleena smiled at the old friend, and took his hand.

"Close your eyes, Karlie."

She did as he asked, and waited. She felt a slight tug on her hand and knew he was leading her forward. She kept her eyes closed, though she expected to walk straight into the wall. After a couple of steps, however, the impact never happened.

"You can open them now."

Karleena did so and looked around. They were inside the Tower. She turned back to the wall and touched it. The wall was solid. "How did you...?"

Jeffa smiled. "You're trying to understand again. Just accept, Karlie."

Just then, Karleena watched as another Mage approached one of the walls and walked right through it without even pausing. "Did he just walk through the wall?"

Jeffa smiled back at her without responding.

"We just walked through the wall?" she asked seeking clarification.

Jeffa only chuckled.

If she was amazed by the size of the area outside, the Tower itself was just as impressive. Fountains flowed with water that took shape and actually danced to music in the middle. A waltz formed before her and danced to harmonics that echoed evenly throughout the hall, though Karleena saw no musicians. Lights illuminated the open air and created images and shapes that were breathtaking to observe.

Even more children and Mages than were on the grounds outside engaged in activities inside the Tower. She even watched as a couple dozen small children participated in training exercises that defied acrobatic abilities. They soared through the sky, landed on a pole or rope, then were airborne again going in different directions. The skills for a group so young were simply amazing.

Jeffa approached a fountain in the middle of the Tower. Unlike the others that had water figures dancing, this was a calm pool of water. "This is where the magic comes from. It was this fountain that first brought magic to the land those many years ago."

"So magic comes from water?" Karleena inquired.

"Not just any water, from this water. At least that is how it all started. Nobody has drunk from this in centuries, yet you can see the Tower is full of Mages."

"I would like to learn more," Karleena said, full of curiosity.

"I'm sure you do. However, the Council is waiting. Perhaps another time," Jeffa suggested.

"Yes, another time." Karleena looked up at the various floors of the Tower, but saw no stairways to ascend. "Lead the way."

Jeffa smiled back at her fondly. "Before we begin, just remember—I won't let anything bad happen to you."

"I don't understand. What could happen?"

Rather than answering her, the ground directly below Jeffa and Karleena began to glow. A small disc of light slowly rose into the air.

Karleena's eyes widened as the disc levitated in the air. "Unbelievable."

"You haven't seen anything yet," Jeffa cautioned.

The disc continued to rise. Karleena observed each level of the Tower as they passed. She saw classrooms with children being taught philosophy, history, and art. She watched groups of students training in combat with various weapons. She saw a library that was so large, the entire palace could probably fit inside.

As she watched all of these things, she once again was amazed at how large and developed the Tower was. In any normal law of architecture, what she was seeing was impossible. The rooms were not located within the Tower, but actually outside of it. The doors to the different halls, classes, and rooms were attached to the Tower, but they opened into worlds far larger than the mind could conceive.

"How is this possible?" she asked again, hoping this time for a real answer.

Jeffa just smiled at her again without replying. The klatia on his shoulder began to hum a tune that grew into a beautiful song as they continued to ascend.

The higher they went, Karleena saw much older Mages. These must be the Masters, she presumed. They were found within halls and residences more spectacular than any room she had ever seen before. Her own bedroom she had felt was excessive, yet as she peered inside, she could see how it paled in comparison.

Looking down, she could barely see the fountain at the base of the Tower. The Mages below appeared no larger than ants to her from this height. She remembered seeing the Tower in the distance from the *Reliance,* but even then, she never would have been able to fathom how high it truly went.

Jeffa gently touched her shoulder. "Looking down may not be the wisest move if you hope to refrain from becoming queasy."

She admitted to herself that he was right. Though she wanted to see everything, looking down was making her a bit queasy and wobbly in the legs. "How high up are we going?"

"The Council of Elders is stationed at the height of the Tower," Jeffa replied.

"That didn't answer my question," Karleena rebutted.

"I know."

Continuing to ascend, the walls of the Tower vanished and they were out in the open. The clear blue sky was all around them. Karleena looked around and could see the borders of Trespias below her. She wondered if Centain could look up and see her out in the open right now. What would he think about in terms of protecting her when she was literally floating through the air?

The glowing disc slowed down as it reached the clouds. Karleena looked up to try to determine their destination, but could see nothing out of the ordinary.

"Only a member of the Council of Elders can ascend this high. The other Masters can merely reach the top of the normal Tower walls unless they have an escort."

Karleena considered this and was honored once more that she was allowed to come to address the Council. Clearly, even among their own order, they valued the status and prestige of this ancient group of leaders. For her to be granted an audience, she knew this was not a meeting to be taken lightly.

Without seeing any difference, the disc entered another structure and halted. Karleena looked around. A grand hall was before her, with marble pillars leading away from the disc up a set of stairs paved in gold.

"This is our stop," Jeffa offered.

"We can just get off? No worries about falling, right?"

"Ah, Karlie. I told you to just accept, and not try to understand. Take a step. You will find this place very solid."

Karleena listened to the man who once fought beside her father, and stepped off the glowing disc. The ground was indeed solid enough.

"Come, follow me," Jeffa indicated.

He walked up the stairs and approached a wall made of crystal. The crystal extended as if large panes of glass, with golden braces holding them together. Jeffa smiled at Karleena, then walked directly through the crystal wall.

"You said to follow me," Karleena whispered to herself, then she, too, stepped through the crystal wall. Inside, she found a circular chamber completely domed and encased in crystal with gold borders like the wall she had stepped through. The room itself had a golden floor with nine chairs of various heights and styles circling the room and facing into the middle of the hall. Beside each chair, a member of the Council of Elders stood observing the Empress.

These Mage Masters all wore similar robes as Jeffa. Unlike the figures she had seen below, the bulk of their robes were gold rather than white, representing their status in the Council.

As Karleena looked at these individuals, she suddenly felt the burdens of her task apply pressure on her once more. Since first walking through the water tunnel, she had felt like a child exploring the wonders of the unknown. Now, she needed to represent the interest of her people and find a way to persuade these nine individuals to assist her.

She glanced at Jeffa and hoped he would help to ease the tension she felt, but he merely walked into the hall and stood by the chair next to Pierce. Glancing around, she tried to determine what outward impressions these individuals held of her.

Standing on the other side of Jeffa was the winged avarian Senix. His smiled widened as she glanced at him, and he used his two feathered wings to whisk him into the air, then glide to her side. "How rude of Jeffa to bring you here and then abandon you. I am Senix."

As she looked at him, his eyes twinkled like a star. He had a full head of blonde hair, with a beard and mustache to match. Karleena had to admit, Senix was a very attractive man. "Hello, Senix, and thank you for the introduction. I am Karleena, Empress of the Imperium."

"And a more lovely Empress I am sure there never has been." Senix nearly sung as he reached over and kissed her hand gently.

The figure closest to Karleena took a step forward. "Okay, lover boy, that's enough. Let her come in peace."

The voice was deep, though not as gruff as she would have expected for a dwarf. This must be Ilfanti, the dwarf who Morex advised her to convince first. He was unlike any dwarf she had ever seen. He had no beard or mustache. His face in fact was clean-shaven. His hair was short in the back, with waves that lifted from his forehead and looped out slightly to the sides. His robes were almost completely gold with only a few slight signs of white threaded within them.

She looked down at the little dwarf and nodded. "My thanks, kind sir. Ilfanti, I presume?"

Ilfanti broke out into a grin that went from ear to ear showing a smile of perfect teeth. "That would be me."

The largest member of the Council leaned forward toward Ilfanti. "Knowing you, I can only imagine what horror stories she has heard." He reached a giant muscular furred paw to Karleena. "I am Hergzenbarung. It is a pleasure to make your acquaintance."

She was amazed at what she was seeing before her. This Master was a lupan, one of the most ferocious beasts in the Seven Kingdoms, yet he had a gentleness that shocked her. His eyes inspired confidence and showed compassion. If not for those eyes and demeanor, she would be terrified by what she saw. Like all lupans, his teeth were large incisors, his claws looked like they could carve through a tree, and his muscular frame could crash through a wall.

An elf called out behind Hergzenbarung. "You can call him Herg. We all do."

Karleena noted that the speaker was severely scarred on one side of her body, as if burned. Her other side was quite attractive, and her light pink hair flowed freely. Karleena wondered what had happened to the elf to disfigure her other side so poorly.

She looked at the speaker. "Why thank you. Herg it is then."

Ilfanti took her hand and led her into the center of the room. "The elf's Cala. Next to her are Ariness, Cinzia, Promithisus, and Pierce."

Karleena nodded to each as Ilfanti introduced them. Ariness was an aquatican. He had blue-pigmented skin, with lime-green hair and beard, both of which were well groomed. He had pointed ears poking through his hair, and appeared very bold and proud as he held her gaze.

When Karleena nodded to Cinzia, she shuddered with a slight hint of pain. The Master was a photon, a member of a race of individuals whose heads combusted and was engulfed in flames since their adolescent years. Cinzia's features were striking and attractive. Her pearl-tinged skin led to light blue flames that emanated from the top of her skull. She appeared indifferent as if more pressing matters demanded her attention.

Promithisus was an albino centaur. He had long wavy white hair trailing down his back. As Karleena nodded to him, she could see by his scowl that this was not one of her allies on the Council.

The final individual Ilfanti introduced was Pierce, the founder and leader of the Mage's Council. Though she was uncertain whether the stories of Pierce's founding the Council were accurate, his name has been found in literature throughout the ages. As she looked at him, he appeared to be no older than a human in his thirties, though his true age spawned the millennia. As an eternal, he was the oldest and most respected member of the Council. His robes were entirely gold, showing him to be the leader of the entire order. The man himself was very muscular and imposing. He had no hair, but shared Karleena's tint of emerald eyes. As he looked at her, it was as if he was peering deep into her soul, and learning all with his gaze.

Pierce did not return Karleena's nod, but instead sat down. As he did so, all other members of the Council also returned to their seats. After all had been seated, he raised a hand toward Karleena and spoke in a deep and demanding voice. "What is it you wish of this Council?"

Karleena glanced around one last time, then stepped to the middle of the hall. "Honored Council members, I come before you during a tumultuous time. The Seven Kingdoms are under siege and the future of the realm may be in peril."

Barely into her introduction, Pierce already leaned forward in his chair and interrupted her. "I have heard a thousand times in a thousand different generations that people lived in trying times. What makes your plea for help any different from theirs?"

Taken aback that she was interrupted so quickly and put on the defensive, Karleena took a deep breath before answering the Master. "Life is always a challenge, and I am certain those before me, and those who come after me, will all have concerns of their own. However, it has been brought to my attention that not only the humans, but the other proud races of the Seven Kingdoms are under siege."

Karleena glanced around the room at the various faces that were listening to her. Some appeared to be listening intently, others with mild interest, and Promethisus with pure disdain. "We are investigating reports of armies being established that will march through the land and conquer all. The Imperium alone cannot withstand these forces. Nor will the independent races. Only united, could we hope to persevere."

Pierce shook his head at her as if she did not have the ability to understand. "Empires rise and fall. I have seen this many times. The failing of the Imperium shall lead to the rise of a new nation. This Council has vowed after losing so many lives fighting the wars of the world outside never to interfere again."

"I can understand your reluctance to assist, honorable Master. However, without a symbol of change and times to come, I fear that the races will fall to these forces."

Ariness spoke out in a calm tone that naturally demanded attention. "Alleged forces."

"I'm sorry?" Karleena inquired.

"You are investigating this opposing army. You are uncertain of its true existence. Thus, it is an alleged force," the aquatican explained.

"Ariness is right. Let this human be gone from my sight," Promethisus spat.

"Calm down, Promethisus," Ilfanti cautioned.

Karleena watched and remembered how Morex warned her that this Council was often at odds with itself. She was confident that her cause was true and just, but if they would not even listen, how could she gain their support?

"Masters, please. I see the concerns you share. The Imperium is just another empire that will come and go in the passage of time. This opposing force may be nothing more than rumors. Still, would this world not be better without the vindictiveness, mistrust, and hatred of other races?" Her words were soft and pure, and she hoped desperately that they would help to sway some of the Council members.

"Oh, please," Promethisus said in disgust. In a mocking tone he tossed her words back at her. "Wouldn't the world be a better place if we could all just get along?"

"Promethisus," Ilfanti said with a deep undertone of warning.

Jeffa looked at Pierce first, then at the rest of the Council. Standing up, he approached Karleena. "Why, thank you, Empress, for your time. The Council shall discuss this matter and inform you of our decision."

Karleena looked at him, puzzled. "I have more I wish to present."

"I'm sure, I'm sure. We are all busy, so please wait outside for our decision." He left no room for debate as he stood with his arm raised toward the wall they had entered.

Karleena scanned the room one more time. She could not believe how poorly things went. The Seven Kingdoms were depending on her, and she hardly was given the opportunity to express her argument. The fact that Jeffa had said nothing except to dismiss her also bothered her. Morex was right about him as well. He was no ally.

She bowed one last time by the wall. "Thank you all for your time. The Imperium appreciates your concern in this matter." Solemnly, she walked through the crystal wall and approached the golden steps. Sitting down, she patiently awaited the decision that would impact the future of so many people.

CHAPTER 38

After Karleena had left the hall, Herg lashed out at the Council members. "She is only trying to make the world a better place."

Cala agreed with her friend and offered her opinion as well. "We could have at least listened to her whole speech before tearing her apart."

Pierce glanced at Herg and then Cala, where he ended with a cold glare. "It is not our place to get involved in the lives of outsiders. This decision will be made quickly."

"Not so fast, Pierce," Ilfanti spoke up. "First off, Herg and Cala are right. Regardless of what you may think of people outside of the order, she is an Empress and deserves some respect."

"Respect. Humph," Promethisus grumbled.

"I was not finished," Ilfanti sneered back. "With the exception of Pierce, I am the only one here old enough to remember the Race Wars. Times were bad. Very bad. A lot of people died. Different races all felt they were superior and those who were different did not deserve to share the same kingdom."

Ilfanti looked around to confirm that people were absorbing his words. Promethisus was clearly ignoring him, and Pierce appeared ready to contradict him. The rest of the Council at least was listening. "The Mage's Council has found a way around such brash prejudices and hatred. Take a walk in the gardens. You see orcs playing with elves. Whoever would have imagined that?"

Cala and Herg were both nodding in agreement to his words. Ilfanti knew that these two close friends of his would agree. Their histories and ties bound them together. Convincing others would be more difficult.

"Yet in the outside world," he continued, "the races outwardly hate and despise each other. Certainly they don't trust. Is this existence? Or is this existing?" Pausing he rescanned the room. "After the Great Wars, the Council at the time vowed never to interfere again. I feel it was a bad decision then, and it is now. We should offer our assistance. All the Empress seeks is someone to help bridge the gap between the races. A mediator. She is not asking us to fight her war for her."

"I agree," Herg bellowed as he pumped his sinewy fist in the air.

Cala nodded her assent as well. "If we can help bring peace to the world, or even keep the races from potential extinction, I feel we must intercede. I vote in favor of assistance."

"We are not voting yet," Pierce admonished.

The centaur Promethisus arose and trotted to the middle of the room. "You all speak of how peaceful things are here. Of how much we trust and respect each other. I tell you this; I saw the destruction that the humans wrought on my people. I will never trust these vermin. Nor will my people."

Senix nodded his head in agreement with his colleague. "Though I feel her position is just, I must agree. I do not see the avarians as being willing to enter into discussions or treaties with the humans. In Estonis, they are safe from any creature that cannot fly. They would not return to the ground and become vulnerable once more."

As he finished his statement, he glanced briefly at Cala who was glaring at him with intense hatred. He quickly averted his gaze and waited to see what Pierce would say.

Regarding the Council members, Pierce beckoned them to quiet and sit down. "This is a debate I do not wish to entertain. I will allow the majority to rule here. If we are to assist and change the decree of the Mage's Council, then so be it. If not, then it shall remain as previously dictated. I vote nay."

Glancing to his left, Pierce indicated that Jeffa would be the next to vote.

Jeffa looked around the Council. "Though it pains me to say this, I feel that the Council members before us were wise when they instituted the noninterference pact. Times do change people, and above all else, we wish not to have the outside world change us. Look at how quickly this discussion has divided this Council! I vote against assisting as well."

Promethisus clapped his hands. "Excellent. Even the human who helped build this Imperium votes against it. Ha! Let it be three against then."

Pierce looked at the centaur. "You will have your turn Promethisus. Senix, how do you vote?"

Senix rubbed his hand through his beard in silent contemplation. Glancing quickly once more at Cala, he delivered his vote. "I stand by my statement. It wouldn't work. Nay."

Herg looked at Senix with a scowl. "You feel that it wouldn't work, so you quit without even trying? How low this Council has fallen. I am almost ashamed to be sitting here and listening to this. I vote in favor of helping."

Ilfanti stared hard at Jeffa. He had not taken his gaze away since Jeffa voted. "I cannot believe you brought her here, comforted her, advised her, then voted against her. You should be ashamed of yourself, Jeffa. I will place my vote where yours should have been. I say we help."

Cala quickly piped in. "As do I."

"Humph. Typical," Promethisus said. "I'd be amazed the day the three of you vote differently."

Ariness raised a finger to his lip to quiet the Council. Closing his eyes, he remained silent for several seconds. The room was plunged into silence as he debated the issue in his own mind. Slowly, he reopened his eyes as he came to a decision. "Her intentions are just and true. She has my support as well."

Ilfanti looked at Ariness and grinned. He did not expect Ariness to vote in favor of assisting the Empress. He was a man who voted logically and rationally, never allowing emotion to sway his decisions. A pleasant surprise to be sure. Looking over at the newest Council member, Ilfanti realized that Cinzia would have the deciding voice.

After hearing Ariness speak, Cinzia looked over at the beaming Ilfanti. "The words of Master Ilfanti have touched me. The races will have to learn to coexist, and without guidance, I do not see that as being feasible. I do not take my vote lightly. I know that my decision will break a deadlock, and I vote in favor of helping."

Promethisus slammed his fist on the side of his chair. "Helping the damned humans? What is wrong with all of you?"

"Enough, Promethisus. Though I am saddened by this Council's ruling, we shall abide by it," Pierce declared. "Who shall we send to assist the Empress?"

"I volunteer," Ilfanti chimed in.

"You would," Senix spat back.

"Excuse me, fly boy? What was that?" demanded Ilfanti.

"You always want to go off on some adventure or another. You'd probably be happy if you never had to sit on this Council."

"Hey, that's me," Ilfanti retorted with a smile. "What can I say, I like to live on the edge."

"You will not leave the Tower, Ilfanti. You are needed here," Pierce declared.

"You telling me that I'm a prisoner here?" Ilfanti challenged the leader of the Council.

"You have responsibilities. Nothing more, nothing less," Pierce replied.

Cala reached over and put a hand on Ilfanti's arm. "This won't solve anything. Save it for another time."

"Very well. We'll talk again, Pierce. Very soon."

"How about Master Dolan?" Jeffa offered. "He has always faired well in diplomacy."

Herg shook his head. "Think, Jeffa, Dolan is human. To make a link with the other races, the Imperium would need a nonhuman symbol to demonstrate their willingness to change."

"Oh, I did not consider that," Jeffa admitted.

"Send Master Korgoth," Promethisus declared.

"Korgoth?" Cala repeated in disbelief.

"Yeah. He'd knock all of those filthy humans into submission, then the other races would be glad to unite together!"

"We're not looking for a master warrior, Promethisus," said Ilfanti.

Ariness stood before speaking. "Cease the debate. I have the perfect contact in mind."

"Go ahead, Ariness. Who?" Ilfanti inquired.

"Master Askari," he declared. "He has some distinct advantages over many candidates. During his Paladin years, he fought alongside his sister Arianna, the Sovereign of Aquatica. This alone is an advantage. He has royalty in his blood and knows how to approach other leaders. In battle, he also gained practical experience of approaching forces of evil. Not to mention, he could obtain his sister's cooperation without extending much effort."

Ilfanti nodded. "I will concur with Ariness. Askari also maintains a strong aura of leadership and respect. When he talks, people listen. I feel that he would be an ideal choice."

"He has an apprentice. You would send an apprentice out before he takes the Trials to enter his Paladin years?" cautioned Senix.

"His apprentice, Cicero, is close to taking the Trials. It would be a little unusual to allow an apprentice to leave the Tower, but he is ready to enter the world. As a wraith, it also provides another diverse race to help display the symbol of unity," Ariness declared.

Pierce spoke up to end the discussion. "This whole session has introduced unusual practices. Cicero will be allowed to go, though he will need to take the Trials immediately upon his return." His ruling was bold and final. He did not leave the selection open to further debate. "Askari is also highly loyal to this Council. He will only act as we see fit."

Pierce reached into his robes and removed a corryby, a small crystalline orb used by the Mages for communication. As he held it, the orb glowed, and the image of Askari appeared before them. "Master Askari," Pierce stated in greeting.

"Master Pierce," he returned. The image above the corryby bowed.

"You and your apprentice shall meet Empress Karleena at the bottom of the Tower. There, you shall assist her in contacting and maintaining diplomatic relations with the various races of the Seven Kingdoms."

"I understand, Master," Askari replied with another bow.

The corryby in Pierce's hand stopped glowing and the image faded. He then returned the orb to a pocket inside his robe. "Bring the Empress back in."

As Jeffa stood up, Ilfanti leapt from his sitting position and spun over his chair toward the wall. "No need to strain yourself, Jeffa. I've got it."

He walked through the wall and saw Karleena sitting on the steps. She looked so sad, as if she knew her attempts had led to failure and all hope was lost. Walking over to her, he squatted down beside her. "We're ready for you now."

Karleena looked up at the small dwarf and searched his face for any sign of what was to come. It was unreadable. Then, without expecting it, she saw his face erupt into joy and he nodded twice to her. "Thank you," she mouthed silently.

The two returned to the hall. As Karleena looked around, she could see that many there were not happy with the decision that the Council arrived at. Seeing their faces, she was grateful Ilfanti had given her a sign that she was triumphant in her pleas.

"Empress Karleena," Pierce spoke as his eyes bored into her for the second time this day. "By a very close vote, this Council has agreed to your request. Master Askari and his apprentice Cicero are waiting for you below to assist you with the attempted unification."

"Thank you, honored Masters," Karleena returned.

"Now go!" boomed Pierce.

Ilfanti, Cala, and Herg all stood up and walked over to Karleena. "We'll see you out."

"Thank you," she said with a smile.

As the three Masters led her back down to the lower levels of the Tower, Karleena felt pure joy and optimism toward the future. The first obstacle had been overcome, and soon, she would be in the position to employ radical changes within the Imperium. Changes that would benefit everyone, even if they did not believe that at first.

CHAPTER 39

"Danchul is really breathtaking this time of day," observed Solara.

Braksis looked around and absorbed his surroundings. They had traveled through Frocomon and were now on the plains of Danchul. As the sun was setting on the horizon, the sky overhead was a striking orange with rays of light reflecting off the clouds. The sun dipping partially below them shadowed the Ventell Mountains, a mountain range stretching throughout the entire kingdom along the shoreline.

"Yes, very beautiful," he agreed.

In the reflection of the light, Braksis could see a large creature flying slightly above the mountains. Though it was shadowed, he knew exactly what it was. "We should find some shelter and set camp for the night."

Solara glanced over at him. "You want to stop this early?"

Braksis pointed at the flying creature. "A griffin."

Solara followed his gaze and saw the beast for herself. "I am sorry I gave in to my distraction. I will be more observant in the future."

"Don't beat yourself up. I didn't see it myself until you told me to look around." Searching the surrounding area, Braksis spotted some rather large rocks jutting from the ground a short distance away. "We'll stop there."

Solara nodded her agreement and the two riders, with Tiot by their side, made their way to the rocky structure. Continuing to watch the griffin in the distance, Solara recalled the story that was told the night they shared with the dwarves. The tale of how a griffin had attacked Theiler and his mount, crippling the dwarf forevermore.

Griffins did not attack humanoids as a rule. However, they craved horsemeat more than any other kind of food. If they spotted a mount, or even a herd, they would become vicious predators, refusing to relent until they claimed their prize. A hungry griffin would be willing to go through many humans to get to a horse.

Arriving at the rocks, Braksis quickly dismounted. "Tie the horses up on this side of the rocks," he instructed. Leaning out as he strapped Blaze down, he was satisfied the griffin had not spotted them, or at least was not approaching them.

"We should cover them, too. Just in case," Solara suggested.

"Agreed." Pulling out blankets they normally would sleep in, Braksis draped them over the horses so they were covered in case one of the mighty beasts flew overhead. "Hopefully this will be good enough. We'll need to be more cautious for the next few days until we reach Vorstad."

"Yeah, if we don't freeze to death tonight. Then we won't have to worry about much."

"You're the one who suggested covering the horses," Braksis quickly retorted.

"Yeah, but we could have gathered some hay, or branches. If I freeze to death, I hold you personally responsible," Solara declared with a wry smile.

"Well, you are supposed to protect me from harm, aren't you?" Braksis inquired with an expression of mischievousness.

Pausing in her reply, Solara exaggerated her answer. "Yes."

"And you fear that we could freeze to death?"

"What's your point?" Solara demanded.

"Well, I guess you'll just have to snuggle up next to me and make sure I don't freeze to death."

"In your dreams," Solara said as she playfully shoved him.

"Ah, but what beautiful dreams." Smiling he watched his companion. "They alone shall keep me warm tonight."

"Well then, Braksis, I'll just have to make sure that I follow the dictates of my order and keep you warm," Solara said matter-of-factly.

"Oh really?" Braksis asked dubiously.

"Really," Solara answered, then walked off with a seductive smile on her face.

"Then where are you going?"

"To find us some kindling." She giggled.

"Kindling?" Watching her begin to accumulate some branches, he looked down at Tiot. "Kindling?"

Tiot jumped up and licked his face twice.

Solara looked over and laughed. "Tiot will keep you comfortable tonight. I have nothing to worry about."

"You don't know what you could be missing," he challenged as he scratched Tiot behind his ear.

Solara paused for a moment to think of the conversation. They were speaking solely in jest, and she was well aware of that. However, she suddenly found herself thinking it would not be so bad if she relented, and they did allow events this night to unfold as they would. The two had been quite close for years since she first vowed to protect his life. Though she never thought of him as anything more than a friend and ally whom she fought alongside, new thoughts had recently begun to gradually sweep through her. Warmth flowed through her body, and she found herself desperately hoping the conversation was geared elsewhere.

Braksis looked up and watched her as she stood there pausing. No retort or rebuttal seemed to be forthcoming. "I finally managed to render you speechless?"

Looking over at him, Solara seemed to be seeing the Warlord for the very first time. He truly was a handsome man, with qualities she found quite admirable. Though she found him a bit serious at times, he still put that aside to smile and joke with her. Yet he also seemed quite taken by Queen Zerilla when they traveled to Suspinti. Though he seemed to move on and remain focused, she was uncertain as to his true feelings for her. The curiosity and sudden anger at the thoughts of the beautiful queen caught Solara by surprise. She never knew she could succumb to jealousy before.

The fact that Angel was able to pick up on it before she did herself also was troubling. Had she been outwardly displaying signals of affection? Was she embarrassing herself?

Braksis moved away from Tiot and toward Solara. She still stood where she was, watching him. "Solara?" His tone was soft and gentle, full of concern. "Are you okay?"

Solara breathed deeply. The scent of nature permeated the air. The ambiance of the twilight was intoxicating. Lost in her thoughts, she realized how seductive these surroundings could be.

Suddenly he was before her. He reached out and gently brushed his fingers against her arms. "Solara?"

She looked up into his greenish-blue eyes. The yellow starburst around his pupil seemed to sparkle. "I'm sorry. My mind was wandering," she finally replied.

Without letting her go, he continued to look her in the eye and saw passion and desire in her gaze. He would never have expected this from his mystral companion, for the mystral themselves had abandoned the normal male and female intimacies. A mystral warrior was a solitary female warrior who was called upon at a certain age to be impregnated by what they refer to as the "Essence of the Dragon." Though he often wondered if Solara or these other warriors had attractions or desired men, he had never seen any indications of that, until now.

"Solara..."

Realizing he must have picked up on the longing in her eyes, she quickly pulled away. "I'm fine. My mind was just wandering." As she turned, some of the kindling fell to the ground. Braksis leaned down and helped her pick it up, keeping his gaze on her the entire time.

"Look what you made me do," Solara accused. "If you kept playing with Tiot, I wouldn't have dropped any of this."

Sensing she was trying a little too hard to change the topic, Braksis envisioned that look once more. He was certain that as she looked up at him, she was hoping and wishing for something more than the companionship they currently shared.

This was troubling. For the same reason he did not wish to pursue Zerilla further, any intimacies between himself and Solara could only result in disaster. The two fought side by side. If they were to become romantically attached, then at a pivotal moment in a battle, one could make a fatal mistake because of their feelings for the other.

There was no way two warriors could enter into relations while still fighting side by side. He knew this instinctively. As he watched her return to the encampment with her share of the kindling, he was troubled even further by the thought that he did not care.

He did not care that life would be difficult or dangerous. He did not care that they had been friends and companions for so long. Watching her, he suddenly realized the two shared a deep bond, and the prospect of enhancing that into a more personal regard was a rather appealing prospect.

Walking back to the camp, he placed his portion of the kindling in a pile close to hers. "Do you want some help?"

"I've got it covered. After all, it's my job to protect you."

Watching her go about her work, he could see she seemed to be purposefully avoiding him, as if she dared not to even look at him.

"Solara?" he questioned softly.

She turned and looked at him again. "Yes?"

"I don't want to lose you," he said in a serious tone.

"You could never lose me. My life is sworn to yours," she replied as sternly as she could.

"You know what I mean." He wanted to get her to stop avoiding the topic. "I saw the way you were looking at me."

She lowered her eyes and stared hard at the ground without speaking.

"Solara?"

"I'm sorry. I don't know what has come over me. It's just that we were playing, then my mind wandered. I'm a mystral. I am sworn to protect you."

Braksis reached out and gently raised her chin. He could see tears in her eyes. "It is a most appealing prospect. There is nobody who knows me better, or who I care for more than you."

As he said it, he opened his arms and beckoned for her to get closer and to hug. Reluctantly, she leaned forward and the two embraced. It was a long and passionate embrace, with neither speaking nor desiring to pull away.

After several long moments, Solara moved her head back and the two lost themselves within each other's eyes. Slowly, they inched closer together leaving all worries and possible consequences behind. All that mattered to them at that moment was the kiss that was about to alter their relationship forever.

"Well, ain't that real sweet-like?"

Immediately alert, Braksis and Solara pushed apart and searched for the unknown voice. Standing atop the rocky structure, three men were glaring down at them, fully armed with a variety of weapons.

One man held a small net, and tossed it toward the growling Tiot, ensnaring him.

"We wouldn't want the wolf to interfere now, would we?"

"What is the meaning of this?" demanded Braksis.

"Well, the meaning is real simple,"declared the speaker. "We are assassins, and you have been designated for termination."

Braksis and Solara exchanged a quick glance, and that was all the two needed. Solara back-flipped toward the covered horses, and Braksis lunged at the trio while they were distracted. He grasped the ankle of the man closest to him, and pulled it toward him, forcing him to fall flat on his back with a yelp of pain.

The second man jumped down on top of Braksis, causing both to topple to the ground and roll. As they were struggling, Braksis tried to turn his head away as the stench of his attacker overwhelmed his senses. The man wore rags for clothes, had dirt caked all around his face and body, and rotted teeth that were revealed as he smiled at the Warlord.

The man pulled a dagger from around his waist, and brought it down with all of his might trying to slice into Braksis's throat.

Braksis closed both of his hands flat and held the blade at bay mere inches from the exposed skin of his neck.

The man on top of him was smiling and snorting as he continued to push down.

Slowly, Braksis forced the blade to the side so that it was only above the ground. Then without warning, he released his grip, and the man rammed the dagger into the grass as the resistance vanished. Braksis then brought his elbow up into the man's jaw, breaking it instantly.

Rolling over, he forced the attacker off of him, and pulled the dagger out of the ground to use as a weapon. Quickly scanning his surroundings, he saw these three men were not alone. Several others were approaching from the plains.

The attacker who had ensnared Tiot was rushing toward Solara, who was uncovering the horses to gather her own weapons. Braksis tossed the blade up in the air and caught it by its tip. Then breathing deeply, he hurtled the blade through the air toward the attacker who now had his hands raised and was ready to thrust a club down on Solara's head. The dagger pierced him in the middle of his back, and he staggered forward, dropping the club behind him.

Solara spun around and tossed him Carnage, the battle-axe Braksis claimed as his own after the battle of Arkham. Catching it, the Warlord quickly looked for the next threat, and stood ready as the attackers moved in on him.

Solara removed her elongated mystral blade, and focused on the attackers herself. She sensed a couple of assassins close to her, but was distracted looking at the several men charging Braksis.

Two men then jumped up from the grass, both holding crossbows. The arrows flew through the air toward the unprepared mystral warrior.

Realizing her mistake and lack of focus, Solara allowed her body to go limp and drop backward, falling barely out of the reach of the oncoming arrows. One flew harmlessly over her head, but the other grazed her arm, leaving a stinging slice. As she fell to the ground, she yelled out in shock, but quickly reclaimed her focused demeanor.

Hearing the scream of his companion, Braksis turned to look, dreading what he might see. Solara was on the ground, but she quickly got up and sent two throwing blades toward the crossbow wielders. The blades hit their mark, dropping the two opponents.

Feeling a sense of relief flood through him, Braksis turned to face the charging attackers, only to realize that he allowed his distraction to delay him for too long. A man with a staff sent it slamming into his stomach, forcing the air from his lungs. He then spun the staff around and slashed down at Braksis's legs, knocking him down on his back.

As he hit the ground, pain seared through him. Deep down, he screamed at himself for allowing distractions to interrupt the battle. He needed to focus and regain the upper hand.

The man with the staff twirled it in the air and brought it down as hard as he could toward Braksis's head. Braksis rolled away, barely missing the fatal blow.

Solara rushed toward Braksis, pausing briefly by the struggling Tiot. Within his snare, Tiot was yelping and growling, struggling to get free. "Easy, boy," Solara cautioned, and cut the mesh netting.

When the opening was large enough, Tiot jumped through and raced toward the attacker and his master. Jumping up, he landed on top of the man with the staff, sinking his teeth into the man's throat.

Solara quickly followed the wolf's lead and confronted one of the other men. She could see the fear in his eyes as he raised his mace, and knew that this would end quickly. Leaping over him, she landed and sent her sword between her stomach and arm, and pierced the attacker in the chest as he turned to defend against her leap.

Pulling her blade away she spun it back into ready position. The man she just killed fell to the ground by her feet. Solara took three quick steps and engaged a sword wielder. This man she noted displayed no fear. He did not even seem fazed that his allies were quickly dwindling. As an assassin, she guessed he probably hoped to get more of the profits for himself.

As he lunged at her, she dropped to her knees, avoided the blow, and brought her sword straight up slicing into his manhood. Screaming in a high-pitched tone, the man faltered and quickly lost consciousness.

Looking for another foe, Solara could see that Braksis had regained his footing and was quickly finishing the final pair of would-be assassins.

Not accustomed to the axe, Braksis felt awkward wielding the hefty weapon. Yet he found that with a full swing, he managed to cleave his opponents' blades in two, just as his own sword, the Phoenix, had been destroyed.

Between the two remaining men, one continued to attack, and the other opted that discretion was the better alternative. Braksis brought the axe down with a piercing thrust and ripped into the man from his shoulder down to his chest. As he plummeted to the ground, Braksis watched as Tiot charged after the fleeing man.

The timber wolf bit into the man's calf and brought him tumbling to the ground screaming in pain. Braksis turned away and approached the man whose jaw he broke. Before reaching him, the night was silenced once more as the man Tiot attacked joined his companions in the afterlife.

Reaching down, Braksis pulled the man with the broken jaw up. "Who sent you?"

With a struggle to speak, the man mumbled slowly. "You broke my jaw."

"I said, who sent you?" Braksis repeated.

Solara walked up beside the two men and pointed her mystral blade at the man's nose. "I can convince him a little. The mystral have learned thousands of ways to inflict pain but keep the subject alive."

The man looked at her horrified. "I'll talk. Please, I don't want to die."

Squinting, Braksis coolly replied. "Then you probably should find a new profession. Now talk."

"We were contracted by the son of Sar-argh."

Suddenly a blast of light struck the man in the chest, cutting off his speech. His entire body convulsed and then combusted from the inside out. Braksis and Solara spun around searching for the new attacker, spotting the last thing they wanted to confront—a Shadow Mage.

Before the two warriors could take a step toward the new attacker, he blended into the shadows and vanished in the night.

"Did you see that?" Solara asked.

"I was hoping I was imagining it," Braksis replied quietly.

He pensively approached the spot where the Shadow Mage had stood, but found no sign of him. "So much for my hope that I killed the only one of these things in Dartie." Looking back at Solara, he glanced toward the man who had been speaking to them. "Is he dead?"

Looking at the smoldering remains, she knew there was no hope. "He won't be telling us anything anytime soon."

"The son of Sar. I wonder what he was going to say. Could it be Winton? The son of Sarlec?" Braksis theorized out loud.

"Possibly, but it could be anybody," Solara rationalized.

"After what just happened, I think I'd rather risk the griffins than stay here any longer. Let's continue on to Vorstad."

Solara nodded her agreement. The sun had completely gone down now, along with, she feared, any chance the two had at passion. Thinking back to the battle, she realized that both had been distracted while looking out for the other. These budding emotions would have to be suppressed or else they both might wind up dead.

As he prepared his horse, Braksis looked at Solara one last time. He found himself deeply regretting not having that kiss they almost shared, but decided that it was probably for the best. Warlords and fighters had no time or place for love.

CHAPTER 40

That same evening, Kai led the pack mule carrying the small child to the same spot where she had previously rested with Braksis so long ago when they met the traveling dwarves. As she looked around, images of that night filled her mind and came to life before her. Even though each faced bleak futures, they were joyous and optimistic.

Walking the mule over to the same branch she had tied her loaned horse once before, she strapped her new mount in and prepared to make camp for the night. Removing the blankets and cooking supplies that had been provided on the mule's pack, she quickly went to work.

After several minutes, she had a fire blazing and tended to her periodic rituals with the child. A little over a week had gone by since the attack at Arkham, and the child still did not rouse from her slumber. Though Kai tended to the injuries, she sincerely wished that Rulysta, or another true healer, were here with the child instead of her.

Seeing no improvement, Kai returned to the pack mule and removed several arrows from a quiver. "I won't be gone long," she whispered as she gently rubbed her hand down the mule's beige mane.

Heading deeper into the Suspintian Forest, Kai hunted for any kind of plant or animal that could be used for sustenance.

Concentrating, the pink elf blended into her surroundings. Her movements were quiet, and her breathing slowed. As she silently moved around, constantly alert, she knew that in this state, she disturbed nothing.

Through a small brush, she spotted a young deer. Quietly, she approached the animal. With each step, she regretted having to resort to killing a defenseless beast like this, but with all things in life, the strong will survive, and if it came down to her or it, the deer would lose every time.

Her mind cleared of all images. All she could see was the deer. The world around her came to a standstill and she moved in slow motion. Carefully, she lifted the first arrow and strung it in her bow. Pulling back, she noted how the bow itself made the first noise since she had entered the forest.

The deer looked up at the sound of the bow being strung but did not dart away. It still had not perceived the threat of danger. Returning to the grasses below, the deer resumed eating.

Kai loosened her grip on the string, and knew that within moments, the deer would fall beneath her attack. Before she could fire, however, the deer darted off deeper into the woods.

Perplexed, Kai knew she had not made any further noise. Kneeling down, she studied her surroundings and tried to ascertain what startled the deer. That was when she heard it.

Deeper in the woods, though a little closer than she would like, she heard movement. By the sound of it, she guessed it was a large group of humanoid creatures. She could hear speaking, but the language was unknown to her.

Feeling that the child was vulnerable by her remaining here, Kai returned to the camp as quickly as she could manage without bringing too much attention to herself. She did not know what was out there, but a feeling of dread overcame her.

Arriving back at the camp, she smothered the flames. The illumination could have attracted those within the forest, and she only hoped they had not yet seen the fire. Preparing an arrow, she stood by the child and waited for any threat that may appear.

Behind her, a voice startled her. "You need not worry. They are moving into the forest, not out of it."

Spinning around, Kai raised the bow at the intruder, but refrained from firing the arrow. "Who are you?"

"Who I am is unimportant. All you need to know is that I am a friend." The voice was soft and smooth. It had almost a hypnotic effect to it, convincing her that she had nothing to fear.

Without lowering her bow, Kai considered the intruder. He wore a black hooded tunic with purple outlining. His face was mostly shaded and dark, but she could see orange stubble on his chin, and yellow eyes that peered at her from the darkness within his hood. His shirt was sleeveless, revealing white small-haired furry arms with orange slashes. Upon each wrist he had laced two black and purple armguards. His pants were tight fitting, with one narrow purple stripe on each black pants leg. His boots were all black and extended to his knees. Though she was certain he was armed, she could not see any weapons clearly displayed.

"I have never met you. How do I know that you are a friend?" Kai inquired.

"You may not have met me, but we have crossed paths before," the intruder replied.

"I do not understand."

"I have been assisting you since you left the tigrel. I am a friend of Hr'Sheesh, and it also suits my employer to see you along safely."

Pondering his words, Kai desired more information. "Who is your employer?"

"Ah, but once again, that particular tidbit of information is unimportant."

"Can I at least refer to you as something?" Kai replied quickly, still keeping her bow raised.

"Yes. That will be acceptable. You can call me Archer. That is all I shall reveal," Archer said.

"Explain to me then, how you have assisted me," Kai instructed.

"I was contacted by Hr'Sheesh to bring your horse to the other edge of the Dimmu Forest and leave it for you. I also brought you the pack mule, fully supplied, while you slept."

"Why did you not reveal yourself to me?" Kai asked.

"Because my employer did not desire it. In our business, secrecy is best. A better question you could ask is why I have opted to reveal myself to you now."

"Very well. Why now?"

A smile could be seen from the darkness around his face. "Very good. Now we are getting someplace. You are traveling to find the fairies. You were told that they have healing powers, and that if you found Shimendyn, you could heal both yourself and Kyria from drinking there."

"Kyria?" Kai asked.

"The child you travel with. Certainly you knew her name?" Archer asked incredulously.

"I'm curious as to how you know any of this. Are you privy to my thoughts and conversations?"

"No, I admit that I am not. My employer finds it within her best interest to know as much as possible. Especially about those who can impact the balance of things in the world. As such, you have fallen under our scrutiny."

"I don't know if I like the sound of that," Kai said.

"Like it or not, we are only helping you." Watching her, he raised a hand toward her bow. "Now that we are speaking freely, could we please do so without the threat of shooting me?"

Kai squinted as she stared at him, then reluctantly lowered her bow. "Very well. You still haven't told me why you are here."

"You yourself heard the creatures in the night. The invasion of the Suspintian Forest has begun. Many races call this forest their home. Not so many will survive the coming onslaught. It is within all of our best interests if you refrain from traveling in the woods yourself."

"Kyria, as you call her, is unconscious. She will not awaken. If the fairies can help her, then I must push onward."

"I thought you might feel this way. I have acquired that which you seek," Archer said.

"Where is it?" Kai asked skeptically.

Reaching behind his back, Archer pulled a small vile from his belt. "Within this vial, there is enough medicine to cure both you and the child of your wounds. I will give it to you freely if you agree to leave this place."

"Nothing is free in the world."

Archer smiled at her. "Impressive. Very intuitive and wise. My employer has selected well in choosing you."

"I still do not understand," Kai returned.

"You need not understand now. One day, perhaps, my employer will call upon you for a small favor. It will not be anything that will go against your conscience or desires, but it will be something that she needs, and you will grant it."

"And if I do not agree?" Kai asked.

"Then the child will remain in her coma, and you will be forced to face an army of raiding hobgoblins to try to save her yourself. I assure you, this is most definitely the lesser of two evils," Archer assured her.

"I still would prefer to know more about your employer. Who is she? What does she want?" Kai demanded.

"You must make a decision with what you already know. I told you that you would learn no more," Archer retorted. "Time is short. You must leave this place soon. What is your decision?"

Kai looked down at the unconscious child. So much emphasis had been placed on this defenseless girl to save the world. Yet, unless she made the right decision here, all may be lost before Kyria was even given a chance. "Very well. You have my word."

"Excellent." Archer tossed the vial to Kai. "Split the vial into two equal portions and dilute it with water. You will see results almost instantaneously."

"Thank you," Kai answered. As Archer turned to walk away, Kai spoke out. "I have one last question."

Archer paused without turning. "Name it."

"You are defenseless. How could you trust that I would not kill you?"

"I have faith in my abilities. You would not kill me." Taking several more steps, Archer spoke one more time. "As for being defenseless?"

Kai watched as he walked away. He pulled a small object from his belt. In the moonlight, she could see it extend both ways from his hand and turn into a staff. She smiled as he walked off and vanished into the night. "Until we meet again, Archer."

Hoping that the vial she now held truly contained the cure for the child; Kai grabbed the water canteen from the mule, along with a pair of small drinking containers. She carefully measured the contents of the vial into two equal amounts, then added the water. Pulling one of Lucky's claws, she slowly stirred each cup.

Looking at the child, she felt hope surge through her. "Well, little one, this is the moment of truth."

Deciding to test the potion on herself first to make sure that it would not hurt Kyria, Kai drank the contents of her cup in one full gulp. Putting the empty container down, she examined her injuries.

"He said it would be instantaneous." Frustrated, she waited, as no effect seemed apparent. Then, a burning sensation overcame her body. She felt as if the sun itself raged within her. The pain was searing and nearly unbearable. Then, as quickly as it had begun, the pain was gone.

Kai slowly opened her eyes and looked at her arm where Lucky had scarred her. The wounds were completely gone. Leaving her walking staff behind, she stood up and jumped around realizing that her legs, too, were better.

"Unbelievable," she whispered.

Carefully picking up the second cup, Kai approached Kyria and knelt down beside her. She raised the child's head and slowly poured the liquid into her mouth. "I hope this works as well on you, little one."

Leaning back, she watched the child intently, hoping desperately for a sign that the child would recover. Then it began. Kyria started to tremble. Her eyes fluttered as if she were in a nightmare. Kai leaned over and cradled her young body, trying to pass along her strength.

Then the shaking stopped, and the blonde-haired girl opened her eyes for the first time since the battle of Arkham. Looking up at Kai, she held a curious look. "Am I dreaming?"

Kai smiled down at the child. "No, you are not dreaming."

"I have seen you before. You are the pink lady from my dreams."

"I have seen you in my dreams as well. My name is Kai," Kai revealed.

"Kyria. What happened?"

"Your village was destroyed. I have rescued you," Kai informed her.

"They destroyed themselves," Kyria stated in a somber tone. "You are here to protect me, aren't you?"

"Yes. We shall talk more later. For now, we must move along. This area is not safe for us," Kai told her.

Kyria understood, and without question about how she got where she was or further detail as to what happened, she stood up and helped Kai pack up their supplies. The two looked at each other, and for the first time, felt optimistic about their future travels. As long as they were together, both felt they could overcome any obstacle.

CHAPTER 41

The visit to Winton from Xyphin, a dark Mage who was a trusted lieutenant of Lady Salaman, was enough to send him spiraling toward defeat and depression. The assassins he had arranged to have murder Lord Braksis had failed. Xyphin assured him the surviving members of the attempt had already been dealt with. However, before they had died, it was possible they told Lord Braksis that it was Winton who ordered the assassination attempt.

Winton was almost in a panic, and Xyphin certainly had better things to do than sit with this sniveling whelp, this poor excuse for a man. The night was almost over, and like all chiroptera, Xyphin was a nocturnal creature and avoided the light as much as possible. To remain here much longer he risked flight in daylight.

His species, the chiroptera, were humanoid bat-like creatures. They were blind, but maintained a strengthened sense of hearing in the form of sonar, which is how they could see the world they lived in. Their arms were attached to large wings, typically black or a dark shade of gray. Xyphin was raised as a Mage, so he had the added benefit of various telepathic and telekinetic abilities, which added to his own heightened senses. Although blind, because of this, he could perceive images quite clearly, even in more detail at times than those with normal sight. However, he still preferred the dark, and remaining out in the sunlight was not his idea of an option.

To Winton, Xyphin was the most intimidating presence he had ever seen. His face was furry with an outstretched jaw filled with incisor teeth. His ears were large, round, and perked up listening to everything. Although blind, Xyphin still had two eyes, though they were clouded and not focused. His fingers were long and pointed, attached to the long gray wings, but even more intimidating were the bulging muscles of his arms. His stomach and chest were covered with the same black fur as his head, with two small legs that also had clawed feet. Winton had no doubt that, like bats, Xyphin could easily hang by his feet from the ceiling or a perch.

Looking at Xyphin with trepidation, Winton attempted to gain his senses enough to try to make this situation redeemable. After all, he was the son of King Sarlec. A prince himself. He had no reason to tremble in fear. Yet his words still came out with great pause and anxiety in his voice. "Since the Hidden Empire failed, is it safe to assume you will protect me? Attempt to kill Braksis once more?"

Xyphin listened intently, but could feel the warming of the air. The sun would soon be up, and he would need to be gone. "You took out a contract. The amount of money you paid was insignificant to purchase top quality assassins. If the mission is a failure, then you should have requested better men. More expensive men."

"But...we had a deal," Winton pleaded.

Realizing that Winton would one day be the King of Danchul, a land that Lady Salaman would be quite anxious to gain influence in, he opted to set up the seeds of control here and now. "Young Winton, you do not understand how business is run in these parts. If you are looking for someone to watch you, we would be happy to protect you."

Looking at Xyphin with hope, but also suspicion, Winton entertained the idea. "I have no more money. I used up my personal accounts to hire the original men you sent. If I used other funds, then my father would become suspicious!"

"Your father will not always be around," Xyphin replied. "We could send some of our agents here to offer protection. You would never even know they were here. No fee at this time."

"At this time?" Winton questioned.

"Exactly. I'm sure that once you become King, a more reasonable arrangement could be designed. Perhaps some land, money, a percentage of profits from your kingdom, or other things of that nature. We could work out the details in good time."

Winton knew that the Hidden Empire was not to be taken lightly. What Xyphin offered was a one-way trip to life as a front to a criminal organization. His lands, votes, and influence would all become those of Lady Salaman. He would no longer have any control himself. Of course, he would be alive. "If I agree, will you also make another attempt on Lord Braksis?"

"When you agree, Lady Salaman will consider how best to protect her investment. She will decide. No guarantees, you understand." Xyphin's bat-like face was full of teeth and a mockery of a human grin.

Seeing no alternative, Winton lowered his head and assented. "Very well. Just make sure I am protected. We will work out terms when I am King."

"Excellent. Lady Salaman will be most pleased." Emissions of the air once again reminded him that daylight was soon upon him. "With that, I must bid thee farewell."

"Wait, when will my protectors come?"

His question went unanswered as Xyphin spread his wings and took to the skies. Protection was guaranteed, as Lady Salaman saw fit. He only hoped she saw fit to track and kill Braksis as well. This was not turning out to be a good morning.

As he slowly walked back toward the castle he called home, his thoughts drifted to Zoldex. With that, he quickened his pace and sprinted to see his mentor. Perhaps Zoldex could find a way to help him out of this predicament.

Without knocking, he opened the door to the basement that Zoldex called his own. "Zoldex, show yourself!" As Winton walked down the steps, he was struck with pitch black. No light at all emanated from the depths below.

Then all at once, the same three candles that Zoldex usually left lit, all burst into flames, causing Winton's eyes to widen in shock, then squint to readjust. "What has transpired that requires my assistance, my lad?" His words were icy cold. As if spoken from a ghost or phantom.

Winton waited until his eyes adjusted, then walked down to the floor and sat. "The assassination attempt on Lord Braksis failed!"

"Yes. I know," Zoldex coolly replied.

"You know? You know?" The hysteria in Winton was increasing. "You told me to have him assassinated!"

"Do not overreact, boy. Things are progressing quite nicely."

"Overreact? I just sold my soul to the Hidden Empire. I am theirs now for all time!"

For the first time, Winton could see the eyes of his mentor since arriving in the room. The appearance of fire flickering sent him shuddering. "That was your own fault for not coming to me first."

"Zoldex, please!" he pleaded. "How do we salvage this?"

"Quite simply. Braksis must die so that none know of your involvement."

Winton shook his head again. "That is easier said than done. We tried. Tried and failed. The Hidden Empire won't try again. They will just send guards."

Zoldex listened intently. "One problem at a time. We shall save this desperation deal with the Hidden Empire for another time. For now, we shall deal with Lord Braksis."

"Desperation deal? Another time? If you back out on your word with Lady Salaman, you wind up dead! There's no other time for this!" Tears flowed down Winton's tanned cheeks.

For the first time, Zoldex took a firm hand rather than mind tricks. "Shut up, you sniveling whelp. Your tears offend me. I shall deal with Lord Braksis for you. He shall perish as I have foreseen."

"Are you certain?"

"I said, shut up! Do not speak again unless I allow it." Zoldex paused to make certain Winton would not speak again. When he was sure his point was clear, he continued. "I want you to take an envoy and return to the palace where you will join your father. Act as if nothing is wrong. The attempt on Braksis never happened. The Hidden Empire, who are they? Nothing ever happened. Do you understand?"

Winton nodded once showing that he understood.

"Excellent. You will go to the palace. Tell your father you were bored here, and that you wish to finally bond with him. To take a more active interest in the Imperium; that you wanted to work together as father and son; to make him proud of you. Are you still following me?"

Winton nodded again.

"This is how you shall remain until I send you a message to do otherwise. Do not question my instructions. Just carry them out. Understand?"

Winton lowered his head. "I understand."

"Excellent. Now go. Prepare for your journey to the palace. Leave me to handle matters while you are gone."

"But Zoldex, how will you handle Lord Braksis?" Winton inquired.

"I said, go," Zoldex sneered.

"Yes, sir. I'm going." In total defeat, Winton slowly walked back up the stairs and left Zoldex alone once again.

Watching him leave Zoldex shook his head and wondered how he put up with that whining, spoiled brat for so long. How would he deal with the Hidden Empire? He'd let them kill the boy for violating their trust. First though, he would allow Winton to live up to his usefulness.

His plan was proceeding quite nicely. Of course the assassination attempt would fail. He made certain that the money Winton put up was insignificant to hire anyone of talent. The fingers were now pointed at Winton, who would quickly have a fall from grace after Zoldex was through with him. The foundation was set.

Now he must deal with Braksis himself, as he always knew he would have to. Not with hired guns, but with individuals with vendettas. Individuals who wished to see Braksis dead with each breath that entered their lungs. A select pair that would succeed where hired hands couldn't dream of going.

He closed his eyes and raised his palms upward. An image appeared above each hand. He opened his eyes and glared at the two individuals. In his left hand, an image from Braksis's childhood was seen clear as day. A man who took everything away from Braksis, creating the man that he is today. A man that Braksis confronted a second time and brought to his knees. A man who now was destined to spend the rest of his life in prison just hoping and praying he would die soon, but not before he learned that his younger cousin, Braksis, was dead first. This man was known as Rawthorne. Life in prison had treated him kind. His muscles had bulged out with little more to do than work out in a life of boredom and misery. The image had a large and bushy brown mustache that trailed from his upper lip and down both sides of his mouth. His hair was also long and flowed freely down his back. In prison, he was respected and feared. There was a story that once he ate a fellow inmate's arm after he had tried to steal food from Rawthorne. Nobody had bothered him since.

In his right hand was an image of a man that was also brought low, but who had fallen even further since. The Warlord who at one time almost killed Braksis if not for the interference of Solara. The man who was responsible for the two to unite in the first place, Durgin. The Imperial troops were unable to keep Durgin a prisoner. Shortly after his capture, he escaped and fled to the swamps of Tenalong. Life in the swamps was not kind. He still towered over most men, but the ferociousness that made many fear him turned into a cower he had regretted since. He dreamed of facing not only Lord Braksis again, but his own inner demons and turmoil.

Two men, both from Braksis's past. Both with reasons to see him brought low and killed. Both would be ideal candidates for Zoldex to bring together for that common goal. With Braksis dead, the two could do whatever they wanted. Until he died, they would both belong to Zoldex. With that thought, Zoldex allowed himself a small sinister laugh, then began to pull the necessary strings to bring his new plan to fruition.

CHAPTER 42

Looking out a window, Karleena watched as carriages approached the palace. Her messages had been received and the royal families had gradually begun to arrive. Pondering how to handle the next few days, she was gladdened by the presence of Morex and Centain.

Both men spent much of the past week with her discussing the upcoming meetings and how best to approach them. Centain suggested that the meetings should reside within the halls of the palace, rather than in the Chamber where meetings like this typically would unfold. He felt that with royal families as well as various races arriving, they would all benefit from the added scrutiny of security checks and isolation, which the palace had over the Chamber.

"Another carriage has arrived," Karleena muttered.

Centain approached the window and glanced out. "That is King Sarlec. He has returned."

Karleena closed her eyes and said a silent prayer for the Danchul king. "I can only imagine how he is feeling after seeing the destruction wrought upon his domain."

"My lady, you are working passionately to bring about these changes. Allow the sadness to help fuel you, but not distract you," Morex cautioned.

"Thank you, Admiral."

"When should we anticipate representatives of the races coming to Trespias? I will need to modify our security measures for their arrival," said Centain.

"Master Askari did not provide any time estimates," Karleena replied.

Morex sat in a chair within the room. "Do we have any assurances as to which races will be represented?"

"The Sovereign of Aquatica has already been contacted and has agreed to come and represent her people personally. She and Askari are siblings. Other than that, Master Askari took his apprentice and ventured off to the other races and ruling castes. I have not heard from them since they departed, though they left me a communication device so they can report in."

A loud knocking at the door interrupted the conversation. Karleena raised a hand to signal the guards at the door to permit the newcomer to enter. As they opened the double doors, Prime Minister Torscen stormed into the room.

"What is the meaning of this? I demand answers!" Torscen screamed.

Karleena watched the Prime Minister and could see his confrontational pose. This man was looking for a fight. Centain inched away from the wall and stood slightly to her side, ready to intervene if need be.

"Calm down, Torscen," Morex warned.

"Calm down? Calm down?" He roared as his temper escalated. "The royal families are being assembled, and I, the Prime Minister and their representative, know nothing of it? This is an outrage!"

Refusing to back down beneath his fury, Karleena held his gaze. "I assure you, Minister, all will be revealed in time. I am not attempting to circumvent you, but there are times when an Empress needs to proceed as she sees fit."

"Sees fit? An Empress? Don't make me laugh! You are but a wee little girl who knows not the ways of the world."

"Torscen!" The shout came from the hall as Sarlec forced his way through the double doors. "I told you not to speak to her like that. Do you wish to incur my wrath?"

Torscen searched the faces in the room and realized he had no allies here. Something he desperately needed. Without replying, he stormed toward the door and past Sarlec. He was determined to find out what was going on, but there were other ways to acquire information. With that information, he would be better suited to manipulate the proceedings.

As he tried to walk by, Sarlec firmly grabbed his arm. Squeezing tightly, he stared into Torscen's eyes, proclaiming an unspoken threat.

"Release me," Torscen declared.

"As long as we understand each other," Sarlec sneered as he released his grip.

Waiting for the Minister to vacate the room and the guards to close the doors, Morex stood and addressed the room. "He is going to try to interfere with your plans. He does still have influence with much of the aristocracy."

"Bah! He should be dropped out of a window and then we would be done with him," Sarlec growled.

Centain smiled at the king. "A rather unique proposition, but I could arrange it."

Laughing softly at first, then erupting into a large bellow, Sarlec demonstrated his appreciation of the joke. "I'm really beginning to like this man."

Karleena approached the king and took his hands in her own. "It is good to see you laugh, my old friend."

"Yes. So much tragedy, almost more than I can bear. I am glad to return here and leave the destruction of Loveskia behind me, though I shall never be able to escape these images in my mind." Taking a deep breath to collect himself, he took his hands back and portrayed the same strong character she had always known. "Enough of that, what news have we here?"

"With the exception of King Garum, all of the royal families are here already," Centain informed him. "No representatives of the races have arrived yet."

"Garum? Bah! He probably can't come until Lady Salaman gives her personal approval," Sarlec declared with spite.

Centain studied the king for a moment. "Should we provide extra security then to make sure that Garum is not being influenced by outside sources?"

Shaking her head, Karleena ended the debate. "Garum is the king of Tenalong and will be treated with respect. I will not authorize added security to single him out."

"Even if he is a puppet?" Sarlec inquired.

"Even then," she responded.

Suddenly looking agitated, Centain looked at his guards. "We are under attack."

Shocked, Karleena looked at him. "What?"

"The docks. Something has the sailors by the docks agitated. They fear we are under attack," Centain continued.

"The docks? My men. Let's go, Captain," Morex said.

Watching this curiously, Karleena spoke up. "How could you know that?"

Already walking out the doors, Centain replied, "It's my job to know everything happening within the palace walls." Then he was gone.

Looking at Sarlec, Karleena saw he, too, was confused. "Let's go. I want to see what is happening."

"Do you think that is wise? What if we really are under attack?" Sarlec asked.

"Then it would be better to face the threat head-on than sit and wait for it like a coward. Let's go."

Sarlec nodded, and the two were off toward the docks at a brisk pace.

❖ ❖ ❖ ❖ ❖

Down at the docks, the *Reliance* rested in the water with crew members running around the deck and scanning the waters below. Orders were bellowed out and weapons drawn.

Imperial Guards filled the dock floorboards, determined to halt any threat to the palace.

From the waters below, a dozen figures slowly emerged from the water. As the naval crew members stared in disbelief, they saw water dripping off of the heads of blue-skinned warriors clad in seashell armor and baring tridents, three pronged swords, nets, and various other weapons.

The figures studied the naval officers and Imperial Guards that now encompassed them. A figure in the middle rose farther out of the water, though she stood on nothing. Her eleven companions closed the gap and encircled her for protection. Scanning the crowd, she spoke regally. "I am Arianna. Is this the proper greeting for the invited Sovereign of Aquatica?"

Receiving no reply, Arianna realized her guards were growing anxious and felt threatened. The land dwellers all bore arms and their intentions appeared hostile.

From a crevice farther in the cavern, two men hustled toward the docks. One raised his hands to his men. "Lower your weapons. They are not a threat."

The Imperial Guards immediately listened to their Captain and lowered their arms. The naval officers still held weapons at bay. One officer stepped to the front of the bridge. "Admiral?"

"Yes, this is not a hostile act. These people were invited," Morex replied.

"Aye, sir. Lower your weapons, men, and get back to work," ordered Harnell, the Captain of the *Reliance.*

Arianna watched as guards and naval men returned to their tasks. She then studied the newcomers. "Where is my brother?"

Morex stepped forward and reached a hand out to the water for her to grab onto. "Master Askari has traveled to visit the leaders of the other races. He should return shortly."

Taking his hand, Arianna lifted herself onto the dock. Like her brother, she had light blue skin, though she had dark brown hair flowing freely. She was garbed only in a one-piece scaly green garment, extending from her bust down to her torso, leaving her arms, hands, legs, and feet bare. For decoration, she donned a necklace, bracelet, and anklet made out of seashells. Upon her waist was strapped a small sword with a coral handle. Her outfit accentuated her naturally fit and trim body.

Releasing her grip, he bowed. "A pleasure to meet you, Sovereign Arianna." As he looked at her, Morex found her quite stunning and impressive. Her eyes were a light brown and full of life. As a man who spent the better part of his life on the sea, seeing this woman, he grew a newfound sense of appreciation of the magnificence of the world of water.

"Likewise, Mr...?"

"My humble apologies. I am Admiral Morex. This is Captain Centain. He will be responsible for your safety while you are here," Morex informed her.

With two short high-pitched harmonic notes, the eleven men who traveled with her leapt from the water and to her side. "I appreciate the offer for protection, but I have guards of my own."

Centain studied the men to ascertain any security concerns. They were more heavily garbed than Arianna, including coral shells that looked as strong as armor for clothing. They also maintained a variety of weaponry. All of them, including Arianna, were very muscular and strong. A natural development for a race that constantly found themselves swimming, he deduced.

"I shall accommodate your wishes, though weapons will be forbidden when truce talks begin," Centain replied.

One of the aquaticans spoke to Arianna in a language Centain could not understand. It sounded like a high-pitched melody from a song. Arianna replied in the same tone, then addressed Centain in the common tongue. "My Sentinel understands your restrictions and we shall agree to them, though he demands at least one of my men be by my side at all times."

Centain nodded. "Of course, Sovereign."

From behind them, Karleena and Sarlec appeared on the docks. Smiling at the aquatican, Karleena stepped forward with her arms open in greeting. "Sovereign Arianna, I presume? I am Empress Karleena. Welcome to Trespias."

The two leaders embraced briefly in greeting, then walked off toward the upper levels of the palace as if they had been friends for years. Kindred spirits perhaps, from one ruler to another.

CHAPTER 43

As they entered the encampment, Braksis and Solara could see that the Imperial forces were bustling with activity. Tents strewn across the plains now had soldiers and medics rushing back and forth tending to the wounded.

Stopping one of the soldiers, Braksis asked for an update. "What happened here?"

The soldier frantically looked up at him and spoke in a confused tone. "Lord Braksis?"

"Yes. What happened here, trooper?" he asked more sternly.

"The orcs were relentless, sir. It was as if there was no end to them. They just kept coming and coming."

"Where is General Kronos?" Braksis demanded.

"They just kept coming and coming," the soldier repeated as if he remained in the battle even now.

"Leave him. He won't have the answers you seek," Solara offered.

Braksis agreed, and they continued on toward the entrance to the caves. As they continued by the tents, he was shocked to see many soldiers, but no officers. This troubled him greatly.

White-armored troops were covered with blood—the uninjured more than the dying, for they were immersed in the blood of their comrades. A panic had overcome well-trained and disciplined soldiers.

A pit had been dug and Braksis could see large mounds of bodies. Not only the human soldiers, but dwarves, orcs, and goblins as well. The stench emanating from the pit was overpowering. The soldiers who brought the bodies there had clothes tied around their mouths and noses.

Seeing the chaos, Braksis rode closer to Solara so that only she could hear his words. "Did I make a mistake sending troops here?"

"Do not doubt yourself. The heavy destruction here only adds credence to the fact that something drastic must be done. Let us hope the effort of your troops was enough to sway the enemy and force a retreat."

"I see no officers. No leaders here. I hope Kronos is uninjured," Braksis commented quietly.

"Look. There is the entrance to Vorstad," Solara pointed to an opening in the base of the mountains where soldiers were still carrying the wounded and dead from the battlefield within.

"We will find our answers in there," Braksis agreed.

Slowly they moved through the chaos. Braksis tried to assess the damages, but until he found his officers, he doubted that he would be able to truly perceive what had happened.

At the entrance to the cave, Braksis and Solara both dismounted and tied up their horses on the branch of a nearby tree. Looking down at Tiot, Braksis spoke a command. "Defend."

With this one word, Tiot was immediately on alert to protect the horses. The timber wolf would attack any threat that approached.

Satisfied that their horses and gear would be safe, Braksis and Solara inched their way past the line of soldiers and into the caves. A long and narrow passageway led deeper into the mountain.

Gradually working against the flow of traffic, they arrived at a large opening. There, both were confronted with destruction even more severe than they could have imagined from what they saw outside.

They could see the crumbling walls of Vorstad, with soldiers and dwarves both alive and dead scattered throughout and around. From the depths of the caves and tunnels, bodies of orcs, goblins, and those who confronted them covered every inch of the ground. As the siege continued, Braksis surmised the orcs had to crawl over their own fallen comrades to continue the onslaught.

Walking through the rubble and deceased, the two entered the Halls of Vorstad. Seeing a dwarf who was directing both Imperial soldiers and his fellow dwarves, Braksis approached him to learn more. "I am Lord Braksis, Warlord of the Imperium. I sent these forces to you."

The dwarf looked up at him. He had a long gray beard, which was caked with blood. An eye patch covered his left eye in what looked like a recent injury. He wore chainmail around his head and below his torn brown garments. Hoisting an axe onto his shoulder, he considered Braksis with his one good eye.

"I am Fok," the dwarf declared in a deep and accented voice. "On behalf of all of Vorstad, I thank you for sending assistance. With pleasantries aside, leave me alone. There are many wounded still to attend to."

"I appreciate your assistance to my men, and your candor. I am seeking the General of the Imperial forces. A man named Kronos. Point me in his direction, and I shall leave you to your duties."

Fok dipped his head in sorrow for a moment. "Your General Kronos is a tribute to your people. He fought valiantly and will be honored with tales of his feats forevermore in the Halls of Vorstad."

"You're saying he's dead?" Braksis asked, a lump forming in his throat.

"He's not dead, but his life is fading quickly."

"Can you tell me how to find him?" Braksis almost pleaded.

Fok regarded the Warlord. "Aye, keep going straight into the Halls of Vorstad. At the third column, take a left. You will find him there."

"Thank you," Braksis said as he and Solara rushed toward the area Fok described. In the background, they could hear Fok barking out orders to those around him. The rescue efforts would continue long into the night, and Fok would not rest until every body was checked for signs of life.

Reaching the third column, Braksis and Solara took a left. Before them, they saw a circle of people, both humans and dwarves. This is where his officers had been.

Approaching the circle, he moved past his officers and walked into the center of the ring. There, atop a stone slab, he saw a weak and bloodied Kronos. Beside him stood a highly ornamented dwarf who could only be Chaddrick, King of Vorstad.

Chaddrick wore a bright red overcoat with blue pants. He had a long gray beard that was perfectly groomed and weaved together in three braids hanging from his chin. He, too, wore chainmail, though golden in color, with a crown upon his brow. One gloved hand held a small scepter, which he gently tapped into his other open palm. He held himself regally, even though his eyes betrayed his true demeanor.

Braksis bowed to the dwarf before speaking. "King Chaddrick, it is an honor to meet you."

Chaddrick bowed briefly in return, though not as low as Braksis had done. "I do not know you."

"I am Lord Braksis, Warlord of the Imperium. I instructed these men to come here to assist you after befriending Thamar and his companions."

"Ah, yes," Chaddrick said. "Thamar. He has yet to return. We fear that he has been lost."

"I last saw him in Suspinti. We shared an evening and an adventure there. I hope that no harm has befallen him," Braksis said.

Chaddrick nodded his agreement. "I would like to hear more, Warlord, though I am sure you wish to see your General." Stepping back, Chaddrick pointed a hand to the slab where Kronos was placed. "He lives, though he is quickly fading."

Braksis stepped forward and held Kronos's hand. It felt so frail and weak in his. The man he had known as a great leader and adviser was lying before him, gasping for each breath. Blood trickled from his nose and from several cuts on his face. In fact, Braksis could see his entire body had been battered.

Squeezing the General's hand, Braksis spoke softly. "Kronos, I am here."

His eyes sputtered open, though he could not focus on the location of the voice. Braksis leaned over so that Kronos could see him without moving. "Braksis," he wheezed.

"Yes, Kronos. I am here," Braksis said softly.

"I have failed you, my lord," said Kronos with a struggle.

"No Kronos, you have not failed. Vorstad still stands," Braksis informed him.

"I could not stop them," he gasped.

Seeing the pain in his friend, Braksis fought back the tears forming in his eyes. "They were stopped, Kronos. You are a hero. Your actions today will help garner in a new age of peace between humans and dwarves."

"Braksis?" Kronos asked, suddenly looking as if he were lost.

"I am here, old friend," Braksis assured him, squeezing his hand gently.

Struggling to speak, Kronos gained a last ounce of strength. "Beware the Shadow Mages. Beware them." His last word trailed off as the life flowed out of his eyes.

"Kronos?" A single tear streaked down Braksis's face. "Kronos?"

Solara walked up and put a hand on his shoulder. "He is gone, my friend."

Braksis turned to consider her, wishing desperately that her words were not so. "This is truly a tragic day for the Imperium."

Two dwarves walked up and placed a thin transparent shroud over Kronos's body. They then bowed to Chaddrick and left the area.

"I want answers," Braksis declared. Looking first at Chaddrick, then at his officers. "I want them now."

One of the Imperial officers dismissed the others. "Return to the encampment and direct the medical efforts there. I shall apprise Lord Braksis of what happened."

As one voice, the soldiers agreed, then marched off to return to the plains.

Chaddrick pointed to a small passage out of the room. "We shall talk in here." With that, he walked through the passage, picking up a lit torch perched on the sidewall.

Following, Braksis, Solara, and the officer went into the room.

"We can speak candidly in here," Chaddrick declared.

"What happened, Mr...?"

"Ritter, sir. Lieutenant Ritter," the officer stated. "We arrived at Vorstad and were deployed along the south wall where the orcs and goblins had been attacking. The assault began at nightfall, and lasted throughout the night and well into the following day. They just kept coming as if there was no end to their forces."

Braksis glanced to Solara and recalled the hysterical soldiers outside, claiming they just kept coming.

"The walls fell, and even with our assistance, things looked bleak. General Kronos came to the lines to inspire the troops to fight harder."

"A noble gesture," voiced Chaddrick.

"His tactics worked. We finally began to push the opposing forces back," Ritter continued.

"Then what happened to Kronos?" Braksis demanded.

"A dead goblin lay on the ground. Then suddenly, it stood up, and before our eyes, it turned into a creature like the one you fought at Dartie."

"A Shadow Mage?" Braksis specified.

"Yes, sir. Well, the Shadow Mage flicked a finger, and hundreds of troops toppled out of his way. Kronos was closest and tried to attack him. The Mage closed his fist, and the armor around Kronos constricted as if he were being crushed."

Noting the pause, Braksis looked at the man as he collected himself.

"I have never heard the sound of bones being crushed like I did then, sir. There was nothing that we could do. Then as quickly as the Shadow Mage came, he vanished, and the dead goblin was back on the ground again."

"What happened then?"

"The remaining orcs and goblins pulled back. They fled, and have yet to return."

Braksis looked at Chaddrick. "Did you send scouts out after them?"

"Yes," he answered. "They are still withdrawing. I can offer no explanation."

Braksis pondered this news for several moments without speaking. Then he addressed Ritter. "We will see to it that Kronos has a proper funeral, then you will take command of the army until relieved by a superior officer."

"Me, sir?" Ritter asked dubiously.

"Yes, Lieutenant. The orcs and goblins may attack again, and we need to be prepared for that."

"What about you, sir?" Ritter inquired.

"I must travel north to Xylona, then on to Falestia. I will send word with further orders after I return to Trespias."

"I understand, sir. I will not fail you," Ritter declared.

Looking at Chaddrick, Braksis bowed, then returned to the side of Kronos.

❖ ❖ ❖ ❖ ❖

Later that night, Braksis stood with a torch before the body of General Kronos. He spoke several short words to those who had gathered about honor, duty, and the symbolism this man fought his whole life for. Then with the words behind him, Braksis lowered the torch and watched as his old friend burned in the night.

CHAPTER 44

Silence. So intoxicating. So soothing. If only it could last forever. Alas, life usually has its own plan, and the quiet calm was disturbed by the world around her. Consciousness gradually came back to Kyria. With her eyes closed, she listened to her surroundings. Birds in the sky, the slithering of some creature along the ground, insects conducting a symphony all around her, the gentle breeze through the trees. Trees?

The realization that she truly could hear trees sent dread surging through her young body. The last thing she could remember was the pain as she was injured in the battle. Dreams as well. Dreams of an elf, unlike any elf she had ever known. Now she was suddenly elsewhere.

Slowly Kyria attempted to open her eyes. Memory of her failed attempts before almost made her surrender before even trying, but she had never been one to give in to despair and surrender. Surprisingly, her eyes did open.

Bright, so bright and hard to see, she thought. Everything around her was a big white blur. Yet her eyes were clearly open. This was definitely progress.

A familiar voice spoke out. The voice was soft, clear, filled with sympathy and concern. Even if the voice were not oddly familiar, she would instinctively trust its tone. "Awake, I see?"

Realizing she was not alone, Kyria attempted to sit up, and fell back over again. She clearly was in no position to move.

The voice spoke again. "Rest, young one. We have traveled far. Though the potion has healed your injuries, you are still weak and need time."

Kyria reached out toward the voice, and attempted to speak herself. "Traveled far?" What came out shocked her. She did sound weak, feeble.

Kai moved closer to Kyria and gently rubbed her hands along her scalp in a soothing motion. She was hesitant to tell Kyria the entire truth, yet if this girl truly was her destiny, she must reveal what happened. "Your village has been destroyed. Everyone else has perished. Don't you remember?"

"I'm sorry," Kyria whispered. "How foolish of me. I was dreaming of that day in Arkham again, and when I woke up, I was disoriented."

"So you do remember everything that has happened since then? Our travels from Suspinti into Dartie?" Kai inquired softly.

"Yes. I remember that now. It's funny, when I first got up, I thought that was the dream," Kyria admitted.

Kai pondered the comment, then spoke sincerely from her heart. "I wish that life was not about to take the path that it will for you. That you could remain happy and joyous as I had once envisioned you in my own dreams."

"We saw each other in our dreams. How odd," Kyria contemplated.

"No, not really. You are a very special and gifted child. It was my destiny to find you, just as it will be to train you and prepare you for the future, where you will be the one to save us all."

"Destiny?" Kyria inquired.

This was the opening Kai was waiting for and also dreading. "The two of us are linked. I am on a quest, one that will save many lives. I do not know how you and I have become joined mentally, but we are part and parcel of each other. Our fates are intertwined. The salvation of my people, and ultimately of yours, rests in your hands."

Sitting up more confidently, Kyria considered the Madrew elf. "I am but a child, frail as you can see by my recent injuries. I'm in no shape to be the savior of our people."

"You will not always be so young, Kyria," Kai stated clearly.

"I will grow, but I have no power or ability that sets me apart from anyone else."

"I can change that," Kai declared.

Confusion set in on Kyria's face. "How could you do that?"

Kai caressed Kyria's hair again. Soothing her. "In my visions of the future, you have the power of a great Mage."

"But I am not a Mage. If I were, the Gatherers would have found me during infancy."

Listening to Kyria's objections, Kai nodded and then continued slowly. "My people have provided me with the ability to awaken magical potential within you. Although I am not a Mage, I can turn you into one, then tutor you in the mystical arts." Seeking any sign of acceptance, Kai paused for a few moments before continuing. "The path I offer will be a hard one. However, if I do not awaken the powers within you, those who would be your future enemies may seek you out and try to destroy you rather than allowing you to ever meet your potential. If we proceed, then ultimately, it will allow you to realize your destiny."

Memories of running through the hills, being so vibrant and alive flooded through her mind, then, realizing how much had changed since that happy day. Even during those happy times, she always seemed to sense dangers within the world. Premonitions like when she saw the darkness surrounding the Carrion Mountains. If what this elf said were true, that she could awaken some latent power within her, should she not take the risk? "Will it hurt?"

"You were already hurt. You may feel some discomfort, but then you will feel more alive than you ever have before." Without another word, Kai watched Kyria nod her head in approval. "Lean back then. The process will not take long, but it is only the beginning of a long road for both of us."

With that, Kai closed her eyes and clasped her hands together in a meditative posture. She began a chant in a tongue foreign to the Seven Kingdoms, that of ancient Madrew. The words were rhythmic, almost akin to a song. The world around her seemed to grow quiet. Almost as if all creatures of the forest were watching the spectacle that was about to transpire.

With a rising crescendo, Kai's entire body illuminated in a blinding white light. A light so pure that those who witnessed this act would feel they were privy to the birth of an angel. The light dimmed around Kai, and slowly encompass Kyria. First the illumination overcame her head, then slowly spread along her entire body until she, too, was aglow.

Time seemed to stop during this mystical exchange, but what was once day soon became night, then day again before the transfer had been completed. Finally, Kai collapsed from exhaustion. Her chanting stopped. Her mysterious dance was all worn out. The glow around Kyria had subsided hours before.

This time, when Kyria opened her eyes, she saw the world completely differently. What was like a blurry black and white the day before suddenly exploded into colors and sensations. Her eyesight became far more crisp and clear than ever it was. She could see movements, sensations, and even sources of small noises. Shifts of the wind and weather patterns became strands of force around her that she could perceive and even manipulate slightly. The world was suddenly an open book to her, and although many things remained foreign to her, she found the sights breathtaking.

She felt completely different, and not just her sight. A feeling of power flowed through her veins. A sense of invincibility, yet also responsibility. The human girl that she was, was no more. In her place, was a young Mage looking to make a difference and save the existence that she cherished.

Looking down at the exhausted Kai, the two switched roles, and Kyria suggested sleep to Kai. Not realizing what she had done, Kai instantly fell into a deep sleep. This new power of Kyria's, unchecked, could be quite dangerous. Hopefully, Kai would be able to tutor her and guide her as promised. For she had a lot to learn.

CHAPTER 45

Deep in the caverns below the Mage's Council was an area that was reserved for those Mages with the gift of sight. These Mages, better known as Seers, could feel any and all new magical presences in the realm, then instantly locate their quarry.

For hundreds of years, the Seers were the hidden group of Mages that allowed new disciples to enter the ranks of the Academy and ultimately the Mage's Council. Whenever an infant was born with mystical powers, the Seers would know instantly, and send the Gatherers out to the precise location to claim the child. Regardless of species, they displayed no bias. They felt the parents of the world should be honored that their children were among the gifted few who would enter the ranks of the Mages.

Although the ethics of this philosophy was debated over the years, the Mage's Council had been accepted as a symbol of peace and prosperity among the land. Over the years, families accepted the loss of their children to this group as a sign that they were gifted to help protect the less fortunate of the world. Those who entered the Mage's Council also received an unparalleled education. Still, giving up one's young is never easy, so whenever possible, the Seers preferred to dispatch the Gatherers quickly to help eliminate any lingering attachment that time could bring.

This particular morning, Lenixum, an overseer of the Seers, slowly sipped his morning nectar wondering what the day would bring. He would not have long to wait. Fifteen Seers were surrounding the circular table on watch that morning, and at once, all of them began to scream.

Lenixum, an avarian, dropped his nectar and quickly flew down to the Seers on duty. He has been working as the supervisor and overseer for several years now and always maintained a calm disposition. His professionalism, order, and organization were inspiring to those around him. Even his features showed careful consideration and efforts to maintain an image of professionalism. Lenixum had a perfectly groomed beard and mustache that matched the lavender hair on his head. His hair was carefully layered back to his neckline. Not a hair looked like it would ever be out of place upon his head. Wearing the traditional white and gold robes of the Mages, he truly was an image of prestige. In one clear, crisp word, he addressed the Seers under his command. "Report."

In one voice, all fifteen Seers spoke. "A spike, sir. Very powerful." The Seers were of a variety of species, and all gifted with the sight. Linked by this gift, they worked as one cohesive unit. The Seers were garbed in all-white robes, displaying no signs of the gold lace outline that Lenixum wore. These gold designs were increased along with the Mage's status. While those who were Seers may be gifted with the sight, they were handicapped in all other aspects of the mystical arts.

"Location?" The routine was second nature to Lenixum. He always maintained discipline and professionalism. Yet, he never recalled the Seers screaming when they found a contact before. The look that they displayed in unison was more of a mixture of agony and terror.

In response to his query, in the center of the table, an image appeared of the Seven Kingdoms. Portions of the image kept vanishing, yet it enlarged focusing on the Dartian Woods. The image continued to flicker and change as it closed in on its quarry, then Lenixum was looking at the image of two figures. One a young girl, and the other what appeared to be elven.

"I see no infant. Confirm."

Once again, speaking together in unison, the Seers confirmed. "The spike is from the young girl in the image. Her spike is off of the charts. More powerful than any Mage currently in the Council."

Lenixum could hardly believe what he was hearing. Not only had a young girl suddenly become a mystic without any prior evidence of this ability, but she was also more mystically attuned than anyone else in the entire Mage's Council!

Flapping his wings twice and elevating into the air, Lenixum glided out of the chamber. If this girl truly were so powerful, then the Gatherers would have to be adequately prepared. Several seconds later, he arrived in the caverns that housed a platoon of the most famed group of Gatherers of all time.

"Tarwas, I have need of you!"

In response to his shout, a large brown sarnal appeared. Tarwas was quite an intimidating presence. He was a little over seven feet in height, and had bulging muscles from head to toe. Like all sarnals, Tarwas had no nose, two slits with eyes that allowed him to see along his sides and in front of him at the same time, and a mouth with the teeth of a carnivorous predator. He had black hair pulled back into a ponytail that reached halfway down his back. His hands, larger than Lenixum's head, had nails that had been rumored to be able to slice through the bark of a tree with ease. His toes had similar nails, causing sarnals to travel without footwear.

His voice was a deep roar that would send many opponents scurrying, yet demanded attention and respect. "Lenixum, my friend. What troubles you so?"

Coming to a perfect landing, Lenixum looked up at his friend and colleague. "The Seers have uncovered a spike. A very powerful spike. More powerful than anyone in the entire Council, they claim."

Folding his arms, Tarwas watched and listened. "Continue."

"The spike is a young girl, not an infant. A most peculiar report. Go Tarwas, bring her back, but be careful."

Tarwas nodded. "All precautions will be taken. The girl will be found."

Lenixum handed Tarwas a trackbar, a sphere that served as a mystical compass. This tool had the ability to compress the Seers' combined abilities and lock in on one specific mystic within the realm. As such, it maintained the image of the girl as well as a locator device keyed into her specific powers.

Tarwas took the trackbar, then turned to address his troops. "Gatherers, let's ride!" With those three words, the chamber filled with activity as the platoon of Gatherers grouped together and rode off. Some by air. Some by land. In a matter of minutes, Lenixum was alone once again.

CHAPTER 46

Sitting in her chambers, Karleena gently rubbed Vaz, one of her white tigers, behind its right ear. She greatly admired her two large pets that she raised since they were cubs. Now, they acted playful with her, but they were also very protective, something she knew Centain was grateful for.

Noticing Vaz tense, she looked at the door as she heard three soft knocks. Vella, her other tiger, peered into the room and gazed at the door.

Though her pets seemed on edge, Karleena knew there were guards stationed at the door, and was not nervous. "Come in," she declared in a commanding tone.

The double doors to her chamber opened inward, and Centain entered her room. "Apologies for the intrusion, Empress."

At the sight of him, both tigers visibly relaxed. Vella returned to the room where she previously had been, and Vaz nuzzled Karleena with his nose trying to get Karleena to rub his ear again.

"No intrusion, Captain. I was merely taking some time to think while waiting for everyone to arrive."

"That is one of the reasons I am here. King Garum has arrived from Tenalong."

"Excellent. I wish to see him right away. Please bring him to my audience hall. I shall be there shortly," Karleena instructed.

"That may not be possible, at least not right away," Centain said.

"Oh? And why is that?"

"Prime Minister Torscen intercepted him at the gate, and the two left together."

"Torscen," she spat. "That man is really beginning to get on my nerves. He is too stubborn and set in his ways. I fear that he is attempting to sabotage what we are looking to accomplish here."

Centain did not reply, though he knew that since the royal families had arrived, Torscen made certain he spoke with each of them individually.

"Send out a pair of your men and bring Garum to me. Don't be forceful, but let him know we anxiously await his report of the orc city in his kingdom. That report takes precedence over any other matter he may be involved in. Make certain he realizes that and doesn't delay."

"If Torscen interferes?"

"As I said, this takes precedence over all other matters right now. Torscen can wait his turn."

"I understand, Empress." Turning around, Centain began to leave but paused at the door. "Do you wish for me to contact King Sarlec and Admiral Morex for your meeting?"

"Not necessary. I shall inform them of what Garum has to say when I see them later. I do not wish for Garum to feel as if we are ganging up on him," she decided.

"Very good. I will have him in the audience hall within the hour." With this promise, he exited the room as his guards closed the doors behind him.

Karleena gently rubbed her white tiger behind the ear again. "Vaz, I think I am going to have to become a little more forceful over the next few days. Too often of late, people have neglected my authority. It is time I showed them I am the true Empress."

Vaz gazed at her in bliss as she continued to stroke his lobes, his emerald eyes sparkling back at her.

Much softer this time, she whispered to herself, "I only hope I don't lose myself by doing so."

❖ ❖ ❖ ❖ ❖

Centain led two of his palace guards down a few side streets to a small tavern known as Krieger's Place. The owner of the establishment, Krieger, marketed his establishment as the one place in Trespias where anyone could frequent and have no questions asked. The reputation of Krieger's preceded itself, and when Centain approached the door, he suddenly wished he had brought more men along with him.

The front of the tavern had two swinging doors that people could easily enter through. Unlike most restaurants, inns, and bars, Krieger's

Place was open twenty-four hours a day, so he never found a need for a door that could be closed or locked.

Entering through the two swinging doors, Centain squinted to try to see within the tavern. Krieger preferred his establishment to be dark, allowing his patrons a sense of privacy. Only a small handful of lanterns by the bar were illuminated. All of the tables were shrouded in darkness.

The three Imperial Guards entered, and the tavern became deathly quiet as all eyes turned to look at the official looking newcomers. Centain pointed for one of his men to begin looking for King Garum along the right-hand side of the wall. His other guard, he gestured to stay where he was by the door.

Krieger eyed them suspiciously behind the bar as Centain slowly walked along the wall toward the left. Reaching below the bar, he grasped a small handheld crossbow that was already loaded and primed to fire.

Noticing that everyone was still staring at him suspiciously, Centain stopped to make an announcement. "Please return to your drinks. We will be out of your way in a moment."

Maintaining his grasp on the crossbow, Krieger continued to watch them as they scanned the patrons.

In a back corner, Centain spotted King Garum sitting with Prime Minister Torscen. He stopped scrutinizing the occupants and approached his quarry, unaware of several large men who were standing or sitting close to the two men.

"King Garum, my apologies for the disturbance, but the Empress requires your presence at the palace immediately," Centain said.

Garum looked up at the Captain of the Guards. "I'm having a drink with an old friend." The voice was full of disrespect and the way he said it implied a hidden threat to Centain if he tried to bring him forcefully.

Centain glanced briefly at Torscen who seemed far too smug and content. He knew the Prime Minister was scheming something. Looking back at Garum, Centain was amazed this man was a member of royalty.

Though Tenalong was mostly swamplands and full of mercenaries, criminals, and the dregs of society, Centain was amazed whenever he saw the man who represented the voice of the people. Garum was short and stocky, with oily black hair that hung down his face in bangs and a matching stringy mustache. His skin was dirty and emitted a foul stench; his poor hygiene could make a man queasy.

To those he faced, Garum appeared to be strong and demanding. He spoke big, and threatened often. He used threats and force in most discussions and diplomatic situations. Yet behind all of that, most suspected that the forty-year-old king was nothing more than a puppet to the leader of the Hidden Empire, a criminal organization. He was the figurehead, but Lady Salaman truly was the one who ruled.

Centain could hear his two guards approaching to display a unified front for their Captain. "As I said, my apologies. The Empress has made it clear it is imperative to speak with you."

"The Empress can wait," Garum declared. "As can you. Outside."

Four men stood behind his guards, with two more stepping in between him and the table. Centain assessed his new opponents quickly. They were large and quite dangerous looking, as were most of the patrons of Krieger's Place. More important, he noted they were not carrying weapons, relying more on brute strength and intimidation.

"My boys will see you out. I shall join you once my drink is through," Garum smiled at the Captain. "Boys."

With the order given, the six men reached out to grab the Imperial Guards and forcibly remove them. Centain yelled out a quick order to his men. "No weapons." He then was in motion, dropping to the ground, and kicking out, swiping the legs out from under one of the men.

The giant bodyguard fell backward into his companion who tried to catch him. "Hey, look out!"

Centain then stood back up and spun around to check on the rest of the men. He quickly saw his two guards being overwhelmed by the behemoths clutching them.

He grabbed a barstool and cracked it over the head of one of the men, who released the Imperial Guard's arm, but only smiled as he looked at Centain. With a deep, guttural laugh, he slowly approached the Captain with his arms outstretched.

Seeing the barstool cracked, Krieger withdrew his handheld crossbow and scanned the fight, wondering how best to break it up. If he killed an Imperial Guard, then Guardsmen or ISIA agents would come to investigate. Yet he did not want his tavern destroyed.

Glimpsing the crossbow in his peripheral vision, Centain dodged the rampaging attack and thrust his foot down on the back of the man's knee, sending him crumbling. Turning directly to the bartender, he raised a finger as if chastising him. "Don't even think about it."

While distracted, the two who initially attacked managed to get ahold of him and bring him down to the ground. The man whose leg he swept was lying right on top pinning him down. "Yous gonna pay for what yous done!"

Centain pulled away frowning. "I assure you, smelling your breath is punishment enough."

Struggling to get free, Centain knew he was unable to move, and that this round went to the thugs. He only hoped that Garum would have them escorted out, and not order them killed.

Then, without warning, the man atop of him was pulled off and tossed over the bar as if he were nothing more than a rag doll. Centain looked up and couldn't believe his eyes. It was Dozzer, the Lumnia star who opted to become a member of ISIA. Garbed in an Authority uniform, Dozzer wore all red with two yellow stripes on the left side of his shirt and down his pants leg.

"Looks like you need a little help, Captain," said Dozzer, reaching out a hand. Centain gladly took it to help himself up. As he looked into Dozzer's face, all he could see was the smile beaming back at him.

"You look like you are enjoying this," Centain stated as Dozzer quickly spun to spar with one of the other thugs. Just as quickly, the man was being hurtled through the air, and Dozzer was back smiling at Centain.

"I am. This is why I decided to take Adonis up on his offer to join ISIA. I get to help make the streets safe for people, rather than just being a source of entertainment."

"Look out!" Centain warned as another thug thrust his arms down at Dozzer.

Dozzer elbowed backward and the thug gasped for air as he crumpled to the floor. "Thanks for the warning."

"Anytime." Centain scanned the tavern again and saw his two men were still conscious, and managed to overcome one of the thugs by themselves.

The last man looked at Dozzer and Centain, then turned and ran out of Krieger's without looking back.

"Looks like some of these hulks actually have brains after all," Dozzer joked.

Centain glanced at him and grasped the joke quickly. He was always amazed by how large and imposing Dozzer truly was. Yet unlike the thugs they fought, he had the heart of a lion and the tenderness of a child. "I'm just glad you happened to be near here."

"Not an accident that I was. Adonis had me watching this place after these two walked in here. Said only to intervene if it looked like you needed help."

"That's another one I owe him then," Centain declared, thinking fondly of his mentor and predecessor.

"It looks like you are okay now, so I'm off to see if I can help out anyone else," Dozzer declared.

Centain smiled back at him, knowing that with a man like Dozzer working for the Authority, every street in the Seven Kingdoms would become a bit safer.

Before returning to Garum and Torscen, Centain approached Krieger. "We didn't come to make a mess. Apologies for the damage." He tossed a few gold coins on the bar, then walked away.

Krieger eyed the coins greedily and quickly pocketed them. Fighting in his tavern was often expected. He rarely profited by such an outburst.

Returning to the table, Centain looked down at the two men. Torscen glared back at him with none of the smugness he displayed earlier. "I trust you are ready to join me now, King Garum? I'd hate to have to keep the Empress waiting any longer."

Torscen stood up first. "This is an outrage. The Empress has gone too far this time, Captain. You have not heard the last of this." He stormed out in a fit of rage.

Garum glared at the Captain. "My men would only have brought you outside. You didn't need to roughhouse them."

"And you didn't need to try to intimidate me," Centain replied coolly. "Come on now, we're leaving."

Reaching down, he grasped one of Garum's arms and hoisted him up. Garum stared at him icily. "A military man dares to touch royalty?"

Centain did not respond. Instead, he handed the slightly intoxicated king over to his two men and led the way back to the palace.

They quickly returned leading Garum, complaining the entire time, to the audience hall where the Empress was waiting. As they entered the room, Centain saw six guards standing along the walls, with two more in the hall by the door. The Empress herself was sitting on an elevated chair awaiting the report from the king.

Centain approached her and knelt down on one knee. "Empress, here is King Garum as requested."

Karleena looked at him with sympathy and concern. "Captain, you require medical attention."

Centain reached up and wiped some blood from a split lip. He knew that by now, his skin would be swelling. "When my duties allow it, Empress."

"Your duties allow it now, Captain. You are dismissed."

"Yes, my Empress." Centain bowed and exited the room.

"King Garum, approach," she instructed.

Garum looked up at her and smiled with an expression she knew was insincere. "Why, my Empress, it is so good to see you again."

"Why is my Captain injured?" Karleena demanded.

"I assure you, I have no idea. He came to get me, then got violent. I must protest, my poor guards were taken unawares and are in far worse shape than the good Captain."

Karleena eyed him coolly and saw straight through his deceptions. Deciding to leave this line of conversation behind her and hopefully having this man leave her presence as soon as possible, she got to the point. "What have your scouts discovered about the orc city in Tenalong?"

"My Empress, my scouts searched far and wide, and they were unable to uncover anything. Whoever you have been listening to, has been feeding you falsehoods and filling your head with dangerous ideas. There is nothing to fear, I assure you."

Watching him for signs of deceit, she realized the man before her made a living excelling in exactly that. Whether the Murky Death clan occupied a large orc city or not, she would not be able to trust the word of the man before her. "Very well. Thank you for your report. I will be meeting with the royal families later this evening. Please take advantage of the palace facilities and bathe yourself appropriately. You may be a king, but your appearance is offensive."

Garum's eyes closed to small slits as he turned and walked out of the room. He purposefully did not offer any sign of respect to the leader of the Imperium. He refused to give her the satisfaction.

Karleena lowered her head and sighed. With men like that ruling a kingdom, perhaps her goals of uniting the people truly was the foolish fantasy of a child.

CHAPTER 47

The trip from Vorstad to Xylona was a silent one. Braksis spent much of the time in quiet contemplation of what he had witnessed at Xylona, as well as regrets and doubts about the path he had followed.

The memory of seeing General Kronos lying there, suffering was enough to send him into despair. The old general should have retired years ago but desired to remain in service to the Imperium he helped forge. Now, one of the great men of the past century was gone, and Braksis felt the burden of that loss.

Deep down, he knew that without the sacrifice of Kronos and the men who fell at Vorstad, Chaddrick's forces would have crumbled, and the orcs' influence would be spreading. Even worse, if Thamar had not informed him about what was happening, Vorstad would have fallen without anyone's knowledge. That thought terrified him.

Solara and Tiot knew he needed time to himself. They traveled slightly behind him rather than beside him as usual. He was grateful for the time alone to think. He would have to speak to Solara later on and explain what he was feeling and thinking, but for now, he only wished to fight his own inner demons.

A yell from behind pierced his contemplation, and Braksis looked back at Solara, who was charging toward him with her sword drawn. Turning back, Braksis saw movement in the trees, right before a hobgoblin jumped out at him.

"Ambush!" Solara screamed from behind.

As the hobgoblin lunged toward his horse, Braksis realized a fight was exactly what he needed. Moping around in self-pity only distracted him from what was important, and that was the preservation of the Imperium. Now, he was returning to his own element. He felt as if he were returning home.

The hobgoblin before him was a burly humanoid standing a little over six feet tall. He had a dark reddish brown hairy hide, and a reddish orange face topped with a light blue nose. His eyes were a dark yellow, almost matching the tinge of his jagged teeth.

He wore chainmail over a bloodred shirt and black leather pants. An iron skullcap rested atop his brow, with long pointed ears jutting out on either side of it. The hobgoblin was twirling a morning star as he approached Braksis.

Braksis quickly sized up his foe and beckoned him to attack. "Show me what you've got, tough guy."

The hobgoblin swung the morning star, bringing the spike-cubed head right where Braksis's chest was. Braksis dropped back and rolled off the saddle, landing on the ground as Blaze galloped away.

The impact on the ground sent jolts of pain up through Braksis. Rolling over, he sat up and shook his head briefly to regain his composure.

The hobgoblin rushed him again with the morning star swinging in the air. Tiot jumped over Braksis's head and collided with the hobgoblin, who dropped his weapon to struggle with the timber wolf.

Braksis reached behind his back and grasped the battle-axe Carnage. Looking around for more foes, Braksis saw he was severely outnumbered. Dozens of hobgoblins were in the bushes and trees around him, some on the ground and some in the branches above. Seeing the insurmountable odds, Braksis took a deep breath, then raised his axe in a defensive posture.

Solara galloped in atop of Myst and looked down at him. "We can't win this; we must flee."

A net dropped down from the branches above, encompassing Solara and her mount. Weights along the side of the net sent the thoroughbred off balance, toppling to the ground.

Braksis looked at his companion and remained in his defensive posture. "I think they insist we stay."

One hobgoblin stepped forward. His hairy hide was more of a dark gray. He raised a sword in the air and spoke loudly. "I am Lutz," the hobgoblin declared in a heavily accented version of the common tongue. "You will surrender, or feel the wrath of the combined clans."

Braksis swiped downward with his axe and slit an opening in the net covering Solara. "I am Braksis, Warlord of the Imperium. I welcome your wrath."

Solara used her own blades to widen the hole and free herself. "I hope you know what you are doing."

Braksis maintained the gaze of Lutz, but spoke to Solara. "Sure I do. I'm going to kill as many of these bastards as I can before they kill me."

"Oh, well, in that case, good plan," Solara said sarcastically.

Lutz lowered his sword in command. "Kill them."

Hobgoblins charged from the brush, carrying primarily polearms and morning stars. Several remained behind with bows and arrows strung and facing inward in case their allies needed assistance.

Braksis had to admit that unlike the mindless orcs that attacked Vorstad, the hobgoblins were an intelligent, organized, and aggressive race. This battle most likely would be his last. Surprisingly, he found that this thought did not frighten him. After seeing Kronos fall, he considered that perhaps only his own death would make amends, in some honorable way. If that were the case, he would die valiantly this day.

The hobgoblins advanced closer, encircling Braksis, Solara, and Tiot, who now returned to his master's side. Braksis and Solara lined up back-to-back so as to cover each other as much as possible.

Braksis continued to watch the attackers as they approached, waiting in anticipation of the first lunge as the assault began. The hobgoblins were moving cautiously. They knew they had the upper hand and were hoping to prolong the slaughter, toying with their prey.

Then the battle began. Several hobgoblins at once lunged forcing both Braksis and Solara to separate rather than remain in proximity to cover each other. Braksis momentarily admired how their foes had quickly divided them, and now were ready to conquer them individually.

Still not completely comfortable without the Phoenix, he raised the Carnage and swung at his foes. The battle-axe he deemed a very slow and sluggish weapon. Even with the sword forged solely for him, these odds would be decisively against him.

A morning star impacted his left shoulder sending prongs of pain through his body. The blades only slightly pierced the armor, but the barrage also dented it and added pressure.

Braksis spun around with his axe and severed the head of the hobgoblin. As the morning star fell, he quickly reached out, caught it, and turned to face his next foe wielding two weapons. Both of which he twirled.

He swung out with the morning star with one arm, then brought the battle-axe ramming down to finish the job. Another hobgoblin fell to his death.

A polearm pierced his thigh, and Braksis fell to his knees, his teeth grinding in pain. Dropping the morning star, he reached out and pulled the legs out from under the hobgoblin.

A whip snapped and wrapped around his neck. A violent thrust pulled Braksis back as he looked up at his adversary. At the same time, another hobgoblin kicked the Carnage out of his hands. Defenseless, he awaited his fate.

Solara was faring little better. She moved quickly around the larger and slower foes, but there were too many of them to avoid for long. A hairy arm chopped down at her neck, and she fell to her knees struggling to remain conscious. Her last sight was of Lutz standing above Braksis with his sword ready to thrust down into the defenseless Warlord.

Tiot jumped up to bite Lutz and protect Braksis, but another net fell and ensnared him quickly. Struggling to free himself, Tiot ripped at the netting, growling the entire time.

Braksis stopped struggling and looked up at Lutz. He stared deep into the hobgoblin leader's eyes with a daring glare, waiting for the final death thrust.

Suddenly, arrows filled the air. Braksis could see the surprised expression overcome Lutz. The hobgoblins spoke rapidly in their own language. Braksis could not understand what was being said. Then he saw Lutz smile and scream out, "Elves!"

With that one word, Braksis and his companions were forgotten as the hobgoblins rushed into the woods after the marauding elves.

A horn bellowed in the afternoon air, and Braksis could hear the sound of horses galloping. Stroking his neck and trying to regain the flow of oxygen in his system, Braksis sat up and looked around at the chaos that quickly ensued.

As the hobgoblins rushed toward the elves, they were assaulted by mounted Imperial troops. Their numbers fell quickly, and the remaining hobgoblins fled deeper into the forest.

Braksis slowly regained his footing, ignoring the pain in his thigh and shoulder. He walked over to where Tiot was ensnared and cut the timber wolf free with a small dagger. When free, Tiot licked Braksis on the face in gratitude. "Easy there, boy, let's check on Solara."

Kneeling down next to her body, a deep sense of fear fled through him. First Kronos, and now Solara, whom he only recently discovered he had feelings for, may have perished because of his decisions. Turning her over, he closed his eyes and sighed in relief when he saw she was still breathing, though unconscious. Barring a concussion, he assumed she would be okay after regaining consciousness.

A mounted rider approached Braksis and looked down at him. "Are you injured, sir?"

Braksis realized it was Captain Travers, the man he ordered to help defend Xylona. The guilt and pain over his decisions to assist the races suddenly left him. Though Kronos fell, clearly by sending his men, he had done the right thing. "I will be fine, Captain, though Solara may need medical attention."

"Begging your pardon, sir, but it looks as if you will need some medical attention as well." Travers pulled out a horn and blew three short notes. Several cavalry troops approached and helped Braksis and Solara onto their horses. "These men will see that you arrive at Xylona safely. You will both receive medical attention there."

Braksis nodded his assent. "Thank you, Captain."

Travers then blew his horn again, and multiple riders fell in line behind him. "Let's go."

With his command, the riders entered the forests where the hobgoblins had retreated and began their pursuit.

Braksis watched as they went, then spoke to the soldier he was riding with. "Why did all of the hobgoblins leave the attack on us so quickly? I thought they would have at least finished us off before going."

The soldier turned to face him. "Yes, sir, though the hobgoblins have their own quirk about them. For some reason, they despise elves above all else. They will attack anyone in these woods, but will just as quickly walk away if an elf is available to attack instead. When we learned this, Captain Travers made arrangements to have several elves join our unit. They provide the distraction, then we mop up the rest."

Braksis nodded. "Very intuitive. Captain Travers is doing well."

"Yes, sir. You should rest, sir. The Captain can bring you up to speed when your injuries are tended to."

"Very well, soldier," Braksis replied, then closed his eyes to try to gain some rest as they traveled the route to Xylona.

He wasn't certain whether he fell asleep or not, but the soldier soon was telling him they were there.

Braksis opened his eyes and looked around. He certainly could not see any elven city. As Thamar had indicated when they met, Xylona was invisible to those who did not know where to look.

What he did see was rather shocking. Scattered around the area were Imperial tents with large numbers of cavalry troops who had remained at the camp. Even larger numbers of dwarves were resting all about.

One familiar redheaded and bearded dwarf stepped forward with a smile from ear to ear. "If my eyes do not deceive me, it is the son of Worren! Welcome, my friend, to Xylona!"

Braksis was helped off of the horse by the cavalry troop and said a quick thanks. Then turning to Thamar, he smiled back just as broadly. "It is good to see you again, Thamar."

Thamar examined the injuries to Braksis, then glanced at Solara. "We will have time for pleasantries and tales later. Let us tend to the wounds of your mystral companion and yourself, then we shall speak long into the night over a bite to eat and mead." Watching a pair of elves descend from the trees, Thamar pointed to them. "These elves, they have the healing touch. You and Solara shall be back to full strength in no time at all."

"Thank you, my friend," Braksis said. Feeling comfort with his friend nearby, he gave in to the pain and collapsed into Thamar's arms.

Thamar caught him easily and looked at the descending elves. In a comforting tone, he spoke softly and gently to the unconscious Warlord. "You will be better soon, my friend. Much better."

CHAPTER 48

Kyria watched Kai working intently on her bow. Ever since she had awakened, she had been stenciling new designs onto the shaft. Allowing her curiosity to finally overcome her, Kyria walked over to Kai and stood watching over her shoulder.

She hoped to speak to Kai about the gentle suggestion that she should get to sleep, and how she then instantly passed out into a deep slumber. Things like that had never happened to her before, and she knew she would have to be very careful with her newfound powers from that moment on.

Looking up at the young savior, Kai smiled. "I like to keep a record of my feats on my bow. Sort of a tale of where I've been."

"That's a koxlen. The fight from my dream!"

Kai stopped her carving and turned to address Kyria. "You mean Lucky?"

"Lucky? I've never heard of a koxlen called Lucky before," Kyria replied.

Kai looked down at the outfit she had made. "He was for me. Anyway, that was no dream. That was a vision. As I mentioned earlier, somehow fate has bound the two of us together. We are linked you and I. You actually saw what was happening to me."

"I have seen others, too, you know. In my dreams that is," Kyria said. "You more so than the others, but there are two other elves I have seen. Both pink like you."

"Yes, that would be the others of the Triad. The three of us were sent to find and protect you. It is our sacred duty to do so."

"Where are they now?" Kyria asked.

"I do not know. I heard a tale that Arifos was in an elven city known as Xylona, but I have not heard anything of Rulysta since arriving here."

As Kai finished her comment, the conversation was abruptly interrupted by a roaring snarl in the trees. Both girls grouped together and stumbled for weapons. "What was that?" Kyria pensively asked.

Then, the chilling roar pierced the wind again, as a large ferocious lupan erupted from the trees and charged straight toward them. It was well over ten feet, all white, furred, and fully barring its teeth and claws.

As the lupan charged, it paused to consider the two humanoids before it. Sniffing the air briefly, the mighty beast roared in defiance and glared at the two. Its feral instincts dictated that these two would be easy prey, though its sense of survival made the creature consider bypassing them.

Watching the creature and sensing that her young companion and herself were not the targets for the lupan, Kai slowly reached for her arrows. If this beast were to suddenly attack, the arrows certainly would not even slow it down, but it might give the creature a momentary pause, convincing it to choose other prey.

The lupan continued to stand there and stare at Kai and Kyria. Eyes bore down into their souls. As Kai inched closer to her arrows, another ferocious roar was released into the windless evening. A cry of defiance and warning so primal, that all creatures in its path would flee in terror.

The seconds slowed down. Time seemed to come to a standstill. This creature stood before them. There was no way to truly defend themselves. Yet it stopped.

Then, without warning, the lupan screamed again. This time, not a roar of warning, of hunger, of anger, but one of pain and shock.

Watching carefully, Kai grabbed her bow and with the speed of years of training, she had three arrows primed and ready to fire. She watched the lupan falter and land on its knees, gasping for air. The look in this proud beast's eyes was no longer that of predator, but of prey that had no hope of survival.

Red blotches of the lupan's blood saturated its white fur. Falling down flat, Kai could see arrows and a spear protruding from the creature's back.

Out of the forest leapt two men identically garbed in red armor. Men she recognized from when she first arrived in this land. Men she felt were cocky, a little reckless, and overall crass. They were none other than the Dartian hunters Boudie and Drew.

Drew quickly moved over to the fallen lupan and hefted his sword overhead, with the clear intention of cleaving the creature's head from its body. As he thrust the sword down, the lupan lashed out with its arm and swiped the smaller warrior at the legs. He fell backward and landed on his back with a grunt.

Boudie laughed uncontrollably, still donning a smile. "Hey brother, you're getting cocky. Serves you right."

With bow still poised and ready to fire, Kai closely examined the scene unfolding before her. Suddenly, she saw the lupan in a new light. This mighty beast no longer seemed fearsome or terrible. Rather, it had simply been attempting to save its own life when it mistakenly stumbled across Kyria and Kai. Now, after its hesitation at seeing them, the two warriors were upon it and clearly were poised to steal the life from the proud beast.

Drew sat up, always maintaining eye contact with his prey. Hearing his brother laugh, a rage overcame his features. "Stop that damned laughing! Nothing can stop me. It only can slow me down." By the end of his statement, he was back on his feet and lunging for the lupan once more.

Again, the injured animal was ready for him. The momentary rest seemed to do the mighty beast some good, as it finally managed to stand up again. With the hunter in a lunge, the lupan spun quickly, sending its tail whizzing through the air and smacking its attacker across the face.

Specks of blood streamed out of Drew's face and spotted the ground. The tail slashed an opening that would take some medical expertise to close up and would scar him for life.

Boudie continued to laugh. "Drew, give it up. You need me. You can't win without me."

To this, Drew glared at his brother, then focused on the lupan once again. This time he opted to use a different weapon. He raised his left hand, which had a crossbow attached to it. An arrow flung out and pierced the eye of the unsuspecting lupan.

Another scream of agony from the beast, and it slashed at the air and wandered around aimlessly trying to find anything it could attack.

As Kai watched, her resentment of the two men continued to grow. They did not come across as particularly noble the first time they met, and this only added to her sentiment. Especially for the one named Drew.

This attack seemed taunting, bloodthirsty, vile, and cruel. A lupan was a powerful creature, but not even a ferocious beast deserved the treatment they were showing it.

In another attempt to flee, the lupan started toward Kai and Kyria once again, claws ahead and slashing at the potential threat. Kai did not want to cause this creature any more pain than it was already in, but her arrows alone would be insufficient to put the poor creature out of its misery.

Motioning for Kyria to get behind her, Kai decided to defend her new ward with her life if need be, but she refused to torment the creature further.

Boudie saw the lupan heading toward the two girls and unsheathed his sword for the first time since he came out of the brush. The smile was no longer on his face. The taunting laughter toward his brother completely halted as he went into action. To look at him now, he embodied sheer determination.

Boudie leapt through the air with his sword poised above his head, the blade aimed toward the lupan. With momentum behind him, he landed on the back of the lupan and rammed his sword deep into the creature's back.

Looking at the lupan from the front, Kai could see the elongated blade pierce the front of the creature's chest. Blood spurted out of the wound, then immediately flowed from both sides of the lupan's body. A look of confusion and defeat became permanently etched on its face. The blade started turning, rotating as Boudie attempted to rid the world of this lupan's presence forevermore. A single tear formed in her eye as Kai watched life drain out of the brutalized prey before her.

Boudie leapt down from the creature's back, satisfied with the kill, then looked at Kai and smiled. "So we meet again." Looking intently at her new wardrobe, he nodded in approval. "A koxlen. Not bad, not bad at all. I like it." Boudie formally bowed toward Kai. "I told you we would share many adventures together, and as you can see, I was right."

Kai stared hard at the man for a long moment. She instinctively did not like his attitude or methods, but had to admit that he was a good fighter. Perhaps he was right, and they would share adventures together in the years to come, though she hoped if that were true, he would gain some redeeming attributes before she lost all patience with the man.

❖ ❖ ❖ ❖ ❖

After several hours in the company of Boudie and Drew, Kai's opinion of them did not change. She found the two to be aggressive, cocky, self-centered, cruel, and wild. They also held the perception that they were the strongest in the realm, invincible and unstoppable.

The first thing Drew had said after the lupan was killed still rang in Kai's ears. He commented that Kai and Kyria should feel indebted to them for saving their lives, and that they would accept compensation in either gold or sexual acts of the flesh. This immediately put Kai on edge, and she personally could not wait for the two hunters to part. Suggesting acts of a sexual nature with her was bad enough, but the thought of one of them, or both, attempting to take advantage of a twelve-year-old child was atrocious.

Although they did not mention this a second time, Kai refused to let her guard down. She had a feeling the two hunters would indeed do as they desired if given the chance. That was a chance she refused to allow them to have.

As she listened to them, their tales of hunting and conquests, she realized more and more how much she despised them. The constant intake of alcohol only made them louder and more boastful.

Looking back and forth at both men, Kai felt relieved that after the battle with the tragon, she had opted to travel alongside Braksis and Solara, and not these two.

Boudie mended the wound upon his brother's face, who seemed overly proud of his newfound scar. At the same time, the two started to bicker about the credit for actually killing the lupan. The prestige and honor of the kill apparently was their primary concern. Something of a challenge between the two of them to see which was truly the better hunter.

She listened as the two went into detail about their history. Originally from Dartie, they first became hunters around their sixteenth birthday when King Palenial decreed that all lupans were to be hunted until extinction. The two quickly had gained fame for being such successful hunters that they craved more of a challenge.

This desire led them to the woods of Suspinti, which was renown for the Suspintian Forest and the people's fear of the creatures within it. Rather than being pure hunters, this feat led them to the life of mercenaries, or hunters for hire. Even then, they became bored with their lives.

No creature could ever stand against them, and they sought the ultimate challenge.

Thus, the two brothers left their lives behind and went traveling to Darnak to find something worthy of their inflated egos. Even here, the dragons fell as prey and left them looking for more, craving a challenge that potentially could best them.

As Kai listened, she remembered her home, the life she led, and how she wished she could still exist in the time of her memories. She thought of how the evil horde had marched down and gradually overtaken whatever they came across. Listening to the boasts of these two, she felt inclined to tell them of the ultimate game. Of the cruelties that life handed to her people. She could give these two a chance to leave with a renewed sense of spirit, and forget about Drew's comments of hints with sexual connotations.

Her decision was made before she even realized she was talking. "I may have the ultimate game that you seek."

Drew looked up at her in a hazed state of inebriation. Even intoxicated, his look of skepticism was clearly evident. "Hey elfie, there aint nothin' that we can't handle." He hiccupped and both brothers erupted in laughter.

Lowering her voice to speak in a spooky tone, Kai ignored Drew's taunts and boasts. "You may think you have seen everything, but I have something that would make you turn and flee in terror."

The two brothers resisted the urge to continue laughing and got themselves under control. Boudie looked at Kyria and then addressed Kai. "If you have a hunt that would be worthy of our name, do not hesitate to offer us this challenge."

With both of them finally appearing attentive, Kai related the story of her past. "Far away from here, I came from a world where there was happiness and joy in the land. Where people knew their place. Where there was no suffering, and there was harmony."

"Damn girl, I'd slit my wrists if I lived in a world like that." Drew's interruption received a backhanded slap across the face from his brother.

"Quiet, you fool, we're listening," Boudie demanded.

With a scowl, Drew sat back up and gently rubbed his face, noticing that he was bleeding slightly again "You opened the damned stitch!"

Boudie glared back at him in warning to be silent.

Kai paused briefly waiting for the brothers to settle back down before continuing her tale. "As I was saying, we lived in perpetual harmony. Fighting was foreign to us. Then one day, when I was a young girl, our entire existence changed."

Kyria moved in closer and sat down next to Kai. As she did so, Kai offered her a smile. She, too, should know all about this, especially if she was the Chosen One, the one destined to help her people. To save the future, she must be cognizant of the past.

"An unknown species, something foreign to us, something we refer to as nothing more than the horde slowly came in. These creatures, were stronger than any in the realm, and soon took over and expanded everywhere."

"What did they look like?" Boudie inquired.

"The horde had many members, some demonic, some humanoid, some large, and some small. It was not any one particular group that was attacking," Kai responded.

Rubbing his chin in contemplation, Boudie nodded his understanding.

As the fire flickered, Kai paused for effect. "The takeover was slow. They began with towns and villages on the outskirts of the realm, but then with a foothold, they spread into the realm itself. Conquering any in their path as they continued."

Boudie leaned closer to Kai. "You say they came slowly and began to conquer the realm. How big was the realm? What about defenses?"

Drew merely laughed in an intoxicated haze at Boudie's question. "No doubt, man, a bunch of weakling pacifists are all that stood before this horde. You and me could probably conquer the realm!" More laughter ensued.

Kai glared at Drew before addressing Boudie's question. "Our realm was far larger than that which is known as the Seven Kingdoms. We also were much more attuned with the mystical arts, yet we fell quickly. Even after we knew that peace was not an option, people kept defending their own homes, not ever mounting a sufficient defense to halt the ascent of the evil horde. Disorganized, we all soon fell."

"If you fell, how are you here? I think you're lying, elfie," Drew slurred drunkenly.

"Shut up!" Boudie demanded of his brother before backhanding him a second time.

With this hit, Drew jumped back up and tackled his brother. A quick fist to the face put Boudie down quickly, as Drew certainly was the stronger of the two. Blood streamed down Boudie's mouth from the split lip his brother just gave him.

Quickly reacting to his brother's attack, Boudie lifted his legs, wrapped them around his brother's waist, and rocked his body, allowing him to reverse positions and wind up on top of Drew. Once there, he quickly pinned his brother down. If Drew had not been intoxicated, this maneuver would never have worked. However, Boudie had been wrestling with his brother for years and knew how to take advantage.

With Drew struggling beneath him, Boudie looked back at Kai and nodded to continue.

"The reason I am here is because my people opted to flee. Many died, but some did survive. Some of us were then sent out to find the Chosen One. The one that has been prophesied to be our salvation." To conclude, she glanced over at the attentive Kyria who absorbed every word.

Boudie was oblivious to the unspoken interaction between the two girls. Rather, he pondered the fame he and his brother could achieve in a realm that was larger than the Seven Kingdoms, by being the guiding force in repelling this evil horde. The two of them alone would be the leaders of a great rebellion. They could even make it a hunt of individual horde members to keep their senses sharp. "Where can I find this realm you speak of?"

With firelight flickering off of her skin, Kai raised her head and stared straight at Boudie. Her eyes looked like they, too, were aflame with the reflection of the fire in front of them. "To get to my homeland, you must travel through the Forbidden Regions."

"The Forbidden Regions? Nobody would take us through there!"

Kai lowered her head again. "It is for the best. The horde would be too much of a challenge." She released a sigh and paused. "Even for you."

Drew pushed his brother off of him in a fit of rage. "Too much of a challenge? Nothing is too much of a challenge for us. Do you dare mock us?"

Dusting some grass and dirt out of his hair after being pushed over by his brother, Boudie spoke to Drew. "Ships would not take us through the Forbidden Regions."

"Then we steal a ship."

"Steal a ship? If we're caught—" Boudie was interrupted by his brother's adamant declaration.

"This is us. If we get caught, we will deal with them, too."

"I thought you did not believe?"

Drew looked down at Kai with skeptical eyes. "I don't believe, but I will not be called a coward."

"She did not call you a coward," Kyria pointed out.

"Irrelevant. I'm ready to go," Drew declared as he stood up and gathered his belongings.

Boudie shook his head. "Brother, if we are going, let's go for the right reasons."

"The right reasons? Man, what the hell would that be?"

"Money, fame, women!" beamed Boudie.

"Now those are my kind of reasons!" agreed Drew.

"Seriously, brother, if we go and the realm is truly as large and in such turmoil, our intervention would bring us instant acknowledgment, fame, fortune, and notoriety. We could do whatever we wanted. All we need to do is what we love. Bring down the beast. The bigger, the badder, the better."

A smile grew on Drew's face. "I can already hear our song sung across the land to acknowledge our triumph. Vanquishing the forces of evil. Boudie and Drew forever!"

Neither Kai nor Kyria said another word. They just watched the two brothers continue to boast of a future of glory and excitement. Kai felt no remorse. These two hunters would find no glory. All they would find would be death. Yet for now, they would leave. That was all that she cared about for the time being.

Without another word being spoken, she watched as these two hunters packed up their weapons and walked out of their lives forever. As they left, she could still hear their boasts, their cockiness, and their sense of superiority. She only hoped they could learn to be humbled before they both died at the hands of the horde.

As the last sign of them vanished over the horizon, Kai whispered to herself. "So much for many adventures together."

CHAPTER 49

Examining the readings on the trackbar, Tarwas continued to zero in on his target. Lenixum had seemed quite paranoid about this particular mystic. Reflecting back, Tarwas did not remember Lenixum ever being paranoid in the past. He had always seemed far more laid-back and relaxed. An avarian stuck in the depths of the Mage's Council. Without a laid-back attitude, one could go mad.

Thinking back himself, the last time he had seen the overseer of the Seers spooked like Lenixum was now, was back on his very first gather. He remembered that mission well. He had just failed the initial Trials that would have elevated him to Apprenticehood. Instead, he found himself in a new direction, was sent to the Gatherers, and joined their ranks. That first mission, he was included in the platoon sent out to recover the newborn Hergzenbarung, current Council of Elders member.

At the time, no lupan had ever been brought into the Council. In fact, Herg had been given his mystical abilities simply because his parents had devoured a Paladin. By digesting this Mage, mysticism remained within the systems of the parents. Then, when Herg was born, he was born with mystical abilities. Naturally, the Gatherers were dispatched to retrieve him.

This first mission, where a young Tarwas was all excited to be out in the real world and desperate to prove his worth to his fellow colleagues, found himself as one of the only surviving Gatherers after confronting the lupan parents.

Although this event took place long ago, Tarwas kept the thoughts fresh in his mind. That mission, they were taken unawares. At the time, he was merely a grunt looking to make a name for himself. Now, he was the commander. It was his job to take his people out and bring them back safe, along with the mystical presence. To do that, he wished to be as prepared as he could be.

As a result of that, he handpicked the platoon that served under him. He selected the best and brightest he could find in the Academy, and tempted them with the benefits of serving as a member of the Gatherers. The thrills, adventure, and excitement they were often faced with inspired many to request to join his ranks when it was time for them to take the Trials.

The most important person under his command was his old Academy roommate, Matrife. Matrife had passed his Trials and continued to prosper all the way up to the rank of Mage Master. When Tarwas was put in command of his own platoon, he went to Matrife and requested his aid in forming a platoon in his own image. Matrife agreed, and subsequently, the two designed and maintained the most successful and renown group of Gatherers in the history of the Mage's Council.

Matrife himself was a wraith, which naturally assisted in gaining information for the Gatherers before advancing. His species had the ability to vanish in the shadows and appear practically invisible. He could blend into his surroundings, regardless of what they were. Without even considering his considerable mystical talents, his natural features allowed him to be the head scout in all missions. Matrife also maintained the second-in-command rank behind his friend Tarwas.

Historically, those who were in the Gatherers were not necessarily the best and brightest that the Mage's Council had to offer. Like Tarwas, they were those who failed the Trials, and did not necessarily have the best affinity toward the education they received, or the magical potential they were embedded with. However, with the assistance of Master Matrife, this one platoon did not follow the typical norm for a group of Gatherers.

If Tarwas had not known Matrife since they were adolescents, he would never have known that his second in command had walked up behind him. Each motion was pure silence and stealth. Truly a magnificent ability that the wraiths perfected. "We are getting close. The quarry is in the Dartian Woods. About an hour's travel more."

Watching the trackbar, Matrife nodded his agreement. "Do you wish me to advance now and scout the situation?"

Tarwas turned to watch his troops. They had traveled hard and fast to get this far. Dartie bordered the Imperial City, but with the sense of urgency Lenixum had portrayed, time seemed to be of the essence. They could all use a little rest before confronting whatever awaited them. "Be cautious, my old friend. Something has spooked the Seers about this quarry. I do not wish to lose you. Observe, then report back quickly. We will be waiting."

Without another word, Matrife was gone. Tarwas looked ahead into the woods, but knew he would never be able to see his friend unless the Mage Master so wished it. For now, it was time to rest his men and prepare for whatever awaited them the following day.

CHAPTER 50

Led by Captain Centain, Karleena approached the hall where she would be meeting with the royal families. King Sarlec and Admiral Morex were already with her, for they desired an update on her meeting with King Garum. Like her, they all felt Garum was either hiding something or outright lying.

Their discussions had lasted the better part of the afternoon, and they all concurred that this upcoming meeting would be a difficult one. Torscen continued to try to manipulate the royal families against them, whereas King Garum appeared to have his own agenda as well.

Though she hoped to avoid dictating their course of action, and would rather see the royal families agree and support her decision, the three decided that if the meeting went poorly, she would need to do exactly that.

As they entered the hall, she looked around at the assembled group. The kings and queens of the Seven Kingdoms were all present, along with Prime Minister Torscen and his cabinet of ministers. Imperial Guards were stationed along each wall, with several other personal guards the royal families had brought with them.

King Euristies of Frocomon was the first to approach and greet the Empress. He was a determined man who struggled along with his people to help his kingdom regain the prosperity it once had prior to the Great Wars. At the age of forty-three, he was the type of man who led by example. Those in his kingdom saw him boarding a fishing boat just as quickly as he would expect them to.

The man himself was extremely muscular and well built, as the life of a fisherman was a strenuous one. Unlike most of the men in the room, he was clean-shaven and quite tanned. His long black hair, which normally flowed freely, was now groomed in a ponytail for the sake of protocol. In his eyes, she could see strong determination, but also deep sorrow.

"My Empress, I wished to express my deepest sympathies and regrets for the vile acts of those under my care. What Arkham did was unforgivable. I only hope that you do not allow the actions of those few to reflect upon my kingdom as a whole."

She could hear the pride in his voice. Euristies had claimed the throne at a very young age, shortly after the Great Wars. His father had perished in one of the sea skirmishes against Conrad and Morex. Due to Frocomon's opposition to the would-be Emperor, their land was reduced, and much of the farmland that the people thrived on came under the banner of Danchul.

Euristies worked hard to try to maintain peace within his land, though the elders frequently cried for vengeance and restitution for what they perceived as wrongs to their land. The king however hoped to steer that aggression into a new trade, namely a merchant and fishing industry.

The younger generation had grasped onto these ideals, and worked hard to be successful in the lives they built for themselves. This was not easy. Dartais had run fishing and merchant operations for hundreds of years, whereas Frocomon was more skilled at farming, or water-faring military vessels. As a result, Dartais often was able to use its experience and developed craft, to be more efficient and drive down the prices on the market, causing even more hardships for Frocomon.

With all of that, Euristies still remained an optimistic leader with a vision that his people would overcome the hardships and regain their prosperity. Not through open warfare or revolt, but through hard work, blood, and sweat. This is why he was particularly outraged by the actions of the people of Arkham.

Karleena gazed deep into Euristies's eyes. "King Euristies, I assure you, there is nothing to seek forgiveness for. As you will see in these upcoming meetings, these are dark times for the Imperium, something we must address. It is possible the people of Arkham were coerced."

"Coerced? I am sorry, but a man is still responsible for his own actions. If they were led astray, then we can address that. The fact that they were willing to be led is something I must address. Again, my deepest sympathies."

Karleena nodded and moved over to an elevated throne. "If we could all bring this together. We have much to discuss over the upcoming days, and I wish to begin."

Those in the hall halted their conversations and focused on the Empress.

"Thank you. I appreciate the fact that all of you took time out of your own busy schedules to travel here and meet with me today." Karleena glanced around the room and studied the faces of those watching her. "What we have to discuss will quite possibly change the way we live our lives forevermore."

"Is the true purpose of this meeting not to undermine the authority of the ruling families?" Torscen bellowed as he interrupted Karleena.

"I am not attempting to undermine the authority of anyone, Mr. Prime Minister. In fact, I am trying to preserve the Imperium and see it prosper for generations to come."

"See it prosper, I see, I see. Then, is it not true that you hope to establish more of a democratic society? One where the people have a say in how the Imperium is being run?"

Unprepared for the vicious attack of Torscen so early, Karleena breathed deeply to regain her composure. As she looked around the room, she could see that several of the royal family members present were aghast by such a suggestion.

"This is an outrage. You wish to remove us from our thrones?" Queen Dornela of Dartais shouted out. "My husband, Rentios, is beloved by our people. He has their admiration and respect. He has always looked out for their best interests. Why then remove him from the throne?"

"Dornela, please." Rentios gently held her arm trying to keep her at bay.

King Rentios was a well-respected member of the royal family. He was truly loved by his people as his wife claimed, and never lifted a finger or made a decision that would bring them harm. In his seventies, Rentios was full of compassion and wisdom, as his eyes and tone clearly portrayed. He had a full gray beard and long hair that still had a few strands of black scattered throughout. His body looked frail and wiry, but the power of his heart and convictions provided the man with a deep sense of inner strength.

His wife, Dornela, however, was a demanding and protective woman. Larger in frame than her husband, many saw her as the physical force of

Dartais. She loved everything they had accumulated; she considered it hers, and was very reluctant to share or risk losing it. Where Rentios was forgiving and compassionate, Dornela was hard and vindictive.

Karleena raised her hands. "Ladies and gentleman, if I may have your attention, please. We should not jump to conclusions. All will be revealed in time. I am not looking to remove anyone from their thrones."

"No, not remove someone from the throne, just give the people enough voice to overthrow the decisions made by the throne," Torscen spat.

"I will not stand for that," Dornela chimed in.

"That is not what we are here to discuss," Karleena commented.

"Do you deny wanting to give the people a voice in the government?" Torscen demanded.

Karleena glanced at Admiral Morex, then at King Sarlec. They were silently offering encouragement, but they both knew she needed to handle this situation on her own. "I admit, I had considered giving the people a voice in the government."

"See! She admits it!" Torscen shouted in joy. "I feel that we should vote right here and now. Let's end this meaningless debacle and send this proposal where it belongs, in the garbage!"

"Prime Minister Torscen, you are making an already difficult situation worse. I would ask you to remain quiet for the next few minutes, or I shall order you removed." Her tone was clear and forceful.

"What? Have me removed? Preposterous," Torscen replied.

With a glance to Centain, the Captain of the Guards moved toward the Prime Minister. "Prime Minister Torscen, if you will come with me."

"I will not be bullied. The royal families themselves selected me. I belong here. More so than a child who succeeded her deceased common-blood father!"

"I will not ask you again, Prime Minister," Centain stated more forcefully.

"And what? Will you bully me like you did King Garum? This court has no respect for history or the way things are meant to be."

"Captain," Karleena said firmly.

He nodded and beckoned two of his guards. Each took one of Torscen's arms and escorted him from the audience hall.

Karleena took a deep breath and addressed the royal families once more. "Now we can continue."

Dornela glared at the Empress. "Will you remove anyone who has an opinion contrary to your own?"

"Queen Dornela, I am hoping to be able to listen to all of your opinions, after I have informed you of why we are gathered here today. Prime Minister Torscen has been growing more and more confrontational of late, and this was a direct assault toward the Imperium. His efforts here are counterproductive, and in truth, self-centered. If he agrees to return and remain composed, I shall readmit him."

"Sit down Dornela," Rentios pleaded.

Eyeing Karleena suspiciously, she conceded and sat down next to her husband.

"As I responded to Prime Minister Torscen, I had thought about providing the people with a voice in the Imperium. The reason for this, was due to the uprisings that have plagued our kingdoms of late in Dartie, and more recently in Frocomon." As she said this, she locked eyes with King Palenial of Dartie, then with King Euristies of Frocomon.

"When I sought information about why there were revolts, I was stalled at every turn with the report that there were no problems. Yet the uprisings displayed otherwise. I felt that if the people themselves could speak and let me know what was going on and why, I would be able to rule with much more efficiency."

"So Torscen was right. You are here to bring voice to the people," stated King Lorrents of Falestia in a steady and calm tone.

"I wish that were so. However, I soon learned of matters far graver than the people's unhappiness. Matters that require swift and decisive action. This is why we are here," Karleena said.

King Garum stepped forward. "Then we are wasting our time. Let me tell you what fantasies she is having. She heard rumors of an orc city in Tenalong with one hundred thousand orcs. One hundred thousand, can you believe that? She feared they were creating an army to swarm the land and slaughter us all. I sent my own scouts to confirm the validity of this city, and do you know what? There was nothing there! So then, why are we here?"

"Is this true?" Queen Zerilla asked.

Karleena looked at the beautiful queen before her. "This, among other reasons, is why we are here, yes."

"I do not wish to insult you, Garum, but Suspinti borders Tenalong. I wish to send my own scouts in to check on the validity of this potential threat. I will not have Suspinti fall because of your motivations," Zerilla declared.

"My motivations?" asked Garum incredulously. "What, pray tell, are my motivations?"

"Forget I said it," Zerilla said. "I still would feel better with my own envoy checking on this rumor."

Karleena watched the exchange briefly, and was thankful for Zerilla's openness, even if she would not outright accuse Garum of being corrupt. "Queen Zerilla, I have heard a motion for further action, and agree that we cannot possibly be too thorough with our resolve. I shall send an Imperial scouting party into Tenalong to verify this threat for ourselves."

"What? You would dare send Imperial troops into my kingdom without my consent?" The expression on Garum's face displayed anger, and very quickly, a sense of hatred for the Empress. "Torscen was right, this is an outrage!"

"As for myself, Empress, I thank you for this additional scouting mission. You have the complete support of Suspinti," declared Zerilla.

"As do you have that of Danchul," Sarlec offered.

"Oh, of course you would be on their side." Garum sneered.

"Do you forget, Garum, like Suspinti, Danchul borders your land? I will not have my kingdom serve as a battleground because of incompetence."

"Incompetence?" Garum shot back. "I do not have to sit here and be assaulted from all sides. I am a king, damn it!"

"Then start acting like one," suggested King Palenial of Dartie, speaking for the first time. "Please continue, Empress."

"Thank you. The rumors of the orc city are but one facet of what is happening within the Seven Kingdoms right now. More importantly for our immediate concerns, are the recent uprisings. It has come to my attention that the people involved in these revolts, are being manipulated and swayed by an outside party. One man who looks to undermine everything we have worked so hard to build over the years."

"One man, you say?" Lorrents asked. "How could one man inspire thousands to revolt?"

"This man is shrouded in mystery. Some believe him to be a god. Who he truly is, we do not yet know, however, his name, the name of Zoldex, has been brought up again and again during these revolts. Coincidence? I think not."

Euristies stepped forward. "My Empress, you know how I feel about people taking responsibility for their own actions. Therefore, even with this one mysterious Zoldex, he had to have a way to open the doors for revolt. We are still personally responsible."

"I agree. I do not know why thousands of Dartian hunters have revolted, but revolt they did. I fear this is a reflection on myself and my rule, not a grand conspiracy," King Palenial offered.

King Sarlec saw the conversation was beginning to churn around the same point, and hoped to move the discussion to the next level. "My Empress, you said this was the first thing. What else is there?"

"Yes, what is the second problem?" King Rentios inquired.

"We have learned that the ancient and noble races are being attacked by united forces of orcs, goblins, and hobgoblins," Karleena said.

"What do the noble races have to do with us? We haven't seen nor heard from them since the Race Wars, and I personally prefer to keep it that way," Dornela stated.

"I admit that through history, the Race Wars were vicious and cruel. Many died, and the Seven Kingdoms were in turmoil. However, we find ourselves facing a common foe in the here and now," Karleena offered.

"A common foe?" Zerilla inquired.

"Yes. The races are being attacked not only by the combined forces of evil, but also by one mysterious man who is leading them."

"Zoldex?" Zerilla asked.

"Yes," Karleena concurred. "Zoldex."

"What would you have us do?" Lorrents asked calmly.

"Whoever this Zoldex is, he has been instigating members of many different races, including humans. These individuals are attacking those around them, though not directly enough to alert all of the races of a direct assault. Instead, they are gradually advancing and wreaking as much havoc as they can. What the end goal is, I do not know."

Pausing for impact, Karleena began again. "Though we are not certain as to the validity of the orc city, the prospect of an army being constructed is terrifying. Warlord Braksis has informed me that our combined military forces would not be enough to withstand an assault of this magnitude."

Karleena noticed Queen Zerilla close her eyes and take a deep breath at the mention of the name Braksis.

"With this being the case, we feel the only way to defend this invading force, is by reuniting the races." Karleena looked around and saw a variety of responses, from shock, to disgust, to acceptance. "This will be a hard path to follow, and we will meet much resistance, both here today, and with the races themselves. A lot of mistrust has been formed between the races, and that is not something that will easily dissipate."

"Both an elf and a mystral helped to save Comonor," Zerilla stated. "I feel that it would be possible to try to work alongside these other races."

"Humph. That from a queen whose kingdom lives in fear of the races that reside within the forests of her land," Garum sneered.

Ignoring Garum, Karleena continued. "To help us with this goal, I have personally approached the Council of Elders of the Mage's Council. They felt that our objectives were pure and just, and have agreed to assist us. A Mage Master and his apprentice have been delegated to us in order to bring about these changes. I am hoping the presence and support of the Mages will allow the other races to at least consider our proposition."

Sarlec decided this was a good opportunity to display his support. "A most admirable course of action. Highly commendable. So when does this Mage team begin its assistance?"

Karleena offered a slight smile to the Danchul king. "They have already begun contacting the races. In fact, the Sovereign of Aquatica is here already. We expect more representatives to arrive at any time."

"Excellent," Sarlec said. "Things are progressing quite nicely."

"I would appreciate the support of those here. I will ask each of you to make any comments you may have. Please do not hesitate, even if you disagree. We shall go around the room. King Rentios, if you will begin."

Rentios gazed at a far corner of the room, lost in thought. Blinking several times, he stood to address his colleagues. "I know that my beloved wife will be opposed to this proposition. However, if the uprisings are really part of a more detailed conspiracy, then we should take every precaution. I am not opposed to at least meeting with the other races."

Dornela stood up. "How well you know me, my love. I have no desire to have dwarves, elves, aquaticans, or whatever wandering through our land. I have worked hard to build a very fashionable chain of islands where the rich and powerful enjoy residing or spending leisurely time. Imagine some filthy creature walking the same shores. That would be an outrage."

King Lorrents stood up and stepped past Dornela. "Well, we see what some people value, don't we? I will vote in favor of the unity meetings, though I must caution everyone here: Make sure our reasoning is sound, and not just overreaction. If we are to return to an age from before the Race Wars, we need to make sure we are doing it for the right reasons."

Queen Zerilla nodded in agreement. "I, too, do not wish to overreact. That is why I requested a second scouting party to validate the rumors of the orc city. As King Garum pointed out, the people of Suspinti have often lived in fear of those who resided within our great forests. To assemble the races and replace mistrust with a working relationship, many individuals will need to change the way they think. I still would be willing to lead my people and try to bridge that gap."

"Pathetic," Garum declared. "All of you, as is this. What happens to your leadership when you welcome the dwarves, who have kings and queens themselves? All we are doing here today is welcoming destruction and a loss of power. And for what, the fantasies of a child?"

"Garum!" Sarlec roared. "We are having a discussion, not a mudslinging contest. I warn you this: If you dare to insult the House of Conrad any further, you will have to deal with me. If that were to happen, not even the Hidden Empire could protect you from my wrath."

Garum looked at the Danchul king defiantly, but sat down without another word.

"As for Danchul, you have my full support. Already, we are making every effort to assist the dwarves in Vorstad, who have been under siege for many weeks. Our actions here can bring in a prosperous new age. I am glad that I was not only a part of the formation of the Imperium, but will also live long enough to see the unification of the races."

King Palenial nodded. "Very well spoken, my friend. I, too, concur, as long as lupans are not included in the mix."

Palenial's wife, Celenia bowed her head in sorrow at the reference to lupans, reminded again of the death of their only child at the hands of the mighty beast. So long ago, but the wounds were still open as if it had happened yesterday. With a tear in her eye, she nodded her agreement.

Euristies stood up and looked around. "As the last person to speak, I have a question to ask first."

Karleena beckoned for him to continue.

"For the past few months, my merchant and fishing ships have been raided by pirates. No matter what we do, we are unable to defend ourselves when they approach. If they, too, are pawns to this Zoldex, then I implore you to include this incident on our list of concerns. I could certainly use Imperial assistance."

Karleena looked over toward Admiral Morex. "Admiral Morex? Can you address this after the meeting?"

"Of course, my lady. I will make every effort to help with this seafaring nemesis," Morex said.

"Thank you, Empress. Admiral," Euristies addressed. "Though some elders in my kingdom would be opposed to this decision, I am in agreement with the meetings. It is time to place the hatreds of the past behind us, and work toward a mutually beneficial future. That goes for all things human, and other races."

Karleena breathed a deep sigh of relief. She managed to convince a majority of the ruling families of her course of action, and would not have to resort to force to mandate her actions. "Do any of the ministers have any comments?"

One minister stepped forward. "We feel that Prime Minister Torscen should have been able to have remained for these proceedings. I assure you, we shall inform him completely of what transpired here today."

Sarlec looked at the minister. "Be sure that you do. Remember to tell him the majority of those present supported the Empress."

"We need not to rehash old arguments again," Karleena cautioned. "I thank you all for coming, and look forward to meeting with you all again over the upcoming weeks as we face the unknown future together."

Centain walked over to Karleena and whispered softly into her ear so that no one could overhear what he had to say.

"If you'll excuse me, it appears we have some more visitors for our upcoming meetings," Karleena stated as she stood up and followed Centain from the hall.

He led her down a long corridor to a smaller room. Two Imperial Guards opened the doors, and three small individuals who were only waist high greeted her. They each had short and stylishly trimmed beards resting below a large, round nose. Their skin was a dark tan, even more tan than Euristies, thought Karleena. The three had various shades of blue-tinted eyes that were looking up at her. Their clothes were relatively simple in brown or green shades, but with intricate stitching, and they wore elaborate jewelry.

Centain extended a hand toward the newcomers. "Allow me to introduce the delegates of Underwood, the three gnomes, Arbuckle, Trivett, and Zeppenfelt."

"That's Zeppenfeld," one of the three gnomes corrected.

"My apologies," conceded Centain.

"Welcome to Trespias. I thank you all for coming," Karleena greeted.

"Trespias, eh? Wow, this city is pretty grand. Pretty grand indeed," Trivett commented.

"Oh yes, we can have a lot of fun here. A lot of little hidey holes we can explore," Arbuckle surmised.

"Hidey holes? Come on, Arbuckle, none of that here, we're guests," Trivett warned.

"Guests, heh, I'd surely like to see what they have here for technology. I might find a few things that could catch my fancy," declared Zeppenfeld.

Karleena stood watching the trio intently. They babbled away and spoke freely, as if they had no concerns in the world. Smiling, she realized she liked these three and would enjoy seeing what they would do in the weeks to come.

CHAPTER 51

As Solara slowly opened her eyes, she struggled to ascertain where she was. Her surroundings were unfamiliar, though she could see she was not bound or imprisoned. The last thing she remembered was the image of Braksis defenseless, with Lutz about to end his life.

"No!" she screamed into the darkened room, piercing the quiet. A sense of failure fled through her as she thought of Braksis perishing, and her being unable to do anything about it.

An elf entered through a small slit in the wall and approached her. He had long brown hair that flowed in perfect strands down his back. His face was full of concern and sympathy as he looked down at her. "You screamed out. We have healed your injuries. Is something else bothering you?"

"I do not understand. Where am I?" Solara inquired.

"This is Xylona. I am a healer here. Jellanos is my name."

"How did I get here?" Solara asked, hoping that somehow Braksis had escaped and brought her here.

"The wielder of Glistrin and his men rescued you. They brought you here."

Looking puzzled, Solara questioned Jellanos. "I don't understand. Glistrin?"

"Oh, I am sorry. The Glistrin is one of the fabled honor blades of Xylona. Captain Travers of your Imperium was awarded the weapon in honor of his deeds against the hobgoblins. He is the one who brought you here."

"Captain Travers?" Solara thought for a moment, remembering nothing after the battle. "The man I was traveling with...Lord Braksis, is he here as well?"

"Yes, Lord Braksis is here, and before your next question, he is unhurt as well." The elf reached out and checked her forehead for signs of fever. "He demanded I help you before tending to his own injuries. A most stubborn human."

Solara smiled at the healer. "Yes, Jellanos, a most stubborn human indeed."

As she attempted to stand up, a bout of nausea overcame her. The feeling flowed through her and her head started to throb again.

"Don't try to get up, you must continue to get some rest," Jellanos cautioned.

"How bad is it?" Solara asked.

"Not too bad. The wound to your head was rather serious, though with some elvish medicines, you will recover. I still would advise you to get some rest and allow the medicine to take effect."

"Thank you, Jellanos. I wish to see Lord Braksis. Could you help me?"

As Jellanos regarded her, he could see the sheer determination in her eyes. She would not be swayed until she saw Braksis was indeed alive and well. To try to curb that need would be a lesson in futility. "As you wish."

He reached down and provided a hand to support her as she struggled to get out of the bed. "Do you know where we can find him?"

"Yes. He is below the city, speaking to one of the dwarves. Thamar, I believe he said his name was."

"Thamar? He's here?"

"Yes," Jellanos confirmed.

As Solara stood up, the nausea threatened to overcome her once more, though the sensation slightly subsided after she was up for a moment. Looking at the door, she indicated she was ready to go.

As they walked out, the beauty and marvel of the city before her amazed Solara. Seeing Xylona from the city itself, one could only stop and admire what they saw. Large buildings were erected and entwined with towering trees. Fine detail and carvings were engraved, depicting years of hard work to present the beauty and magnificence of the city. Walkways were stretched from building to building and around all of the trees for transportation. Candlelight glimmered in the night sky, delivering a sense of serenity and peace.

As she absorbed the city before her, she was unable to fathom how this city could be under siege for so long and show no signs of violence or destruction. Truly a marvel that Xylona remained as it was.

Smiling knowingly, Jellanos approached the side of one building where there was an opening. "You find Xylona to be impressive."

Solara continued to scan the city and watch the bustle of activity. "That is an understatement. Breathtaking is more like it."

"Yes, it is. Even after living my whole life here, I still look around in awe at times." Pointing toward a small opening between the building and the bridge, Jellanos indicated how they were to get down. "We will descend here."

"How?" inquired a puzzled Solara.

"Just trust me," Jellanos replied. He reached over and opened a small lid on the wall beside the opening. He then removed a thin strand of vine attached to the cabinet. "I assure you, this is stronger than it looks."

"I certainly hope so," Solara stated.

He wrapped the vine around her waist one time, then brought her close to him and held on tight with his other arm. He squeezed the vine twice, and they began to descend from the city.

"How is this happening?" Solara asked.

Jellanos smiled back at her. "It's a Xylona trade secret."

Slowly they descended. As they did so, Solara looked up and struggled to see the city. From below, Xylona truly was hidden. The underbelly of the city resembled foliage and branches. "Remarkable," she said.

They continued to descend, slowing down slightly before reaching the ground. As they touched down, the impact was gentle and calm. Jellanos unwrapped the vine from around Solara, then squeezed the vine again. After releasing it, it returned to the city above.

Solara watched it return to where they had come from, and wondered once again how something like that worked. Hearing Braksis speaking, a sense of elation flowed through her and she quickly forgot all about the Xylonian form of transportation.

Jellanos led her through the trees to a small opening where she saw Braksis and Thamar sitting by a fire, drinking spirits, and speaking of things that happened since they parted.

"Then Travers and his men came and saved us from the hobgoblins. If not for them, we wouldn't be here for this reunion," Braksis concluded.

"And what a reunion it is, eh, friend Braksis?" Thamar bellowed. Glancing up, he pointed behind Braksis. "And another reunion you will wish to have right now, I would think."

Braksis turned to look behind him and saw Solara standing there with Jellanos. "Solara!" He jumped up and ran toward her, bringing her into a full embrace.

She held him tightly, as a small tear flowed from her eye. A tear of happiness to see that he was still alive.

Braksis quickly released her and looked at Jellanos with concern. "I'm not hurting her, am I?"

Jellanos smiled back politely. "Your actions just now probably did wonders for her."

Solara slapped Braksis on the shoulder. "Shouldn't you be asking me that? Besides, don't ever make me think that you are dead again! I won't take it too kindly."

Looking at the mixture of emotions in her eyes, Braksis nodded. "Very well, I promise never to leave you thinking that I am dead."

Behind them, Thamar began laughing. "A joyous reunion this truly is. Come, Solara, join our fire and listen to my tale."

Braksis gently took Solara's hand and walked her over to the fire. The two sat down, monitoring each other's injuries as they did so.

Jellanos bowed to the trio and then went on his way.

"Songs will be sung of the two heroes who tackled an army of hobgoblins!" Thamar declared.

Solara shook her head. "Is it a comical song? We lost."

"Ha, ha! It will be a valiant and bold song. One that shows that heroes-true face insurmountable odds, then, when all seems lost; our heroes are joined by their own allies and reign triumphant. A magnificent song this will be."

"I'll take your word for it, Thamar. As long as you don't try to sing it for me now," Solara commented.

"Ha!" Thamar laughed. "She is regaining her true wits. A very good sign."

Braksis reached over and gently squeezed her hand in a sign of affection. "A very good sign indeed."

Not desiring all of the attention, Solara looked straight at Thamar. "If I am not mistaken, you were about to tell us a tale of what happened to you since we parted."

"Ah, yes. Yes, I was," Thamar declared. "Then grab your drinks and get comfortable, because I hope to speak eloquently and true."

"After we parted ways, we continued north toward the Blackstock Mountains of Falestia as we had planned. For three days, this trip was uneventful, if slow moving. On that third night, things changed.

"As you, son of Worren, warned, there are indeed creatures known as kriverlings in the mountains of Falestia. Unfortunately, we were not careful enough."

Braksis looked at the bold dwarf. "Is everyone all right?"

"Unfold in time that shall. I won't allow you to get ahead of our story."

"My apologies. Please continue," Braksis said.

"Listening to your warning of the kriverlings, I sent Grosskurth ahead to scout out our route for us. He was instructed to learn as much as he could, but not to be detected. On that third night, he never returned."

Pausing to create a sense of foreboding, Thamar continued. "The rest of us packed our gear and went out in search of the tracker. Fortune herself must have favored us that night, for we managed to find a torn fragment of Grosskurth's outfit. With that in our possession, we spotted footprints and followed them into subterranean depths.

"As we descended the caverns, fear gripped many a dwarf. Yet continue onward we did. None of us wanted to go into the kriverlings' inner sanctuary, but we refused to leave Grosskurth behind if he was still alive."

"A valiant objective," Braksis offered.

"Yes, valiant," Thamar agreed. "We found an opening in the depths of the caverns and found hundreds of these creatures sleeping. Males, females, and children scattered all about. They appeared to be powerfully built and were clad only in filthy rags. They had thick, scaly, black skin with long, dark, stringy hair. Let me tell you, the stench of the caverns and the sight of these creatures were appalling.

"At the other end of the opening, I could see Grosskurth strapped to a wooden pole, above bones and other scraps. A fate I would not allow him to suffer. However, I was uncertain how to proceed.

"Then it hit me. Kriverlings were rumored to be blind. Yet they supposedly had highly developed senses of smell and hearing. I surmised then, that if we could mask our own stench and be more like the foul odor from below, we could walk among them unimpeded.

"Disgusting it was, I had us all roll around in the waste and much of the cavern floors. Let me just say this to you: Never enter the caverns of creatures so foul if you can avoid it."

With her nose wrinkled in disgust, Solara quickly agreed.

"After dirtying ourselves, we entered the cavern and moved slowly toward Grosskurth. Many a kriverling stirred with their heightened sense of hearing, sniffed the air in our direction, then returned to their slumber.

"As we reached Grosskurth, I knew we had managed to pull it off and was gladdened by this revelation. Yet when Grosskurth saw us, he laughed out in glee. A mistake, I assure you.

"Many kriverlings jumped up and approached us. The situation seemed dire indeed. We released Grosskurth, and darted as quickly as we could deeper into the depths of the unknown. The kriverlings charged after us, gaining with every step."

"Obviously you made it though, Thamar. What happened?" Braksis inquired.

"Ah, you wish to know the ending without the suspense. I can understand this as well. I tend to speak long and detailed, though with your injuries, you both probably desire sleep. Thus, I shall end this tale sooner than I typically would."

Solara sleepily smiled her appreciation.

"As we fled, the kriverlings got ever closer. We knew not where we were going, and the advantage was definitely theirs. Though dwarves have excellent vision in the dark, even we struggled to see where we were heading.

"Before we knew what to do, we wound up at a dead end. The kriverlings slowed down and approached us in bulk. There was no way to escape. We had to fight our way out."

Thamar scanned his audience, then continued. "The battle began in earnest. We fought well, and then..." Pausing, Thamar tossed the remaining contents of his ale into the fire, which resulted in a short eruption of flame.

Braksis and Solara both leaned back at the burst of flame, then focused on Thamar, who was smiling at them.

"And then, just as we thought that all was lost, we heard loud, thunderous bangs. The kriverlings stopped, and if they could look scared, I assure you, they were terrified. Behind them, a large club swung, and dozens of kriverlings flew through the air as if they were no more than leaves blowing in the wind.

"We retreated to the wall and tried to determine what was happening, then we saw them, a trio of rock trolls! They came in fast and strong attacking the kriverlings. These massive creatures were powerful, and the kriverlings fell quickly to their bulk and might.

"Seeing an opening to one side of the cavern, we snuck past the warring factions, and made our way through a different passage. One rock troll did spot us and attempted to stop us, but a couple of kriverlings got in its way and it attacked them instead. Once again, fortune was shining on us."

"Yes, I would say so," Braksis agreed.

"The remainder of our journey was uneventful. We arrived at Tregador and King Kendall sent four hundred dwarves—which you can see scattered around here—with us to fight these wars."

Braksis glanced around again to see the vast number of dwarves resting below the city of Xylona. "How about the elves? Did you attempt to gain their assistance as well?"

"If not for the elves here at Xylona, I would spit at the whole race. Visit Turning Leaf we did, and they merely turned their backs on us. Not their problem, they said. Self-centered egotistical fools. Don't they realize that even if they are not being attacked now themselves, they ultimately will be if we fall?"

"Many times, people only consider their own needs. Though you and I, what we have accomplished in such a short time, this could be the first step to bridge the gap between the races," Braksis stated.

"A just cause, I agree, though much resistance we shall encounter. That does not bode well for peace between the races," Thamar said. Seeing someone walking in the distance, Thamar jumped up. "If you'll excuse me for a moment, there is someone I think you should meet, my friend."

Sprinting away, Braksis watched as Thamar approached a pink-skinned elf and brought him back. Slightly darker in tinge than Kai, Braksis surmised that this must be Arifos, one of the Triad sent here to find the savior.

"Son of Worren, Solara, allow me to introduce you to the greatest warrior ever to grace these trees, Arifos."

Arifos lowered his head in a slight bow of greeting. "Thamar is too kind with his praise."

"Hah! Say that now, but see you fight I have!" Thamar returned.

Braksis stood up and extended his arm to Arifos. The Madrew elf clasped arms in greeting. "An honor to meet you."

"And likewise. Thamar informs me you have information regarding the Chosen One?" Arifos inquired.

"Yes. I saw Kai at Arkham, a small town in Frocomon. She had found the child and was looking to keep her safe."

"How did they fare? My dreams were plagued with images of the child in pain."

"Both were in pain. It appeared as if they both had extensive injuries. However, we pointed Kai toward the fairies, who have uncanny healing abilities."

Arifos considered these words. "Images of pain have left me. I can only assume that Kai succeeded in helping the child recover. This is good news indeed. A huge relief since I felt inclined to stay here and assist these brave souls."

After witnessing the assault of the hobgoblins firsthand, Braksis could understand how opposing them could become intoxicating. Those from Xylona and their Vorstad allies were so full of life and joyous, yet these creatures looked to utterly destroy them. He, too, felt he could stay here and fight, though his sense of responsibility demanded that he move on.

Reaching out to Thamar, Braksis offered his farewells. "Thamar, my friend. Arifos. If you will both excuse us. Fatigue is claiming us this night, and we were instructed to rest as much as possible. We shall speak more before we depart in the morning."

"Yes, my friend, we shall speak more later. For now, regain your strength so we can claim victory once more by each other's side," Thamar announced.

Arifos stepped forward and helped Solara to her feet. "It was a pleasure to meet you both. May good fortune travel along with you."

Touched by the sincerity, Solara smiled at Arifos and watched as he turned and resumed his prior task. Braksis walked over to assist her, and the two walked to a tent that was erected for the duration of their stay. Though, unless inhibited by the injuries, she knew they would continue their travels at daybreak.

CHAPTER 52

"Concentrate, you can do this." The encouraging words hit Kyria like a breath of inspiration. Redoubling her efforts, she attempted to fire the arrow at the target. "You need to see the target, to visualize it, to know exactly where it is, and exactly how much force you need to put into the arrow."

"This would be much easier if I wasn't blindfolded," Kyria rebutted.

"That may be so, but I have been able to shoot blindfolded and hit my mark using just my senses. With your newfound mysticism, you should actually be able to see even though you are blindfolded. You just need to feel it. Visualize it. Your senses will not betray you."

With that, Kyria fired another arrow off into the distance. She listened for the penetration of her target, but it never came. The arrow missed its mark as it had all morning. "This is impossible."

Shaking her head, Kai walked up to stand behind the young girl. "If you think it is impossible, then it will be. Open your mind to the possibility that you can do this."

"I'm trying, really, I am." The words came out as a whine.

"Kyria. Listen to my voice for a minute. Just concentrate on my words. The world around you is alive. Everything has life, senses, sound, and touch. Even though you are blindfolded, you can experience the world around you. Now listen and tell me what you hear."

With a huff and pout, Kyria listened and tried to hear her surroundings. At first, she heard nothing. Stubbornness, more than anything, was keeping her from truly experiencing the world around her. But then she allowed herself to open up and truly concentrate.

There was a bird chirping in a tree. The leaves swaying in the morning breeze. The trees and branches they were connected to creaking in the wind. Even on the ground, she could hear beetles, ants, and worms digging. Was that a bee flying?

Suddenly, her eyesight returned, as if her blindfold had been taken off. She could see the bee. Watched it as it flew to a flower, landed, and crawled inside the petals. She glanced down and saw underneath the ground. As clearly as if she were underground watching it, she could see the worm she heard digging a new tunnel. Then she looked up and saw the bird singing happily. What a beautiful bird, she thought. Its head was light blue with a red beak. Its back was a shade of yellow trailing all the way down to its tail feathers. The bird's belly shared the same shade of blue as its head. The wings were truly magnificent, a myriad of yellow and red at the stem of the wings, with white, black, and yellow feathers stretching wide. As she watched it, the bird spread its wings and took to the sky.

Kyria then looked at the target that Kai had set up for her between the trees in the distance. She really could see it. She could see everything around her. Not as lifelike as when she had her eyes open, but she could still see everything as if the world was a glossy haze. She noticed she could feel everything as well. Sensations flowed through her body, leaving her invigorated and happy.

Without so much as even thinking about it, Kyria raised the bow and released another arrow toward the target. This time, the blindfold did not matter; for she could see the target, feel the patterns of the wind, and knew precisely which angle to use and how much force. Then she released the arrow and watched it soar through the open air. Just as she had foreseen, the arrow made subtle shifts and turns from the wind. Everything flew exactly as she had anticipated. As if she could see the future patterns of the wind and anticipate them when she fired. Finally, the arrow landed dead center as it pierced the target.

Removing her blindfold and opening her eyes for real, she could see the smile on Kai's face. An expression filled with pride and warmth for her young pupil. "Very good."

"I, I did it." She surprised herself with the shock and disbelief that crept into her voice.

Patting Kyria's back, Kai tried to comfort her. "Like all things in life, practice makes perfect. It took me a long time to learn how to fire accurately when blindfolded, and I don't have the senses that you now do. You have far more to learn than I ever did. You will need to concentrate.

To always remain focused. To experience the world around you, to take everything in, but to allow it to remain calm and not overwhelm you."

"If you did not learn the ways of the Mages, then how can you teach me what I need to learn?"

The question was indeed a valid one. Kai had contemplated this many times. She maintained the inner peace the Mages required, but beyond that, she did not know how to truly open Kyria up to the world of mysticism. To bring her to the fruition and development she needed to truly be the savior. Times like this, she wished that Rulysta were here to take over Kyria's training, helping her to become a great Mage.

Kai knelt down and looked at the ground as she spoke. "To be honest with you, I am not certain how your development will progress. I have been assigned to find you, and to help you along your path, but as you state, I have not gone through this myself, so what I can teach would be limited."

Kyria knelt down with her friend. "I appreciate your candor. I feel that you are doing a great job with what you are showing me so far. I have been opening up. I just don't know what my potential is, or if either of us would know that."

"I see visions. I have seen you garbed in a suit of armor that appeared alive, flowing over you. I have seen you as the savior, the Chosen One. I know that is your destiny. How to get you there, that I have not seen."

"What else can you tell me about this?" Kyria asked.

Kai breathed slowly. "I saw you with a sword. The blade appeared from nothingness, and remained ablaze with a pure white light. Then you seemed to tear a hole in the fabric of reality, and by entering it, you ended up elsewhere. The image is so confusing, but crystal clear as well. Some of my people have the ability to teleport individuals, but it is very draining and requires immense effort. From my vision, you appeared able to do this with relative ease and no fatigue. I know that in time, this will be so, just as I knew how to find you."

Kyria stood back up and put her blindfold back on. "Well, if I am to be the savior, and truly turn into this vision that you see, then first I need to learn as much as I can. I want to try again."

Without picking up the bow, she concentrated. Much more quickly this time, the world around her came into her vision. The target was like a beacon begging her to pick up the bow and launch another arrow toward it. Something was different. She could feel something. Something she did not notice before, something at odds with the world around her.

Concentrating harder, she slowly turned around in a circle. Then she saw it. Him rather. Somebody was watching them. A shadow-like creature that blended into the world around him. She instinctively knew she could be looking straight at him and not even see him standing there. Only her heightened state of perception allowed the onlooker to be uncovered.

Focusing on this new presence, Kyria saw further. She began to know who he was and what he was doing there. She could see inside his soul. He was a passionate person with strong ideals and worthy of respect. Yet he was there to capture her, any way he could, and that included the potential of violence. She now knew that he was one of what was known as the Gatherers. An advanced scout sent to identify his target and determine how to proceed.

Others. There were others. Kyria turned around slowly. Then she saw them. Much further away, perhaps an hour's travel by foot. A whole group of them awaited a response from this shadow creature, this wraith. Kyria counted the new contacts, instantly knowing them like she did the one who was sent to spy on her–Matrife. Their backgrounds, lives, desires, hopes, and prayers. All became apparent to her young mind. She knew all that they knew. This revelation brought a newfound desperation. This group would not rest until they had her, and that was something she hoped to avoid.

Holding her hand above the bow, she concentrated, using her newfound abilities to levitate the weapon into her waiting limb. In one quick motion she had an arrow nocked and ready to fire. She could hear Kai asking her what she was doing; however concentration was important. She must not allow her focus to waiver.

Pulling back on the string, she could see all obstacles between her and Matrife. The trees she would need to fire between, the bushes swaying in the wind, and even the patterns of wind itself. All parts of the tapestry of life that she now comprehended and could utilize. Exhaling slowly, she released the arrow along with her breath.

The arrow traveled quickly through the air, narrowly missing several trees, exactly as she had anticipated. As it closed in on its target, she was struck with confusion. The arrow slowed, then come to a complete halt and hung in the air. At last, the arrow fell from the sky and landed flat on the ground.

She watched as her target jumped from his perch in the tree and returned toward the remaining Gatherers at their camp. Disbelief and disappointment that she missed flowed through her, but she realized this, too, must be one of the powers of a Mage. The ability to control physical objects with nothing more than a thought. Her actions were instinctual, but she had a lot of learning ahead of her.

"Kyria! What are you doing?" By this time, Kai had been yelling. She had been unable to get the attention of the young girl, who seemed to almost be stuck in a trance. She had watched as Kyria levitated the bow and fired in what could be considered pure poetry, as if she had been born with a bow. What was the target? The arrow stopped in mid-ascent. How was that possible? Kai contemplated.

Finally Kyria removed her blindfold and spoke in desperation. "We need to go. Now."

"Go? What's wrong?"

"The Gatherers are coming for me. They will not stop until I am in their possession. Even if that means your death." The seriousness in the twelve-year-old's tone was unmistakable. Her youth had been lost to the events of the past few weeks. She was maturing quickly. Learning the true way of the world. Kai prayed that would not scar her too badly as she continued to grow. For her experiences would have the potential to turn her heart cold as ice, to create a destroyer rather than a savior.

CHAPTER 53

Back at the Gatherer's camp, Tarwas maintained a constant vigil, always watching and waiting for any sign of danger. The calm before the storm, as he considered it. Growing closer, he could hear the rustling of the leaves. Someone was moving quickly in his direction. As he concentrated, he ascertained it was only one person. No need to alert his troops, at least not yet.

Out of the trees, ran a shadowy image, then before his eyes, the image grew into focus and revealed itself as Matrife. Out of breath, the Mage Master had clearly been running hard, rushing to arrive here. Most unusual, pondered Tarwas. For all Mages in the Council, physical training was a daily requirement. Mages usually were in exceptional shape and could often perform immense feats without the detriment of weariness or fatigue.

When Matrife was within earshot of his commander, Tarwas barked out his command. "Report, my friend."

Coming to a stop and trying to catch his breath, Matrife closed his eyes and attempted to regain his inner calm. To find the spot that would allow him to regain his composure more quickly. Taking in deep breaths through his nose, and out through his mouth, he straightened back up to full height and with his composure intact after about a minute of breathlessness.

Addressing his old Academy roommate, Matrife reported his findings. "The girl is being tutored by an elf from outside of our realm."

"Outside of our realm? How did you ascertain this?"

"She was pink pigmented. Unlike any elf we have ever seen," Matrife deduced.

"Understood. Continue."

"The girl struggled at first with what the elf was attempting to teach her, but then mastered it quickly. Indeed she is powerful."

"What makes you say that, Master?" Tarwas offered Matrife his official title of Mage Master as a sign of respect.

"This small child, this girl managed to sense me. I could feel her touch. Gentle and inexperienced though it was, she was able to probe my mind. There was nothing I could do. She slipped right past my defenses."

"A child managed to get through your defenses?" The disbelief poured off of Tarwas's words. "I find that hard to believe."

"You are not as intoned to your mystical abilities as I am, Tarwas. After she was finished with me, she found all of you as well. We would be wise not to underestimate her."

Scowling, Tarwas turned to look at his men. "So she knows we are here. We still outnumber her, and as you said, she is inexperienced. What does the scene look like in terms of resistance?"

"Just the two females, but as I've been saying, the young one uncovered me. Discovered me. Fired an arrow at me that would have pierced my heart if I had not used my magic to deflect the shaft."

"I cannot even see you when you are in the shadows, and we grew up together."

"Yes, Tarwas, but this girl uncovered me easily. For those Gatherers with lesser mystical abilities, they may not be able to avoid the girl's blows." Pausing briefly, he mentioned one other thing he had noticed. "There was also a dead lupan in their vicinity. If she was able to overpower a lupan..."

"I understand. We must go in fast and furious then. Strike quickly and render the girl unconscious. Once she is within the walls of the Mage's Council, there will be those who know how to help her adjust and develop. I will not lose my men to a child." Spinning around and entering the camp, Tarwas roared his orders gaining the attention of the platoon. "Gatherers, our time has come. This is the hunt that will prove we are truly the best of the best. We shall strike fast and hard. Do not underestimate your quarry. If you can render the girl unconscious, do so quickly. Now, Gatherers, let's ride!"

His speech ended, the platoon quickly sprung up, ready to go into action. Whether on horseback, in the air, through the trees, or along the ground, they all moved quickly toward their intended target.

CHAPTER 54

Captain Centain sat cross-legged in his quarters, wearing nothing more than small vines of the Harlocten tree laced around his neck and woven down his body to his waist. With his eyes closed, he gently rubbed the foliage on his chest as he listened to what it revealed.

Voices flowed through his mind in silent whispers. He could not truly hear what was being said, but experienced vibrations and emanations, allowing him to feel the words. Entire conversations throughout the palace were playing throughout his mind.

He heard the head chef discussing the afternoon meal with his staff; several guards discussing the aesthetically pleasing appearance of Sovereign Arianna; Sharnesta providing the Empress's handmaidens with instructions for her care for the day; and a conversation that was most troubling.

Stroking the Harlocten vine, Centain concentrated on this last conversation. Two people speaking, but the tone, feeling, and emotion in the room displayed darker, ulterior motives.

"Xyphin, I trust that Lady Salaman will be pleased with my efforts to undermine the Empress."

"Lady Salaman questions your motives."

"My motives?"

"Yes, you seem to be influenced by another, not just your master."

"I am the slave of nobody."

"If you feel that way, then this meeting is over."

"No, wait, I didn't mean it. Please do not tell Lady Salaman of my insolence."

"You offend me, Garum; you are fortunate Lady Salaman has need of you. See to it that this need does not outlive your usefulness."

"I'm sorry. I will cooperate."

"Excellent. Now, why were you assembled here?"

"The Empress is attempting to unite the races."

"Unite the races? This is most interesting, though such an enterprise would be most disruptive to our business. I trust that you will make every effort to sabotage these efforts."

"Yes, just tell Lady Salaman I am cooperating."

Hearing enough of the conversation, Centain opened his eyes and stood up. Stepping toward his bed, he quickly placed garments over his muscular form. He only hoped he could reach King Garum's quarters before Xyphin was allowed to escape. If not, then he had no true evidence to accuse the king with what he now knew.

Completely dressed, he ran out his door and toward the guest quarters. Garum was located in one of the palace towers, leaving a long and winding stairway to climb for Centain to reach him.

As he darted through the halls, he spotted several guards and instructed them to join him. Finally reaching the door to Garum's room, Centain touched his chest briefly, closing his eyes to concentrate. They were still there.

He nodded to his guards and they tried the door. Garum had it sealed from within.

"What was that?"

Centain could feel the panic within, and heard the conversation come to an end. He spun around and kicked the door open, leading his guards into the room.

King Garum approached him with a scowl on his face. "What is the meaning of this? How dare you interrupt me this way?"

Centain brushed past the king and checked the balcony. In the distance, he could see a dark figure flying away. Turning to face Garum, he beckoned two of his guards. "King Garum, I am detaining you for consorting with known criminals and attempting to undermine the Imperium."

"Detaining me? I am a king! You cannot detain me!" Garum roared.

"When within these palace walls, you are under the complete jurisdiction of the Imperium. I am sworn to defend this palace and that jurisdiction. This matter will be brought before the Empress for review. For now, take him away."

The guards took the resisting Garum by the arms, issuing threats and profanity as he left. Centain turned to look out the balcony window once more and silently chastised himself for not being quick enough to visibly catch Garum and Xyphin together. That one detail, he feared, would allow Garum to go free and possibly force his own resignation.

CHAPTER 55

The sight in the hills was truly breathtaking. With the morning light shining behind it, a unicorn stood proud and scanned the land. Its mane, a sort of bluish glimmer that trailed from its head down its back, appeared to sparkle in the sunshine. The mystical horn atop its head reflected the light and dazzled the senses. The horn was predominantly white, with traces of sparkling silver spiraling throughout. The unicorn's body was also white, though with slashes of golden markings.

The travelers, Lord Braksis and Solara, along with Tiot, watched the unicorn off in the distance with awe. Even the way the sun was shining down on the steed gave it the impression of holiness. A creature stemmed from the gods. Truly beautiful and a gift to all of terra. A welcome sight after all they had witnessed of late.

As Braksis watched the unicorn turn and walk into the Suspintian Forest, he was glad they had decided to leave Xylona so early. If not, they would have missed this spectacular sighting.

Before leaving, the elven doctor Jellanos had examined both Braksis and Solara once more. He stressed that they still needed some rest and should take it easy, though they both were on the quick road to recovery.

Seeing firsthand the destruction and hostile actions since they left the battlefield at Arkham, Braksis did not wish to delay their journey to Ferceng's any longer. He had wanted to check on his troops at Vorstad and Xylona, then move on toward Ferceng's lair, which would be an additional fortnight's journey. However, he felt an overwhelming desire to complete his journey and return to Trespias as soon as possible.

With this goal in mind, Braksis decided to take a path that was much quicker but also more dangerous. He would lead them straight through the Suspintian Forest. Although Solara was a mystral, and her people lived within the forests, he knew that as a human, he could attract the attention and hostilities of many races. Still, that was a risk he was willing to take.

Presuming that they were not delayed by further assaults, Braksis estimated they could pass through the forest and arrive at Ferceng's within the next three to four days. A much better time frame than fourteen, though with the added danger, that estimate might be a bit off.

That morning, Thamar had expressed many reservations about Braksis' taking this route. He had just traveled through the forest himself, though he had the advantage of marching with four hundred dwarven warriors. Even then, Thamar said the forest had many eyes, and he often felt threatened by creatures lurking within.

Solara quickly agreed with their dwarven friend, reminding Braksis that she used to live in the forest and was well aware of the dangers within. Regardless of these warnings, he knew that the time saved would be invaluable. His first priority now was to return to Trespias and inform the Empress of everything he had learned and witnessed on his journey. To stay away longer would be futile.

Reluctantly, Solara conceded, and they began traveling shortly after a breakfast feast with Thamar, Travers, and several others at Xylona. Since then, the trip had remained uneventful, and relatively quiet, leaving both riders to their own thoughts.

These were interrupted by a loud crack, followed by voices in the distance. With all that had happened of late, Braksis instinctively grabbed Carnage and braced himself in a defensive posture, listening intently. He heard voices again, followed by cheering.

Looking over at Tiot, he could see the timber wolf with its hair up on end, growling off at an unknown threat in the distance. Tiot would stay unless instructed by Braksis to attack. His obedience and control were never in question. Braksis whistled in a low tone once, and Tiot rushed into the forest to find the source of the disturbance.

Braksis dismounted and took to the woods after Tiot, with Solara close behind him. Running, he quickly came upon the voices he had heard. Slowing down so as to assess the situation, he found six men attempting to capture the unicorn. The steed was in a hole that clearly had been dug out as a trap. The men tossed ropes around the unicorn's neck, binding it down.

The men themselves all wore dirt-covered clothing, with assortments of older weapons. As he scanned them, he knew that these men were poachers, most likely from Tenalong. Disgusted, Braksis quickly analyzed how to go about this mission. With Solara's head injury, he preferred not to have her involved, but he, too, had been injured. Though he was confident he could overcome six men, especially these six men, he decided that the best course of action would be to lull them into a false sense of security and take them unawares.

Looking at Solara, he beckoned her to one side, then released a pair of short whistles to Tiot so that the timber wolf would move to the other. Then, he slowly removed his armor, leaving on only his black leather pants and a loose-fitting white shirt. No marking remained to indicate who he was, or what he represented.

Reaching down, he picked up some dirt and rubbed it onto his outfit, leaving blotches of caked mud upon his shirt and pants. Stepping into the clearing where they could see him, he stumbled and acted intoxicated.

The first of the poachers to notice Braksis quickly brought his colleagues' attention to him. "Brothers, we are not alone."

Braksis stumbled a little more and dropped his axe, giggling the entire time.

Another poacher approached him slowly. "Hey, brothers, he's not even wearing shoes. He must have sold them at the tavern for more booze!"

"Either that, or some backstreet whore ran off with them after filling him with ale!" All the poachers started to laugh.

"What say you, stranger? You seem most unkempt. What is your story?"

Braksis sent out the impression that he was trying to regain his focus, as if the whole world was blurry. "Pretty horsy," he slurred.

This comment sent the poachers into laughter once more. The one closest to him turned to face those nearest the unicorn. "What do you think? Can we get anything for an intoxicated fool?"

The others laughed at this, too. One man stepped forward, clearly the leader of the group. "Marcalis, kill him and be over with it."

The man closest to Lord Braksis, now identified as Marcalis, reached down for his chipped and rusted sword, only to discover that it was no longer there. Lord Braksis used some of the subtleties of his mystral companion to remove the blade from its sheath unnoticed. As Marcalis turned to look, the blade was thrust into his stomach and drawn up. The look of shock permeated his face as his life faded away.

Braksis then stepped on the handle of Carnage, raising it in the air slightly. He grabbed it quickly and sent it hurtling at the one he identified as the leader. The blade hit its mark and sent the man propelling back with the force of the blow.

The other four forgot about their intended prey and armed themselves. This barefoot man only had Marcalis's old and battered sword left. One against four, they would kill him, then split the profits of the unicorn four ways instead of six.

Two charged, and as they did so, found it peculiar that the brown-haired man merely smiled at them. He ducked the first assault, sending the blade sidelong into the stomach of one poacher, then spun up and around, slashing down at the second man. Both fell to the ground dead.

The two remaining poachers could not believe their eyes. This man had just killed four of their fellow hunters, and now they, too, risked death at his hands. Discretion is often the better part of valor, and the two opted to flee in order to survive for a future hunt. They didn't make it far. Solara hung upside down from a tree by her knees and sent two daggers hurtling through the air toward the last two poachers. Both blades hit the men in the chest, piercing their hearts with precision.

She released her knees and flipped before landing erect. Walking over to her daggers, she removed both from the poachers' chests, wiped them off on the men's shirts, and then approached Braksis. "I thought we were going to take them from three sides at once."

Braksis laughed as he walked over to the unicorn and cut it free of the ropes that held it in place. Tiot walked into the opening and stopped by Solara's legs. "Teaming up on me? How unfair."

"You could have at least kept your armor on."

"Why? You aren't very protected with your outfit." Making the statement, Braksis's eyes wandered as he quickly scanned Solara's body.

A playful smile was the only answer he received. After their years together, quick banter such as this became expected. Especially now, in light of all that happened, a lighthearted approach allowed the two to remain focused and not give in to the despair of their discoveries.

As Braksis finished freeing the unicorn, it stared in his eyes as if it were looking into his soul. He whispered to it and tried to calm it, telling the unicorn everything he was doing and why. It seemed to understand every word, and did not move a muscle while he was working. With the last bond severed, the unicorn jumped from the hole, looked at Braksis briefly, then turned and disappeared deeper in the Suspintian Forest.

Solara walked to Braksis's side, watching the unicorn as it vanished behind several trees. "There's gratitude for you."

"Yeah. What did you expect? I save its life and it stays by my side forever?"

Solara shot him a look of disbelief at his analogy.

"Hey!" Solara retorted to Braksis's jab.

"What? What did I say?" Braksis pleaded innocently.

"Maybe I should just run off into the night, too," she challenged.

"Go right ahead. But you'd miss my world-famous cooking. You hungry?"

"Yeah. Let's have lunch." With that, the two returned to the horses with Tiot trailing close behind. As they walked, both continued to bicker and joke with each other. Both secure in the fact that they faced yet another threat and overcame it. Neither aware, that at that exact moment, at their destination, old adversaries were plotting their downfall.

❖ ❖ ❖ ❖ ❖

Rawthorne and Durgin, two large elements from Braksis's past, had joined together for the first time. One whisked away from the prison where he was sentenced to spend the rest of his days, the other found rummaging through the swamps, afraid of his own shadow.

Both men, in their day, had managed to overcome a younger Braksis, then faltered as they themselves were vanquished. As a result, they were the perfect duo to plot and plan the demise of the man they hated so intensely.

This was the reason Zoldex pulled some strings and brought these two together. He knew no mere assassin–but rather an image from his past–could overcome the Warlord. Old enemies fueled with rage and the taste of vengeance. Where assassins failed, these two men would succeed.

To improve their odds, Zoldex also provided them with a way to summon a nearby clan of goblins. A race that had no love for humans, and also had a hatred of their own for Ferceng, the troll who Braksis considered his father.

The two men arrived in Falestia first, with Rawthorne immediately taking command of their partnership due to his feelings of natural superiority, as well as familiarity with the surroundings of his prior home.

Pointing at a small opening in the rocks, Rawthorne opened dialogue to dictate their plan. "That is where Braksis will be going."

Following the pointed finger, Durgin scanned the cave that led to the home of the Mage. "We must be careful we are not discovered."

"We will not be discovered. I know this area like the back of my hand. We will wait up there." He pointed to an area on the mountain that was jutted out with a flat outcrop behind it so that they could remain hidden. "We'll wait for Braksis, then strike when he least suspects it."

Durgin looked at his companion, full of confidence and control. He remembered when he, too, used to be that way. Before being brought down by a naked woman with some stones and a branch. A time when he was on the top of the world, feared by many, and considered a true Warlord in every way. Now, he only wished to atone for his past mistakes. To put his demons to rest and live out the rest of his days without fear or regret. The only way he felt he could do that was by killing Lord Braksis and reclaiming his honor and name.

Zoldex promised that it was written in destiny. They would be victorious. Durgin could practically taste the sweet nectar of victory already. With Braksis dead, he would then go after Solara and make her suffer for what she had done to him. Perhaps then, he would hunt down the mystral everywhere. Wipe her whole species off the face of the planet.

Rawthorne looked at his companion and questioned once again why Zoldex brought the two together. Durgin was large and imposing, and he was sure, at one point in time, quite intimidating. However, now, he flinched at his own shadow. A fraction of the man he once was, he was pitiful. Rawthorne had no need of this excuse of a human being. He would take control, kill Lord Braksis, then take steps to try to reclaim his throne. When Zoldex freed him from incarceration, he assured him no strings were attached. Just kill Braksis, and he was free to go. He planned on following those instructions to the letter.

At Rawthorne's lead, both men ascended until they arrived at the selected perch. Once there, they unpacked weapons and dreamed of how they would kill the man they both had hated and despised for so long.

CHAPTER 56

Trees flowing past the two girls in a blur as they ran, Kai and Kyria ultimately lost all sense of direction. Where they were, where they were going, both sites blurred as quickly as the trees around them.

Slowing down, Kai reached out to the young girl. "Kyria, stop. We are growing tired and are lost."

Kyria closed her eyes and turned around in circles. Her breathing calmed as soon as her eyelids shut. This amazed Kai. Truly, this girl was growing much more powerful. Her ability to adapt and master magic so quickly just confirmed that she was truly the Chosen One.

As Kyria spun around, the world clarified again. She could see the Dartian Woods, and even go straight through them. She could see the Gatherers and how close they were to them. At the pace they were traveling, they would probably arrive at their current location in about twenty minutes. That provided a little breathing room, but not much. It was a good thing that they decided to leave the mule behind, because it would only have slowed them down. "We have maybe twenty minutes before they will be upon us."

Kai gazed off in the direction that Kyria was looking. "Can you find any place we could use as sanctuary?"

Looking around again, Kyria focused further, allowing her senses to probe the woods deeper and more clearly. Then she saw it. A chance to escape. Or at least, a chance to elude their pursuers for the time being. "There is an opening in that direction. What looks like an old temple."

Kai nodded her assent. The temple was their only hope. The Gatherers would continue after them relentlessly until they found the child. She knew that they would be unable to outrun them for long. Eluding them. Hiding. Laying a trap, that was the most favorable avenue available to them. "That is where we will make our stand then."

Looking like a child again for the first time since she discovered Matrife watching them, Kyria gazed up pleadingly at Kai. "Will we make it?"

"We will have to, won't we?" With that, Kai ran in the direction of the temple. Her lungs felt ready to burst with their constant and swift pace, but she refused to allow these Mages to take the Chosen One away from her without a fight.

❖ ❖ ❖ ❖ ❖

The point of the Gatherers was led by a cornal, a member of a canine race with enhanced senses of smell and hearing. These enhanced senses helped to offset the black and white sight that plagued all cornals. Covered from head to tow with fur, they also had elongated jaws with a nose at the tip of the mouth. Their ears stood erect and pointed, with hands and feet, or rather paws that consisted of only three fingers or toes.

This particular cornal, Nerwasa, had been hand-selected by Tarwas since he had tested as extremely gifted in the hunt, but not in other practical attributes. Nerwasa quickly grew into his role as a Gatherer and had often been utilized as the point man or advance scout. His tracking abilities were unparalleled in all the ranks of the Gatherers. Nerwasa was furred in a shade of light brown with a patch of creamy white circling his left eye. He usually spoke little, instead focusing on the task at hand.

As Nerwasa moved into the clearing, he could taste the scent of the elf and girl on his tongue. They had been here recently, he thought to himself. He slowly moved around the wooded area, and found some stirring of the leaves which looked as if someone had been standing in place and going around in circles. There was also another indentation in the ground where the elf had been standing. By his estimation, they were here not even fifteen minutes ago.

Lifting his snout into the air, Nerwasa took in several deep breaths of air through his nose, looking for the scent of his prey. It did not take long; he could sense them heading off in a northerly direction toward the Horned River.

Nerwasa removed a corryby from a pouch hanging over his neck. Upon his touch, it began to glow from within. A clear image of Tarwas appeared above it as if a smaller version of him was actually standing there.

The image looked straight at him and issued his command. "Report."

Nodding his head, Nerwasa spoke to the orb. "Commander, I have found the trail of our prey. They are heading in a northerly direction toward the Horned River."

"They could be hoping to use the current to flee more swiftly. Then attempt to lose us at Cupton Ridge or Lake Cupton." Pausing, Nerwasa could see Tarwas turn and order his men who had the ability to fly to go on ahead to Cupton Ridge as lookout scouts. The image of Tarwas then returned to Nerwasa again. "Continue."

"By my estimations, they were at my current location approximately fifteen minutes ago, sir. We shall close in on them quickly."

"Excellent. Continue tracking the two. We shall be with you shortly. Tarwas out." At the end of his transmission, the crystalline orb ceased its glowing, and the image of Tarwas faded. Nerwasa then returned it to his pouch and resumed his journey toward his quarry.

As he continued to close in on them, their scent became clearer, allowing him to increase his pace and shorten the distance between them. Crossing through bushes, trees, even a small stream, Nerwasa did not slow his pace, or lose track of his prey.

Up ahead, the trees opened up into a clearing. That was where the scent was leading him. Slowing down, he approached the edge with a little more caution. Perhaps it was a trap. Why would prey go out into the open?

As he approached the edge of the forest and only had open ground in front of him, he scanned the landscape. No apparent deception was evident. About a hundred yards away, he spotted a massive structure that appeared as if it were hundreds of years old. The trail he was following indicated that the girls had come this way and gone right up the stairs of the temple.

Still looking for a potential trap, Nerwasa observed the ruins of the temple. Portions of the once mighty structure lay scattered along the ground. The temple itself had crumbled stairs leading up to an opening. Along the sides of the stairs were large statues of creatures that he was unfamiliar with. The statues portrayed the heads of what looked like bulls, but were elevated and standing like men. Each statue held giant spears and other weapons in what appeared to be a guard detail surrounding the stairs of the temple.

Nerwasa slowly moved up the stairs, his senses on full alert. He was confident he would hear his prey before they could ever spring a trap on him.

As he approached the opening, he noticed there was a choice of paths. He could go down one of three dark passages, to the left, right, or straight. Oddly, he could no longer smell the two girls. His senses were betraying him.

Looking at the three dark caverns, he desperately hoped to find some sign as to which way to go. Then he heard something fall, a scream followed by an echo. The sound came from the left, so that was the direction he chose.

❖ ❖ ❖ ❖ ❖

Slowly traveling through the caverns of the temple, the two girls were surrounded by darkness. Even then, Kyria still was able to see everything, regardless of the lack of light. She also instinctively knew which way to go. As they entered the temple, there were many paths to choose. The inner corridors proved to be a labyrinth, giving them multiple options at just about every turn. Without slowing her pace, Kyria confidently knew the way she wanted to go.

Rounding another corner, the ground beneath Kyria crumbled and fell out. As the ground gave way, she screamed in shock. Plummeting into the darkness, she desperately reached out to find anything she could hold on to. At last, catching a piece of rock jutting out, she slammed into the sidewall of the hole.

Kai quickly twirled her bow and jammed it into place between the two side walls, creating a beam to support her weight. “Hold on.” Even as she was speaking, she was wrapping her legs around the shaft and lowering herself into the hole.

Looking up, all Kyria could see was darkness. How close was Kai? She couldn’t tell. She wondered how it was that she could see so clearly a minute ago, and now struggle so much? Concentration, it must be concentration. Just then, she could feel something light and string-like touching her face.

Attempting to focus, the world around her began to take shape again. Directly in front of her was an upside-down Kai smiling at her.

"Need a lift?"

Kyria smiled back at her friend and mentor, feeling ashamed that she had given in briefly to her fear and allowed her concentration to slip. "Yes, please."

Kai then reached out with both arms and lifted Kyria up. The strain and the creaking of her bow with the extra weight were quite noticeable. "Climb up me."

"Will it hold the weight?"

"Don't worry, we Madrew know how to make good weapons. Though I wouldn't recommend trying this with any other bow, it should hold," Kai said to comfort her.

Kyria slowly climbed up Kai's body until she could feel the bow where Kai's legs were entwined. She then grabbed ahold of this and leapt to the other side of the cavern, avoiding the hole in the ground. "I'm up."

After hearing that Kyria was safe, Kai twisted and raised her body up, grabbing the bow with her arms. As soon as she had ahold of it, she released her legs, and allowed herself to sway back and forth. As she shifted to one side, like a pendulum, she then motioned toward the side where Kyria had landed, springing up and landing solidly on the ground. While in the air, she released one arm, but twisted with her other, removing her bow from the ledge and bringing it with her.

As she landed safely on the ground, she heard Kyria scream out. "Look out!" The shout of warning came an instant too late, as something solid collided with her and sent her toppling to the ground.

Kai could feel some kind of furry beast atop of her. It was growling and bringing its head closer to hers. Warm saliva was dripping out of its mouth and landing upon her brow. Using all of her strength just to keep the carnivorous jaw from biting her, she felt her options fleeting quickly.

Kyria ran to Kai's side and started hitting their attacker on the back. Releasing his grip, Nerwasa lunged toward the unarmed Kyria. She instinctively held out her hand trying to keep him away, and miraculously, an unseen force pushed Nerwasa off of her.

Kai jumped up and headed toward where Nerwasa had fallen. She clenched her fists, extending the koxlen claws she had attached to her gloves. Making sure she could hear the cornal to determine its exact position, she slashed her arm and heard a yelp immediately following her motion. She then punched the Gatherer several times. With each punch, the four blades per fist would puncture her attacker. Deep down, she thought this may be brutal and bloody, but survival and escape was all that mattered.

She could feel the warmth of Nerwasa's blood dripping down her fingers and arm. Reaching down, she realized he was still breathing, but was clearly unconscious. "Let's go before he gets back up, or his friends catch up to us."

Kyria reached out to take Kai's blood-soaked hands, then walked slowly through the depths of the labyrinth once more. The others would soon be upon them. She could feel them getting nearer with every heart-beat.

CHAPTER 57

"What kind of reaction can we expect from this?" Karleena asked, fearing for the worst.

"He is a king, my lady. The other royal families will not be happy with his incarceration. Especially after you removed Prime Minister Torscen from diplomatic proceedings. They may view this as a direct assault against any member who opposes you."

King Sarlec jumped up quickly. "Bah! Morex speaks well, but I can assure you of this, I am one member of the royal family who thinks that dirty bastard got what he deserves!"

"Captain, do you have any evidence of his involvement with the Hidden Empire?" Morex inquired.

Captain Centain lightly rubbed his chest, then shook his head. "I know for a fact that he was meeting with Xyphin, one of the Hidden Empire's lieutenants. As for proof, I have none."

"I see no other alternative then. Without physical evidence, we'll have to release him," Morex declared.

Frowning, Centain stepped forward. "I only wish I were fast enough to have caught them together. Then you would have your proof." Looking toward the Empress, he knelt down on one knee. "For this failure, my Empress, I humbly offer my resignation and place my life in your hands."

"Stand, Captain," Karleena ordered. "Your resignation is not desired, nor will it be accepted. We will release Garum and deal with any public outcry that may come up."

"Too bad he can't rot in that cell for a bit longer," Sarlec stated.

"I think you misunderstand me, King Sarlec. I said release him, but not when. We are not meeting again with the royal families until more representatives of the races arrive. I think we can leave him in his cell for a few days." Looking at Centain, she instructed him further. "No communication with others. I want him to feel guilty, then maybe he'll admit it on his own."

Sarlec let out a loud bellow. "I like that. I like that very much. Let him be his own downfall!"

"You mentioned more races. Do you have any indication as to when others shall arrive?" Morex inquired.

"I received a communication from Master Askari right before our meeting. He arrived at Xylona this morning and they were quite receptive to sending representatives."

"I would think so, especially with Imperial troops helping them right now," Sarlec commented.

"Yes, well, he said that representatives of Xylona, the dwarves of both Tregador and Vorstad, as well as a member of the Madrew elves will be leaving for Trespias today."

"Impressive. That will expand our current ensemble quite significantly," Sarlec concluded.

"Yes. Also of interest, Askari indicated that he had just missed Lord Braksis, who spent the prior night at Xylona. Apparently, Braksis and Solara were both injured, and told tales of sorrow."

"Sorrow?" Morex questioned.

"General Kronos was killed defending the Halls of Vorstad from an orc invasion," Karleena replied.

"This is most distressing," Sarlec said. "Hopefully the representatives of these races will arrive soon. We must unite, or more problems like this will arise."

"I cannot agree with you more, Sarlec," said Karleena. "What other developments are there?"

"I have sent three Imperial Gallies to Frocomon to defend the merchant and shipping fleets. If these pirates attack again, they will have a surprise waiting for them," Morex reported.

"Excellent. I am sure King Euristies will be elated by this news," she commented. "King Sarlec, anything from you?"

"Nothing to do with business right now. My son has joined me here. I think this is good news. He has been so reluctant to show an interest in the Imperium up to now. Maybe he is finally maturing."

"That would be welcome news indeed," Karleena replied.

"Well, since he is here, and of royal blood, perhaps the two of you would be willing to say, have dinner together?"

Blushing, Karleena looked at him with a startled smile. "Sarlec, I am shocked."

"Not so shocked. You know I have been trying to get him to take an interest in the Imperium. If that interest led to an attraction to you as well, all the better."

Morex placed a hand on Sarlec's shoulder. "Old friend, you better not let the boy hear this, you would embarrass him."

"Bah! He should not be so easily upset. He will learn to grow a thick hide like me."

In the distance, a large explosion erupted, shaking the entire palace.

Grasping onto her chair, Karleena looked worriedly at Centain. "What was that?"

Centain dropped to his knees with an expression of pain and worry. Clutching his chest, he tried desperately to regain his composure. "Gone. They're all gone."

"Who is gone? Captain? What is going on?" Karleena demanded.

"The third tower, the explosion was there," he announced.

Leaping from her throne, Karleena led the way out the door and toward the third tower. In the halls, Imperial Guards and staff were running back and forth in confusion. Nobody seemed to know what was going on or what to make of it. The palace was in utter chaos.

As she continued toward the third tower, she could hear Morex and Sarlec warning her not to go there. It could be a direct attack on the palace, and she should be brought to safety. Though their words were feasible, all she could think of was an attack on the representatives of the races. The gnomes had been quartered in the third tower.

Reaching the stairwell, she saw large gaps where walls once were. Bending down, she ripped her dress so her legs could have full movement and not worry about the frill catching on anything.

Captain Centain grabbed her arm and looked at her desperately. "I will have rescue crews explore the wreckage. You need to get to safety."

"We do not have the luxury of time. I will do everything in my power to try to help the gnomes." Karleena brushed his arm off and climbed the remains of the stairwell. Smoke filled the corridors and hindered her vision. Behind her, she could hear Centain coughing as he followed her closely from behind.

Determined, she continued upward. About halfway to the top of the tower, she found two of the three gnomes. They, too, were making their way up toward the top. "Are you all right?"

Arbuckle looked up at her with an expression like he was in trouble. "Why me? Sure, I'm fine. Nothing wrong here. No worries. No problems. What wouldn't be all right?" As he spoke, his words rolled on into one elongated babble.

"Idiot," Trivett declared. "This whole stairwell is about to fall apart, we have smoke in our eyes, no clue as to where Zeppenfeld is, this place is in shambles, and you say that nothing is wrong?"

Bending down to look the two directly in the eye, she spoke briefly, but with a tone that left little to discussion. "Go back downstairs. We will find Zeppenfeld. This is not safe for you now."

Frustrated, Trivett started to walk back down the damaged stairwell. "See what you did? If not for you, we would be up there with Zeppenfeld right now. Maybe the greatest discovery of all time, and here we are going back downstairs and missing it."

As they vanished in the smoke, Karleena could hear the back-and-forth banter continue at a heightened pace. Curious about what Trivett said about a discovery, Karleena pushed that to the back of her mind as she continued upward.

With her next step, the stairwell collapsed slightly and shook below her. "Centain, go back. The stairs can't hold the weight of us both."

"No, Empress, I will not leave your side. There may be danger," Centain replied.

"I am in more danger if you stay. I am lighter and the stairwell will hold me; this is not open to discussion. Go."

Watching her, he couldn't help but feel helpless. If she were to get killed, or even hurt, he would never forgive himself. As he took a step toward her, the stairwell shook again, dislodging several steps from the wall.

"Captain, this is an order," Karleena declared.

"Very well. Please be careful," he conceded, then walked backward down the stairs so that he could watch her as long as possible. He lost sight of her quickly through the smoke.

Moving back up, she was glad to see that the stairwell was not as shaky with her alone climbing it. Reaching the doors to the tower, she checked the handles for heat. Though warm, she deduced there was no fire on the other side.

Opening the double doors, a dark black cloud of smoke fled into the now open hall causing her to cough and choke. Waving in front of her face for air, she could see past the smoke, and entered the room.

The ceiling was in tatters, as well as the walls. In the center of the room, she saw a large crater with streaks extended from it. Searching desperately for the last gnome, she saw him sitting on the floor looking directly toward the crater.

Rushing to him, she peered to see whether he was severely injured or not. "Are you okay?"

Zeppenfeld sat there, covered in soot and grease. His hair and beard were both frazzled and blackened by the explosion. Two small round goggles, the lenses of which were also covered with a black substance, covered his eyes.

Slowly reaching up, Zeppenfeld pulled the goggles from his eyes, revealing the only clean spot on his body. The awe in his eyes was apparent.

Karleena put herself directly in front of his gaze. "Are you okay?" she repeated.

He smiled joyously. "That was cool."

"Cool?"

"Oh, wow, I have to remember that one!" he exclaimed as he searched his filthy clothes for something to write on.

"Remember what?" Karleena asked.

"The formula. Yes, the formula. Was it two ounces—or three? I can't remember," Zeppenfeld spoke quickly.

Watching his reaction, Karleena was taken aback. "You mean to say, you caused all of this?"

"Yes, yes. Wasn't it brilliant? I hope it wasn't an inconvenience."

"An inconvenience? An entire tower of the palace has been decimated," she said angrily.

Pausing from his thought, Zeppenfeld looked at her as if for the first time. "Yes, yes, I see how that would be most unsettling. Apologies I would offer, but sincerity it would lack. A war we prepare for. Yes indeed, a war. I may have just invented a concoction that will help us win. But was it two or three ounces? Why can't I remember?"

Surrendering, Karleena sat down and watched as the gnome continued speaking to himself and rattling off elements from his experiment. Though the tower would take a long time to repair, nobody was hurt. If this experiment would provide them with an advantage over an adversary, then the damaged tower would be a small price to pay.

CHAPTER 58

Raising his right arm, Braksis signaled Solara to remain quiet. He heard something in the depths of the forest and preferred that whatever it was not be able to locate them easily.

Quietly, Solara dismounted and approached Braksis. "What is it?" she whispered.

"I thought I heard something," he responded.

Looking down at Tiot, Solara could see that the timber wolf showed no sign of warning or danger. "Tiot doesn't agree with you."

"Since I fought the poachers alone, he's been ignoring me. It would be just like him to allow me to ride into danger without a warning."

"Why don't we stop then? It's starting to get dark. We can rest here tonight, and arrive at Ferceng's midday tomorrow," Solara suggested.

Nodding, he agreed. "Very well. I want to check the perimeter first."

"I'll do that. It's your turn to set up the camp."

"Very well," Braksis said. "Be careful."

With a devious smile, she was off, quickly lost in the cover of the bushes and trees.

Dismounting, Braksis removed his pack from Blaze's back. He unrolled a small blanket and laid it upon the ground. He did the same with Solara's pack, placing them both near a small clearing where a fire would be set.

Seeing the panting Tiot, Braksis removed a small bowl and placed it by his faithful companion. He then unstrapped a leather canteen filled with water, and poured some of the contents for the wolf.

Tiot immediately lapped at the water happily. At the same time, Braksis scratched the wolf behind its left ear.

Returning to his work, Braksis removed several other items, including pots and pans, to prepare the night's dinner. They still had a good amount of provisions remaining from Xylona, and he planned on cooking Solara a meal that would make her mouth water.

As the minutes passed by, a slight unease crept over him with Solara gone for so long. After all, he had thought that he heard something. Concern quickly ended all thoughts of dinner and the camp, and he unlatched Carnage from his saddle.

"Tiot, stay here and guard the camp."

The timber wolf looked up as if to acknowledge the command, then went back to the bowl of water.

Braksis headed off into the woods after Solara. How exactly he planned on finding her he did not know. She was much more skilled in stealth than he, and that more than likely meant she would leave little to no tracks for him to follow.

Not wishing to yell out, he moved through the trees quickly, scanning back and forth as he went. With each step, a growing sense of desperation pierced him. This trip had been so tragic already; he could not stand the thought of losing his mystral companion as well.

Stopping, he realized he wasn't thinking clearly and needed to focus his attention. He could see a steep incline about forty yards away, and hoped that from there, he could see more of the woods.

Sprinting up the incline, his heart was pounding as a myriad of thoughts, wishes, and fears flowed through him. Reaching the top, he looked out and saw a small spring on the other end, but no Solara.

Turning in a circle, he observed each side, every movement of the forest caught his attention. Then, without warning, his footing slipped and he fell back down the incline. Wet leaves and grasses gave way to a muddy slide sending him racing uncontrollably down the hill toward the spring.

Reaching for anything that could slow his descent, Braksis found nothing. Plummeting quickly, the ground vanished beneath him, and he found himself hurtling through the air toward the spring.

Waving his arms in a valiant attempt to slow himself, Braksis plunged into the water feet first. The water was cold and jolted him as his momentum sent him deeper. Grateful the water was deep enough so as not to injure him with impact on the ground, Braksis kicked up toward the surface.

Reaching the top, he burst through the once-calm water and gasped for a breath of air. Looking out, he saw Solara looking down at him with concern.

"Are you okay?"

"Only my pride is hurt."

"That is all that should be hurt," she responded.

"What do you mean?" he asked as he stepped out of the water.

"This is Shimendyn. Home of the fairy folk. The waters have healing arts. This is where we sent Kai."

"Fairies? I don't see any," Braksis said as he looked around.

"They have the ability to look into people's souls and determine whether they are good or evil. If you were evil, I assure you that you would not be walking out of the water so easily."

Caressing his shoulder and leg where he was recently injured, he looked at her with amazement. "The wounds are gone."

"As should we be. We are disrupting their home. Come, let's return to the camp," Solara suggested.

Along the way, Braksis kept glancing at Solara until he could not stand being silent any longer. Before he could speak, she did herself.

"What were you doing out here? I thought you were setting up the camp."

"Yes, but I feared you were gone too long. I wanted to make sure you were okay."

"Oh really?" She asked. "Is that why you slid down the hill and plunged into the waters of Shimendyn?"

"I'm not kidding, I was concerned," he said in a serious tone.

Regarding him, she could see he was trembling. "Are you cold?"

"Just wet."

"We should get you out of those clothes. It will do you no good to be too sick to travel."

"I'm fine."

"Male bravado," she uttered in jest. "Seriously, we should get you out of those."

Reaching over, she unfastened his cloak and put it over her arm. "This alone will take hours to dry."

Braksis gazed deep into her eyes as she was helping him.

"I bet this is just your attempt to make me get the kindling again. Always trying to get out of doing work yourself."

"Solara," he said softly as he reached out to her.

For the first time, she allowed herself to return his longing gaze. She could see the passion and desire deep within his eyes, as well as the fear that she knew both were feeling.

As she leaned into him, his cloak fell from her arms to the ground. The two shared a slow, soft, passionate kiss. All doubts and fears faded with the tenderness of their embrace.

All around them, life slowed down. The wind seemed to swirl a little less quickly. The water dripping from his wet body froze in the moment in time. A bird returning to feed its young seemed to hover in place in the air. The moment was all that mattered to the two lovers.

Gently, he lowered her to the ground, both lost within each other's eyes and touch. He leaned forward and softly kissed her bare neck.

Solara arched her head back as warmth flowed through her, a raging inferno demanding to be unleashed.

Reaching out, she started to work at the links in his uniform. "We still need to get you out of these."

Braksis bent back up and raised his arms as she pulled off his breastplate and the shirt underneath, and dropped them to the side.

Gently caressing his bare right shoulder, she was in awe that the scar he received when he first met her had vanished. Moving her other hand slowly to his left shoulder, the wound from the hobgoblins attack likewise was gone. Admiring his fit and muscular form, she smiled seductively at him.

Returning her smile, Braksis leaned back down and kissed her passionately on the lips. Moving slightly, he worked down her body, gently kissing her neck and her shoulders. As he did so, he unfastened her one-piece mystral body armor. Slowly he pulled it down and off as he kissed each spot now uncovered, leaving her with only her gauntlets and boots on.

As he removed each knee-high boot, she untied her gauntlets and tossed them to the side. Scanning her naked form, Braksis had to stop himself to simply admire how breathtaking she was. Never before had he seen or been with a woman so beautiful and intoxicating.

She sat up and helped him with his pants and boots, as he nibbled on her ear, distracting her. As his pants came off, she noted that the injury to his thigh from the hobgoblin was gone as well. In fact, every inch of his body was flawless as if the waters of Shimendyn turned him into the perfect male. His muscles were bulging in desire for her, and the excitement within her turned into a raging inferno as she absorbed his features.

Cupping her breasts, he gazed deep into her eyes and smiled again, then bent down and gently licked her nipples. He smiled as they hardened beneath his tongue, then he covered his mouth over them and sucked gently.

Solara let out a slight gasp of pleasure and reached out to pull him up to her.

As he lay atop of her, he kissed her passionately, then pulled back slightly. "Are you certain?"

Kissing him once more, she looked him in the eye and nodded. "I have never been more certain of anything in my life."

She helped guide him inside her, and both released a gasp at their initial joining. Slowly at first, he moved as she clenched onto his back and allowed the sensations to flow over her. To fulfill her.

Gradually increasing the speed and intensity, both bodies flowed together with caressing, kissing, and torrents of pleasure. Every movement was blissful, yet both craved more.

Rolling him over, Solara got on top, tightened her legs, and moved in a gentle waving motion. Below her, she watched as Braksis's mouth opened and gasped with pleasure.

She could feel him tensing below her right before he finally erupted. She moved even faster as each motion sent waves of pleasure pulsating through his whole body. He was holding onto her hands and squeezing tightly with moans emanating deep from within him. A cloudiness came over his eyes, and she leaned down and passionately kissed him once more, still moving on top of him, feeling him shudder each time.

She, too, quickly gasped for breath as orgasmic bliss flowed through her. Drained, she finally couldn't move anymore and lay still on top of him. They held and cuddled each other, both out of breath and with hearts pounding.

Gently caressing her arm, Braksis kissed her forehead. "We are joined now in more ways than one."

"Yes," she agreed. "It seems that fate has us bound more tightly than as a protector."

"Solara," he said clearly. "I could not bear to lose you."

"Nor I you."

"I love you. I have for years, though I never realized how deeply until this journey began."

"And I love you. Though not the way of the mystral, I can find no happiness anywhere but within your arms."

Pushing his fears and doubts aside, Braksis gently rubbed his hands through her hair. "Though this is certainly not the appropriate way or time to do so, I can wait no longer to ask this of you."

"You can ask me anything," Solara said as she took his hand and interlaced her fingers with his.

"Would you give me the honor of being my mate? Forever being known to all as each other's?"

Solara smiled and kissed him passionately. "Yes. Forever only for each other."

Relieved, Braksis leaned back down and sighed. "It's strange how life works. So much death and destruction of late, yet we can find a moment like this with pure peace and harmony."

"This is life's way of letting us know that you need to work through the trying times and fight for a better tomorrow. A tomorrow when we will be together, with a family of our own."

With this, he kissed her again, and for the second time, the two experienced pure bliss and solace within each other.

❖ ❖ ❖ ❖ ❖

Several hours later, the two finally got up and dressed. Their desire for food was beginning to overwhelm them, and Braksis promised to make a grand feast for dinner.

From out of nowhere, the unicorn they saved the day they left Xylona stood on its back legs and neighed a warning. Then it stormed off into the woods. Braksis and Solara watched the beast with curiosity, and then heard many voices, grunts, and branches bristling in the distance.

Quickly placing the remainder of their equipment on, the two silently approached the sounds. Crawling through the grasses, they stopped by a large tree and looked out at an opening, shocked to see hundreds of hobgoblins nearby.

Close by them was a scouting party with their backs turned. The small group was looking at the unicorn, which entered the opening, and they charged after it.

"We need to help it," Braksis said.

Solara placed an arm on his shoulder to convince him to stay down. "Don't you see, it helped us? It's returning the favor from when we saved it. Those hobgoblins would have come across us when we were unprepared, and we wouldn't have survived."

"Then we must help it even more so. If it is hurt trying to help us..."

"The unicorn is a guardian of the forest. It will be fine. Better than we will be if we don't leave. Let's go."

Seeing the wisdom in her words, Braksis reluctantly agreed. As he took one last look at the hobgoblins, he remembered Thamar's words of how the elves would not help, and wondered if they realized they would be next if the war entered the Suspintian Forest. There were two elven cities nearby, Turning Leaf and Wild Wood. As he crawled away from the hobgoblin forces, he hoped that both would be prepared and able to hold off the attacking masses. If not, the loss of the elves from their hopes of unifying the races would be tragic.

CHAPTER 59

Cautiously approaching the front opening of the temple, Tarwas looked at his old roommate. "Matrife, do you have a mental fix on our quarry?"

Matrife looked into the tunnel and saw the three passageways. "I believe they went to the left. I cannot pick up anything from the girl and elf, but I can feel Nerwasa. He is in pain."

Tarwas clenched his fists and ground his teeth. "Idiot. He's supposed to be the point man. Not a one-man operation. He should have waited for us."

Matrife nodded to his friend, then looked down at the remaining troops. The Gatherers capable of flight had been dispatched to monitor Cupton Ridge, so they had just seven men left, excluding Tarwas and himself. Of course, that would be more than enough to capture any quarry, any normal quarry that is.

Taking a step into the temple, Tarwas raised his hand chest high. The air around it ignited in bright bluish flames. "Matrife, you can see best in the shadows. Find Nerwasa. Everyone else, follow me."

Without another word, the wraith entered the temple and quickly explored the left tunnel, the direction where he could feel the pain of his colleague Nerwasa. Tarwas waited several seconds and then entered the dark tunnels himself, his seven remaining Gatherers in tow.

❖ ❖ ❖ ❖ ❖

"Kyria, this temple is a maze. We've taken so many twists and turns, are you sure you know where we are going?"

"Yes. I know exactly where we are going," Kyria replied confidently.

"I hope so." Although she logically knew Kyria was the Chosen One and it was her destiny to save Kai's people, still she instinctively had trouble depending on others. She had always been a loner who managed to stay one step ahead of the game. In this situation, she found herself following blindly, and she did not particularly like her role. However, for the sake of her people, more than anything else, her true role right now was that of protector and guide. She would gladly sacrifice her own life fighting the Gatherers if it meant that her charge would escape and survive.

Kyria closed her eyes again. She could see her destination clearly. She knew exactly how these events were going to unfold from the first minute they stepped into the temple. This temple had a system to it. It was an intricate labyrinth designed to dissuade intruders. As she concentrated, she could see the water flowing along the side of the tunnels. Could hear it as if she were already there. Of course, they hadn't gotten far enough to actually find the water yet, but they would be upon it soon.

The water was a beacon. It would lead them to an inner sanctum of the temple. This inner area then dropped off where the water would flow into an underground river below the temple. In the middle of the structure was an additional area that would hide a mighty beast who would ultimately help them, a beast she would soon call friend.

As they turned the next corner, she could hear the running water along the sides. "Is that water I hear?" Kai inquired.

"Yes. Up ahead there will be an opening. That is our destination." Once again, the sound of certainty in her voice left little room for doubt. The statement was not a prediction. Not an assumption. It was a fact. Once again, Kai realized that this young savior would soon outgrow her. Soon be more powerful than she could even conceive possible.

A couple of quick turns through the darkness, and the two found themselves on a ledge. The water streaming beside them did indeed flow right off of the ledge and down into a small body of water below them. Looking around, there appeared to be several tunnels that would lead to this area, but none that contained a bridge to get them across.

In the middle of the body of water, was another stone structure, the central spot in the temple. The top of it was covered with vegetation and trees. The inner framework of the temple was massive, very deceiving from the outside, but internally quite large and rather beautiful in design. Whatever was over there, if anything, could be hidden easily.

As Kai examined their surroundings, she ascertained that this central structure could be of immense strategic value. There was no easy way to gain access, which would allow her bow to come into play for any Gatherer attempting to get at them. The vegetation also would provide cover, so they could defend against the oncoming foes. This area would be perfect.

The only question that remained was how to get across. Kai reached into her quiver and removed one of the arrows designed to pierce armor. The arrow would dig deep into whatever it connected with on the other side. Now, all she needed was something to tie to it that would support their weight and allow them to climb across.

Looking around, she could find nothing strong enough to support both her and Kyria's weight. All she wanted was a rope. One good rope and they could manage to get across. Either that or another arrow with cable wire like the one she used to save Solara from the tragon.

"What about that?" Kyria pointed inquisitively.

Looking toward what Kyria was referencing, Kai managed to detect a whip. The whip could likely support their weight. Unfortunately, it was on the structure itself, not within arm's reach for the two to utilize. "That could work, but there is no way to get it."

Closing her eyes again, Kyria concentrated on the whip. She visualized it clearly. Could feel the contours of the design in her mind. Then she imagined the whip coming to her. Without really knowing what she was doing, the whip twitched at first. Then it started to slither along the ground as if it were a snake. Finally, it leapt through the air, not plummeting into the waters below, but landing gently in Kyria's hands. "I think I'm starting to get the hang of this."

She handed the whip to Kai, who checked it for length. It just wasn't long enough. Pulling out her dagger, she sliced the whip down the middle cutting it in two. She then repeated the process with both halves making four smaller strands of rope. After she completed cutting, she tied the ends together, attaching one side to the armored piercing arrow and the other to her dagger.

Checking the tensile strength carefully, she was quite pleased with their makeshift line. She then lifted her dagger high above her head and thrust down as hard as she could, digging the blade into the ground below her. Pulling on the line to test it, she was satisfied that the dagger would hold.

She then took the arrow and fired it across to the structure, impacting the ledge cleanly and deeply. Once again confirming that the line would hold, she was confident they would be able to make it across.

"Are you ready?" Looking at Kyria for any sign of doubt or fear, she found none.

"Yes. Let's do this." Kyria then leaned over the ledge, and approached the structure in the middle of the temple. One hand over the other, slowly moving forward, she made steady progress toward the other ledge.

Kai did not wish to apply too much pressure by having both cross at the same time. She monitored Kyria's trip across, and maintained a constant check on both the arrow and dagger, anticipating any kind of loosening.

As Kyria reached the other ledge, she wrapped one arm around the whip, then used her other hand to gain hold of the edge. When her grip was secure, she released the whip altogether, lifted herself onto the inner structure, and sat down facing Kai. "I'm across. Come on."

Lowering herself down, Kai gripped the rope with her front arms and slowly went over the ledge. After a couple of motions away from the dagger, she brought her legs up to provide even more support. Moving in tandem, hands and legs in motion, she quickly crawled to the other side.

Unnoticed by either, the dagger shifted and pivoted with each move. Slowly it crept up out of the ground with the weight. Kai looked ahead. She would need about four more movements before she would be on the other side.

Mere inches from making it, Kai could feel the line begin to give some slack. Looking back at the other side, she saw the dagger pull out of the ground, and the whole line start to fall down toward the waters below and swing to the side of the ledge she was heading for. Bracing herself for impact, she hit the structure hard, injuring her right arm and falling a little farther down before she managed to tighten her grip.

Kyria dashed to the ledge and looked down. "Are you okay?"

Kai held on, waiting to catch her breath. She would need to scale the wall. This should not be a problem, though her arm was now throbbing. A bigger concern, she felt, was that the arrow might not support this much weight alone. "I'm fine. I just hope the arrow doesn't give way also."

Looking intently at the arrow, Kyria concentrated. She could see inside the ground where the arrow was imbedded. She could see it slowly sliding out of the hole it had made when it pierced the structure. Putting all of her heart and soul into it, she concentrated on that arrow and managed to halt it from moving. "Hurry, I don't know how long I can hold it."

Kai began her ascent up the wall. Hand over hand. The pain seared through her injured arm. The pressure was immense. Still, she would not be found wanting. Slowly she crept upward. As she approached the arrow, she felt a sense of amazement looking at it. By all rights, she should have plummeted into the waters below. The arrow was practically completely dislodged from the wall. The only thing truly keeping her from falling was Kyria's determination and will.

Reaching the top, she grabbed the ledge, and pulled herself up. Kyria released her mental grip on the arrow, and reached down to help support Kai. As soon as she did so, the arrow came free and fell into the waters below. "I've got you."

With a little help, Kai managed to get up to the ledge herself. Taking several deep breaths, she looked at the young savior. "Thank you. I would not have made it without you."

"I would not be here without you, either," Kyria calmly stated. "We need each other. We're bonded to each other. Complete each other."

Listening to her words, many of the doubts that Kai had been experiencing faded. It was not relevant that this young girl had powers she did not. They were a team. The strengths of one could offset the weaknesses of the other.

With a renewed vigor and sense of determination, Kai looked around at the vegetation. "We can hide there. We will have a clear view of three entrances as the Gatherers try to come in." Looking back at the other entrances, she looked Kyria in the face. "Could you warn me if they are coming from any other direction?"

Kyria nodded her assent. "However, we will not need to fight them alone."

A look of puzzlement crossed Kai's face. "We won't?"

"No. We will have help."

Almost as if her words were prophetic, a large creature landed in front of them. He was quite intimidating, and resembled the statues on the steps of the temple. Overall, he was at least eight feet tall. He had short brown fur covering his entire body. His head resembled that of a bull, and the body that of a man. It had bloodred horns, and eyes to match. Its upper body was extremely muscular and well built, with legs that seemed fit and trim. The feet were red hooves, and a tail with red fur at the tip twitched behind its back.

Staring down at Kai and Kyria, the foreboding beast acted with intent to harm. A light mist trailed out of its nose with each breath. Taking a step forward, it kept its predatory gaze on Kai and Kyria.

Standing up sternly, Kyria walked over to the creature. "I can feel your pain. We shall share it now. All of us."

Befuddled, Kai watched this exchange. Could this creature be the foreseen ally Kyria had been referencing? If so, they may just be able to survive the next few minutes after all.

❖ ❖ ❖ ❖ ❖

As Tarwas continued to illuminate the path before him for the Gatherers, he could see the bright yellow eyes of Matrife reflecting back at him. "Did you find Nerwasa?"

The eyes of his friend slowly scanned the remaining Gatherers. "Yes. I have him, but he needs a Healer quickly." Holding his comrade in his arms, Matrife could feel the lifeblood draining out of him. His flicker of life was quickly dimming. He had several wounds that pierced his outer skin, and internal injuries as well. Without a mystical Healer to repair the damage, chances of survival were unlikely.

A sense of dread and peril permeated the air. As long as Tarwas commanded his own platoon, never had a Gatherer fallen. This mission was quickly changing that. "Bring him back the way we came. Contact the airborne troops. Have them return and fly Nerwasa back to the Council."

Matrife nodded, then moved quickly to bring Nerwasa to the entrance of the temple. As long as he did not get lost in the labyrinth, there was a slight chance of saving this warrior whose life was fading quickly. He would not—could not—fail.

Feeling the anger increasing deep inside his body, Tarwas growled to his remaining troops. "Let's go." With the order out, he turned and took a step, falling into the hole that Kyria had plummeted into just minutes before. He quickly straightened out his arms and legs catching the side walls. Taking a deep breath, he looked up. "How far have I fallen?"

One of the younger troops in his command, an elf named Hurnelo, responded. "It looks like you fell about fifteen meters. Can you climb up?"

"It would help if I could see. Right now I'm just holding on. I can't ignite the flame in my veins or I may plummet farther." Trying to focus his eyes, Tarwas began to see the white eyes of young Hurnelo looking back at him. "Could you ignite a few arrows and shoot them into the walls?"

"Aye, sir." Leaving the crevice for a few seconds, Hurnelo came back with flaming arrows and a bow. He fired several shots into the pit, illuminating it for Tarwas.

Hurnelo had always had an affinity for seeing in the dark. An excellent marksman, Tarwas trusted nobody more with the task he just had Hurnelo perform. His eyes, though young and innocent, had the experience of the ages in them, wisdom beyond his years. Even his hair was pure white as if he were an elder. Yet when not on a mission, all could see that Hurnelo was truly a young and gifted individual who enjoyed having a good time through song and playing practical jokes.

Repositioning himself, Tarwas pushed his back against one side of the pit, then his feet against the other, allowing himself to slowly shuffle his way up. "Hurnelo, have Crecix come over here to help me up."

"Aye, sir. Crecix!"

Moving toward the opening in the ground at a crawl, Crecix leaned over the edge. "You be wanting me, boss, sir?" Crecix was not one of the smartest Gatherers under Tarwas's command. He was an orc, and compared to the rest of his race, he would be considered an intellectual genius. Yet his intellectual prowess was not why Tarwas requested his assistance now.

Crecix stood approximately six and a half feet tall. Only Tarwas himself was taller. Orcs were also naturally gifted with immense strength and physical abilities. Crecix was green-skinned and bald. His mouth had two teeth jutting from it and pointing upward toward his nose. He had been serving under Tarwas for several years, and never had any problems. He was obedient and loyal, even if a little slower than the others. He helped create the backbone of Tarwas's team.

"Crecix, when I am close enough, reach over, grab me by my shoulders, and hoist me up." Even as Tarwas was commanding his troop, he continued his ascent toward the opening.

"Aye, boss, sir, I not be letting you down." Through the flicker of the firelight, you could see an intensity drawn across Crecix's face. He had a mission and he refused to disappoint his commander.

Reaching out, he grabbed Tarwas by his armpits and quickly yanked up, pulling Tarwas clear from the pit and on top of him. "How be that, boss, sir?"

"Very good, Crecix." Igniting his hand again, a stream of blue flame launched out of his fingers toward the pit below. The edges caught on fire, illuminating the pit and tunnel for all to see. "Be careful of the pit. I don't want to have an encore performance. Let's move out."

The Gatherers slowly crept along the side of the opening making sure none fell into its gaping mouth. One at a time they circled around. The process was slow, and the prey was being given too much time to find a way to escape.

When all of the troops were safe and clear, Tarwas addressed them again. "Remember, they have now been granted a substantial lead. We do not know what lies ahead of us. We saw what was done to Nerwasa. Take no chances." He looked at each of his troops as they nodded their assent. With that, they were back on the hunt once more.

❖ ❖ ❖ ❖ ❖

Images flowed. Came together. Histories intertwined. As Kyria touched both Kai, and the brown-furred minotaur—who they learned was named Grazlin—the three became connected. Running through the hills, playing with Nezbith. The attack on Arkham. The explosion. The fear. The solitude. The desperation. The defeat. Then suddenly Kai came to save her. Hope. A vision. A prophecy. The awakening of uncanny mystical abilities. Then fleeing for their lives all over again.

All of these memories flowed out of Kyria, allowing Kai and Grazlin to experience them as if they themselves had lived through the days Kyria was relating.

Then the scene changed. A young elf, learning the ways of her people. An invasion. The conquering horde. The darkness. Fleeing into the night and risking the unknown by venturing into the Forbidden Regions. Finding an island enshrouded in the mist and fog. Making a new home in seclusion. Living in constant fear and turmoil. Volunteering to be part of the Triad to bring the Chosen One back, the savior that was prophesied. The visions of a young girl. The realization that she would find the object of her quest. The new friends she met since arriving in the Seven Kingdoms. The attack of the koxlen. The sense of time running out. Of all hope resting on her ability to persevere. To pushing herself above and beyond, and finally finding a young Kyria close to death. Helping her. Introducing the mystical arts into her body. Awakening her potential. Then the constant struggle ever since.

All the being that had been Kai, now also belonged to Kyria and Grazlin. The images so clear, crystal clear. A tear formed in Grazlin's eye as he lived two lifetimes of experiences in mere seconds.

Then the image shifted again. This time to the temple they were in. To a proud and strong race of minotaurs. Dating back to the early Race Wars when humans attempted to conquer the Seven Kingdoms, and nearly succeeded. Mages were also there. Human Mages.

Elders placed a spell on the temple. A spell of confusion. Those who entered the walls would have their senses scrambled. The strongest Mages could still feel impressions, but more often than not, a Mage would be head blind in this labyrinth. As for minotaurs themselves, they became completely mystic-blind. Having no existence in the mystical arts.

Even with all of these attempts to mask themselves and hide within the great temple, the humans kept coming and killing off as many of the minotaurs as they could. The once proud and strong race falling limply on the stone floor with only memories and the remains of their temple to prove their existence.

The images shifted as a young baby cried out in the dark. A young minotaur that somehow was spared. An old woman raising the child and teaching him of his people's history and heritage. Of a young baby growing into the full aspects and attributes of the proud warrior before them. A life of solitude. Seclusion. Yet here, now, his inner sanctum was being disturbed, and his mark would be made on the world.

As the images ceased, Kyria removed her hands from Kai and Grazlin. All breathed for a minute, saying nothing. In that brief contact, all that they had been, all that they were, was now shared between them. Joined in a way that no other ever had been before. Experiences, hopes, dreams, desires, and fears. All shared and understood by all.

Grazlin was the first to break the silence, speaking in a voice that boomed like thunder, as he turned his attention to one of the entryways. "They are coming. Prepare yourselves."

Not a second later, a Gatherer appeared at the ledge looking in toward the inner structure. Grazlin jumped up, leaping over the crevice and landing on the ledge on the other side. With a flick of his head, he rammed the Gatherer and sent him flying backward into the tunnel.

Another foe faced him, a large green orc. He grabbed Grazlin and attempted to wrestle him. Dropping to his knees, Grazlin launched straight up holding the orc and sending his head crashing into the ceiling above. Consciousness was immediately lost.

Roaring out in defiance, Grazlin took a look at the other Gatherers quickly coming toward him down the tunnel, then he jumped back to the other side. Without a word to his two newfound companions, he raced to the center of the temple and knelt down before a statue of a large minotaur.

Seeing Grazlin flee, Kai prepped her bow and arrows and awaited the assault. "Stay down, Kyria. This could get dangerous. I don't want you hurt." Glancing back to see if her young charge had listened, all she saw was blonde hair running into the foliage toward Grazlin. "Kyria!"

Before she could follow, a couple of Gatherers arrived at the ledge. Kai launched arrows in their direction hoping to discourage them.

Kyria ran over to where Grazlin knelt. As she looked at the statue, she understood immediately. "It is time, Grazlin. You have lived here long enough. It is time to leave. He would want it that way."

Grazlin glanced down at the young girl, so full of courage, compassion, and understanding. "I was always told that if ever I needed to leave, to pull down on the statue's spear." Reaching up, he took a firm hold of the spear and applied pressure. The spear easily moved downward, and noises of gears turning filled the room. "Now, it is time."

Picking up Kyria, Grazlin carried her back toward Kai so that the trio could leave.

Back by the ledge, Kai aimed another armored piercing arrow. The creature in the doorway–a sarnal–appeared to be their leader. Shortly after her attack began, this Gatherer took the point and created a shield of pure fire. All of her arrows combusted and were destroyed before hitting him. This arrow, she aimed at his heart.

Aiming carefully, she prepared to release the arrow. As she did so, she was lifted up from behind, sending the arrow harmlessly launching toward the ceiling. "I could have had him."

In his thunderous voice, Grazlin shook off her words. "No time. We must go. Now!" With that, he jumped in the air, the two girls closely gripped between his bulging arms. The leap took them right off of the landing in the center of the temple, and toward the waters below. "Deep breaths. Saturate your lungs with air. Now!"

As they fell through the air, the three breathed in and out quickly, filling their lungs with air. The waters below were spiraling into a whirlpool. No longer the calm waters that were flowing when they first entered the temple.

Across the way, the sarnal launched projectiles of fire out of his hands toward the trio, failing to connect with any of them.

As the water came up, all three took one last deep breath, then submerged, diving deep with the momentum of their fall. Kai and Kyria instinctively tried to break Grazlin's grasp and head back toward the surface. However he refused to release his grip. Spinning in the water so his head was aimed down, he kicked, propelling the three farther into the depths.

The lungs of the trio swelled and throbbed. Air was needed so badly. To stay under any longer would be certain death. Yet Grazlin kept kicking. Kept moving toward the bottom. With eyes beginning to blur, and senses starting to fade from lack of oxygen, the three struggled to keep from opening their mouths and facing certain death by drowning.

Kyria closed her eyes and tried to concentrate. Then she could see it, their destination. At the bottom, the water was flowing out in a hole. The spear had set up a chain reaction that opened the gates to allow the water to flow out of the temple and into the Horned River. They were almost upon it.

Concentrating harder, she could see that at the end of the tunnel, they would come upon a waterfall, and find themselves miles away from the temple and the Gatherers. If only they could hold their breath that long.

Then she focused further. The air molecules on the other side of the waterfall. She could see the chemistry of them. The particles of air. Reaching out, she grabbed a handful of oxygen, and brought it into the water racing upstream toward them.

As Grazlin continued to kick, the three finally were caught in the current and dragged down into the opening in the floor. Their speed picked up immensely. If only they could hold out until they reached the other side.

Kyria continued to concentrate. It was almost there. She could see it. Feel it. Breathe it. Then the oxygen she had grabbed was upon her. She willed a small bubble around each of their heads, and forced the oxygen in. Thinking to her companions to try to get them to trust their senses, she sent a mental command. "Breathe. You now have air."

Reluctantly, Kai and Grazlin opened their mouths underwater, and discovered that the waters that encompassed them did not drown them. There truly was a pocket of air surrounding their heads. Air that never smelled or tasted so good. Taking deep breaths, they re-saturated their lungs, then continued on the pressurized ride toward the waterfall below.

Shooting quickly through the tunnel, the darkness opened up to the light of the day, as the three flew out into the open and down a cliff into the waters below. Flowing over the waterfall, the three screamed out, ultimately plunging into the waters at the bottom of the ravine.

❖ ❖ ❖ ❖ ❖

Tarwas watched in disbelief as the three plummeted into the waters below and were sucked down into the whirlpool. Surely, they would have a watery grave. Yet he would need to confirm that theory. He needed an aquatican to pursue them into the water, but his only aquatic Gatherer, Zenelca, had been attacked and rendered unconscious by the brown-furred minotaur.

Regarding his troops, Tarwas was in a state of misery. Zenelca had a concussion and needed medical attention. Crecix was also unconscious from the minotaur's assault. Two others had minor injuries as well. Not to mention their depleted numbers, since his airborne troops were already attempting to take Nerwasa to the Healers.

He needed to take the wounded out of here and get them back to the Mage's Council where they could receive proper care. So far, none of his platoon had suffered casualties, but he had lost many members to injury. He refused to let another Gatherer fall this day.

"Take the wounded. We will return the way we came. We will recall the rest of the troops to take the injured, then resume the hunt with those we have left." The remaining Gatherers did not say a word. They all nodded to Tarwas, then helped carry the wounded back through the labyrinth in silence.

CHAPTER 60

Lifting her father's sword, the Ochroid, Karleena imagined she could feel the presence of her father standing beside her. Raising the sword over her head, she thrust the blade down, cleaving a practice dummy in two. Spinning around, she lunged at a second target, then dropped to her knees and slashed at the supports of a third.

Standing back up, she looked at the three damaged targets and contemplated how she would be able to do against a real-life enemy. Something she always felt protected against, though in these desperate times, she feared that mastering the blade would be pivotal to her survival.

Startling her, Sovereign Arianna stepped out of a corner and addressed her. "You are slow with the blade, and your moves are clumsy."

Looking back at the three stationary targets, she had to agree with the aquatican ruler. "I've had some of the best teachers in the Imperium. Lord Braksis, Adonis, and Centain are all excellent swordsmen. Still, I never did do more than dabble at the art of swordplay."

Arianna reached her hand out to Karleena, who handed over Conrad's sword. "The blade is heavy. Much too heavy for you."

"It was my father's," Karleena replied.

"Sentiment will get you killed," Arianna declared. "Let me tell you a little story, then offer some advice. One ruler to another."

Karleena smiled at the aquatican, approached a bench, and sat down.

"This story begins long ago. My family has ruled Aquatica for generations. The elder child of my lineage would assume control when their parent was no longer able to perform their duties, or when they died." Sitting down next to Karleena, Arianna continued.

"This was our tradition right up until my parents passed on. You see, Askari is my older brother. Not by much, only a matter of minutes, but he is indeed older. However, he was also a Mage, something that no other member of the royal family has been. Being the older child, our father was reluctant to part with him, but ultimately gave in and allowed Askari to be raised in the Mage's Council, where he could gain far more knowledge and training in his destined path than our people could even hope to offer."

"That decision is certainly advantageous to the Imperium today," Karleena stated.

"That may be very so. However, in Aquatica, many of the people felt it was a betrayal to surrender the true heir to the throne to outsiders. First there were protests and public statements. Soon, they grew into an outright rebellion."

Looking over at Karleena, Arianna smiled briefly. "I was not much older than you at the time. A new Sovereign in a kingdom that wanted nothing to do with me, which is something that only led to self-doubt, and ultimately, my parents' death and my banishment."

"I don't understand," Karleena began. "What happened?"

"My father left Aquatica to me, but the rebellions continued. I doubted whether I truly should have accepted the throne, or whether I should have abdicated. Seeing my indecision, the people openly attacked the palace, killing my entire family, and banishing me with nothing more than my tattered clothes."

"That is horrible," Karleena said.

"Yes. It was truly difficult. However, I struggled to survive. I vowed vengeance, and decided right then and there that I would return one day and reclaim the throne." Arianna's words were full of conviction, as well as a touch of sadness over the loss of her parents.

"I found I still had many loyal supporters. They assisted me and became my army. We returned to Aquatica and challenged those who had claimed the rulership for themselves."

"Is that when you reclaimed the throne?" Karleena guessed.

"If only it were that simple. The battles were long and hard, and stretched over several months and the deaths of many aquaticans. We were finally beginning to turn the tide, then my brother returned, helping to completely crush the enemy."

"What happened to those who led the rebellion? Are they dead?" Karleena asked.

"It was a man named Kor who murdered my parents and took the crown for himself. He was one of the most famed warriors in all of Aquatica, but for some reason, he turned against us. Whether he is dead or not, I know not. My brother unleashed a mystical spell, boiling the waters before him. Kor had been leading his troops, and was hit by the heat blast. Many aquaticans died or were tragically disfigured from the attack, but Kor's remains were never found."

"That ended the war?" Karleena inquired.

"Yes. After my brother unleashed the heat blast, all remaining antagonists lowered their arms and surrendered."

"What happened to them?"

"We tried them and found them guilty. Rather than executing them, we banished all as they once had banished me." Arianna looked down at her feet for a moment. "I am sorry to say, I lost track of them after that. They could be plotting my demise even now and I wouldn't be aware of it."

Reaching out, Karleena placed her hand on Arianna's shoulder. "Whatever happens to either of us from now on, we will be there to support each other."

Looking up, Arianna stared deeply into Karleena's eyes. "I learned from a young age to fear and distrust humans."

"We, too, have that embedded in our minds about other races. What we do here now will hopefully change that."

"Yes. That would be nice," Arianna said.

"Friends?"

"Friends, and more," Arianna responded. "Now, as for that advice I offered, be certain of what you want to do, and never let anyone see you display weakness. Whatever happens, it is exactly what you anticipated. These will be trying times, but I am confident that you, just as I did before you, will prosper."

Karleena considered the words, and realized there were a lot of parallels between the two rulers. Where Arianna had lost power through her own self-doubt, Karleena had been in jeopardy of the same thing through the attacks of Torscen and the doubts that were creeping up.

"Now, for something more useful, would you like some instruction with the blade?"

"Very much so. Thank you."

"First then, lose the sentiment. This sword appears to be a mighty weapon, once wielded by a mighty warrior. Too mighty for you," Arianna declared. Standing up, she walked to the wall and removed two wooden practice swords. "First, we will work on your skills, then we can find an appropriate blade."

Arianna tossed one of the swords to Karleena, then immediately stood in battle position. "In battle, you must be prepared. Watch your enemy and anticipate their moves. Gaze into their eyes and learn what your enemy will do before they know they will do it."

"How do you do that?" Karleena asked.

"I will show you. Attack me," Arianna instructed.

Karleena stepped forward cautiously, then lunged at the aquatican.

Arianna sidestepped easily and tripped Karleena as she went by. "See, I anticipated your move and countered it. Try again."

As Karleena stood up, the back door opened. She looked over as Admiral Morex entered the room.

"My lady, Sovereign, apologies for the intrusion," he said properly.

"No intrusion at all, Admiral. The Sovereign and I were merely getting better acquainted, and she offered to help me with my sword skills."

Morex looked at Arianna and nodded. "Many thanks for these lessons, Sovereign."

"She is strong and determined, a good leader. I would hate to see harm come to her because she was unable to defend herself," Arianna responded.

"I concur completely." Looking back at Karleena, Morex presented his report. "My lady, it troubles me greatly to learn that the three Imperial Gallies I sent to Frocomon were destroyed, along with an entire merchant fleet that was under their protection."

"That is horrible," Karleena gasped. "Is King Euristies aware of this?"

"If he is not, he will learn shortly."

"How do you plan on proceeding, Admiral?"

"Though I must say that it is with great reluctance, I fear I will have to leave the palace and these vital negotiations. Whatever threat was able to overcome three of my best ships is substantial enough for me to address personally."

"Of course, Admiral. Do not even hesitate. The negotiations will be fine," Karleena said.

"I merely did not wish to abandon you when you needed support the most."

Stepping next to Karleena, Arianna smiled at the Admiral. "She will have my support to carry her through these trying times. Your place is on your ship, Admiral."

"I agree with Arianna. Go, Admiral. Protect these people and stop these attacks."

"Very well. The *Reliance* is being prepared as we speak. I shall be leaving within the hour."

"Best wishes, Admiral. Do be careful," Karleena advised.

"Yes, my lady. Sovereign." With that, Morex bowed to each and left the two alone once more.

Sitting down again, Karleena looked up at Arianna. "Will it never end?"

Arianna shook her head. "No. Life is a constant struggle. Sure, we may triumph and the war will be behind us, but something else will surface and wreak havoc in your life."

"Comforting thought."

"A realistic thought," Arianna corrected. "Shall we continue with your training?"

❖ ❖ ❖ ❖ ❖

Several hours later, battered and bruised from sparring, Karleena returned to her chambers to refresh herself. The training was long and arduous, but well worth it. She knew a few hours wouldn't turn her into a swordsman, but Arianna was a patient and insightful instructor, and she sincerely felt she had improved.

As she reached her door, she stopped and thought of Admiral Morex leaving to face this seafaring threat himself. Even though all the races had not yet arrived, she decided that to delay the meetings any further would be an exercise in futility.

Turning around, she opted to visit King Sarlec and discuss her plans.

One of the two guards stationed by her door watched as she stopped and turned around. "Empress? Is there something I can help you with?"

"No, thank you. I seek an audience with King Sarlec before I retire for the night."

"Allow me to escort you, my Empress," the guard offered.

"That will not be necessary. I know the way. Thank you."

As she walked down the hallway, she rehearsed her opening remarks to the assembled royal families and delegates of the races. She knew she had to set the right tone from the start, and show her resolve and determination in the matter.

Reaching the door to Sarlec's chambers, Karleena knocked. She waited a few moments, but nobody answered. She knocked several more times and yelled out Sarlec's name.

Wondering whether she was waking him from a deep sleep, or possibly not even finding him in his quarters, Karleena decided to peer inside. Sarlec was one of her most ardent supporters, and he treated her like family, so she hoped he wouldn't take offense at the intrusion.

As she slowly opened the door, she thought to herself that if she saw him sleeping, she would quietly walk back out and leave him alone.

Stepping inside, she could hear no noise, including the thunderous snoring that her father and Morex had always teased Sarlec about.

"Sarlec? Are you here?"

Walking in, she checked the bed and could see that it had not yet been slept in. Looking at the bathing room, she knocked again on the wall separating the two rooms. "Sarlec?"

Walking into the adjoining room, Karleena screamed out as she saw King Sarlec lying flat on the ground with a goblet of spilled wine inches from his hand.

"Sarlec!" she screamed as she dropped to his side and searched for a sign that he was only unconscious. Checking for his pulse, she could find none.

"Help! Somebody help me!" she screamed out.

Turning the obese king over, Karleena could see his open eyes staring blankly at her. "No, oh no," she pleaded.

"Karleena?" The voice came from the bedroom. "Empress, where are you?"

"Centain, in here," she responded in panic.

He ran into the room with his sword drawn. Seeing Sarlec sprawled along the ground, he knew immediately the king was dead. "Karleena, come with me."

"I can't leave him like this."

"There is nothing we can do for him now. Come with me. Please."

She looked up at his outstretched hand, and reluctantly, took it. "What do you think happened?" The shock was subsiding and tears began flowing from her eyes in torrents.

"I shall send for Adonis. ISIA will investigate, then we shall have some answers," he informed her.

"Adonis? Yes. Send for Adonis," she agreed.

"Leave that to me, Empress. Let's get you back to your room and have you get some rest. I'll have Sharnesta make you a nice drink to help you sleep."

As he led her away, she kept looking back at the man she had known and respected for so long. A great man who had always put the Imperium first. A man whose strength and resolve would be sorely missed with the trying times that approached.

CHAPTER 61

The closer they got to the Northern Mountains of Falestia, Braksis took on a whole new personality. Rather than the normal demeanor that people would expect, he turned light, happy, even joyous. He was returning to the place of his birth, and although the memories were not all pleasant ones, he still found the mountains breathtaking. No place in all of the Seven Kingdoms was as beautiful in his opinion as the mountains that had once been called home.

The mountains themselves soon encompassed them. Spanning the entire northern mountain range, Falestia was one of the largest kingdoms. Coming through the Suspintian Forest, the mountain peaks could be seen from a distance above the trees. The mountain itself was full of green vegetation from the bottom stemming upward. The top was covered in a foggy mist, and capped with ice and snow.

Beyond the Northern Mountains, depending on where one stood, one could see vast oceans, a small chain of islands, and the Falestian Mountains, which served as the border between Falestia and the barren ruins of Darnak. Darnak was at the northernmost point, and beyond the highest of the mountains. Most people avoided this area for fear of their own safety. The sides of the kingdom though, presented a view that could bring a tear to ones eye.

Their destination, the home of Ferceng, was located at the base of the mountains, closer to the western side of the kingdom. Ferceng made this his home many years ago, during the time when he was a Paladin on his quest for understanding. On this quest, he met and fell in love with the troll who would become his wife and bear his child. Though he did return to the Tower and take on the status of a full Mage Master, he left all he knew behind for love, and that love soon turned into tragedy.

The Race Wars were not kind to the nonhuman species of the realm. It also led to immense feelings of prejudice and superiority. After suffering the loss of his wife during childbirth, Ferceng's son also was to be taken from him by a lynch mob of humans. Ferceng was not certain of the details, but by the time he found his young son, he had been tortured and brutalized.

Braksis remembered all of this. The stories he was told. He knew how much pain these memories brought to Ferceng, but also that he would never doubt his decision to start a family. Ferceng many times would say that the love of the moment would be enough to last a lifetime. He had no regrets toward the decisions in his life.

Though he had always listened to the stories and claimed to understand, he realized now that he really did not grasp the concept. For him, family had been full of betrayal and death. Now, with Solara, he knew he would sacrifice all for a simple moment of happiness in her arms.

With a grin full of playfulness, Braksis challenged Solara. "I'll race you there." With that, he pulled on the reins and stormed ahead of her.

Solara shook her head wondering how this man could be feared by so many, but also have such an inner child and joy that could come out when they were alone. If the Seven Kingdoms knew him as she did, his famed intimidation would become irreparably tarnished. "Come on, Tiot, let's give him a run for his money." She, too, pulled on the reins and Myst galloped after Braksis, Tiot running alongside.

With his lead, Braksis whooped and hollered the entire way to the caves where Ferceng dwelled. The grin on his face grew to a full smile from ear to ear. He was home and enjoying every minute of it. The man was gone, replaced by the child who once roamed these very paths.

Arriving at the mouth of the cave, he jumped down and turned to wait for Solara. When she arrived, he merely grinned and proclaimed his victory. "Beat ya."

Solara dismounted, walked over to Braksis without saying a word, then tickled him along his sides. Braksis began squirming immediately. "Beat me, did you? You cheated!"

"Okay, okay, I give up. I cheated. I admit it." The laughter and mood of the moment was infectious. Both of them started to giggle with the absurdity of their behavior. "Let's head on in. Let Ferceng know we're here."

The two tied their horses down, then with Tiot by their feet, hand in hand they entered the caves that Braksis had once called home.

❖ ❖ ❖ ❖ ❖

Watching the events unfold, Rawthorne attempted to determine how to proceed. A well-thought-out plan would be required. He did not trust his companion with the smaller details, so he needed to devise it himself.

"Why didn't we just go take care of him right then? They were laughing and joking. Oblivious to us. We could have killed them both and have been done with it."

Rawthorne glared at his companion with contempt. "We need to bide our time. Not rush things. We will know when the time is right."

"The time was right then," Durgin insisted.

"The time will be right when I say it is right. Not a moment before. Do we understand each other?" he sneered. With that, Rawthorne stood up and moved further from the ledge to relax. "Now rest. We don't want him to have an advantage because we were too tired to confront him."

Rage was growing in Durgin. He remembered who he once was, and despised what he had now become. Even the treatment from Rawthorne reminded him how low others thought of him. That would soon change. Soon enough. He would kill Braksis and his bitch, then move on to more important things after his confidence and reputation were restored. He would reclaim all he had lost.

❖ ❖ ❖ ❖ ❖

As they walked into the cave, Braksis was yelling out. "Don't anybody move. This is a raid. We're coming in."

"Why are you saying that?"

"Ferceng hasn't seen me in a few years. Figured I'd see if he remembers me."

Without another word, two large arms reached down from the ceiling and pulled Braksis up by the shoulders into the air. "How could I ever forget my son?"

"Hey, hey, let me down. I'm not a kid anymore," Braksis jokingly retorted.

Solara watched the exchange in awe. She was beginning to see sides of Braksis she had never been privy to before. Sides that only increased her love and admiration for the man she wished to spend all eternity with. "If my vote counts, I like him better this way. Out of control. Hold him there for a while."

"Oh, thanks a lot. Some bodyguard you turned out to be. Dad, let me down."

Ferceng released his grip on the ceiling and spun down. He and Braksis landed on their feet, hugging. "It's been too long, boy." He looked over at Solara and then whispered into Braksis's ear. "She's a looker. I like, I like. Good for you."

Restraining a smile, Solara regarded the troll who raised Braksis. Ferceng was about eight feet tall, with long curly gray hair flowing down his sides and back. A similarly tinted beard and mustache hung down his chest. His nose was thick and long, resting atop a smile that paralleled Braksis's at the moment. His eyes were vibrant and alive, yet full of compassion and love. His frame was solid. Strong. He may have seen many years, but he still came across as one who could hold his own in a conflict. Wearing only a simple brown shirt and matching pants, he did not display any indication that he was originally from the Mage's Council.

Ferceng bowed down to Solara in the gentlemanly style of one raised through aristocracy, honor, and respect. "Welcome to my humble abode, madam. I am Ferceng. If you have need of anything, merely ask, and it shall be yours."

"Why, thank you, kind sir," Solara replied with an attempted curtsey of respect herself.

Laughing at the attempt, Braksis could not resist commenting. "Keep this up, Solara, and we may need to introduce you into high society."

"Ha, ha. Very funny."

The smile never leaving Ferceng's face, he watched the two bicker and thought of how wonderful it was to have Braksis home. Even if for just a little while. He was proud of his son, and wished to know what was going on in life. "Why don't we have something to eat? I myself am famished. Then we can catch up."

"Sounds like a good idea," Braksis said. Glancing back at his companion, he whispered, "Don't worry, it may not look pretty, but Ferceng is truly a great cook. He taught me everything I know."

"I heard that! Not look pretty? Humph. Judge your food by looks, do you, boy?"

"I was trying to give you a compliment, but prepare Solara in case she had a weak stomach."

"Weak stomach?" Ferceng bounced back, picked Solara up in a big hug, and then looked at his son. "I think the lady and I will be quite fine. If your stomach can't handle the sight of my fine cuisine, you are more than entitled to cook something on your own."

"I didn't mean—"

"Enough, I know what you mean. After all these years, you think you are wise in the world. Some fancy Imperial chef has prepared your food for you, and now you look down at your poor father's attempts. But I know that when you were a boy, you always came back for seconds!"

Doing her best to repress a giggle, Solara covered her mouth. Ferceng picked up on it immediately and let her down gently. "No need to cover your mouth, madam, feel free to erupt with laughter. I won't take it offensively." With that, he boisterously laughed himself.

After enjoying the moment for a while, Ferceng turned and walked deeper into the cave. With a snap of his fingers, the cave illuminated as if they were still standing out in the daylight.

Solara sought out the cause of the illumination. She could find no lanterns or candles. "Where is the light coming from?"

Slowing down, Ferceng looked at his guest. "Well, it certainly wouldn't do for you to get lost in these caves. They can lead you all the way down to the molten magma of terra, you know."

"I still don't see any source of light," she said.

"Well, I may have given up my life in the Council, but I am still a Mage."

Leaning over to whisper into her ear, Braksis spoke softly. "Don't you feel like the idiot now?"

"Stop it," she replied, playfully sending her elbow lightly into his stomach.

"What did I do?" he quickly responded.

"Now, now children. No violence in the caves," Ferceng chastised.

With mocking obedience, Braksis replied. "Yes, Father."

Ferceng led them to what appeared to be a boulder blocking their path. He walked up to it, and motioned his hand at the wrist from left to right. The boulder slowly rolled out of the way revealing an inner sanctum that could put a room at the palace to shame. This inner area was what Ferceng called home. There were several large rooms all beautifully styled. Colorful, fashionable, and luxurious. "Welcome to my humble abode."

As Solara looked around, she was amazed. The furniture was handcrafted and intricately designed. There was a couch with handwoven upholstery designed to resemble sparkling diamonds. The detail was breathtaking. On the floor there was a velvet carpet with similar diamonds sewn into the sides. Everything in the room stood out as a symbol of aristocracy, wealth, prestige, and pride. Yet to look at the man, he did not seem to fit in, in his brown garments. "Very impressive. This must have cost you a fortune."

Bashfully, Ferceng replied. "Actually, I made it all myself."

"Yourself?"

"Yes. When I decided to spend my life with my dearest wife, I wanted to provide her with a life of luxury. I then crafted everything you see here in this cave for her comfort, pleasure, and pride."

"I bet she loved it."

"Actually, I think she would have been happy if we slept on the floor as long as she was with me. A magnificent woman. I never could have asked for better."

"That is so sweet. I hope to find the same happiness myself one day." As she said it, she smiled at Braksis and winked.

Looking at Braksis briefly, Ferceng smiled. "Perhaps you have already met him and just don't know it."

"Dad," Braksis quickly slurred under his breath in warning.

"Sorry. Just an old man fantasizing. Regardless, I hope that both of you find happiness, and that it will last you a wee bit longer than mine."

"I'm sorry," Solara offered.

"Do not be, madam. I have no regrets. Not a single one. I cherish every moment that I had. Even if so brief. I would make the same decisions if I had them to do over," Ferceng sighed. "Solara, do you mind getting a quick drink from the kitchen for an old man?"

"Of course not," she stated as she approached the kitchen.

Braksis looked at Ferceng for a moment with confusion. "What did you do that for?"

"I wish to speak for a moment to my son, is that so bad?"

"No, sir, not at all."

"All joking aside, I see the way you have been looking at each other. Holding hands, too, when you first arrived. You two have gone beyond the typical boundaries of a life debt." It was not a question.

"Yes, sir, we have. Only recently, but now, I can't believe how much time we have wasted by being apart."

"I approve. You have made a good choice. She is a lovely girl. She'll also keep you on your toes. I definitely approve."

"Thank you. I am glad you are the first to know."

Solara walked back in to see the two embracing. "Am I interrupting something?"

"Of course not," Ferceng quickly replied.

Solara handed him the water. With a wave of his hand, the glass turned into a bowl and he put it down for Tiot. "The poor wolf seems more tired than all of us. I think he deserves this the most." Ferceng motioned toward the table. "Sit, I shall prepare a feast for us. It's not every day my son returns home! Even less that he returns home with a beautiful woman who has captivated his heart." With that, he was off toward the kitchen area where mouthwatering scents quickly filled the air.

❖ ❖ ❖ ❖ ❖

As dinner came to an end, the trio, along with Tiot, was stuffed. Just as Braksis described, the food did not exactly look all that appetizing, yet if you closed your eyes and took a mouthful, it was pure bliss. Perfection to the taste buds. Ferceng truly was a magnificent chef.

For hours they sat talking. Telling stories of their pasts, the present, and hopes and dreams for the future. Ferceng often did most of the talking, but just as quickly switched gears to listen to what his son and guest were saying. Ferceng told stories of a young Braksis being raised, full of comical adventures and embarrassing memories. Solara laughed freely, and even more so when she saw her companion turning beet red.

Solara spoke briefly of her life as a mystral and what ultimately led to her meeting Braksis. How he saved her life and she in return swore her life over to him as his protector. Even though he repeatedly declined, she followed the dictates of her people and would not be swayed. In time, they grew closer and turned into faithful friends and ultimately into the lovers they were today.

Braksis spoke more of the current problems in the Imperium. He left out little detail in his story, beginning when he first marched to the Dartian plains to face the uprisings, straight through until the prior night when they discovered the hobgoblins marching in the Suspintian Forest.

"I wish that I could see what was happening with everyone. I feel so out of touch," Braksis concluded.

Ferceng rubbed the beard on his chin and smiled. "Then tell me who you want to see, and see them you shall."

"What? How?" Braksis asked.

"I am a Mage. Even the youngest Mage learns how to create images! Who shall we look in on first?"

"Well, the Empress. Karleena."

With a wave of his hand, an image appeared in the air before them. Karleena sat there, her eyes red and full of tears.

Braksis leaned forward for a better view. "She's crying. What's happened?"

Ferceng closed his eyes to concentrate, and the image spun to another view. There, Braksis could see Karleena kneeling beside the body of King Sarlec, desperately trying to wake him up.

"King Sarlec is dead? How did this happen?" Braksis demanded.

"I can only show you images. You must interpret them on your own."

"I didn't see Admiral Morex. Where is he?"

The image shifted again, this time, to the sea where Admiral Morex stood on the deck of the flagship, watching merchant ships in the distance.

"Well, I don't know why he was away from the palace, but he looks unharmed. How about the rest of my command staff and armies?"

The image of Morex dissolved into multiple images, showing Braksis all of his forces. From Sevlow in the Dartian plains, to Hinbar and Lowred in Tresias, to Ritter in Vorstad, and finally to Travers in Xylona. Only in Xylona was there activity, where he watched Captain Travers fighting yet another band of hobgoblins.

"I didn't see Thamar at either Xylona or Vorstad, where is he?"

The multiple images flowed together, and Braksis saw Thamar, Theiler, and Arifos, accompanied by a trio of elves and a dwarf, traveling atop horses and ponies.

"They seem fine, but I wonder where they are going?" Braksis pondered.

Solara shook her head, uncertain as well. They definitely were not on the path from Xylona to Vorstad. "What about Angel? Can we see how she is doing?"

To her question, the image swirled again, and they saw Angel, with her newly crafted mystral armor and swords, directing a group of women in various fighting techniques.

"Well, she certainly seems to be making progress," Solara concluded.

"Yes, she was a good find for the Imperium," Braksis agreed.

"Anyone else?" Ferceng asked.

"Yes, show us Kai," Braksis responded.

The image changed again, and Braksis watched as a minotaur lifted a drenched Kai and Kyria out of the water. They seemed tense, but not afraid of the minotaur, so Braksis assumed that he was not a threat.

"Thank you, father. It is hard to be away, and these images have troubled me even more."

Turning serious after hearing Braksis speak, Ferceng looked him straight in the eye. "Well, tell me, boy. With all of this going on, I know that you didn't take time off to just visit your dear old dad. This certainly is not a personal visit, so let's stop with the pleasantries and get you back to where you belong."

Braksis stood up and walked over to where he placed his armor and gear. He removed the hilt from his sword, the Phoenix, and the axe he had taken from Guldan after killing him. "In the last revolt, this axe shattered the Phoenix is one swing. The hilt is all I have left."

"Bring it here. Let me see." As Braksis handed the two weapons to him, Ferceng studied them hard. "This axe has been mystically protected."

"Mystically protected?"

"Yes. A definite spell on it. It reeks of magic use."

"A Mage was supporting the uprising? Could it have been another one of the Shadow Mages?"

"Possibly, though I think this is the work of a Master. Humph. To fight a Mage, you'll need a Mage. Or at least an advantage."

Studying his father, Braksis considered his reply. "Are you offering to come with me? To return to the Imperium?"

"If you ask, I shall come. However, I have a few other ideas to help you as well."

"What do you suggest?"

Ferceng looked at the hilt he had designed years before and smirked. "When I designed this sword for you, I made it perfect. Illistrium, the strongest metal forged from the molten magma of the planet terra itself."

"Yes. I am aware of that."

"Well, I did not provide it with any mystical abilities because I felt that would give you an unfair advantage. You had honed your skills. Practiced for years. To give you a weapon with added abilities, I felt would demean your progress."

"I can understand that," Braksis appreciatively replied.

"This advantage would no longer be unfair. Some other Mage is providing your enemies with mystical weapons. It seems only fair that you, too, have a mystical weapon to counter with."

"Something like the axe? Stronger? Unbreakable?"

Solara watched the exchange with interest. A mystical weapon could be an immense advantage regardless of whom they were facing. Although her counsel was not requested or required, if either man questioned her, she would toss in her full support of the suggestion.

"I could even go a step further." The smile on Ferceng's face was growing with each thought.

"Further? Explain."

"Your sword was the Phoenix. You wear the emblem of the phoenix. The symbolism of rising from the ashes. Your past life was ended, and your new life rose from it. A masterful selection if I do say so myself."

Pausing for effect, Ferceng then lifted the hilt into the air. "Imagine the blade of the Phoenix being reinvented. A new Phoenix, even more powerful than the last. You want unbreakable? Done. You want stronger? But of course. However, I'll also add the symbolism of the phoenix. The fire. The heat. The intensity. Your blade will not only be a sword, but a weapon that will respond to only your essence. A blade that will burn at your merest desire, and in time and practice, even launch the molten lava of its origin out to strike an enemy from afar."

Watching the expression on Braksis's face, Ferceng continued to smile. "This is the advantage that I offer you. This is what my gift to you shall be."

"That's...that's more than I would ever have expected. Thank you."

"Think nothing of it, boy. Now, it's going to take me a while to craft it. I will need to go deep into the subterranean caverns of the Northern Mountains to find what I seek. Why don't you two get some rest and I'll get started. If you wish, you can even return to the palace and I will deliver it to you when completed."

"Thank you again, Father. We shall rest tonight. We will debark for the palace in the morning. After a full night's sleep."

Ferceng started to leave, then paused. "I almost forgot. I need one more thing." In one swift motion, he reached over and pricked Braksis's arm with a pin, quickly catching the blood in a small orb.

"What did you do that for?" He yelled as he caressed his arm.

"I need the blood so that the mystical blade will be able to react to you and only you."

"You could have warned me!"

"Bah, what fun would that have been?" With a laugh, he turned and walked out.

"He could have warned me," Braksis whimpered.

Shaking her head, Solara walked over with a towel to put pressure on the puncture wound. "You are a man who has been cut, sliced, hacked, shot, and any number of other injuries, and you are whining over a pinprick?"

"I'm just saying he could have told me he was going to do it."

"Does it hurt?"

"Yes!"

"Humph. Men." Gazing intently at her work, she looked him in the eye. "It's not even bleeding anymore! You're fine." Tossing the towel into a corner, she kissed his arm where he was pricked, then walked over to the couch and lay down. "I'm going to try to get some rest. Stop whining and get some yourself. It's going to be a long ride back to the palace."

Looking down at her, Braksis could not refrain from smiling. He wasn't hurt. The pinprick did not bother him at all. He just found himself acting more and more playful ever since he got home. Perhaps he would need to come home more frequently.

Not really tired yet, he hoped to catch the sunset before he left. Seeing it from the mountains of Falestia just added to the beauty of the moment. "Care to watch the sunset?"

In retort, Solara faked a few snores to let him know she wished to sleep.

"It would be romantic." Seeing that she was indeed falling asleep, he placed a blanket over her and gently kissed her forehead. "We'll have plenty of mornings for romance." Smiling a second time, he put on his boots and headed back toward the entrance to leave.

CHAPTER 62

Frustrated with the lack of progress his search has taken over the last several hours, Tarwas decided to check on his injured comrades. Both Nerwasa and Zenelca had been rushed back to the Tower with serious injuries. Crecix remained a little groggy, but desired to stay until the young Kyria had been captured. Tarwas feared that with numbers severely depleted, success of this mission would become questionable.

He reached into his pouch, removed his corryby, and attempted to contact the Mage's Council. The corryby began to glow, and an image of Pierce appeared above it.

Shocked to see the father of all Mages respond to his inquiry, Tarwas dropped to one knee and bowed to the Council of Elders chairman. "Master Pierce, what great honor it does me to speak to you directly."

"Arise, Tarwas. You do not have to kneel to me. Your reputation precedes you."

Tarwas nodded once and then stood back up to full height, intrigued by this communication. "How may I help you, Master?"

"This current mission you are embarked upon has come to my personal attention. Your quarry is a very special individual. Very powerful. We do not yet understand how this has happened, but her inclusion into our ranks will be of a great benefit to our future." With every word, Pierce relayed pure confidence and determination. His words came across not as opinion, but as facts that were not to be taken lightly.

"I understand her value to you. However, the girl and her companions have left me at half strength." Commenting on his reduced numbers, Tarwas noticeably cringed at the thought of making excuses to the elder Pierce.

"Companions? Tell me more."

"She travels with an elf of unknown origin. We have never seen her ilk before. More recently, she has been joined by a minotaur."

Cutting Tarwas off in mid-explanation, Pierce sounded his disbelief. "A minotaur, you say? I believed them to be extinct for well over three hundred years. The last group was hunted down and killed during the Race Wars."

"Nevertheless, sir, a minotaur it was. Further, this new ally is the one responsible for the injuries to several of my men. He single-handedly thwarted our last advance."

"So, a minotaur yet survives. Very interesting. How many troops do you still have under your command?"

"With the severely wounded escorted back to the Tower, I have eight Gatherers remaining, including myself. Several members of this group are also injured, but willing to continue with the mission."

"Eight. Eight should do. Eight should do quite nicely." Pausing for a moment, the image of Pierce turned above the corryby as he addressed someone outside of the transmission. "The eight of you will distract the minotaur and elf. That is your new mission."

"Distract, sir? We are not to apprehend the girl?" he asked, with confusion clearly articulated in his question.

"That is correct. I am sending out one of my own trusted colleagues, an eternal that has fought by my side since before Mages even existed in the Seven Kingdoms. An eternal who helped me design the Council as it is today, and was the first of the Gatherers."

"You mean...?"

"Yes, Commander. I am sending Master Zane to assist you. He and his special group of Gatherers will be responsible for apprehending the child. That is no longer your concern."

"I understand and obey, Master Pierce."

"Very well, happy hunting. I will see to it that your part in this is properly rewarded. Pierce out." With those last few words, the corryby stopped glowing and the image faded.

Matrife approached Tarwas. "So he is replacing us?"

In frustration, Tarwas turned and sneered at his old friend. "Yes. He is." Walking over to his other troops, he picked up the trackbar to home in on and track down Kyria. "Gatherers. Our mission has changed. We have finally picked up the child's signal again, but she is no longer our objective. We are to create a diversion and distract her two companions.

Be careful and cautious. I do not wish to lose any of you in an attempt at folly."

Looking around at each of his troops, his brave men—those injured who remained on the hunt because that was why they were here. Suddenly, their reason for being, their purpose became a question. Their roles were redefined. Yet that was the wish of Master Pierce, leader of the Council. Then that was what they would do. "Gatherers, for the future, resume the hunt."

❖ ❖ ❖ ❖ ❖

Crawling away from the water, Kai looked over and watched as Grazlin carried Kyria to a tree to rest. Reflecting back on their ploy to escape, she was amazed that they were all still alive. They definitely had run out of oxygen, but somehow Kyria managed to bring air for them to breathe while they were still underwater. Remarkable.

"We should move quickly," Kai advised. "No telling how soon they will be upon us again."

Standing erect, Grazlin shook rapidly to try to free his fur of all of the water. "I concur. Many hours have passed already and we are well away from the temple, however they will be able to track the water flow and arrive here quickly. Especially if they have flyers."

Closing her eyes, Kyria concentrated on those who pursued her. Attempting to catch a glimpse of her future, she saw herself surrounded by golden figures with wings and a man with long lime-green hair. She was fighting. Fighting with a sword. Where did the sword come from? she wondered. Instinctively, she knew that the sword was a part of herself, part of her own essence, her soul.

Focusing on the battle, she realized that Kai and Grazlin were no longer a part of it. Looking around for images of events that had yet to occur, she found her two friends bloody and battered. Close to death. "No!" The gasp came out as a scream, turning both Grazlin and Kai around to stare at her.

"What is wrong, child?" Kai knelt down to comfort her.

"I saw the future. The two of you were—"

Cutting her off in mid-sentence, Grazlin interjected his views. "Enough talk of the future. Whatever will be, will be. Besides, I do not think that my future will have to follow whatever you have dreamed about it."

"But–"

"No buts," Kai offered. "Grazlin is right. We must go." With that, Kai stood up and walked along the river away from the waterfall. Grazlin and Kyria quickly joined her, but the sense of impending doom and foreboding would not leave the young girl's thoughts.

❖ ❖ ❖ ❖ ❖

"The signal is coming in clear, sir. They are right down there in the valley by the river."

"Thank you, Hurnelo. We shall advance soon. For now, allow them to think they have escaped our grasp." Turning, Tarwas gave a look to his old friend Matrife that clearly showed he, too, wished to go down and personally finish the hunt. That was his prey. His right as a Gatherer was to find his quarry; not to bring it back to the Council would be considered the ultimate failure.

"Patience, Commander. Our time will come soon."

"I know, old friend, I know." As Tarwas walked past Matrife, he patted him on the shoulder.

"See, Tarwas–here they come now."

Following Matrife's finger, he looked up to see a large contingent of avarians flying in. He counted twelve in all, flying in a triangular pattern, with a larger creature in the middle.

As they closed in and came to a landing, Tarwas could see them more clearly. The lead flyer was riding a griffin. The body and tail of the griffin were beige in color, and resembled those of a powerful predator akin to a koxlen, or another strong and ferocious beast. Its head was white and feathery like that of a great bird, with a strong yellow beak. The claws of the beast also resembled that of a predatory bird. Large wings protruded from its back and flapped effortlessly in the wind, keeping it soaring through the sky.

Riding the griffin must be the one known as Master Zane. An imposing man who closely resembled Master Pierce. The two could have been twins from afar. Unlike Pierce, this eternal had a full head of lime-green hair that, when he was standing, would freely flow down his back. The same tint covered his face in the form of a mustache and a single stream of hair on his chin. Although he had lived for several thousand years, he resembled a human around the age of thirty. Zane was garbed in golden armor covering his body from neck to toe. Around his shoulders and hanging in back was a cape of white with golden designs around the edges. For that much gold to be portrayed, Master Zane was clearly a strong and experienced influence in the mystical arts.

Those accompanying him were also garbed in the traditional Mage colors of white and gold, but they all were wearing golden armor rather than the normal robes. The avarians, however, had a white tunic that wrapped around their chests and flowed below their belts. Underneath the white cloth was pure gold. They also wore golden helmets upon their heads, with pure white wings stretching out at each side. With a little more white displayed than Zane, they were not as experienced as their leader, but still extremely adept Mage Masters.

In unison, the griffin and twelve avarians came to a flawless landing. Master Zane jumped off of his mount and approached Tarwas. He was taller than he looked riding the griffin. His build, although mostly hidden by the armor, was associated with someone who took great pride in his body. Someone who would work out regularly, and always attempt to improve his own physical fitness and prowess.

He stepped before Tarwas, looked once, then moved to the edge of the hill to watch the trio attempting to flee below. "Take your men straight down and follow them from behind. Be loud and obvious in your descent."

"Begging your pardon, Master Zane—do you not wish an update on the situation?" The spite he felt for the man who clearly looked down upon him was pronounced with each word.

"I need no update, Commander. I can see that you and yours have failed. We are here to succeed."

"We have not failed," Tarwas roared.

"Oh no, Commander? Should I even call you Commander? That will be in review, as will your entire strategy on this mission." Turning to actually look at Tarwas for the first time, Zane continued in his condescending and arrogant tone. "You will not presume to even speak to me further, Commander. As of this moment, I am in command."

Clenching his fists and grinding his teeth, Tarwas controlled his urge to lash out at the man who originally formed the Gatherers so long ago. He had taken this mission with dedication and determination. From beginning to end, he executed each command with one eye on the goal, and one on the safety of the men under his command. To be questioned, insulted, and attacked by Zane was beyond redemption.

"Now, Commander, I do not like to repeat myself. As I said before, take your remaining rabble down the hill and make plenty of noise as you do so. Create a distraction, and we will do the rest." As Zane returned and mounted his griffin once more, he looked back at Tarwas, puzzled. "You're still here? Were my orders unclear? Move!"

Emitting a low growl, Tarwas turned to his troops. "You heard the man—let's move out."

With the respect of his platoon still intact, his remaining Gatherers quickly fell in line and descended toward the trio below.

❖ ❖ ❖ ❖ ❖

Moving along the river, Kai continued to feel as if she could not get enough oxygen into her lungs. Her sight continued to blur, and a vision overcame her. In this hazed vision, Kai could see an older Kyria. Still young, but a woman nonetheless. This was the second time she had seen an image of Kyria encased in a skintight suit of shiny silver armor wielding a blade that glimmered and released an aura of pure and blinding white light.

Kai tried to concentrate further to see who Kyria had been fighting against. What was she doing? She heard Kyria begin to speak. "Kai, they found us."

Trying to comprehend the words the older Kyria was saying, Kai remained lost in her vision. They found us? Who? What is she talking about? I need more. Tell me more.

Grazlin shook Kai lightly. As she opened her eyes and looked up at the minotaur, she could see the intensity in his eyes. Kyria was screaming as well. "Kai, did you hear me? They found us!" The voice had changed back to that of the young girl. Or had it always been the young girl? she pondered. Was her last vision nothing more than a fever dream?

Straining to see what Kyria was yelling about, Kai saw the Gatherers in pursuit mere minutes away from them. "Grazlin, thank you, I am fine now."

Beginning to object, Grazlin repeatedly shook his head no. "You are in no shape to fight."

"I merely had a vision. I am fine now."

Reluctantly, Grazlin let her go and turned to face the oncoming Gatherers.

Immediately assessing the situation and taking charge, Kai resumed her normal role. "Thank you. Now, Grazlin, you and I are the first line of defense. I will attack at a distance with the bow. Those who get past me, are all up to you. Kyria, I need you to stay behind me so they cannot get to you."

Grazlin took several steps toward the oncoming Gatherers and lowered himself to be out of the line of fire. Kai placed arrows at her sides for easy and quick access. Kyria knelt down behind her to watch her friends risk their lives to protect her.

Kai wiped her eyes and tried to focus. She needed her senses to be sharp and heightened, as she had been trained. A lack of focus now could be tragic. She could see seven Gatherers approaching them. "I see seven. A sarnal, two trolls, an orc, a centaur, an elf, and a simian."

Kyria pointed out to the right of the group. "There are eight. The one that spied on us before, the wraith, is trying to circle around us."

Following Kyria's finger, Kai could see a slight blur in the surrounding atmosphere. Definitely a wraith. This would have to be her first target. They could lose sight of him quickly in the oncoming melee, and that would not be advisable.

Remembering the last time they uncovered the wraith, he had stopped Kyria's arrow in mid-flight. She must find a way to overcome that. "Can you create a distraction? Something to get his attention?"

Kyria nodded and then began to concentrate, focusing on the near-invisible opponent. She found a small bee in the vicinity, then focused on it. She could feel the bee. Relate to its purpose. Its reason for being. Then she focused on the wraith again. Sent an image to the bee that this attacker was dangerous and would attack the hive.

A small smile appeared on her lips. "You are about to get your distraction. Be ready."

Kai drew the bowstring, arrow set to launch. Then she saw the wraith appear as clear as day, and turn around feeling his neck, as if stung by a bee. Releasing the arrow, it hit its mark on the distracted Gatherer, sending him falling back with an arrow jutting from his chest.

An immediate cry came from the sarnal. "Matrife!" She could hear the pain in his voice. This was clearly someone of great value to him. That being the case, he would be even more determined and dangerous.

Reassessing the situation instantly, Kai targeted her enemies. The elf and simian were not real physical threats. The sarnal clearly was. The centaur would reach them the quickest, but also should be no problem for Grazlin. The trolls and orc were probably the strongest of the remaining group. The three of them, along with the sarnal, would have to go down next.

Aiming again, she launched an arrow at the rampaging sarnal. In his rage, he did not even defend himself. The arrow pierced his left shoulder, yet onward he continued. She aimed a second arrow at the sarnal but never got off the shot. An arrow hit her chest high, propelling her backward into a state of shock almost immediately.

Kyria leaped up crying. "No! Kai, no!" Pain and anguish in her voice.

Kai looked up at her, unable to ascertain what had happened. She could see Kyria crying, looking down at her. Why was she crying? she wondered. Then she could see the arrow sticking out of her. How odd for it to be there. Out of place. Straining to see the advancing Gatherers, she could see the centaur and two trolls atop of Grazlin and attacking brutally. Then she saw the enemy she underestimated. The elf. The elf shot her, just as she had been targeting the others.

Slowly, her vision blurred again. A sense of failure permeated her consciousness. Then there was a light. A blinding light. She could hear Kyria again. Struggling to open her eyes, she could see that the light was coming from Kyria. Somehow, she had found a sword. The same sword Kai had seen in the visions. The blade glimmered and released an aura of purity. A pure white light that was burning on the blade itself. The hilt sparkled of silver. A silver that Kai noted also covered the fingers of the young Kyria. Wondering what this meant, her eyes closed once more as she passed into unconsciousness.

Three against one, Grazlin fought valiantly. The centaur was on him first, kicking his hind legs. Grazlin had enough. He grabbed the two legs and used the centaur as a weapon against the two trolls. Spinning the half-man, half-horse around, he managed to knock both trolls down. While doing so, a weapon from one of the trolls impacted the centaur, producing an earsplitting scream as his life flowed away. Seeing Tarwas charging, Grazlin sent the lifeless husk of the centaur hurtling through the air and into the oncoming sarnal.

Hearing Kyria's scream, Grazlin quickly opted to finish this conflict, fall back to his two friends, and remain there. Something had clearly gone wrong. Kai had planned on taking several of the opponents out, evening the odds. Instead, she only managed to bring down one, and barely injure a second. The odds were clearly against them.

The two trolls were back on him first. With his prior assault, he had only knocked them down. The first one lunged at him, and Grazlin dropped and flipped him over his head. The second one stood there watching and had little time to prepare as Grazlin extended up and lunged at the troll, barreling headfirst into his stomach. Grazlin's horns pierced the Gatherer, sending him faltering backward spitting up blood. Disbelief was clearly in his eyes as he looked down at the two holes in his stomach left behind by Grazlin. In an instant, it was over and the troll collapsed into death.

From behind him, Grazlin could hear the other troll screaming. "Brother! You killed my brother!" His second attack was even less effective than his first. As he ran into Grazlin, the minotaur braced himself and grabbed the troll's head. With the troll pounding him with his fists, Grazlin sighed and snapped his neck in one swift motion.

Anxiously running back to his friends to try to find out why Kyria screamed, he could see her wielding a blade that was glowing with pure, blinding light. Kai was lying at her feet, an arrow jutting out of her chest. When he got to the two girls, he could see the tears in Kyria's eyes. Not taking her eyes off of her friend and mentor, she asked. "Is she dead?"

Grazlin bent down and could feel her pulse. "No. She yet lives." Without hesitation, he pulled the arrow from her chest. "Quickly child, use your flaming blade to cauterize and seal the wound."

Puzzled, Kyria did as Grazlin asked. She cringed when she heard the moan of pain emitted from Kai's mouth. "I'm hurting her."

"No, child. You are helping her." Grazlin stood back up. "That is enough. If we survive the next few minutes, she will make it. She just needs to rest now." Turning, he saw his opponents approaching. The sarnal, orc, elf, and simian were almost upon them. The other four were not there. At least three he had felled personally, and potentially four were down with the one that Kai managed to shoot.

As they closed in, Kyria's young heart started to pound. She did not know how she managed to bring this sword out of thin air, but she had it and knew that it could help, but not as a weapon. She could feel that. Instinctively. Then she understood. She was the Chosen One. The one that could bend reality at her will. Time. Space. It was all within her realm and domain. How else could she save Kai's people? "Grazlin, I know how to get us out of here."

Turning back, he looked her in the eye. "Speak now, child, they are almost upon us."

Rather than responding, she took her sword and slashed it through the air. A ripple appeared, a rift in space, an opening. "We can escape through here."

Unable to perceive what he was witnessing, Grazlin looked at this tear in the fabric of reality, a gateway to the unknown. He hesitantly stepped toward it. Put his hand in, saw that it vanished, then pulled it back out. "Impossible. What is this?"

Kyria confidently responded. "Grazlin, this is the way that fate was written. This is the future. This is our escape. Remember, the three of us will prosper as long as we are together. We will always be connected. Bonded."

"You are talking in riddles, girl."

"There's no time. They are here. Quick, grab Kai and go. I will be behind you to close the rift."

Grazlin still hesitated, but the intensity in her eyes convinced him this was their only hope. Swooping up Kai, he looked at Kyria one last time. "I will see you on the other side." With that, he stepped into the rift and vanished from reality as it was known.

Kyria smiled. "You will see me on the other side." She then stepped toward the rift herself, but felt her world go dark around her before she made it. She started to fall and saw the rift close. The sword vanished as it fell from her grip. As the darkness overwhelmed her, she knew that everything ended the way it was meant to. You cannot rewrite destiny.

❖ ❖ ❖ ❖ ❖

Standing over the unconscious body of the young Kyria, Master Zane stood triumphantly. "Not going to escape that way, little one." In his hand, he held a blowgun, a handy weapon that had been invented centuries before, which he used to send paralysis and unconsciousness to the youth. Sometimes, the easiest methods are the most effective.

Looking to one of his avarian troops, he issued his orders. "Return to the Council with her immediately. Pierce wishes to examine her personally. I shall be behind you shortly."

The avarians nodded, then scooped the girl up and took to flight. Zane watched them as they grew smaller and smaller flying off into the distance.

Tarwas stood before him. Anger and sorrow mixed in his eyes. Blood flowed from his arrow wound. "Congratulations. You got the girl. Perhaps if you were not so reckless with my platoon, I would not have lost half of my men."

Turning to address Tarwas with contempt, Zane stared him down and sneered. "Your men are expendable. Only the mission was important. We accomplished the mission. However, I will see to it that their sacrifice will be remembered."

"Will be remembered? How can you say that? Four of my men are dead! Because of your orders! If we did things the way we were trained to, without this reckless behavior you demanded, they would still be alive!" The rage in his voice increased with each word as he thought of the losses his unit suffered that day, including his closest friend, Matrife.

"So certain are you, Commander? Tsk, tsk." Zane reached out with his hand and exaggerated a yanking motion. As Tarwas turned to look, he saw Matrife floating through the air to them. "You need to develop your inner sight a little better, Commander. He yet lives. A trip to the Healers, and you will never know that he was even hit. That, my dear Commander, is why I remained behind with several of my own men. To provide assistance to you and your fallen comrades."

"Your actions were still reckless. The casualty list only totals three rather than four."

"Tarwas, Tarwas. You need to see the big picture here. Would I be here if this girl were not seen as special to the Council of Elders? No. I wouldn't. You would have been left to do your job as always. But I was called in. Called in to make the tough choices and get the job done. The girl is special and powerful, very powerful. The sacrifice of your own will become legendary through the Council as this child grows and develops. Your names will not be forgotten, Commander."

Looking down in shame, Tarwas lowered his voice. "My apologies and thanks, Master. I presumed the worst based on the situation. It will not happen again."

"Of that, you are right, Commander. It will not happen again. I will see to that personally." Zane then signaled to his remaining troops, dispersing them to pick up the wounded and fly back to the Council. "Your names may be connected with hers forevermore, but your outright disobedience to authority, disregard of my orders, and pursuit of this hunt from the onset will all be brought to light."

An avarian moved over to help carry Crecix back to the Council. Refusing to simply go, he looked out at Tarwas for approval before leaving. He had opted to stay to finish the mission, but with the hunt complete, he now could receive the medical attention he required. Still, he would not leave without the blessing of his commanding officer. A nod from Tarwas, and Crecix, too, was ready to go. "See you soon, boss, sir."

Tarwas stood alone, watching as his men were flown back home. Hurnelo and Chendra, his simian companion, remained behind and walked over to his side. Yet he still felt alone, more alone than he ever was before. The hunt was done. Perhaps, too, were his team, and his own command. More than half of his platoon was either injured or dead. He hoped for their sakes that this girl truly was as gifted as Pierce, Zane, and Lenixum preached. Regardless, he would remember this hunt as being the turning point in his life. The point when he lost his faith in his own ideals. The point when he was ashamed of what he did, and who he was.

CHAPTER 63

Standing on the bridge of the Imperial flagship *Reliance,* Morex looked out at the various ships traveling along the shipping lanes. Even without the help of his optical enhancers, he could see several fishing vessels, two merchant ships, and another Gallie.

He personally decided to take the same patrol route that saw the demise of his other warships. Whatever it was that was attacking them, he hoped they would come after him directly, and allow his tactical mind to resolve the situation as quickly as possible.

It was a beautiful day. The sky was blue with white clouds scattered about. The wind was gently blowing, but strong enough to allow the ships to move swiftly. The waters themselves were calm.

Observing everything, Morex had too much time to consider what was happening in the Seven Kingdoms, and what may be happening back at the palace. He knew that he needed to be here personally, but he sincerely wished he could be beside Karleena as she continued with her efforts toward the unification.

Disturbing his solitude, Captain Harnell made an inquiry. "Begging the Admiral's pardon, sir, but why exactly do we have ten ships out here to watch a bunch of fisherman and merchants going about their business?"

"Something has been attacking these people, Captain, something dangerous enough to destroy three of our Gallies. I'd say that warrants our attention."

"Yes, sir, but the men are getting restless. They all know that there have been attacks upon the Imperium, and truth be told, they want to face a physical enemy and help do something about it. Just sitting here on a bright and sunny day is maddening."

Morex rubbed his eyes. "Yes, this is a frustrating assignment. However, we are all military men. We will maintain our vigil until we overcome this threat."

"Well, I for one would just be happy to see something happen."

On the horizon, Morex watched as a clear sky turned dark as night, in mere moments. Storm clouds approached with lightning striking from the sky. The clear waters gained in turbulence as they rushed toward the waiting ships.

"It looks like you may get your wish, Captain." Using his optical enhancers, Morex was astonished by the rate the storm was coming in. "Send the command to prepare for a storm, battle stations as well. This feels wrong. Whatever that is, it is not a natural phenomenon."

"Aye, Admiral." Stepping away, Captain Harnell barked out orders to the men. Immediately, they rushed to prepare for the storm.

Admiral Morex continued to watch the clouds. They moved swiftly and methodically. In mere minutes, the storm was already upon one of his Gallies. The waves towered high above their masts and came crashing down, leaving the ship in splinters.

Lowering the optical enhancers from his eyes, Morex was stunned by what he was witnessing. Everything he just watched was impossible, yet he just saw it with his own eyes.

Looking through the optical enhancers again, he could see a ship directly behind the waves. He could not distinguish the design, but as he watched, he knew that this was his true enemy. The storm raged around this ship, and acted as if under the vessel's control.

The fishing vessels and merchant ships all were destroyed as the waves crashed through them, or lightning struck their bows.

Seeing that they would certainly perish by doing nothing, Admiral Morex started issuing commands. "Captain, I want the catapults turned to thirty mark two."

"Thirty mark two. Yes, sir." Stepping toward the bow, the Captain yelled out. "Catapults turned to thirty mark two."

Below, several men turned the catapults to the specified coordinates, then signaled the Captain when completed.

"Thirty mark two, sir, as ordered," Harnell relayed.

"Fire," Morex stated with his fist pumped.

"Fire!" Harnell repeated to the gunnery crew.

Artillery filled the quickly darkening sky and rained down toward the oncoming storm and the vessel it nearly hid. Morex watched in dismay as lightning struck each shell out of the sky.

For the first time in his life, he was at a loss. He could see no strategic way to overcome this foe. Clearly, they must have the assistance of Mages. There was no other practical explanation for what he was witnessing.

"Captain, issue the retreat," he said somberly.

"Retreat, sir?"

"Yes. Get us out of here, Captain." His words were clear and perfectly calm, as was the man's demeanor itself.

"Helm, turn us about and get us out of here," Captain Harnell ordered.

"Aye, sir."

The *Reliance* slowly turned away from the waves, which were rising in height and intensity as it approached them. Crashing down, the waves hit the spot where the flagship had been, barely missing them, but propelling them further away at an accelerated speed.

Morex watched as the ship in pursuit resumed the chase, closing the gap between them.

The helmsman looked backward at the storm and the rising waves coming after them again. "We're not going to make it."

"Cease the defeatist attitude, Ensign," Captain Harnell demanded.

Morex considered the exchange. "A defeatist attitude perhaps, but he also happens to be right."

Harnell looked at the Admiral in pure disbelief.

"Captain, plot a course to the Forbidden Regions."

"The Forbidden Regions, sir?"

"Yes, Captain," Morex confirmed sternly.

"Sir, nobody can survive in the Forbidden Regions."

"We aren't going to survive here. Now get moving," Morex declared.

"Aye, sir." Looking at the Ensign, Harnell nodded. "You heard the man, set course for the Forbidden Regions."

With the order relayed, Morex could see that those near him were beginning to show signs of strain. All mariners knew to stay away from the Forbidden Regions. The area was so dense and thick in fog, that you literally could not see your nose on the tip of your face. With rocks, whirlpools, and numerous other unknowns, no ship had ever returned from the Forbidden Regions, and here he was ordering them into the unknown and certain death. Tension was definitely high, and he knew that it would only escalate further.

Behind them, the storm was still approaching, gradually gaining upon them. He wondered whether they would make it to the Forbidden Regions in time.

"Captain, we need to slow them down. Reposition catapults and continue firing until ordered to stop."

"Aye, sir." Looking down he yelled out, "Reposition those catapults! Quickly, quickly."

The artillerymen dragged the catapults across the bow toward the stern of the ship. Once there, each crewman looked up at the Captain.

"Fire!" he yelled.

The catapults launched shells back toward the storm. As it hit the waves, the shells vanished into the fury of the storm. Lightning shot out in greater frequency knocking other bursts from the sky.

"It's having no impact, sir," Harnell reported.

"Look again, Captain, the storm has slowed down. Keep firing," Morex ordered.

"Aye, sir."

Turning, Morex looked ahead and saw the edges of their destination. The white mists were the first thing to greet them into the Forbidden Regions. Looking back, for the first time he was optimistic that they would make it in time.

"Straight ahead, Ensign. You are doing fine," Morex encouraged.

"Aye, sir," the Ensign responded.

As they entered the mists of the Forbidden Regions, Morex could see the storm dissipating and the ship begin to turn to leave. He knew the Captain of that ship must not be crazy enough to follow them.

"Cease artillery. Lower the sails and begin rowing. I want a dinghy attached in front leading the *Reliance."* His orders were issued calmly as he maintained his posture and tried to reassure his men.

"Aye, sir," Captain Harnell responded. "Cease artillery! Lower the sails! Deploy oars!"

Admiral Morex allowed his thoughts to return to the Empress one last time as he lost all visibility to the fog of the Forbidden Regions. Under his breath so no one could hear, he said his final farewells. "For the preservation of the Imperium, may the unification be true and everlasting."

CHAPTER 64

"Report," Centain stated as one of his messengers returned.

Bowing briefly, the Imperial Guard greeted the Captain. "Sir, Adonis is not in Trespias."

"Where is he?"

"There has been a murder in Korland. He took his unit to investigate."

"Korland? That's northern Suspinti. He won't be able to get back here at least for a fortnight." The frustration was evident in his voice.

"What are your orders, sir?"

"Dispatch Geist to Korland. The death of a king is paramount to anything else he may be investigating. I just hope that if there is any evidence of foul play, Adonis and his crew can still detect it after the long delay."

"Yes, sir."

"Dismissed," Centain said with a quick wave of his hand.

"Yes, sir." The young messenger turned and walked away.

Addressing the other man with him, Centain issued further orders. "Commander, I want guards posted at this door. Until Adonis arrives, I want no one to disturb King Sarlec's quarters."

"What about the King himself, sir? The Empress has planned a ceremony for later today."

"The ceremony will have to be without Sarlec. Adonis may not be able to do anything two weeks from now, but I want to give him the opportunity to see things as they are now."

"The body will decay, sir," stated the Commander.

"I know. Regardless, my orders stand." Leaving the chambers of King Sarlec, he continued. "Until we know whether this was from natural causes, an accident, or murder, I want security doubled around all of the royal families and the delegates of the races."

"Yes, sir."

Seeing that the Commander did not leave to begin issuing the orders, Centain turned to look at him. "Is there something else, Commander?"

"Yes, sir, there is. King Garum remains in the dungeon. Will we be releasing him for this afternoon's ceremony?"

Taking a deep breath, Centain considered Garum and his treachery. Though he was locked away, he still remained a key suspect. After all, through an association with the Hidden Empire, he could have had one of their agents assassinate the King. "For the time being, leave him where he is. I'll want to question him personally after the ceremony."

"Yes, sir."

As the Commander left, Centain considered the suspects and possibilities. He did not hear anything through the Harlocten plants that would incriminate anyone, but he still felt uneasy. Instinctively, he knew that foul play was indeed involved. He was uncertain how.

❖ ❖ ❖ ❖ ❖

A cloaked figure approached the entrance to the palace and looked up at the statues of Emperor Conrad, Admiral Morex, King Sarlec, Mage Master Jeffa, and the other heroes who led to the formation of the Imperium. Pausing to study these proud figures, the man knew that his actions today would very likely alter the scope of the entire Imperium.

Moving ahead, he approached the doors to the Chamber. As the gateway between Trespias and the palace, he knew that this circular structure would be the place where he would first encounter his opponents.

A palace guard approached with his hand outstretched. "I'm sorry, the palace is off limits to all visitors today."

The cloaked figure did not respond with words, but with actions. Swiping his arms out to the side, he knocked off his cloak, revealing the warrior beneath. His body was as dark as the night sky, and just as with a cloudless night, constellations and stellar phenomena swirled throughout his body. The effect itself was remarkable, leaving the man almost transparent. He wore very little clothing, only dark shorts, gloves, and boots.

As the Imperial Guards looked him over, they quickly armed themselves, seeing the apparent threat. This visitor was fully garbed with a variety of weapons. Visibly, two swords crossed along his back, with a case full of arrows and a bow in the middle. He had a wide belt full of pouches and other attached weapons, including two small crossbows and a pair of scimitar-shaped knives. On his right leg, completely encircling his upper thigh, was a laced casing surrounded by arrows for the crossbows. His left leg had a parallel holder, but contained multiple small throwing knives. Each of his lower calves also had serrated knives strapped to them.

"What do you think he is?" one of the guards asked another.

"I don't know. I've never seen anything like it," came the reply.

The first guard took a step forward. "Okay, buddy, back up or we'll have to do this the hard way."

Speaking for the first time, chills were sent through the spines of each of the guards. The voice was full of ice and inspired terror. "I am Nitorum, let me pass or die."

The first guard turned to look at his men, then readdressed Nitorum. "I think you are mistaken. There are fifteen of us in the Chamber alone, and more than a hundred Imperial Guards in the palace. Now why don't you come with me and we'll make sure that nobody regrets what happens here today?"

Nitorum did not say another word; he merely reached into one of the pouches strapped to his belt, and removed a small organism that looked like a round tube with cilia protruding from it. He squeezed it gently, and it emitted a porous gas.

The first guard coughed and then struggled to get his helmet off. Several others moved up to try to help him, but stopped in their tracks when they saw the helmet finally come off. The man's face was decomposing right in front of them, leaving only skin and bones as he shrieked in terror for the final moments of his life.

Dropping the organism, Nitorum leapt toward the shocked men with his two scimitar knives, slashing and cutting each guard in unprotected areas, such as the arm pits, their sides, and behind the knees. His motions were quick, and the Imperial Guards writhed upon the ground in agony.

Twirling his knives, in one quick motion, he placed them back on his utility belt. Reaching into a second pouch, he removed another small organism and tossed it at the few remaining guards. The organism hit the ground in front of them, then exploded in a plantlike growth, binding each of the men. As they struggled, the vines tightened, crushing the armor and bones within the men's bodies.

Nitorum nodded at the fifteen men he felled in under a minute, then ran off toward the other end of the Chamber. This doorway led to the drawbridge of the palace. Nitorum saw the bridge was up, with a gap of about thirty feet between the Chamber and the palace.

Looking down, he saw a deep and treacherous ravine that would certainly lead to a fatal fall. Reaching into the pouch behind his back, he removed two small poles, then clasped them together. Stringing each end, he had a longbow. He selected an iron arrow from his pouch, which had a small device attached to its head, a clamp with a roller. He took a steel cable and attached it to the doorway of the Chamber, placed the other end on the clamp, then fired the arrow toward the palace.

The arrow impacted slightly above the drawbridge. Nitorum opened a small lever from the end attached to the door, and cranked it several times, reducing the slack in the line. Testing it, he stepped on top of the narrow line and walked across it toward the other end.

Upon reaching the other side, he reached into one of the pouches on the back of his utility belt, and removed two claws that he fastened on the palms of each hand. Lifting his right arm, he rammed the claws into the palace walls and lifted himself slightly. He did the same with his left arm, and started crawling up the sheer face of the wall itself.

He moved along the walls quickly, and directed himself to a windowed room by one of the towers. Reaching there, he climbed slightly above the window, then swung directly into it, shattering the glass and landing inside.

Rolling with the impact, he was up and in a defensive posture scanning the room. Seeing that he was alone, he placed the two claws back into his utility belt, and removed two more poles from the pouch along his back. He fastened both of these together and held a weathered staff.

He opened the door and walked into the hallway, searching for any sign of activity. Nothing thus far, so he headed down the corridor approaching his destination.

❖ ❖ ❖ ❖ ❖

Karleena stood next to a stone altar with Winton by her side. She had delivered a heartfelt speech about King Sarlec and how they would all desperately miss him. The ceremony was attended by all of the royal families, with the exception of Garum, the ministers, the delegates of the races, staff members, and a vast number of Imperial Guards.

One by one, they all approached Winton and Karleena after her words and stressed their own sorrows and sympathies. The mood was somber for all, but Karleena could see that both her supporters and opponents appeared to offer her strength and words of encouragement even in these tragic times. Torscen himself even acted remorseful and respectful.

She wished that King Sarlec's body itself could be here for those present to see one last time, but Centain was adamant about not moving it until Adonis and his ISIA crew could examine it at the scene. She truly hated that thought, but if he was really murdered, she did not want to lose the culprit because of her desires to respect and honor the man. Far better for him to be brought to justice, she felt.

Thinking of Centain, she looked back and saw he was no longer standing guard behind her. Scanning the room, she finally saw him in a back corner speaking to several Imperial Guards. They then ran out of the room, and he moved on to the next station to talk.

Curious, she wished she knew what was going on. However, etiquette and protocol demanded that she stay beside Winton and meet with everyone within the room. Whatever was happening, Centain was more than capable of handling it.

❖ ❖ ❖ ❖ ❖

The guards rushed around the corner with weapons in hand. Nitorum stepped back and raised his staff. He lunged forward striking the first guard in the stomach, twirled the staff back, then swung it head high knocking the guard to the ground unconscious.

Twirling the staff again, he thrust it down at another guard, then brought it up between the legs of a third, sending him hurtling backward into a fourth.

With the first four down, the remaining two approached more carefully. Nitorum squeezed the staff, and a blade popped out of each end. Leaping into the air, he somersaulted over both men, cutting each as he twirled the staff between them.

Landing on his feet, he turned, squeezed the staff a second time so the blades resheathed, then resumed his pace down the hall, never bothering to look at the bloodied and battered troops he left behind.

Each time he encountered the Imperial Guards, his actions were swift and flawless, and all fell before him, regardless of their superior numbers.

❖ ❖ ❖ ❖ ❖

"Barricade the door," Centain instructed several of his men. "He's still coming,"

The gnome Arbuckle stepped up and faced Centain. "Trouble, I think; yes trouble indeed."

Centain looked down at the small gnome. "You should return to your seat. We are handling this."

"On edge. Something is coming. Something you haven't been able to stop. Yes, definitely something sinister I think. Time perhaps to tell all here?"

Centain smiled at the gnome. "Arbuckle, my thanks. It is indeed time to inform everyone." Stepping forward, Centain approached the altar where Karleena stood.

Once there, he clapped his hands to try to gain everyone's attention. As the crowd quieted down, he spoke out. "Ladies and gentleman, I do not wish to alarm any of you, but someone has infiltrated the palace and is making a path toward this room."

"An intruder? Why haven't you stopped him, Captain?" Dornela demanded.

"We have been trying. Unsuccessfully. However, this room has been barricaded and is well protected. Whatever the threat, your safety is our utmost goal."

"Little comfort in that, I think," Torscen sneered.

Just then, the doors to the hall exploded. The palace guards and guests who were near them were lying scattered along the ground, either dead or unconscious.

Centain watched as his remaining guards moved toward the doors to stop the new threat. Nothing was there.

Behind them, a portion of the ceiling collapsed, and Nitorum dropped to the floor in a crouch. Unlike earlier, all of the stars within his body had faded, leaving him dark, shaded, and hard to see when he moved away from the light.

Holding both crossbows, he launched two arrows at the closest guards. In fluid motion, he dropped the crossbows, which were still strung to his utility belt, and removed several throwing knives, which he hurled with deadly accuracy.

Several guards broke off and tried to move the royal families and guests away from the battle for their protection. Arianna and her own bodyguards were struggling to get free and enter the fray themselves.

Nitorum tossed several of the organisms toward the bulk of the remaining Imperial Guards, and like their comrades in the Chamber, vines sprouted out and bound them.

Back-flipping, Nitorum positioned himself, heading directly for Karleena and Winton, who remained at the altar with Centain.

Finally freeing herself, Arianna stepped in front of Nitorum, blocking his path. With that, the guards did not bother to try to stop her honor guard, who now flanked her sides and prepared to face this oncoming threat.

Nitorum reached into his utility belt and removed a small cylinder. Pushing a button, an intense steam shot out at the group of aquaticans. Their bodies hardened and cracked as all water drained from them. Those closest fell quickly, with Arianna being dragged away by her Sentinel. The few remaining aquaticans desperately looked for water to try to replenish the liquid in their systems before they perished.

Stepping in front of Karleena, Centain drew his elvish blade, the Nocplest. "None may touch the Empress unless they get past me first."

Nitorum stopped and bowed slightly in acceptance of the challenge. He then removed the two swords strung across his back and moved toward the Captain of the Guards.

Centain stepped cautiously. Not only had he seen this man in action, but he also had heard his troops falling quickly through the Harlocten plants vibrations. He twirled the Nocplest once, then braced for the attack.

Nitorum moved in swiftly, bringing both blades at him from different arcs and at different times. His movements were practically a blur, with deadly efficiency.

Very quickly, Nitorum had Centain fighting a defensive battle. Centain faltered backward struggling to simply block each attack. This foe before him seemed impervious to any kind of harm, and a master in all arts of fighting.

Attempting to go on the offensive, Centain dropped to the ground and swiped with the Nocplest at Nitorum's legs.

Nitorum jumped up, and landed squarely on Centain's back, stomping down. Centain could feel his ribs breaking.

Two of the Imperial Guards who were protecting the royal families rushed to their leader's aid. Nitorum stepped off of the Captain, sent one blade into the chest of the first guard, and swung head-high decapitating the second.

As he turned around, the Nocplest was swinging for his own head. Nitorum raised his arm and took the brunt of the impact there. His blood, a bright and glowing yellow liquid, spurted from the wound.

Nitorum stepped back as Centain swung his elven sword again. This time, Nitorum parried the blow and then kicked Centain in the stomach, sending him reeling over.

Centain fell in pain. His ribs broken, his air gone, and blood flowing from his nose and mouth. Seeing Karleena in his peripheral vision, he attempted to rise once more.

Nitorum removed one of the serrated blades from his calf and rammed it into the captain's stomach.

Shock hitting him first, Centain looked down at the blade lodged in his stomach, and tried to concentrate on it as the world around him lost focus. Dropping to his knees, he reached for his sword one last time. Grasping the hilt, he used it to help himself stand, then toppled over and succumbed to the darkness.

Karleena stood her ground and stared at Nitorum as he walked toward her. She refused to run in terror of this murderer.

Winton stepped in front of her with his fists raised. "Run, I'll slow him down."

Nitorum backhanded Winton across the face and sent him hurtling over the altar. Reaching out, he grabbed Karleena and glared deep into her eyes.

As she stared back, all she could see was an endless abyss of nothingness.

Several of the members of the royal family moved forward in an attempt to help the Empress.

Nitorum faced them all and merely glared. "Emperor Wei Lau sends his greetings." His dark form suddenly burst into radiating light, momentarily blinding everyone present.

As their vision cleared, Nitorum was gone, and with him, Empress Karleena.

CHAPTER 65

Waking, Rawthorne could hear his companion snoring. Taking a minute to reorient himself, he quickly grew infuriated. Both of them were sleeping, and in the distance, he could see Braksis sitting atop a peak looking out toward the sea. Throwing a rock at Durgin's head, he screamed. "Wake up, you idiot! You were supposed to be on watch!"

"Ow! That hurt!"

"That's not the only thing that is going to hurt if you don't do what you're told!" The desire to leave Durgin behind and face Braksis alone was overwhelming. He was amazed that Zoldex had insisted both men band together. However, Zoldex did break him out of prison, so if that meant dealing with a cowering fool, so be it. "While you were supposed to be watching, Braksis came out on his own. We missed him!"

"What? Where?"

With contempt in his voice, Rawthorne pointed toward the peak where he saw Braksis. "There."

"We'll still get him. There is as good as here," Durgin attempted to rationalize.

"We had an ambush spot set up for a reason. Now we will need to try to sneak up on him. All because you couldn't do as you were told!" Grabbing his mallet, Rawthorne ascended the trail to where Braksis lay waiting. "Send the signal to the goblins. Can you at least handle that without failure?"

Attempting to regain the confidence he once exuded, Durgin placed a sword in its sheath by his side, and also hefted an axe that was similar to the one he used to have when striking down his victims. The stencils of skulls were not etched into his new blade, but with luck, Braksis would be the first symbolic death of his new reign of tyranny.

As he started after Rawthorne, he picked up the small pod that Zoldex had given them. It was no larger than a small pea, but they were told that by breaking it, the goblins would know to come. Not truly understanding how it worked, he tossed the pod in front of him and mashed it with the heel of his boot as he walked along.

❖ ❖ ❖ ❖ ❖

As he approached the molten magma, Ferceng produced a Mage protection spell that moderated the temperature of his skin to keep him from passing out from the heat. The spell also enabled a small layer on top of his skin to protect him from any lava that might inadvertently splash out and catch him by surprise. This was not the first time he had been here, so he knew what precautions needed to be taken.

The first step of forging Braksis's new blade was to find the right elements. Some chose metals they could craft. He, too, desired metals, but metals that could withstand far more pressure and abuse than steel. Although he did not know the alchemy of the illistrium he used, he knew that it could create a blade so powerful it was nearly impossible to dent, chip, crack, or break when retrieved in this intense heat. Though the ore could be found embedded in the caverns this deep, he knew that it was more potent when taken directly from the magma.

The first blade he designed, the original Phoenix was of this same material. It had lasted until the mystical axe of Guldan shattered it. He would put magic into the new Phoenix, too, but he wished to have the material be as strong and resistant as the original. Especially since the power he was putting into the weapon would stem from the molten magma itself.

Ferceng closed his eyes and concentrated on the flowing lava. The flames bursting throughout the caverns. The air pressure that would be impossible to breathe if not under a Mage's protection spell. He saw deeper. Under the murky red surface. Searching slowly and meticulously for the rare metal which he desired.

Time in the cavern lost meaning. Seconds. Minutes. Hours. Whatever it was, the only thing Ferceng could concentrate on was probing beneath the magma surface for his goal. Then finally, he found it.

With a deep breath, he increased his concentration and attempted to lift the object from the lava. He could still see it clearly in his mind as it slowly rocked back and forth. Slowly moving and trying to dislodge itself from where it lay nestled on the wall under the river of molten lava.

With a pump of his fists, the boulder came loose and slowly rose to the surface. Ferceng opened his eyes for the first time now and watched the object as it broke free of the magma and floated in the air toward him. The object was almost as large as he was. Molten lava dripped from it on all sides, and flames danced all around it.

He set it down on the clear path next to him and encircled the sweltering boulder, studying it. "This will do quite nicely. Quite nicely indeed."

❖ ❖ ❖ ❖ ❖

Elsewhere in the home of Ferceng, the hair on Tiot's back stood on end. He quickly jumped up and growled, sensing danger. Something was not quite right. Tensely he crept over to where Solara slept soundly and barked twice.

Awakening immediately, she saw that Tiot was on edge. Battle instincts taking over, she flipped off of the couch and back-flipped over to where her weapons sat. Removing a sword, she looked around the room. Nothing seemed out of the ordinary. "What is it, boy? What do you sense?"

Continuing to growl with his hair standing on end, Tiot looked one last time at Solara, then ran toward the door.

Not truly comprehending what was wrong, but trusting the wolf's instincts, she quickly donned her armor plating and weapons. Whatever was bothering Tiot, she would be ready to face the threat as well. As she clamped her armor in place, she was already moving toward the door and after Tiot.

Hustling after him, Solara watched as he circled around, smelling the ground. With a pair of barks to focus her attention, he was off and running again. She watched as he ascended the mountains on what appeared to be a trail. Straining her vision, Solara could not see anything that would have attracted Tiot's interest. Senses still aware of her surroundings, she followed the wolf farther, hoping desperately to find Braksis and confirm that he was unharmed.

❖ ❖ ❖ ❖ ❖

The two former foes of Braksis crept closer to him, quietly and stealthily. They watched as he looked out over the horizon and lost himself in thought. They would be upon him soon. Only a few minutes more.

Even with thoughts of victory dancing in his head, the displeasure of having to sneak up on his quarry like this was infuriating. In that time, Rawthorne plotted the demise of Durgin upon this battle's conclusion. If not for Durgin falling asleep while on watch, this mission would already be completed and Braksis would be dead.

Sensing the increasing anger in Rawthorne, Durgin knew that when the deed was done, he would need to flee quickly. Although that would reinforce the cowardly nature he was looking to dispel, he knew that Rawthorne held him responsible and wished to retaliate. This was after all, his fault.

Lost in thought, Durgin did not notice a branch stretched across the path. As he stepped on it, the branch snapped, releasing a loud crack. He also stumbled forward and collided with Rawthorne, knocking both men down.

Surprise was lost. As both men glanced up, they saw Braksis looking down at them. He knew they were there. Subterfuge aside, it was time to attack and complete their mission. The two men stood up, and without the words that either was thinking, they charged up the remainder of the path toward the unarmed Warlord.

❖ ❖ ❖ ❖ ❖

Catching up to Tiot, Solara saw an indentation in the rock face. There were clear signs of a camp, as well as scattered weapons and supplies. Someone had been there. She looked down and saw that whoever had been perched here had a clear view of them when they first arrived. With Tiot's reaction, intentions of aggression were the only ones she could consider.

Looking down at Tiot, she saw that he was sniffing around and gradually moving up the path again. He had found the hideout, now he was looking for the men. She looked up the path and could see three men in the distance. They were too far to clearly distinguish, but one was definitely Braksis. An unarmored and unarmed Braksis.

Desperation quickly crept in as she ran up the trail as quickly as she could. Even so, they were high up on the mountains and it would take her too long to get there. Still, Braksis was skilled and talented. She just prayed that he could hold them off until she arrived.

With her running, Tiot quickly joined her and darted up the path. Their master was in danger. They would do their best to get there, even if it would be too late.

Then, disaster struck, causing an even larger delay. From the rock face itself, goblins leapt out at Solara and Tiot, attacking ruthlessly. Ambushed, Solara drew her sword and braced herself as dozens of the small four-foot creatures came at her.

She knew that a goblin was no match for her, but they had the advantage of numbers, surprise, and even more importantly, time. Time was of the essence, and she was desperate to get past them and up to Braksis.

"I have no time for you. Be gone!" she barked out, but her only reply was the small creatures garbed in dark leather charging her. Some carried spears or maces; only a few had short swords. Solara spun into action and desperately attempted to make her way through the attackers with swift moves and a deep brutality.

❖ ❖ ❖ ❖ ❖

Braksis looked around for something that he could use as a weapon. The only thing he could find was small rocks and stones. Certainly not the types of weapons he would chose to fight against two men with axes, mallets, and swords.

As they approached him, he could clearly see who they were. Both were images from his past. One, his evil cousin Rawthorne, a man who was supposed to be in prison and who had been responsible for the death of his entire family. He, too, would have been killed if Rawthorne had his way. Fortunately, Ferceng rescued him.

The next time the two relatives had crossed each other's paths, Braksis had been empowered by Conrad to act in the Imperium's behalf. As a result of that conflict, Rawthorne was removed from the crown and imprisoned. To see him suddenly here was a shock.

The other man was the one who had been responsible for months of physical training and recovery. At the same time, he was also responsible for bringing Solara into his life. The vile Warlord Durgin. Although, by looking at him now, Braksis could see that Durgin no longer had that sinister and cocky arrogance that had accompanied him. In fact, it looked like he was shaking a little. Timid even.

"If it isn't Rawthorne and Durgin. To what do I owe the pleasure?"

Rawthorne slowly approached Braksis, never taking his eyes off of him. "Why, hello, cousin. Just thought I'd pay a visit and let you know I was out of prison."

"Oh really? So why bring useless over there with you?"

"Hey!" Durgin retorted. "I took you down once, and I'll do it again! You don't have your bitch to protect you this time!"

Durgin charged with his axe held above his head. Lord Braksis watched without moving. Not even appearing to notice the advance.

Rawthorne shook his head. "Idiot." He, too, then charged Braksis.

As Durgin was about five feet from Braksis, he pitched one of the rocks that he had picked up and instantly broke Durgin's nose. The man fell down with blood pouring out between his fingers as he tried to cover the pain.

Jumping over Durgin, Rawthorne landed with a laugh. "You won't best me so easily, cousin. This fool was useless as you said. I however, am more than enough to bring you down."

"Sure, sure. How many times have I heard that one? You think because I'm unarmed I can't do anything?" To prove his taunt, Braksis dodged out of the way as Rawthorne lunged with his mallet. Braksis then dropped to his knees and spun down to Durgin, standing up and removing the sword from its sheath in his belt.

"Hey, that's mine!" Durgin objected in a muffled tone.

Ignoring the wounded behemoth, Braksis turned just in time to dodge another attack from his cousin. Rawthorne was stronger and far faster than he remembered. Prison clearly did not have a mal effect upon him.

Braksis kept dodging, trying to remain a step ahead of his larger cousin. His agility now was his greatest strength. He needed to be quick on his feet and manage to stay away from the powerful mallet.

Rawthorne thrust the mallet at Braksis, and was rewarded by a slash of Durgin's sword across his shoulder. Blood instantly soaked through his tunic. "First blood is yours, cousin. I'll still win this day."

"Keep on dreaming. This day will end with you either back in prison or dead. Either is fine with me."

In his peripheral vision, Braksis saw that Durgin was once again up and looking to attack him. He pivoted so that he could see both men, but was taken unawares when Rawthorne released his mallet into the air and it barreled into his chest. He could hear his ribs cracking with the impact and knew that the tide had definitely turned against him. Any chance he had was slowly leaving him. Thinking that he may finally die, he remembered his promise to Solara about not letting her think he was dead and leaving her. Slowly attempting to move, he wished desperately that he could keep that vow.

❖ ❖ ❖ ❖ ❖

Deep in the depths of the caverns, Ferceng was hard at work on the boulder. He was making solid progress. The hard part had been completed. He managed to strip the molten lava from the metal he wanted. Now he needed to mold it into the shape of the blade. Although this shaping was artistic and time-consuming, he enjoyed this portion of the work. The locating of the material and stripping it was the hard part.

Concentrating fully on his task, a random shriek of pain pierced his concentration. He grasped his chest and felt like he had received a physical blow. Reaching out, he concentrated. He could feel his son's pain. Closing his eyes, he was desperate to focus and see what was happening. Regaining his calm, he waved his hand, and an image appeared of a battle between Braksis and the loathsome Rawthorne along with another man. He watched as Braksis fell and the two jackals closed in for the kill.

Shrieking out in terror, Ferceng left the caverns below as quickly as he could. He knew that he would not arrive in time, but the thought of losing a second son was too overwhelming to bear. Tears flowed down his face. He continued to concentrate and reached out so that in that last minute of his life, Braksis would not be alone.

❖ ❖ ❖ ❖ ❖

The goblin assault slowly began to overwhelm Solara and Tiot by mere numbers alone. For every one they cut down, two others jumped out and took their place. In a random moment when she had a chance to catch her breath, she managed to see the mallet hit Braksis. He fell and she knew he was down. The two men were closing in. She needed to be there, but knew that she would not arrive in time. Vows of vengeance flowed through her brain. Braksis may fall to these men, but they would join him in the afterlife before his body even grew cold.

With renewed vigor, she charged ahead, cleaving limbs from bodies without slowing down. Even with their massive numbers, the goblins gave pause, and that was all the time that Solara and Tiot needed to break through their ranks.

Suddenly, the goblins were behind them and fleeing back into the crevices from which they came. The two sprinted as quickly as they could toward Braksis, hoping beyond hope that they would arrive in time.

❖ ❖ ❖ ❖ ❖

Lying on the ground, Braksis attempted to concentrate. He needed to get up. Needed to keep fighting. Everything seemed so clear all of a sudden. His entire life seemed to make sense as it flashed before his eyes. He could even see his parents smiling and beckoning him to join them. Giving in to this temptation would be so easy.

The warmth of Ferceng soon entered him, and he knew that his surrogate father was with him. Keeping him company in his final moments. His fate was inevitable. Perhaps he was foolish not to wear his armor when he left the cave. Perhaps he was foolish not to bring a weapon. Yet how could he predict something like this happening at the place he called home? Perhaps he was too cocky and overconfident. Never considering the fact that he could truly fall in the face of an enemy. If he had time to do it again, he would make sure that overconfidence did not get the best of him.

Thoughts of those he would be leaving behind flooded his mind. Karleena would grow into a great Empress. He hoped that she managed to do so without him. It meant she would need to be strong and unite the races on her own. The thought of Ferceng losing another son was heartbreaking. A man filled with such tragedy and warmth, he deserved happiness, and this certainly would not bring him any. Thoughts of Solara and her sudden regrets of not going with him to watch the sunset, leading to feelings of remorse and guilt, wondering if she could have protected him if she were there. He also wondered whether she would begin to regret their decision to be together, or whether his death would devastate her.

Thinking of the people he would be leaving behind, he struggled to stand up. He refused to just lie down and die. The pain was immense, but he was trained to be stronger than that. Opening his eyes, he saw Rawthorne picking up his mallet from the ground. Durgin was above him laughing with his axe raised. This was the immediate threat.

Moving his legs through excruciating pain in his chest, he kicked Durgin behind the knees and sent the Warlord toppling down. This quickly got Rawthorne's attention as he turned to resume the attack.

Braksis used the sword to hoist himself up and glared defiantly at his cousin. His eyes were bloodshot. His nose leaked blood like the flow of a river. His chest heaved with pain. Yet he would remain standing and fight. He would not leave Solara so soon after he had finally found her, nor anyone else who depended upon him.

❖ ❖ ❖ ❖ ❖

Ferceng continued to run. He saw in his mind's eye his son standing to face his enemies. Realizing that he could do far more by concentrating, he sat down and slowly meditated, clearing his mind of everything but the events happening so far above him. He used his powers to try to create a bond around the broken ribs. To try to help Braksis calm himself and concentrate. The effort was immense, but he would not falter.

❖ ❖ ❖ ❖ ❖

Braksis could feel his chest easing. The pain was still there, but something was clearly helping to relieve the pressure. He felt strength returning to his body. The grogginess and sense of certain defeat was quickly evaporating. Before facing his enemies again, he quietly thanked Ferceng for trying to help.

Rawthorne kept swinging his mallet at a distance and tried to knock Braksis down again. Surprisingly, Braksis managed to dodge the swings and with the last one, strike Rawthorne's arm with his sword causing him to drop the mallet.

"Argh! I'll have the last laugh, not you! You're dead. You're just too stubborn to admit it!" Rawthorne screamed.

Durgin jumped in and took over where Rawthorne had left off pressing the attack on Braksis. His axe was swinging through the air and landing hard, causing Braksis to jump back further with each swing. Nearing the end of the cliff face, Braksis looked down and saw he had no farther to go. From where he was perched, only the rocky shore was below him. A fall from this height would be certain death.

In the distance, Braksis could see Solara and Tiot rushing to his aid. If only he could hold off for a few more moments. They were almost there.

Rawthorne recovered his mallet and opted to let nature handle Braksis for him. Durgin was in the way, but he despised the man anyway. Slamming the mallet down as hard as he could, the rock face cracked and the ledge where Braksis and Durgin stood began to tilt toward the waters below.

"Stop!" Durgin screeched as realization hit as to Rawthorne's motives.

"I was going to kill you anyway. Might as well take both of you down now." With pure hatred in his eyes, he raised the mallet a second time and brought it slamming down on the precipice.

Durgin jumped back toward Rawthorne and perpetual safety. Braksis tried to move to get off of his perch as well, but the nagging pain slowed him down. The rocks tumbled, and in an avalanche of rock, Braksis quickly disappeared as the cliff below him crumbled.

Durgin managed to maintain a grip and did not suffer the same fate. As he looked to find Rawthorne, he could see the former king fleeing. Solara was closing in on them and he wanted nothing to do with her. Durgin concurred and quickly moved to make his escape.

As Solara ran to the ledge, she ignored both opponents, although she made a mental note as to who they were. Disgust filled her as she realized that one was a man she should have killed years before, and now he had managed to take not only her mother, but her lover and companion as well. She looked over the ledge and watched as Braksis fell through the sky and plummeted into the waters below.

Certainly a fall from this height would mean instantaneous death. Especially after being injured in a conflict. She could always track down the two murderers later. Now, she only wished to search for her mate. His life was all that mattered. Her decision was instantaneous as she quickly descended the trail again so that she could search the waters below.

❖ ❖ ❖ ❖ ❖

Sitting in meditation Ferceng could feel the low glimmer of life that was the man he considered his son. He hoped and prayed for his safety, but as the rock face collapsed, he knew that death was probable. In a last-resort effort to help, he mentally employed the same protection spell he used upon himself as Braksis fell into the waters below. Whether this was enough to protect him or not would remain to be seen. The spell certainly was never intended for a drop of that magnitude.

Reaching out with his heart, he could not find Braksis anywhere. He either had perished in the fall or lost consciousness. Hoping beyond hope for the latter, he jumped up and rushed to the water's edge. He managed to beat Solara there by mere moments as the two were possessed with attempting to locate Braksis. Together, they began the search in earnest.

❖ ❖ ❖ ❖ ❖

Hours later, even after the sun completely dipped down and night encompassed them, the two continued their search. The unspoken truth that Braksis was indeed dead never entered their throats or was voiced for fear that it would be true.

With each passing minute, Solara resumed her vow that she would hunt down these two men and kill them. She knew one to be Durgin. The other was unknown to her, but she would find him, and she would let him know as she killed him that Braksis had the last laugh.

Refusing to give in to despair, Ferceng decided that he would finish the Phoenix. In denial over the death of his son, he felt certain that Braksis would return. When he did so, the blade would be ready for him to reclaim whatever it was that he lost here today. Like the phoenix, Ferceng became convinced that in time, Braksis would rise from the ashes and return more powerful than ever.

EPILOGUE

Deep within his lair beneath the Danchul capital, Zoldex sat in perpetual darkness, with only his light blue images to cast illumination in the room. He watched with mild satisfaction as his plans came together magnificently—the death of King Sarlec, the demise of Admiral Morex, the kidnapping of Empress Karleena, and the downfall of Lord Braksis. Even Centain, one of the strongest supporters of the Imperium, had fallen, an added bonus for the scheming mastermind. He was very pleased with the outcome of the bounty hunter's assault.

With a flick of his wrist, all of the images vanished, leaving only the aftermath in the audience chamber of the palace alight before him. He could see the royal families scrambling in chaos. A chaos he knew would be escalated once they learned of all he had manipulated throughout the Seven Kingdoms, successfully removing the head of the realm.

Focusing on the new king of Danchul, Zoldex sent his thoughts through the image, hundreds of miles away. A simple message jolting the young man back to consciousness: "Get up."

Zoldex watched as he struggled to stand up. Sending his thoughts to the boy again, he forced Winton to stand. "This is the moment we have been waiting for. Working for. You will not miss it because of a slap to the face. Get up!"

He saw that Winton propped himself up and was satisfied his pawn would perform his task admirably. After all, a void at the top of the Imperium demanded to be filled, and Zoldex planned on having Winton do exactly that.

With a wave of his hand, he summoned images of his other forces. He watched multiple images of orcs, goblins, and hobgoblins performing a variety of activities, some of which had been engaged in combat. He then focused on the two assassins from Braksis's past whom he had sent out to deal with the Warlord, and was surprised to see them separated. Rawthorne was traveling west, with Durgin east. No matter, he thought. If he had need of them again, he would be able to find them wherever they may go.

With an idle thought, all of the images flickered out and Zoldex was left alone in the darkness once more. Then, with a burst of light, ten new diamonds of pale blue light cascaded through the darkness. Zoldex regarded each of the figures the images represented, including one eternal, and in an icy voice, relayed his instructions: "It is time."

The images replied in different manners, but all acknowledged the order and faded out again. Zoldex smiled in the darkness. The foundation had been set. Soon, his legions would lay claim to all of the realm. His sinister laugh echoed long into the night, sending chills up the spines of any who heard it.

The Imperium Saga

The Age of the Imperium is almost at an end!

The true intentions of Zoldex have yet to be revealed. Follow the heroes who survived in the aftermath through their struggles as the fate of the Seven Kingdoms hangs in the balance.

This epic saga continues in

Fall of the Imperium Trilogy

Book II

THE CHANGING TIDES

by

Clifford B. Bowyer

The Imperium Saga

Fleeing from their homes, the survivors of the once mighty Madrew are refugees searching to rebuild their civilization. The Elders have prophesied one individual, a child, who will defeat the threat of the tyrant Zoldex and return the Madrew to their former glory. This child is Kyria, the Chosen One.

Follow the adventures of Kyria in her own series intended for young adults.

This series begins in

The Chosen One
Book I

CHILD OF PROPHECY

by
Clifford B. Bowyer

Tarlesktaztrin
MOURNING MOUNTAINS
Vohlmuth
FALESTIAN MOUNTAINS
Arenberg
RED MOUNTAINS
SENYA FALLS
Reuland
KREBLAH
LAKE SENYA
BLACKSTOCK MOUNTAINS
LAKE SUPRETTA
Turning Leaf
Tregador
NORTHERN MOUNTAINS
Wildwood
Underwood
Korland
PIRROS RIVE
ISLAND OF NO RETURN
HORNED
Shimendyn
LAKE OF TEARS
DRYNAN RIVER
BLOODY RIVER
FORBIDDEN PEAKS
TENALONG
Bimbadine
SUSPINTIAN FOREST
NEKROS LAKE
FORBIDDEN FOREST
Fenland
SUSPINTI
BLACK PEAKS
Border Town
Comonor
DIM
RIVER OF TEARS
TENALONG EVERGLADES
ARDAN RIVER
NORTH HORWOOD FOREST
Xylona
Purington
Lareridge
LAKE CRESPEN
DANCHUL
SOUTH HORWOOD FOREST
DANCHUL RIVER
Vorstad
VENTELL MOUNTAINS
Estonis

N
ADLAI
ORDELL MOUNTAINS
OLBRUS RAPIDS
DARTIAN WOODS
Faylinn
BOLE RIVER
DARTAIS
LAKE CUPTON
DARTIE
LAKE PERCOTI
Bellmore
PERCOTI WOODS
Edgewood
Trespias
Kramden
Arkham
Loveskia
Aquatica
FROCOMON
GREEN MOUNTAINS
CARRION MOUNTAINS